THE LAST TEMPTATION

The last temptation is the greatest treason:
To do the right deed for the wrong reason.
—T. S. Eliot's *Murder in the Cathedral*

The Last Temptation

by Joseph Viertel

SIMON AND SCHUSTER, NEW YORK

PUBLISHED BY SIMON AND SCHUSTER, INC.
ROCKEFELLER CENTER, 630 FIFTH AVENUE
NEW YORK 20, N. Y.

MANUFACTURED IN THE UNITED STATES OF AMERICA

For Daisy and Jack

The backdrop for this book is already written into history and cannot be unwritten or idly tampered with. However, all the persons in this volume, without exception, are entirely fictional, completely the product of my own imagination; and all that befalls them in this book is also fictional.

One

Although the morning was hot with the wind blowing from the desert, Deborah Marmorek lay with the sheet pulled over her head, listening half-awake to the unfamiliar, treacherous silence which the night had brought. The siege was over, but it was not easy to grow accustomed to. What promise was there in thirty days of uneasy truce?

She was thirsty. Her stomach rumbled. She could half hear the gurgle of it in her sleep. And Lord, she was filthy. Everywhere she itched.

She opened her eyes. The silence was there all right. It was truly cease-fire.

There would be water again, enough for a full bath. And white bread. Perhaps two cigarettes, one for her and one for Vic. Now see how depraved her mind was becoming! She'd just about trained herself not to think about cigarettes at all. Eight hours of peace and she was going soft.

She had arranged with her brother Karl and Lilith for the four of them to be together again tonight like old times, to celebrate. Perhaps they would go to Expresso or Hesse's and who knows what they might discover at a restaurant these days. Perhaps a bit of meat. If there could be cease-fire, anything could happen. A convoy might come through soon on the new road—Vic's new road. He'd been bursting with the secret of it when she saw him last. Now everyone knew about it—miles of military secret, hacked out of the mountains, built up through wadis, fashioned by wrecked bulldozers and men who worked like the pyramid slaves of old Egypt. In many ways it seemed silly. How could they keep a road secret? It was like trying to hide a river or a mountain, but there it was, and when it was finished there would be convoys from Tel Aviv again, Arabs or no Arabs, lorries with food and clothing, arms, and, yes, eventually even shampoos and lipsticks. And if everyone did not know yet that Vic had done it, they would know it soon. Someday soon. Right now she only wanted him home again.

She could still feel Vic's suppressed anticipation when he'd said, casually, before he left last time, three weeks ago, "If the truce comes off, I'll get back to town somehow. I'll try to rustle up the loaf of bread and jug of wine. You just bring thou." Their old German *du*. Then he'd been gone in the truck's roar, her tall warrior, waving. She was sure he'd keep his promise if he had to come home on a donkey. She wondered whether he was well and as tired and hungry as she. He would be fine, of course, well fed, she couldn't imagine him otherwise. She stretched her arm across Vic's side of the bed.

Oh God, how long had it been? Weeks, almost four months! Since the day Vic left for the Road. That was no night for love. They had simply forced themselves, because Vic was leaving; it hadn't been really nice, mostly bravado.

But tonight would be better. Methuselah! Tonight she could be her old cheerful self again. No fears, no tensions. Once he came, he would stay.

David would be happy to see his father again, too. He'd been asking for him often lately. David! With a suddenness that reflected her change in thought, she straightened and pulled the sheet down to her chin. David was not in his cot, the little devil!

Debbie peered from her second-story window into Gaza Road. An old woman, Noah Mendoza's grandmother, was making her way in sudden darts from one doorway to the next toward Polachek's grocery across the street. Polachek hadn't a blessed thing on his shelves, of course, but that wouldn't stop the old lady. And would people ever accustom themselves to walking the streets again instead of scurrying and clinging close to masonry?

At the sound of footsteps, Debbie turned around. Elsa Schumacher, her broad-beamed friend who was also her supervisor at the hospital, stood in the bedroom doorway, dressed and ready to go out. Elsa, who had lived in Debbie's flat since her own was bombed out, shook her head woefully. "I don't know why God wouldn't let me sleep," she said wryly. "Hard to relax without the mortars. Coming, coming, coming. They had their own music, didn't they?" Deborah was only half listening. It was Debbie's theory that gloomy Elsa had entirely missed her calling. Instead of a nurse, what a rabbi Elsa would have made! As far as she was concerned, everything was up to God.

"Is David in your room?"

"No." Elsa patted her paunchy stomach tenderly. "I'm going out to scrape up some food now, God willing. I'm hungry. I go to bed hungry and wake up hungry. And still there's no improvement in my figure. I've lost twenty pounds and look at me. It's not scientific. You see, science can't explain everything! What keeps me so inflated? Must be gas."

It was true. She bulged and protruded everywhere. Her straight gray hair, chopped hurriedly about her oval face, and her narrow nose bent in a clean obtuse angle at its bridge did nothing to enhance her appearance.

"I'll bet that boy of yours is out in the street. If you ask me, Deborah, he's entirely too wild."

Both women called him from the window now with some urgency, but their cries attracted only Tani from the kitchen. The little brown Yemenite maid was a creature whose age and status would be hard to guess. She looked old, but she was only thirty-three. On the other hand she was a grandmother.

"Should I go out and find him?" Tani asked. "I told him to stay inside but he won't listen to *me*. After all who am *I*?"

Debbie sighed and slipped into her dusty heavy-duty shoes, not congruous on her small feet. She stood before the cracked mirror and brushed her hair quickly. Each time she looked at herself she seemed to be getting shorter. Her small, pretty and finely freckled Slavic face with its surface-set blue eyes and high broad cheekbones frowned back at her and she wrinkled her snub nose disapprovingly. When she was well fed, her face looked almost plump, but the pallor of subterranean life and heavy sleepless lines marred her otherwise young cheeks, and hunger made her drawn. She looked with revulsion at her hands which were rough, the nails cut short, and the balls of her fingers laced with thousands of tiny parallel lines.

"Heavens to Methuselah, this war is positively my last. I must remember to get word to Ben-Gurion and Lake Success. It hasn't done a thing for me. Look at me, Elsa, my hair, see the gray ones?" Her hair hung straight and black, almost shoulder length, but there were a few gray strands if one looked closely. "See, Elsa, I'm getting old before my time. I think I've shrunk. Do I still look five feet tall to you? Only twenty-eight years old and I look at least a hundred and twenty-eight, don't I? Seriously? And to think Papa used to say I was the prettiest girl in Vienna, and Papa did know every dancing girl in Austria." She sighed. "Wherever do you think that boy has gone? I've got to get him to school."

Elsa was incredulous. "School? It doesn't seem possible they'd open the schools so soon."

"That's what Mrs. Van Bern told me. Our school anyway."

"How do you like that?" Elsa said. "Have you ever heard anything to match it? Half the dead aren't buried, and we're so short-handed at the hospital. Why don't they get these teachers to do something useful for a change? Empty bedpans at least. But does this make sense to the glorious military mind of Colonel Steinmetz? Everyone's starving, we're exhausted, no water, no electricity, we're cut off from the rest of the world, so this great genius scratches his head. In such a desperate situation, what is the logical thing to do? What will save us? It's obvious. Open the schools!" Elsa's voice had risen perilously high and was filled with righteous agitation, but there was a thread of pride in it.

"I'm going out to find something to eat. If I see David I'll send him home." She started down the stairs.

"Oh, Elsa!" Debbie called.

She'd better speak to Elsa about the delicate matter of tonight. In the old days the subject might have been embarrassing, but there were no such niceties left after two months of siege, waterless toilets, sleeping in public halls and six to a room.

"Just for tonight, Elsa dear . . . may we have David sleep in with you and Tani? He sleeps quiet as a mouse. I'm sure he won't disturb you. Vic and I—"

Elsa, the fifty-nine-year-old spinster, held up her hand in that exaggerated way which means I'm as clever as the next fellow, say no more, and clomped downstairs.

Just then, from the direction of Terra Sancta, Debbie saw a troop of four boys marching in exaggerated arm-swinging British military style; David led them. He was tall for his eight years, with Debbie's Slavic features, but without her freckles. "Halt, men!" David's shrill command carried through the street in the silence of the morning and on toward the hills behind Jerusalem. He threw a fist-sized stone down the center of the road, as if it were a hand grenade. "Take cover, men!" The boys scattered realistically, crouching in entryways.

"David, come upstairs this minute."

"Dismissed, men," David snapped. "My mommy wants me."

"Look at you!" Debbie ran her fingers lovingly through David's straight brown hair. "You're nearly as big as I am." It always struck her as ridiculous that she, who was so small, should have borne this mammoth creature. "Look at your face and clothes. What's to become of us, we all look like pigs. There, in the bucket next to your cot, wash your face and don't splash. We have none to waste."

Carefully, out of long habit, she parted and combed his wetted hair and dusted his shirt and the seat of his khaki shorts.

"Why did you run out without telling anyone? I told you you had to go to school this morning."

She knew he was secretly pleased to go back to school, although it was fashionable to insist that he hated it. There were certain people he would especially want to see after all these weeks—Miss Even for one, and Tamar, of course. She spruced him up because she knew he would want to look his best for Tamar.

David hunted patiently in his room for his books, moaning and groaning in the exaggerated way boys have groaned for centuries over having to go to school.

"You have everything?"

"I s'pose."

"Would you like to take the concertina?"

"No. Not today."

"Well, come along. Miss Even is probably waiting breathlessly for you."

Two

As they started downstairs, Rose Epstein opened her door on the landing and called after them. "Good morning!" Her voice had more heartiness than she had shown in weeks. "So no more sleeping in the hall, eh? Gershon and I'll be lonesome for you in our little dormitory and, of course, your friend, Miss Schumacher; my God, but she was a loud snorer. What adenoids! Like a railroad train, you know? Magnificent!"

David laughed.

"We'll miss you too," Debbie said.

"Will your husband be home tonight?" Rose Epstein was a curious woman and she lived vicariously even though she had a full life of her own.

"I should hope so. I'm beginning to feel neglected. He promised he would try anyway, and that's a step in the right direction."

David said, "He built a new road, you know, my dad." Then turning to his mother, "Am I allowed to mention the road now?"

"You've just mentioned it, dear."

"My dad built it. He and a few friends in the Haganah. Of course, they had these machines. Bulldozers."

Rose Epstein laughed a light cackling laugh. "Imagine! All this time you've been keeping this secret from us! A real military secret! They learn so young."

For a moment Deborah and David stood in the sunlight before their doorway at 32 Gaza Road in Rehavia. Their house was the last on the right of the street, a typical modern, unimaginative four-family, two-story building with its inevitable balconies. Beyond them was nothing. The road ended and there were only bare, rock-littered lots, future apartment sites, which became within a few hundred meters the barren Judean foothills. Far beyond, in a gray haze, rose the Mountains of Moab.

The *hamseen* had grown worse, since early morning, this sticky, hot, dry, parched wind, penetrating everywhere, irritating the membranes, the tongue, the eyes, the gums—a reminder that Jerusalem rose to its mountain retreat from the dry sands of the great surrounding desert. But in spite of the *hamseen* and in spite of the siege, each courtyard or terrace they passed had its ridiculously bright daisies and anemones and geraniums, its palms and its fruit trees. Debbie could not resist the temptation to snatch a few flowers, which were in such contrast to the shattered masonry, and she handed them to David to give Miss Even at school.

Along Gaza Road they could see the domes and walled perimeter of the Old City, now without a living Jew in it, mostly hidden by the ghastly gray smoke smudge which clung to it after all these days, a dead battlefield.

The New City, too, lay battered and uncomfortably quiet, like a great sand-colored beast, unconscious, but far from finished. Her pale buff buildings, hot in the dust, sprawled in the bright morning light among the towering buff hills, the terraced Judean slopes, as though the buildings had been there as long as the hills themselves, instead of a few short years. Jerusalem lay grievously wounded, clinging to her mother mountain. Only the barbed wire and the high-piled sandbags and the ugly, menacing concrete pillboxes and security walls seemed vital and alive. The black burnt-out trucks and jeeps carrying armor that was not armor told their own stories.

On the wall of the monastery she noticed the familiar poster, a picture of two huge drops of water and the single word, "SAVE." As if anyone needed to be told! And alongside it an Arab with a huge ear. "DON'T TALK! THE ENEMY LISTENS!" There had been a great many rumors about spies lately. Real terror over spies.

On their walk David grimaced at the brown blood stains in the gutter not far from Terra Sancta and remembered the three bodies, two men and a small girl, he had seen lying in the road last week in fresh red blood. He remembered long ago in Rome when he saw his first corpse, and the days of the ship and what happened to Mr. Shapiro. He wondered aloud how the bodies were disposed of here in Jerusalem. They were too big for the garbage. Debbie told him they were put in great holes under the ground in a big green field like a park. The Arabs did it in the Mamillah Cemetery and that was certainly a mess. The garbage would be easier, or burn them, as he'd heard Daddy say was most sensible. Still, would they burn? They didn't seem dry enough.

Now as they walked, slowly all Jerusalem stirred like a great giant. Debbie could see it awakening everywhere. Faces, taut and pinched, tired, hungry, irritated faces peering from windows. Military vehicles careening through the street; a Chopin mazurka being played on a piano could be heard from a nearby window; complete strangers smiling and saying Hello, is it really true? The streets beginning to come alive with people. A casual friend, another, each neighbor a wonderful discovery. Distant, distracted smiles, asking about others, afraid to ask about too many. What do you hear from Victor? And your brother Karl? Hello, David, how big you've got! Other kids dashing through the streets, liberated by peace.

Indestructible Jerusalem stone, crushed to powder. When Debbie had first come to the city, she had resented the monotony of the buildings, so unlike Vienna's or Prague's loved Baroque, or the Carrara marble of stately Rome, these squat structures, punctuated by dome or spire, and literally all built of the same rough-faced sand-colored stone. She preferred prettiness, and Jerusalem was not pretty. Still, she had learned to look more closely, and Jerusalem's stone grew golden, she could find tints of rare rose and amber, even blue in the sunshine or in the twilight. Now Jerusalem was sore and hurt, but still alive, and, dimly she perceived, somehow victorious. It was odd to think this prostrate city was triumph. She thought of her patients at Hadassah, destroyed, wasted, the hard young boys and girls, fifteen, sixteen, even fourteen, or the unpolitical men, women and children, all brought bleeding into emergency operating rooms—dungeons at the English Mission—to be bound up, for morphine, catch as catch can, some just to die. Row on row of beds, mattresses on the floor, two patients to a mattress, at Hadassah A, the squalid makeshift that could never take the place of the beautiful gleaming hospital on the Scopus. What would young men like Noah Mendoza do now? Peace was not for one-legged boys.

Nevertheless, she felt better about herself today, about Vic, about David. She realized that the going of the British made a great personal difference to her, even though she knew it meant she would probably never see Redge or Enid Walker again. She wondered how acutely Vic would miss the Walkers.

On Ben Maimon Street they passed the woman who called herself Sadie Jerusalem, the only professional call-girl she knew by sight. Debbie could scarcely recognize her, her face was so pinched and gray; the bounce of her buttocks was gone. Debbie could hardly resist the satisfying thought that she had greater qualifications today than poor Sadie. As they passed, Debbie nodded a pleasant hello, as though it were something that she had been doing socially for years. Sadie, flattered at the recognition, smiled back.

Suddenly, quite suddenly, Debbie felt the impact of the day and the moment. She could not remember a more exquisite time in her life. There was peace. A thirty-day truce might last forever. And they were all alive and well, their tight little trio. They had staked their lives and won. So many others were mourning their dead, but they were all still alive.

"Come along, David, I'll race you to school." When Debbie ran, it was a dance, in spite of her ridiculous shoes. There was a young unbridled wildness in her that infected passers-by who watched. Such energy when everyone else had trouble climbing stairs! Her hair flew, her eyes shone, and she laughed as she let David pass her because she knew he would be very touchy about losing a race to his mother, or about losing anything to anybody for that matter. "Oh, I'm getting to be a slow old woman." She knew her resistance was low and she did feel strained and exhausted by the effort. Not enough calories these days.

David said, "Oh, you're not so old," and he tapped her arm magnanimously. David was a great winner, a fine front runner.

They stood for a moment catching their breath outside the school building. Oh, David! I feel so good at last. Relieved and good. We've had it, haven't we? We deserve a little something special now, golly, we do. Well, here you are now, David, going to school this morning like any normal boy anywhere in the world. It could be London or Vienna.

The familiar Rehavia school was a two-story quadrangular affair built about a central courtyard. Half the yard was the children's garden, protected by a wood and wire fence; the other half a hard-surfaced playing field, where now about thirty-five children were playing. A few girls jumped rope. Other boys and girls were busy throwing a soccer ball from one team to the other. The more competitive boys were in a wild basketball game, screaming and scrapping. The bedlam was quite satisfying.

In the planting beds, many of the vegetables, untended for weeks, seemed still to be healthy, although some had gone to seed, and all the corn had withered. Near the fence several rows of tiny evergreens strained skyward.

Vic and I must really have another baby now, she thought suddenly. A *sabra*, a child born in the East. And the pattern of her morning's rambling thoughts came sharply into focus. She would buy a couple of bottles of wine from old Baumerstock, who had hinted to her that as a special favor for a special friend, and at a special price, even wine could somehow be located. The old goat. She and Vic and Lilith and Karl would eat at the Vienna Café or Expresso or Hesse's or somewhere, whatever they could get, and afterward at the flat, just the two of them would open the caviar can they'd been saving and the wine. And there would be talk and warmth and love, but not only for pleasure. It was all to come to something. A *sabra*. Theirs. Girl or boy, no matter.

Three

"David! It's old King David!" One of the boys had his arm about David's shoulder. The children crowded round, asking questions, screaming everything they could think of, miscellaneous tidbits of news of which he could not make head or tail.

"No arithmetic today, David," a dark pigtailed girl cried, obviously seeking his attention. "Recess all day!"

"Good," David said. "Recess is my favorite subject. Tuvia! Throw the ball!"

"Where's the concertina?"

"Left it home. Throw the ball, Tuvia!"

"Children, children!" Miss Even called, clapping her hands for attention. "Come along, David." She stretched her hand toward him. He was wild and unruly sometimes, but one of her favorites. "Say a proper hello to your old teacher."

David moved cautiously. He had been shocked by the ugly security wall scarring the handsome modern front of the school and now he saw that Miss Even was dressed in the uniform of a soldier of Haganah.

To Debbie, too, Miss Even seemed different. It was not only that the tam-o-shanter gave her a rakish look, but the quick smile came more slowly now to her young, heart-shaped face, and her eyes seemed more furtive than they had before. Her darkish blond hair was cut even shorter, and her light pink cheeks were rosier and drier and a little chapped, almost indistinguishable in color and texture from her lips. The uniform skirt and the khaki socks made her look somewhat shorter and perhaps a trifle older than her twenty-two years.

"We must remember our manners, mustn't we?" Miss Even was saying in her soft, musical teacher's voice. As she shook hands, David handed her the flowers, and she bent and kissed him. It was a special kind of kiss and he knew exactly what it meant. It meant Thank You, God, Because David Is Not Dead. And he was glad Miss Even was not dead too. You could see that in his reddened face.

He blurted out, "My father's in Haganah now. Engineers. And my Uncle Karl, too. Transport."

"No more Haganah," Miss Even said. "The Army of Israel."

"Did you kill any Arabs?" David asked. "Can you throw hand grenades? My dad once showed me, he had a whole briefcase full of hand grenades. And I know how to throw them, too. Where's your gun?" The other children who had restrained themselves all morning—noticing the uniform, but not asking about it—joined in the chorus of questions.

"Children, children, please!" Miss Even held her hands up in mock horror. "If you don't stop shrieking, I'll—I'll—"

"Tell us what you did. Tell us, tell us!" The chorus rose swiftly.

Miss Even looked trapped, but not displeased. "All right." The children surrounded her. "All I did, really, was carry messages from one place to another." Faces fell. This was scarcely up to expectations. "Of course, they were messages from one Commanding Officer to another," she added hastily. "From Katamon to Rehavia to the German Colony, from Ramat Rahel to the Center."

"Were you in Notre Dame?"

"But naturally." They felt better already. "And while the messages were *little* they were rather important."

"You can't do *anything* without messengers," David proclaimed. "You can't win a war without messengers. Everybody knows that." She could see the need being filled in the faces of the children.

Two had their mouths open. Several boys and girls of ten and eleven had their thumbs firmly in their mouths. The one boy with religious side curls tugged nervously at them. Eight-year-old Rosa sat by herself in the sandbox, running her fingers through the sand, not interested. But most of them were crowding Miss Even against the garden rail.

"Were you in the fighting at Ramat Rahel?"

"But of course."

"Were you wounded?"

"No. They missed me."

Thirty-five children who had hid under their beds or in public halls or shelters for nearly forty nights and days listening to the mortars crash about them, and seven of whom had lost a brother or a sister, a father or a mother, thirty-five boys and girls from everywhere in the world stood silent and in awe at this wonderful fact, this delicious fact they had never known before, that Miss Even, their teacher, was a soldier, a secret soldier of Israel.

"You're all so *disappointed,*" she cried, "simply because they missed me. I'm terribly sorry. I apologize."

They laughed. One ten-year-old girl whose baby brother had been killed last week laughed so hard it made tears run down her cheeks.

"That's all about me," Miss Even said. "Let's finish our game, and then we must get on to our planting. Look at the gardens. What a mess of weeds! We have to get to work. And tomorrow we start new cypress trees."

Reluctantly they went back to their games. Tuvia tossed the ball to David, and all the kids began their familiar chant. "Here, David, throw it, David, you can't hit me, cockeyed David, can't hit me."

Miss Even came over to Debbie, who felt tiny beside her. They had always liked each other instinctively, although the only time they ever met was at school.

"I'm afraid they'll get too wild," Miss Even said. "Everything strikes them so funny or so terrible, it's going to be hard to keep them under control."

"I think you're spectacular," Debbie said. "I'm sure they'd drive me out of my head, really. All those high voices meet at one spot in my poor brain, and it's like chalk squeaking on a blackboard."

Miss Even said softly, "It's a question of getting used to it. Although I do feel out of practice. Army life seems almost peaceful by comparison." She smiled down at Debbie. "Of course, we're not having any formal classes today. Miss Baruch and I got our C.O. to let us come over. He's Dr. Yassonovsky, you know, the Professor of Education at the University, so he's sympathetic. We thought we'd give the kids a chance to get together and play in the open and be a little normal. And at the same time give you mothers a rest. Tell me, how's David's shoulder?"

"Oh, it's fine now. It healed beautifully."

"And Mr. Marmorek, is he well?"

"Yes, fine," Debbie said fervently. "Just fine." She knocked the wood railing at the edge of the garden. "The last time I saw him he was bubbling over with his great secret. He's working on the new road, you know."

"Yes?" Miss Even registered the slight beat of Debbie's uncertainty. Debbie threw off a premonition that possessed her for a flashing moment. Her mind had become suddenly morbid with the coming of peace. She must really train herself to stand prosperity. Nothing had happened to Victor, nothing, and she felt for an instant that she had to reassure Miss Even on this score and erase that barely perceptible skepticism.

"We'll keep the children till five if we can stand it," Miss Even was saying. "Somehow we'll find lunch for them. Miss Baruch is out foraging now. You should have seen her, she looked so silly going off for food in an armored lorry, as if she were carrying gold."

The children were shrieking so that the two women were now shouting to make themselves heard.

"I think you and Miss Baruch are wonderful," Debbie said, "I couldn't do it."

Miss Even smiled. "And I don't think I could put up with what you do at the hospital. Every girl to her own knitting. Some of the boys in my outfit are still talking about you, you know. Poor Noah Mendoza did an impression of you in charcoal; it has everything but wings and a halo. He has you down as his own personal heroine."

Debbie shrugged. "Heroines, heroes, wherever you look. I can't say I care much for it." She sighed. "It was never like this in old Vienna, you know, when I went to school. In old Vienna life was more—more cozy, somehow, and you had to look mighty close to find heroes in those days." She waved and went back out through the building to the street. As she left the screaming children and Miss Even, her mind wandered back. . . .

She was seeing her own school in Vienna, Frau Morgenstelle's School, and especially Fräulein Froelich's class.

Four

The classrooms in Frau Morgenstelle's exclusive establishment had huge windows along one wall facing Döblinger Hauptstrasse, and in winter it sometimes grew fearfully hot with the windows closed and the steam heat going full blast. Fräulein Froelich in the Sixth Grade was an impetuous woman. When the room grew hot, she threw open the windows and turned off the heat. In half an hour the girls began to shiver. While she maintained fresh air was good for the lungs and for health in general, she finally ordered the windows closed and the heat turned on full, and slowly the classroom grew stifling hot. This heat irritated her to the point where she turned the heat off and threw the windows wide open.

The windows in Fräulein Froelich's class were thrown open at least four times a day during the months of December, January and February. Half the class was frequently home with grippe, colds or influenza, which Fräulein Froelich appeared to take as a symptom of national decadence. Fräulein Froelich was a pinched old woman—positively ancient to Deborah, although she was probably in her late forties—who seemed to regard the children through her pince-nez spectacles as some unsavory kind of specimens. It was not unusual for her to burst into angry tears in her efforts to quiet them and she sometimes called them little tormentors or devils.

Debbie could never quite forget the small croak in her voice when she would command them to sit absolutely still and think. *Think!* With their hands palms down on their desks. And she would quietly but ostentatiously place a thick fifty-centimeter wood rule within closer reach on her desk. Those had been grim contests of endurance. For twenty minutes or more nothing would be taught or said. The girls were thinking. And then finally there was the inevitable titter or whisper. This was the moment when Fräulein Froelich became terrible. Seizing the rule, she would march in cruel sudden steps to the offender, whom she inevitably spotted with her uncanny sixth sense, and with what seemed amazing speed and strength would smash the rule down on the backs of smooth young knuckles. The girls would cry out—twice, three times, until the cry came shrill, usually followed by a soft whimpering; and then Fräulein Froelich would relax, as though some soothing drug had eased a mysterious cramp, and invariably she was pleasant the rest of the day. Sometimes almost gay.

And then the inevitable morning—it seemed inevitable now—which had to come in one form or another. It was during religious study, and they were discussing the Last Supper. "Jesus and His Disciples were having their last supper together, as a group. Can anyone tell us what they were celebrating?" Gussie Goldenberg raised her hand. "The Passover." "Good, the Jewish service of Passover. Now what exactly does the Passover celebrate? Perhaps we can have a Jewish girl tell us. Which of you are Jews?" Gussie's hand went up. Everyone knew Gussie was. She looked it—plump and dark, and her thick glasses behind which she constantly blinked made it worse. Deborah hesitated, barely an instant of hesitation. She could remember it, feel it to this day. The humiliation of having hesitated. And the far greater moment of humiliation as her hand went up. It was like plunging into icy waters.

"Ah, Deborah Pretsch." Fräulein Froelich seemed surprised, but mysteriously pleased. "Can you tell us about Passover? The significance of Passover?"

"I . . . really don't know much about it."

She could remember so clearly Fräulein Froelich's voice, too cool and too soft, explaining, "Of course, there are many who believe that the Jews are not exactly a religion. Many Jews know very little of their religion. Deborah Pretsch, is your family Jewish by religion or race?"

Deborah liked Christmas carols and she had been to Oberammergau when she was ten to see the Passion Play with her parents. Judaism was as unfamiliar to her as it was to Fräulein Froelich.

"Stand up, Fräulein Pretsch. I am talking to you. Can you tell the other girls about Passover? Or of your other rituals? They seem strange to many of us. Many of us just don't understand them."

Blushing, stammering, nibbling nervously at her pigtail tip, she hoped a miraculous hole in the floor would open.

"Stop biting your braids. It's a disgusting habit. Apparently, you're not of the Jewish *religion*. You're simply a Jewess. Gussie Goldenberg may explain the Passover ritual."

In one of the endurance contests of thinking and silence after the Easter holidays, the rule was used across Debbie's knuckles when it was plainly Alvina, the girl beside her, who had giggled. It seemed quite clearly Alvina, but Fräulein Froelich thought it was Deborah. Several times again during the following weeks it happened. Alvina smirked across at her and no girl was willing to call Fräulein Froelich's attention to the injustice, not even Gussie who knew it as well as any of them. In fact, many of the girls seemed rather pleased with the injustice. Papa raged, of course, but only at home. Mama came to school to complain; but poor Mama was no match for Frau Morgenstelle. The principal said she was being treated like every other child. There were certain kinds of people who expected special treatment for their children . . . Frau Pretsch must realize she had a difficult child. Debbie, the mouse, a difficult child! She had to smile, remembering it.

It was not much, really, looking back from the far side of twenty-eight across Europe's tortures and gas chambers and six million dead. It was not much to what came later to Mama and Papa or friends like Gussie Goldenberg, it was not much to the stories Elsa liked to tell (yes, she believed Elsa *liked* to tell them), especially the gloomy one of the old rabbi who was dragged behind a cart through the streets of Linz and whipped to death by his own two sons under the direction of the Brownshirts.

Fräulein Froelich and the little persecutions she perpetrated were not so much when you came right down to it. But the other things had never happened to her, and Fräulein Froelich had happened to her.

Debbie was glad of Miss Even who was genuinely fond of David. And it was nice to know, besides, that Miss Even was a Jew herself, and was satisfied to be one.

Five

The streets had begun to bustle; more children were coming to school, some with their mothers. Soldiers and their girls, usually soldiers too, walked in the bright sunlight as though brushing up a lost art. There was so much sunshine; yet everyone wore the same sick yellow pallor. Acquaintances and utter strangers smiled and said Hello and sometimes My you're looking well, which seemed to be the universal compliment, perhaps because, although everyone looked so bad, they were nevertheless still alive.

Debbie knew she ought to rush home, finish her shopping for tonight—if there was anything to be bought—and then get to the hospital, but she dawdled partly because she was mentally tired and partly because she preferred to put off coping with Elsa or Tani at home. Elsa, whom Heaven knows she loved, had become trying lately, not at the hospital where she was busy, efficient and happy, but at home. If you said black she said white, and she argued endlessly, without even enjoying it. As for Tani, she was so helpless when Debbie was home, she never gave a minute's peace. Honestly, if it weren't that she needed Tani for David it would be easier to do the housework herself. She smiled to herself now, remembering her mother's perpetual self-satisfied complaint: "Help—they're really more trouble than they're worth," but poor Mama had never had fewer than four in service. Still Debbie was lucky. Practically no one in Rehavia except the Marmoreks still had a maid.

She would stroll a little before going home. She had no idea that at that moment she was being sought by a Haganah man who had called earlier at her house; then, having missed her there, followed her to school, and having missed her again by minutes was returning to the Agency, after visiting with Elsa and Tani, Baumerstock the grocer, and later at school with Miss Even. It was only because he had missed her in each place that she was able to wander happily down to King George Park beyond the security wall where she heard the sound of music and singing.

She found a crowd watching a twelve-year-old boy play the accordion. He was an older version of David and his concertina, the way he bobbed his head with the rhythm. A group of Haganah boys and girls danced the *hora* around the young accordionist, conducting themselves as if they were at a party. Flirting was a favorite pastime. One large bearded youth, not more than nineteen, made the rounds, ritually kissing each of the girls in turn and occasionally a smiling grandmother. Two bashful girls squealed at him and the crowd laughed and applauded as the young accordionist started up another tune for the dance to begin again. The bearded boy insisted that Debbie join the circle and be rewarded with one of his great hugs and whiskery kisses. It suited her mood to be accepted by these youngsters and she was thoroughly satisfied and exhausted when during the fourth dance she stole away. There was a little flush of color in her cheeks. She felt almost pretty again. The street dancing and celebrating made the cease-fire seem less unreal.

On Gaza Road in the semi-basement which was Baumerstock's grocery, four steps down from the sidewalk Mr. Baumerstock was sitting in his doorway greeting not only his own customers, but Polachek's and Goldstein's as well. Baumerstock was a clean-shaven, thin little man who wore his black skullcap simply to conceal his baldness, and even for a grocer seemed always a bit more vague and remote than absolutely necessary. His mind rarely proceeded in any one direction but meandered, while the details of his grocery business were beneath his contempt. His main interests were the study of the Talmud and human nature as exemplified by his customers.

Since the moment he had opened his door and set down his stool in the sun he had been surrounded by a knot of would-be buyers, to whom he spoke in mocking but not unfriendly tones. "Oh, what a shame, Mrs. Lowenthal, but just today I ran out of fresh eggs. Ten minutes earlier and you could have had a dozen. But I just this minute ate them. That's why I'm sitting here—to digest. Shells and all, of course. Who had the time to crack them? Still, Mrs. Lowenthal, I see you're alive and I'm happy. Milk, Mrs. Heller? How many quarts? I'll have the boy deliver positively not later than next New Year's Day."

The women let the man have his little say; and he had no objection to their wandering about the shop peering, searching through the empty shelves.

There was a cautious change in his manner when Deborah came. He nodded solemnly and formally over the heads of the other women. "Mrs. Marmorek, you wish something here?" To be sure, she had observed an armed truce with Baumerstock these last two years, but they had got on well enough and lately his attitude seemed less reserved, like his hints about the wine. But there was no joking to his solemnity now, and an instant of perplexity brushed across her consciousness. She smiled at Mrs. Heller as if to say He's a weird old duck, isn't he? But Mrs. Heller had turned away.

"Mr. Baumerstock,"—she could be as formal as he—"isn't it a scrumptious day? How's business?"

"One should never mention business in the house of a man who has been three times bankrupt. You see my trouble, my customers are all cleverer than I. And those who are not, are married to men who are cleverer. Some are married to men who are too clever. They have money, they have position, they are promoted into bigger and better positions. Surely they must have food. I have none. Perhaps you have a tin or two *you* could sell *me*. You must have quite a bit stored up which maybe your English friends gave you before all this trouble?"

The little man scarcely looked at her and spoke almost in a monotone; Deborah could feel the flush of anger and mortification flooding her face, but some of the other women who overheard seemed to take it for Baumerstock's usual joshing.

Deborah felt she ought to make something of a joke of it. "Of course, Mr. Baumerstock; you should see my stove right now. A thick American steak direct by plane from Chicago where all the best steak comes from, you know. If they would turn on the electricity my stove would work and the steak would sizzle. And fried potatoes. Fried in chicken fat, of course. And nice gefüllte fish. If I say so myself I whip up a fancy gefüllte fish."

Baumerstock made an elaborate belch. It was not particularly amusing. "Never mention American steak in the house of a man with Bulgarian ulcers. All I want is mutton. Some of that nice English mutton. Surely you must have that, a woman of your position. And plum pudding."

Baumerstock was not the only one who had made snide comments about Redge and Enid Walker, but his digs were the most offensive. However, since the English Exodus even he hadn't mentioned them until this moment, when he was being pointedly unpleasant. Mrs. Heller was gossiping and whispering hand to mouth, and the other woman listened and shook their heads and peered curiously at her.

Debbie ignored them and became business-like, speaking in an undertone below the gossip of the four other women, confidentially. "Would you have two cigarettes to sell, Mr. Baumerstock? I'd be so happy if I had just two cigarettes. I'll pay any price you ask. Five piastres apiece. Ten." Baumerstock grunted. "You mentioned wine last week also. Real Rishon Le Zion—red and dry. A port." Ordinarily she would have told him it was for a celebration, but he seemed so unpleasant she decided to save her breath. Instead she drew out of her pocket her roll of five-pound notes. Money never failed to move Baumerstock.

"I said for a special friend, of course. I remember." He made no attempt to move from his seat in the sun and quite suddenly his voice rose abusively, "See, plenty of money; that kind of money I wouldn't take, not the whole roll. Put it away. Put it away. Such money." And he spit.

"Mr. Baumerstock, yesterday—"

The man rose and flung his arms upward in a gesture of violent dismissal. "Yesterday I was a blabbermouth, a boaster, but not today. Today I have no wine, I have no wine."

Deborah thought it best to leave before the eccentric old man made a ridiculous scene. The other women were looking at her with expressions which were strangely unsympathetic, except for one girl, a newcomer, who smiled and seemed to say, "It takes all kinds to make a world."

As she backed hurriedly up the steps, Baumerstock waved his arms again. "They are looking for you," he cried. "They've caught up with you. The man was just here."

Baumerstock's riddles were not new to her, but Debbie was troubled—curious and on the verge of asking who was looking for her when Baumerstock grasped the stool in one hand, and fiddled in his pocket for the store key.

"Store closed, store closed," he chanted. "With my volume of business, the overhead is killing me. Eating me up alive. Who can afford such overhead to sit here all day?" He walked inside, pulled the corrugated metal shade down over the entire storefront, and the final sound of the key in the door told the women on the steps that the shop was absolutely closed.

She knew there was no use trying Polachek's or Goldstein's. They would have nothing. She could only hope that Vic would be able to bring something for the celebration.

Her uneasiness could not be suppressed altogether. Who was looking for her? If only Vic were home; really she depended so on him. Nothing could have happened to him, could it? Oh God, not her indestructible Vic!

Before she had time to explore her nameless fear, the water lorry lumbered down Gaza Road, its familiar tank a welcome sight to the cheerful but orderly crowd following it. The driver honked the horn continuously, long and short honks like conversations, as if to say, Get your water today without worry. No shrapnel today. Just queue up and stand in the middle of the street. Really a pleasure today. And from every building they came, crying Water! Water! Women, some with babies, old men and teenagers, swinging their buckets or bottles or water cans, vases and laundry tubs, anything that would carry water. Debbie was too far from home to go for her pails and be back in time, but surely Elsa would come. Up the hill they tramped toward the truck, in slacks and skirts, shorts and halters, every size and shape. Down the hill came the others following the slow truck like a gay cortege, patient, waiting for it to stop. There was no sign of Elsa.

In the basement areaway in front of Baumerstock's shop two Coca-Cola bottles stood empty and unclaimed. Two pints would be better than nothing. At least Vic could shave; there would be some to drink for them all; she could sponge herself. There had been no water for several days and what was left was beginning to smell. The old water could be used to flush the toilet. Debbie was in the middle of the queue, one empty bottle in each hand, watching the familiar, efficient old civic guard, Moshe Ben Saul, behave like the preoccupied professor he was, muttering, "Come ye to the waters, come ye," as he filled the buckets and kettles with the hose. He had a prodigious memory for names and faces, doubtless acquired at Sachshausen, where he had had similar responsibilities. With each nod he mournfully intoned the name of the family; it was a ritual he obviously enjoyed, and he knew everyone. Grab, swish, deliver. The efficiency was marvelous; the water was handled like fine brandy: no drop fell to the ground.

Before she knew it Debbie was being handed back two full bottles. "Marmorek," droned old Ben Saul. Debbie did not know whether she imagined it, but there seemed to be a fleeting hush, the merest brush of silence that swept through those near enough to hear Ben Saul, a flick, and then it was gone.

Perhaps she would still have time to take these home and get a full bucket before the truck moved on to Talbieh and the German Colony. She explained her situation to Ben Saul. "Why not?" he shrugged. "You are entitled to a full share like everybody else. But you will have to hurry. I can't wait."

She started swiftly toward her apartment shouldering her way through her neighbors in the road. She had got almost to the edge of the crowd when suddenly she felt herself falling—falling, foolishly falling, sprawling and awkward. The bottles! Instinctively she grasped them, holding tight, falling forward. She heard a splintering crash, and felt a sharp pain in her left hand. That bottle was smashed. The one in her right hand was intact, but nearly empty. Her clothes were wet and her knee burned badly. For a few seconds she sat on the curb, dazed. A teenage girl tried to help her to her feet, but she sank back, winded. She felt so stupid. Whatever possessed her to fall?

"She tripped you," a little boy said. "Her over there," and he pointed to Mrs. Heller who from ten feet away watched her with a sullen, unfeeling, almost stupid interest. She wore a dimly remembered expression; Debbie had seen that look somewhere, where had it been? Mrs. Heller was a spare, tall woman with a gawky body and scarecrow face, her bone structure so clearly discernible beneath the flesh that it made her skeleton-like. But it was her dull listless eyes that made the expression. There was no sign of remorse. Mrs. Heller only said gloomily, "It was my fault. I'm clumsy."

Now Deborah remembered the look from deep in the far recesses of her mind. It was the expression she had seen that March day in 1938 on so many faces on Josefstadter Strasse when two Jewish women had been set to scrubbing the gutter. It was a look that said, It probably serves her right and if not, who cares? It's a spectacle and I must remember to tell the family about it.

Debbie wanted to escape, to run, run fast, just as she had wanted to do that day on the Josefstadter Strasse. Her heart was pounding, her face was hot. "Lord, look at me!" She started to giggle and foolishly smeared her sleeve across her face to wipe her eyes. "Arab snipers never touched me. The mortars never touched me. First day of ceasefire and look at me. I'm wounded. I'm bleeding all over, look at me. I'm a mess. I'm a comedienne. Isn't it a scream?"

A young man was washing the gash in her palm with a cloth he had wet from her bottle, and the cloth became quickly bloody, but the sight of blood, even her own, was something she was used to. Dimly she realized the water truck was lumbering away, but she had no strength to try to stop it. She had so wanted water. Just some clean water. She felt on the verge of tears. Perhaps all these people in the circle about her, watching with curiosity, many of them neighbors she knew, perhaps they would go away now. Perhaps Mrs. Heller would quit staring at her. The young man washing her cut put a comforting hand on her shoulder and she realized at last it was Noah Mendoza, the boy who had lost his leg at Kastel. Laboriously he rose, hobbled to a pail, picked it up and made his way back toward her on his crutch, the pail swinging ridiculously, clopping the crutch with every step. "Miss Deborah," he said, "please let me give you some of mine. I can get along fine with half a pail till the next ration . . ."

"Don't do her any favors," Mrs. Heller called. Noah was not agile, still struggling with his crutches; he was slow to turn toward Mrs. Heller, and before he could answer, her voice rose shrilly. "Marmorek! You'll hear the name again. Everyone will hear it."

Debbie rose to her feet, unsteady at first, confused, but through her vague sensations of pain, curious.

"What are you driving at?" But Mrs. Heller shrugged as though she had said too much already. "Is it my business? Why should I bother myself?" Like Baumerstock she shut Debbie out, turned away, marched into her apartment. Noah Mendoza laughed uneasily. "What's eating her?" He filled Debbie's bottle from his pail.

"Goodness, Noah, you're nice! What's got into that old witch, do you suppose?"

Noah shrugged. "She's got a vile word for everyone, and especially pretty girls. People who hardly know her say she's the absolutely nastiest woman in Jerusalem, without exception, but it's only when you get to know her very well that you realize it's no exaggeration."

Debbie was relieved to hear Noah's banter, although she could not throw off this growing fear which was beginning to affect her physically. She was queasy.

She left Noah and started downhill to her house, walking deliberately, carefully, the way she had walked long ago along the Josefstadter Strasse, hoping no one would notice her, clutching the bottle of water to her as she went. If only she dared run! How she wanted to run, although her knee ached and she knew her palm was still bleeding and the emptiness and churning in the pit of her stomach was only partly hunger, but she walked slowly and carefully. She had to control herself, for why should she run? It was only her imagination. Calm, calm. Mustn't get rattled.

The flat was empty. Elsa was still out, probably after food tins. She had no idea where Tani could have gone. She wanted time to think. What was Baumerstock driving at? And Mrs. Heller? Someone had said something about her. They knew something. She tried to imagine what it might be.

On the basement level behind their house was a small but sunny terrazzo courtyard, in the corner of which grew a single large evergreen. Here Debbie sought out her old secure and quiet corner. Her canvas chair was still there, almost forgotten after two months, and she settled herself in the shadow-mottled sun under the tree. Not ten feet from the chair lay an immovable, unexploded mortar shell, its nose buried in a small evergreen bush. She remembered the day Vic had removed the fuse.

She would sit and rest for a few moments and then go to the hospital. It would be nice to rest a bit longer, her first opportunity to sit in the sun for a month. But she knew she had to go quickly, they still needed the extra pair of hands at Hadassah.

Three years ago, when they had first come to Jerusalem, Debbie had loved to sit here, when the tree was small, watching David learn to play, first by himself, and at last with the neighbors' children. How long it had taken to make David secure! How carefully his small social life had to be nurtured. Debbie had never realized what a frightened boy he had grown to be—and it was not easy to fathom the reasons, for she had always made great efforts to shield him in his infant and baby days from the slings and arrows which an outrageous fortune had saved specially for the children of twentieth-century European Jews.

It was under this tree that she had seen his courage grow, too. He had not only made his first friends here, but had fought his first fight. She had started by holding him in her arms in this courtyard and singing him his familiar baby chant, the chant he had loved because he could fill in so many of the words, his well-remembered nursery song sung to a staccato, choppy little tune that was somewhat different with each rendition, for Debbie was no silver-tongued soprano nor a very consistent composer.

She closed her eyes, rested her head back. The tree's shade comforted her; there was no letup in the *hamseen*. It had been almost three years since she had last had to sing that chant to David. How did it go?

"Someday, yes someday we're going on a big . . . *trip*"—David liked to fill in his words with a singsong emphasis—"A big trip far, far away till finally we come . . . *home. Home at last!* David and Mommy and Daddy will all go together on a big, big . . . *ship* and home is the place that is ve-rry . . . warm because the sun shines all day long and everyone is ve-rry . . . *happy*. Because everyone is . . . *friends*. David will have hundreds of friends and David will go to a great big . . . *school*. And the children will play and read stories and sing songs . . . and *go swimming and ride horses* and all the teachers will love all the children . . . *especially David*. And when David grows up he can be chancellor or king or . . . *a fireman or a soldier or a policeman with a big big club*. Because David will be home with his . . . *friends*. And *here we are!*"

Yes, everything had been worth it, the filthy ship, the ghastly dysentery, the revolting food, and back, back in the dark corners of her mind, the unreal days in Rome, the fear of discovery, the deception of everyone, yes, even Victor, perhaps herself too. Those weird, exciting, tortured nights when Vic was at the power plant and she . . .

It was strange that she still thought in terms of blame. There were no pangs of guilt, exactly, or remorse for herself or Vic or even for Angelo. Fear and pride could provoke behavior without honor, without dignity, and almost without shame or blame. Almost, but not quite. For some, rationalization might be necessary, self-justification. Others simply did what they had to do. Like prostitution, she thought with annoyance and amusement. Once you embarked on the business of staying alive, once you were committed to survival, there were no proscriptions in morality or behavior—only things which were good for business or bad.

That change had come so suddenly, so without warning. After a childhood at Lindenhouse and the year in the neat Prague flat with

Victor, nothing that had ever happened in her life could have prepared her for the obscenity of the one-room cellar dungeon in Rome. She had never seen rats before; here they simply stood in the sink and bared their teeth, saying, Here the rat is your equal, here you keep your distance and have suitable respect for the rat, who is also one of God's creatures and a proud one.

Still, you grow accustomed to everything, and when you compared the Roman flat to the good ship *Petah Tiqva,* it was really quite a sweet apartment after all, with a certain fresh charm and dignity, especially after the coat of paint. There was a separate place outside in the hall for natural functions, for instance, and you could frequently get the door to stay closed to minimize the stench. There was a sink in the flat with running cold water that frequently ran. And no one ever died on the floor or threw up all over your clothing the way they did on the ship. In many ways the Roman room was nice. It had meant life, and to stay alive had seemed as important in those days as in these, and no less difficult.

She supposed it was possible for things to be even worse than the *Petah Tiqva* itself; no matter how bad things got, they could be worse. This viewpoint, she realized, could make you an optimist or a pessimist depending on which side of the coin you preferred.

In many ways it was difficult, almost painful, to look back, whether it was to the bright days at Lindenhouse or Vienna when she had seen only a little cloud no larger than a man's hand, or the hectic year in Prague, or the oppressive days in Rome, or these last three wonderful years, or the past four grim months in Jerusalem. Each was painful in its unique way. There was a great sense of relief to be here now . . . if she could ever find the time and peace and quiet to enjoy the relief. It was nice to be able to sun herself here. A little wine would go sweetly now, or brandy would be better, but where was a girl to get any? Anyhow she felt almost light-hearted without it. Hunger, she thought absently. It made the mind light and wandery. Rome was so far away, another life and yet not quite. Could lives be neatly partitioned as so many people in Jerusalem tried to do? Many went the whole way, changed their names, put blinders on their memories, and how often had she heard, "That was a different life. Better not to think of it, better to forget it." What nonsense, and they knew it even as they said it. Was Gussie Goldenberg in a different life from Elsa or the Epsteins? Or Angelo? Silent brooding Angelo, her enemy and master. She remembered mostly his black eyes and his gleaming teeth when he smiled, but it was difficult to really picture him. How he tried to scare her and please her and how she had twisted him round her finger in the end. . . . And if Angelo had been her nemesis, Karl had been her comforter. Karl, the beginning and the end. She was surely in a reflective mood today. Whatever had set her off? David's school, perhaps.

But then surely this was a time for reflection—and looking forward, too. The end of the war and the beginning of something brand new—a new life in a new nation. A girl could surely be forgiven some aimless memories before putting on the harness. To think that it was all because of Karl, her being here. That hardly seemed possible. All because of Karl.

Six

The day Karl had first revealed his intention to leave home was still vivid in her mind. They were living at Lindenhouse, the Pretsch summer place at Puchberg near Snow Mountain, and she had just got back flushed and exuberant after horseback riding with Victor late one hot July afternoon. How old was she then? Nine, nearly ten, in braided pigtails. Yes, that would be about 1930. They were all in the library—Mama, Papa, Karl and even Axel, the collie. She knew at once that something was wrong. Papa sat on the edge of his chair rubbing his stubby hand absently over his gleaming bare head brushing nonexistent hair out of his eyes, with the theatrical page of the paper rolled into his other hand like a weapon. Mama leaned against the huge teakwood desk, dabbing at her eyes with her lace kerchief. And Karl, short for seventeen and painfully thin, still bare and dripping from a swim in the pool, stumped barefoot back and forth over the Persian rug, his white terrycloth robe trailing.

Mama stopped dabbing long enough to say, "Put your slippers on, dear, you're getting the rug all wet."

"I don't know why you're so upset." Karl shrugged. "You'd think I was about to die or something."

"What did you expect us to do," Papa said, "dance a jig?"

"Has Karl said something to Paula again, Mama?" Debbie asked, stuffing a forbidden chocolate into her mouth.

"Stop that, dear, you'll spoil your appetite."

"Karl wants to leave home and go to Palestine," Papa said. "We've been talking."

Papa sounded gruff and worried.

"Oh," she said, "I thought it was something serious."

Vic sat in the small leather chair, picked up the news section of the paper and studied it. Though he was a cousin and they all treated him like a member of the family, it struck her as a little wrong for him to sit listening like that behind the newspaper to what was obviously an intimate family quarrel. Debbie had not quite made up her mind about Cousin Vic. He came from Prague each summer to teach her and Karl to ski, swim, and ride, to work on Karl's tennis, to coach him in algebra. Mama said they were to mind him in every detail, yet Papa paid him just as he used to pay the nursemaid, and that disturbed her because it put him on a level with Willie the chauffeur, or Paula the cook. Still he sat comfortably cushioned like Jove, in the corner of the library, immaculate in his riding habit, listening like a cat.

"Where's Palestine, Karl?" she asked. "Can I go with you?"

"I'm going there to live, Debbie."

This was beyond her.

"All by yourself? Without Mama and Papa?" Karl said nothing. "But who'll take care of you?" Karl only smiled sagely. "Will you have to go to work then? Oh, Karl, please!"

"Of course I'll work. Everybody works there." Karl's close-cropped sandy hair seemed to bristle, his eyes were fiercer, and he looked as if he were trying to be taller.

The idea of Karl's leaving home was preposterous to Debbie; she boldly helped herself to another candy. "I don't think it's a good idea, Karl. Hilda Braunstein will be furious. She'll never let you do it anyway." Hilda was Karl's current girl and so sweet she made Debbie absolutely throw up. Always telling her what cute freckles she had. She knew Debbie hated freckles. "She'll work you around. 'Please, pretty please. Just for little old me, for little old fat, pasty stupid Hilda?' "

"I'm not an unreasonable man, but my God," Papa said, shaking his head. It was clear that Papa took the matter more seriously than she did. Papa, as a rule, scarcely listened to Karl. "The absolutely barrenest spot on earth, no civilization, no music, no literature, no movies, not even a language anyone can speak. Do they have a Reinhardt? Do they have a Bergner? Or even trained seals? In fact what *have* they got?"

"Can I say something?" Karl said. "That's a great criterion for a country! Theaters! Trained seals! Movies! Only a man in the theater business could think like that."

"Now something's wrong with my business! A man works, gives his children an education, a nice home, a position in the community, and in the end he's below standard." He snorted, mostly at himself.

"Is Palestine near where Jesus lived?" Debbie asked brightly. "With all the Jews and things?"

"See, a child, a ten-year-old child knows."

"I'm no child," Debbie pouted, "I'm more grownup than you, you skinny goat."

"You know something?" Karl cried. "You're more grownup than lots of people. At least you know there *is* such a thing as Jews. Do you know that you're a Jew, Debbie? You, personally? I may as well tell you, because no one else around here ever will. They're all Austrians, or Czechs—but never Jews. God forbid! Until someone else spits it out at them as they did to me at the *Gymnasium!*"

"Who?" Papa said. "I'll see the headmaster! I don't stand for such nonsense!"

"What good would it do?" Karl said, exasperated. "What's the good of fighting windmills, Papa?"

"Karl, quiet your voice."

"I suppose in a way I've failed somewhere," Mama said, "or you wouldn't be carrying on so, Karl dear."

"It's not you, Mama." Karl reached toward her helplessly. "It has nothing to do with you." There was an embarrassed quiet.

"Does Karl want to be a Jew?" Debbie asked solemnly to break the silence.

Karl threw up his hands in surrender. "See? No wonder we're confused. And now this man Hitler from Munich is making pretty propaganda. Well, I can't listen to it. I'd rather be doing something useful, building up a new land, restoring the earth."

"So," Papa said grasping the straw, "a very worthwhile task for the Russians and Poles. They were driven to it by pogroms. Believe me, Karl, I'm sympathetic with your spirit. It's something fine to be a pioneer. I understand how you feel. But usually people are not pioneers unless they are forced to it. The world can't live on pioneers alone. There must be those who carry on. And as for Palestine, can't we do more for them from here?"

"How?" Karl was suspicious.

"They need money, don't they? For plows, tractors, shovels—I don't know exactly, but they must need tools. I've been thinking for a long time of making a substantial contribution to the Zionists." He turned to Mama. "Believe me, many of the things he says are wiser than we like to admit."

Karl was taken aback, a little flattered. "Papa, are you serious?"

"Of course I'm serious. Would I joke about such a thing? The fact is I've been playing with a figure of two hundred thousand schillings. Haven't I, Bertha? We talked of it only a few days ago. And next year, we'll send more. Meanwhile, you stick around, Karl, at least till you finish school and then if you still want to go—"

Karl was unhappy, not sure whether to say any more. Finally he blurted, miserably, "I've signed up to take the training course. In six months I have to leave. We're starting a new farm settlement—a kibbutz—sixty of us, all Austrians."

Then Papa really lost his temper.

"Look how wretched you're making your mother! And how do you suppose I feel? Haven't you any sense? We need you here. Why, I don't know, but we do. Mama and I in our fumbling way have become attached to you. Very attached! Why, I'll never understand, but it's a fact. We're attached. Of course this new country sounds glamorous. Of course, pioneers, settlers. But it's a desert, a Godforsaken hellhole of a desert. Be realistic, boy. We don't ask much. Stay with us at least till you're twenty-one. After that, do anything you please. You can go on with your music here. You have a great talent there. My old friend Dr. Bonner expects you at the university next term. We've planned on it." He put his arm affectionately about Karl's shoulders and they made a pathetic picture: the short bulldog man who always had things his own way and his short, skinny blond son, wet and bare beneath the open terrycloth.

Then Vic folded his newspaper, and spoke with the calm voice of authority to his young charge and cousin. Vic was twenty-two then and smoothly handsome in his boyish, unworried way.

"Karl's only suffering from the same thing we've all suffered with one time or another—if we only admit it to ourselves. The old question. What sets us apart from the others? How are we different?

"There are only two possible answers, Karl. One, you look the question in the eyes as I did when I was your age, and you see clearly there *is* no difference. We have eyes, hands, feet like anyone else. We bleed, cry, make music or money, and starve just like anyone else. Then what sets us aside? Only a word. That's all there is to it. Is there a real difference between an Englishman or a German, a Czech or a Jew? Nothing but geography. Otherwise we're all people. They put their shoes on one at a time just like us. As soon as you realize that, you can relax.

"But if you give yourself the other answer—that there *are* differences, you'll find you're trying to define the differences, you'll go on and on, carrying the chip on your shoulder, worried every time someone says the word. You'll go looking for your religion, reaching for a kind of fictional Jewish culture, to anthropology, to racialism, to the Hebrew language. And before you know it, you'll have *made* the difference. Then it's there, and you have to cope with it.

"Haven't our families been happy and accepted everywhere? The problem's just hit you personally for the first time. It's upsetting when it first comes into focus. But it's damned important which decision you make."

"Oh, my God," Karl said when Vic had finished. "That's the kind of stuff I can't stand. Everything that ever happened, I suppose, it was all just words. Kishinev, the Inquisition, this fellow Hitler screaming for blood, they're not real, just nonsense!"

Mama said, "Karl darling, you're all upset. Go upstairs and change your clothes, and after you calm down, we'll talk about it."

Karl became overquiet. "Can I say something, please? Without excitement?" He was pale and his face was drawn. "I love you very much, Mama, and Papa too and Debbie, and I'm even fond of Vic here in my childish way. He's a terrific tennis player anyway, and he sure knows his algebra. But I'm a big boy now, seventeen, that's pretty big. You were married at seventeen, Mama."

"But I'm a girl," Mama said.

"Can I say something?" Karl said. "It was the toughest thing I ever did, making up my mind to go. I've been happy here. I love Lindenhouse, my family and all. But I'm a house pet, a lucky little cat with a nice home. Now I'm learning to think. It's probably unfortunate, may get me in trouble, but I can't help it. Some of my friends at school are ambitious to become rich. They're working like dogs. Some of the others are joining secret political clubs, Nazis a lot of them, some Communists. Me, I've been visiting a man named Jabotinsky. Quite a man. We've been to his house half a dozen times. He's had speakers from Palestine. Did you ever hear of Rutenberg, Vic? You should see the Palestine Electric Corporation stuff, out of nothing! And all done by Jews! A handful, for the benefit of those who'll come later."

"Only nobody will go later!" Papa shouted bitterly. "I can't understand it. Hitler screams Germany for the Germans, and your people are crying Palestine for the Jews. Isn't it all the same nonsense? Isn't the world for people? Vic is right."

But Karl was now agitated beyond reasoning with. "Let them have their Hitler! We have our Herzl and our Weizmann!"

Papa shook his head. "It's in the air, a kind of craziness in the kids. A kind of mass desire to *be* a mass. What is it? Why is it?" He put his arm about Mama's waist and they stood facing Karl, uncertain and afraid.

"Please, Karl," Mama said, "keep an open mind . . . that's all I ask. . . . We'll talk about it later."

"All right, Mama," Karl said reluctantly.

"I don't understand it," Vic said, "I really don't. You have as much right here as anyone."

"Right to what?" Karl was back on familiar ground. Mama and Papa upset him but with Victor he could debate on a doctrinaire level. He made great wet tracks back and forth across the Persian rug while Paula, the cook, scurried in to see what the commotion was about and was shushed back into the pantry by Mama, still dabbing at her eyes.

"Look around you, Vic, get away from your tennis long enough to open your eyes. You read the papers; try to understand them! What do you see? Starvation! Unemployment, soup kitchens! You must see it also in Prague. Look at faces, man. The sick faces, the twelve-year-old girls soliciting on the Ring. There's hate in those faces. We're no longer wanted, Vic, and it's not only wild kids my age, but adults too. Isn't it always so in times like these? Read your history. Oh, this fellow Jabotinsky opened my eyes!"

"But *you* aren't starving," Vic said. "You're comfortable here."

"Sure, I'm so comfortable I can't stand it any longer. Austria's one great poorhouse, and look at us with our cars, a chauffeur, this house. When I look around, you know how I feel about myself? Enough to make me positively puke! I want to go where I can really work. And I'm not going *off* to Palestine, I'm going *back—back home*—where the land will be me, and I'll be the land!"

"Karl, now don't be stuffy. This is your home right here. And there's so much for you to do right here. Not just for Jews, that's much too narrow a viewpoint, but for everyone. Does your running off feed anyone starving or cure anyone sick? By staying right here you can help, with your brains, your work, yes and your money."

"And how are *you* fighting this good fight, old boy? Skiing at Snow Mountain! Teaching Debbie to swim!"

"Karl!" Mama said. "Is that a way to talk?"

Vic was unruffled. "You know quite well this summer's my last. You know I start next month with the Light and Power Company in Prague. And that's exactly how I'm going to do *my* fighting, by sticking to my job and doing a good job, and I'll be good. Expansion of cheap power, transmission of cheap power, that's one of the fundamental answers to depression."

"Bravo! Very fancy. You know, I feel sorry for you, Vic. You'll always do the easiest, most comfortable thing and then prove to yourself a thousand ways that by doing it you're a benefactor to mankind."

"Karl, isn't that exactly what *you're* doing? We've got to stay and fight for decency against lunatics like Hitler. And I don't know why you're so disgusted with material things, with good old-fashioned comfort. Most people work all their lives to get it. This summer house, the pool and the rest. What's so revolting about them? Your father worked damned hard for them, and his father before him. I'm sorry *my* family could never afford those things. I can't think of anything that would make me walk out on all that."

"Well, I'm walking."

Vic said slowly, "I hate to say it, Karl, but I hope you're not running simply because you're scared of that comical Mr. Hitler."

Karl glared at Vic and without a further word slammed out of the room. Those were the days for fine melodramatic gestures.

Mama turned angrily on Vic and cried, "All your fine arguments, Vic. So academic. You're driving him away! Don't argue with him about it again!"

Debbie wondered what everyone was getting so worked up about. After a while Papa calmed himself and soothed Mama. He was only a boy, only *talking* about going away. Quite clearly he was not this moment going and he would never go. He would only talk, talk, talk.

Then came the Sunday Karl left for Trieste, a day so different. Quiet and frost and snow in the streets made the ride to Franz Joseph Station peaceful. Karl looked wistfully about as they rode, trying with his eyes to photograph Vienna. And the old city was particularly beautiful that day: the cozy crowd before old St. Stephen's, the stately buildings on the Ring, and especially the university. It was no day for recriminations. Only love and good-bye. Write often and we'll send food. Be a good boy, Karl. Wear your woolens if it gets cold. Don't forget this, Mama. Don't forget that, Papa. Good-bye, Debbie. *You'll* come to Palestine to see me, won't you?

"But, of course, Karl, when I'm big enough to get married, if my husband will take me."

"Insist on it! I'll expect you."

He left her a present. A gold Star of David on a gold chain—to hang about her neck, but Mama would never let her wear it and it was lost years ago.

"Good-bye. Until we see each other again."

He tugged her pigtails as he kissed her cheek.

"Karl, Karl! We almost forgot to give it to you. Open the door, dear. Hurry. Fruit. A nice basket of fruit for the trip. You'll try to keep on with your music? God bless you, Karl."

"Don't worry, Mama. I'll be all right."

Papa reached into his inside coat pocket and handed Karl a check. "We wanted you to have this, both of us. We hope you'll use it wisely."

Karl stared at the check a long time, expressionless. Then took out his handkerchief and blew his nose, and she was sure he was crying. Her impression—she had to smile now when she thought of it—was that Karl was weeping because the check was so small.

"God bless you, Karl." Mama was waving, looking more fragile than ever. The engine hissed. "Attention! All aboard."

They waved, Mama, Papa, Debbie, Willie the chauffeur, and even Axel pointed his long lean collie face to the rear of the disappearing train with a sad expression.

Mama broke into lamentation. "Oh David dear! Karl, our little Karl from the wet diapers, from the kindergarten, Karl our ski jumper . . . I hope he'll be happy . . . I hope he doesn't completely give up his music . . ."

"Bertha, honey, don't. In a year he'll be back, I promise you, maybe sooner. It's only a stage. Right now he's in a crazy Jewish stage and it's not entirely his fault. After all, we were Jews way ahead of him. Come, come on, the car is waiting. Debbie dear, come along, he can't see you waving any more."

Later came Karl's letters and photographs. Karl at the farm, running a tractor, milking a cow, with his farmer friends, boys and girls; his pictures looked happy.

Then Karl in Jerusalem. By that time Debbie was past fourteen. Karl as a bus-driver, a privileged position in Jerusalem, he wrote. A cooperative, a company called Egged. He was to have a share, whatever it meant, which he bought with part of Papa's check.

"A bus-driver," Papa snorted, his bright eyes popping and his bald head wagging with aggravation. "Here he could have been much greater—he could have been a taxi-driver! I could have sold a few theaters and bought him a taxi. You meet a better class of people that way. Hah, some way to build up a country! A genuine pioneer, a bus-driver!"

And then Karl married. The pictures showed a disappointingly plain, unadorned girl in nurse's uniform and cap. Lilith, an odd, pretty name, Lilith. Originally from Budapest. The daughter of a veterinary and a ballet dancer. "It's funny," Debbie said to her friend Gussie Goldenberg on the way home from Frau Morgenstelle's school one afternoon. "I have this sister-in-law in Jerusalem I've never even met. A Hungarian girl. Look." Gussie was more impressed with the snapshots than she. Palestine seemed always to have glamour for Gussie.

When Karl became rich, and he was rich from bus-driving, he moved to the nicest section of Jerusalem—Beth Hakerem—and in letter after letter, pleaded with them to come, if only for a visit. But Papa would never hear of it. He was Austrian and stubborn.

Seven

What had Karl *really* been doing and thinking all those years when Debbie was growing up? What had he become, living in faraway Jerusalem? For in spite of his letters and the photos she had no clear idea, and the meaning of his letters grew hazier and hazier to her as their centers of interest separated. It was absolutely beyond her imagination to think of him driving a bus anyhow. And if she told herself the truth she hadn't as much interest in Karl and in Palestine as a dutiful sister ought, perhaps because she was living in an age of crisis, and while Central Europe was having hers, Debbie was going through what Papa called one great Debbie crisis after another. And crises keep a growing girl's mind occupied.

In those rare periods when there was an absence of crisis, Lindenhouse in the summer, or the two-floor apartment on Rotenturm Strasse during the season, was aglow, packed in the evenings with theatrical people, writers, directors, managers, musicians, conductors, actors and actresses, critics and occasionally minor politicians who would come all the way down to Puchberg at Snow Mountain to meet this or that celebrated figure in the theater or cinema. Mama was a famous party-giver. Weekend evenings in the summer Papa showed films in their little motion picture theater on the grounds to which not only the guests came, but also all the help. And in the winter they used the more compact projection room in the apartment.

During the days, Mama, small and helpless as she looked, was usually deep in the details of some charity affair attended by countless good ladies of whom Debbie could never keep track. Her impression was that the ladies came to the apartment or to Lindenhouse to gossip, eat, stare, and leave large donations. And that Mama, after adding her own, distributed the money like a good fairy to abysmally poor and grateful children or old crones or blind men who, she was sure, fought to kiss the hem of Mama's skirt. Mama also sent large sums to Lilith's hospital in Jerusalem. Everyone said she was a wonderful woman and in fact no one could help loving Mama, who, although not unusually bright, toiled fiercely to be good and selfless and kind. Debbie had no choice but to help Mama after school with her charity affairs.

So it was not possible to give Karl much thought, even if one didn't consider the recurring crises, which had very much to be considered. Among the major and minor ones were such matters as the terrible Cold-in-the-Head Crisis the week before she was to play Kathy in *Karl Heinrich* at Frau Morgenstelle's School and how with the help of aspirin and cognac she came through like a true daughter of the theater; the Unfair-Final-Exam-in-Algebra Crisis, a subject no normal girl could possibly master anyhow; the mortifying Crisis-of-the-Descending-Panties during the opening waltz at the first formal at Dancing School and the abandonment of fat old Hans Vogel in the middle of the floor without explanation, resulting in Great Disgrace; and months later Papa's cruel and inhuman punishment—a week's house confinement—for staying out until All Hours with the same Hans Vogel, a young swain of whom Papa disapproved, but who was only Very Boring; Fräulein Froelich's-Persecution Crisis in Sixth Grade, which made her think fleetingly of Karl and his ominous warnings; the occasion when she and six other Girl Scouts had been lost in the Vienna woods for nine hours, with police and a dozen frantic parents out hunting for them until they were located by the fire Debbie had built; the cutting of her long hair and the beginning of artificial curling; the Skiing Accident when she was thirteen and Victor took her to the Krknos not far from Prague for a weekend and she went down the great slope all by herself early in the morning while Victor was still asleep, though Victor had strictly forbidden it; the results of which were not only that her broken arm remained in a cast for months, but that she had to come vigorously to Vic's defense with Papa, who had the primitive notion that a man who took charge of a thirteen-year-old girl was responsible for what happened to her, and in spite of her spirited defense and Papa's forgiveness, Victor had remained unhappy and never forgave himself. It was a Great Mess.

And most important there was the tragic time when she was nearly fifteen and their collie Axel was run down by a truck and killed, and Debbie remained inconsolable for a week, until six days later Cousin Victor, whom she had written about it, and his father, Cousin Jan, the doctor, paid a surprise visit and brought with them the sweetest, friendliest, most helpless little spaniel puppy in the entire world and gave it to Debbie for her very own. The pup was called Spots for the black speckles on his back, and formed an immediate attachment to Debbie, who in turn loved him instantly and forever. But the puppy was only the end of one Debbie crisis and the beginning of a much more important one.

Cousin Victor, on the first afternoon of the visit, quite unexpectedly looked up from the paper he was reading, folded it, and suggested that he take her out for the evening since his father wanted to spend some time with the Pretsches and catch up on family gossip.

Everyone seemed instantly delighted with Vic's suggestion, including Papa, who suppressed any mention of homework and merely said that the car and Willie would be at their disposal, and he also happened to have passes to a fetching Lehar operetta.

As Mama helped her on with her gown, she scolded, "Heavens to Methuselah, Debbie, stop squirming. Stand still a minute till I finish. I don't know what's got into you." And when Debbie applied her lipstick with a heavier hand than ever before, Mama made her take it off. "Plenty of time for that. Just be yourself, act natural, I'm sure Victor will be most proud of you that way. Now have a lovely time, dear."

"I'm not nearly the child he may think I am," Debbie pouted. "Or that you may think either, Mama. In many ways I feel quite a bit older than you, actually. Sometimes you're so *naïve*, Mama."

Mama smiled her innocent girlish smile. "Thank you, dear. That's one of the nicest things you've said."

Debbie tossed her head back in such a way that she could see herself better in the mirror. She was glad she had got rid of her childish braids. Dressed in her white evening gown and wearing her expression of cold, aloof sophistication, she looked fetching even to herself, although her tiny bosom and insufficient hips were no help toward the womanly look for which she yearned.

Dr. Marmorek, Mama, and Papa kissed her good night and Papa insisted on having her turn about so he could see her from all sides. "Just as I suspected," he said proudly to Dr. Marmorek, "the best looking girl in Vienna. And I don't exaggerate."

"Oh, Papa!" she said, "you're such a promoter!"

Willie drove them downtown and in the back seat of the huge black limousine beside Victor she felt more like a great lady than she ever had before or ever would again. Victor took her to the Three Hussars, a restaurant on the Ring, where she had been before with her parents, but the captain and the waiter had a different kind of respect for her tonight. They bowed to her as nicely as if she had been Elisabeth Bergner or Jeritza. She was conscious of the eyes on them for they must have made a remarkable couple—Vic so handsome and massive, glowing like a knight in the black armor of his tuxedo, and she, half his size, delicate and glistening in white.

"Now tell me all about yourself, Vic," she said, emboldened by the dinner champagne, which she ordered and drank for the first time in her life with such *savoir-faire*. "Your work, I mean, it must be quite intriguing. Of course, I don't want to pry into your private affairs. That's not what I mean. But I often think of all that electricity in Prague and I wonder what you're doing with it." She felt terribly flippant and alluring.

Vic was tactful. He smiled and said he thought it would be difficult for her to understand, that it was really quite dry and technical and that probably she would be bored.

"Oh, I'm good at algebra and all that sort of thing," she lied blithely. "Try me."

He did, reluctantly at first, as if to a child, but she reacted with fascinated attention from beginning to end. And each time he said, doubtfully, "You're sure you understand what I mean?" or "I'm not boring you?" she nodded carefully, smiled harder than ever and said, "I think it's absolutely *fascinating*, isn't it, and it sounds like such fun." She did understand that he supervised the extension of electric service to new homes and factories and to entirely new areas, and that he had a number of crews working under him, but when he tried to explain high and low tension lines, substations, feeders, transformers, radial and network systems, these only tumbled together to give her the lovely impression that her cousin was not only handsome and a great athlete and teacher, and kind and thoughtful, but also terribly intelligent and wise and clever and scientific in a quiet way which put to shame all the showy sophisticates who came to visit Mama and Papa.

She loved him. And she understood at that moment in a flash of insight why all the boys her own age were awkward and silly and Terrible Bores.

After dinner they went to the operetta. Some of the music was nice and lilting and put her in a gay party mood. When the show was over Vic asked Willie to take them to the People's Prater, the great midway of shows and games, rides and slides, ice cream and candy; and although she was furious to be brought to such a childish place instead of a nightclub like the Kahlenberg or even for a sip of Heuriger and outdoor dancing at the wine gardens of Grinzing or in Stadt Park where he would surely have gone with a *woman*, she pretended so well to be having a wonderful time that she soon was having one. Victor loved everything. They rode in a huge tunnel, something called a "Ride with the Devil," in the pitch dark. She shrieked and giggled at the jumping ghosts and sudden lights. They gambled and played games and won prizes—a blue stuffed bunny, a kewpie doll, and a can of coffee.

They went to have their picture taken together on the rear platform of a papier mâché train that had a sign proclaiming it to be the "Honeymoon Express." Debbie clutched all the prizes to her, and at the photographer's instructions Vic put his arm about her shoulders and they looked into each other's eyes. His, she noticed, were so brown and soft and serious, even though he was smiling cheerfully.

While the picture was being developed they rode on the great ferris wheel, and high above the fairground lights they were so alone that for a brief instant it seemed to Debbie that nothing in the world was impossible. His protective arm about her felt comfortable and she snuggled her head happily on his shoulder and looked up at him. Lord, he was beautiful! Grinning down at her like a satisfied uncle with a six-year-old niece, the same grin she remembered when she first mastered the crawl for the full length of the pool, at eight. How could she ever make him realize she was now a mature person, practically a woman, even though she might be only fifteen calendar years old? It was so frustrating, really!

Before they left the Prater Vic remembered the picture. It came out rather nicely of them both. When he looked at it he squinted and screwed up his face in an amused puzzlement that was only fleeting. "Honeymoon Express!" he laughed. "My God, you look grownup enough to really *be* my wife. Look at you!"

She did. Her high heels which had been plaguing her all evening made some of the difference. But part of it she knew was just wanting to. "And we look as if we love each other dearly too," she said brightly. "I'd say, we'll be very happy together."

"Yes, I guess we will," he said and quickly slipped the photo into his side pocket. "Come along, Girl Scout, it's late and we'd better be getting back. Dad and I have an early train to make." He bought a morning paper and they went to find Willie and the car.

When they reached home and Willie opened the door, Debbie had the sinking feeling that the most wonderful evening of her life was over.

Mama and Papa and Dr. Marmorek were asleep. But before they went to bed Victor suggested that they get tea and crackers from the kitchen as they used to do summers in the country when Karl was home and Debbie was a child.

In the kitchen, Vic asked about Karl; and Debbie, remembering how close they had all been, realized with some shame that neither of them had mentioned Karl all evening. She tried to be enthusiastic about the letters from Palestine. "Some day," she said absently, "I'd like to go visit him."

"Oh, I don't know," Vic said, "I hear Jerusalem is a dreary place—the Wailing Wall and all that. I just don't think I could go in for all that wailing." She giggled. "Come on, girl, we'd better get off to sleep. I've kept you up way past your bedtime and way past my own for that matter. You must have school tomorrow too. Upstairs now."

The guest room was downstairs so he went only to the foot of the stairs. "I'm leaving very early so I probably won't see you. You and the family must come to see us in Prague though—soon."

"Love to," she said, "invite us soon." She stood hesitant, arms loaded with the bunny, the kewpie doll, and the red balloon.

"Good night, Girl Scout."

He kissed her on the mouth as he had done since she was eight; that was the terrible trouble, you couldn't find significance in the most significant things. Her knees grew weak, and perhaps she kissed him back harder than she ought to, but if he noticed it he said nothing.

"Vic," she said softly, "may I have the picture? I ought to have something to remember the evening by. Such a nice evening, did I say thank you?"

"But you have the bunny," he said slowly. "You have the kewpie doll. What a hog you are! What will I have? Besides I have to study it more carefully. It's a rather interesting picture."

She turned and ran upstairs to her room. Her clothes were strewn everywhere by the time she got into her pajamas, and she curled up on the bed with the bunny, pensively stroking its long funny ears. There was no one to talk to, no one she could tell anything to, certainly not Mama or Papa. She was too old to talk to a toy bunny. It suddenly occurred to her that it would be nice if Karl were home. She began to pull a comb angrily through the snags in her hair, and when she felt composed she sat down at her writing desk and wrote Karl a letter, which, after she scratched in a few corrections, said:

Dear Karl:—

Poor old Axel ran out on the road and a truck struck him and killed him right away. Luckily he didn't suffer, but of course I've been absolutely miserable and so have Mama and Papa. I know how you loved him and I'm sorry we have to tell you this.

Your photos and letters have been so worn out from thumbing over that you'll have to send more. Your new house is very nice. Do you own the whole thing or is it divided into apartments like your last one? Beth Hakerem sounds like a lovely neighborhood, though it must be very boring to live with so many bus-drivers. At least when Papa talks shop, it's fascinating, it's even glamorous, but when you bus-drivers talk shop what ever can you talk about? The price of petrol is about all I can think of. Is it high or low? Heavens to Methuselah!

Now, I think Lilith's work sounds much more interesting. I've always loved nurses. Secretly I've always wanted to be a nurse myself. It's what Victor would call my Girl Scout instinct.

I haven't told you the latest about Victor, have I? He came to visit and brought us a new puppy to take Axel's place. The darlingest little thing you ever met. He's a spaniel, only six weeks old.

What would you think if I should some day marry Vic? After all he's a *fourth* cousin. Practically a *fifth* cousin the way I figure it, so it's not exactly *incest*, I wouldn't think. Anyhow, I believe I may. Don't mention it to anyone, especially not Mama or Papa. No one knows anything about it yet, not even Vic. The only one who knows is I. And now you.

With all my love,

Your loving sister,
DEBORAH

It was to be two years before Debbie and her parents visited Victor and his father under circumstances that could never have been foreseen; meanwhile after three weeks Karl replied disappointingly to her letter:—

As for your personal matter, Debbie, I can only keep your secret and hope it remains one. As a big brother who is so far away that you can't spit back at me the way you used to, I guess you can't keep me from offering a little unpleasant advice. I hope you will find a nice young fellow your own age, with at least half your native courage, who is a Jew and who knows it; and then I hope you will take the first boat out here with him. Or better still, why don't you persuade Mama and Papa to come right away and if that's impossible, which I suspect it is, knowing Papa, why not come out yourself? You're only a year or two younger than I was when I came and it's much easier here now. If a husband is what you are looking for (at your age!) we'll find you several to pick from, right here in Jerusalem. Somehow I'll manage to get certifications. There isn't much time, you know. We are getting quite a number of Germans here now and they tell us of the frightful conditions in Berlin, Munich, Breslau and other cities. How long can Vienna be safe? I'm not trying to be gloomy, but please think seriously of all this. Lilith sends greetings and love.

But Debbie was having none of Karl's advice. He was living in his own dream world. It was amazing how few people dared to face truth. Even Mama and Papa took to the shadowy world of everyday mundanities—fantasies, actually, to a truth-facer like Debbie—paying bills, buying groceries, going to business, worrying about Hitler.

But no truth, large or small, could escape Debbie's inner eye. None but she could read between the lines of Vic's long lovely letters. When, in her sixteenth spring, she strolled languorously with Mama along the Ring, none but she could see herself sitting before the fireplace in one of the window displays, older and breathtakingly beautiful, while Vic, in a silk smoking jacket, floated beside her, masterful but tender, and the governess brought the pink children to be kissed good night.

Vic was with her at bedtime too, suddenly shrunk small enough for her to hold in the crook of her arm, beneath three blankets on cold winter nights. He was only a boy, and she comforted him when his mother died, and promised to try to take her place.

During assemblies at Frau Morgenstelle's they played tennis together or went skiing in soft mountains of warm cottony snow. Vic teased her from between logarithms and applauded the splendor of her Czerny exercises. When, at dancing school, she waltzed with bumbling Hans Vogel, by simply closing her eyes she could swim into Vic's welcoming arms. The rest was mirage.

She wrote him once, saying, "I think of you always," but that seemed too obvious, so she changed it to "We think of you often." Vic would know. How could he *not* know?

During Debbie's days of transcendental longing and delight, she could not be expected to listen with more than half an ear to Mama or to Gussie when they continued to fret over gruesome vexations like what to do about Hitler. She knew neither Papa nor Vic would ever expose her to any danger like *that.*

Eight

Indeed, during the summer the Olympic games were held at Berlin and the anti-Jewish policy of the German Government was relaxed. To Papa it was confirmation that Karl was an alarmist. Meanwhile they read of Arab uprisings and riots in Jaffa and Jerusalem. Life in Palestine, Papa observed, was no bed of roses and they had always to worry about Karl.

At home there were a few concessions to the times: one was the gradual disappearance from Mama's table of her tastiest dishes—matzoh balls, gefüllte fish, and cheese blintzes. It seemed that she could not mention these dishes to Paula the cook, who sometimes listened to Hitler's broadcasts from Germany, without a blush of embarrassment, and rather than be embarrassed she stopped ordering them. Also a few of the friends who had been frequent visitors like the actress Olga Perelli openly proclaimed themselves to be Nazis and were not again invited. But for the most part everyday routine remained unchanged.

It seemed as though they were perpetually planning to visit Victor or have him down, but one thing or another always interfered. Once it was the mumps, a mortifying thing to befall a grown girl, and another time Papa had to change their plans because of business. They had still not visited when on Debbie's eighteenth birthday the tall, scholarly Austrian Chancellor Schuschnigg was called on the phone from Berchtesgaden and in a melancholy March afternoon was forced to surrender Austria to the tender mercies of the Third Reich. The little birthday party Mama had arranged came to a sudden end when Schuschnigg made a surprise announcement over the radio from Ballhausplatz: "Austrians! Chancellor Hitler has asked President Miklas to cancel the plebiscite and has asked me to resign. If we do not give in within the hour, German troops will invade Austria. President Miklas has asked me to tell the Austrian people that we have yielded to force. To avoid bloodshed and destruction I have submitted my resignation. God save Austria!" That poor, unhappy, sad voice. Silence and then music—"Deutschland Über Alles"!

Within five minutes swastika-marked planes were overhead, dropping leaflets. Gussie Goldenberg left the party, and went into the street; when she returned, her face was as white as the sheet of paper she carried. The pamphlet said, "Nazi Germany welcomes Nazi Austria!" The streets were full of wildly cheering people, and from the Graben and Kärntner Strasse they heard the frightening rhythmic roar which until that day had never come from anywhere but the radio: "Sieg Heil! Sieg Heil! Heil Hitler!" coming in waves of cheering. And the crash of breaking glass.

To Debbie the Nazis had all the unreality of a bad cinema. The brown hordes with the red swastika armbands seemed to come from nowhere and everywhere. People had not time to prepare themselves, and if they had they wouldn't have known what to do. On the streets there was a tremendous excitement, shouting, and a feeling of new strength and good cheer, but at home and in her own heart there was only a chill fear.

The first day of school after the Anschluss some ruffian kids were waiting in the street with rubber truncheons which they used on Gussie Goldenberg and two other Jewish-looking girls, beating them across the backs all the way to the tram stop. Teachers looked the other way. After a while Fräulein Froelich asked the boys sweetly to stop. But the boys never noticed Debbie, who didn't look Jewish and walked slowly and deliberately. Those who ran fastest, she saw, attracted the heaviest blows.

It was on the Josefstadter Strasse when she was coming home from

Frau Morgenstelle's, the third day of the Nazis, when school had been let out early for the parade, that she herself saw the smashed shop-windows hastily boarded up, and the two women in mink coats forced by Brownshirts to scrub the gutter with bucket and brush while a smiling, detached, appreciative crowd looked on as if they were watching actors in a play and expected the actors would presently rise, take their curtain calls and go home. She walked, but not too quickly, to catch the bus home, her heart pumping. The car was no longer available, for Willie had turned out to be a Nazi; Willie whose son, Fritz, Papa had put through college!

How Papa arranged it she never knew, but on the fourth day of the Nazis he announced he had been in touch with Cousin Victor, who insisted they come for a visit and that arrangements had been made to do so—a long overdue visit too. Debbie tried to be decorous and not dance about the apartment. Mama was more openly delighted. "It will be nice to get away, a lovely change for all of us. I've been so depressed since Willie left, you've no idea. Not only that he turned out to be one of those—those terrible creatures all this time, right in our house too, but I know it will never be possible to get another chauffeur like Willie nowadays. I believe people are afraid to work for us. You'd think we'd done something wrong!" Mama liked to face things squarely, but she generally faced in the wrong direction. Imagine! She had run an ad for a new chauffeur, but there were no responses, dejecting her more than ever. "And I do so hate the idea of going out," she rambled. "Prague will be a nice change."

"Little Willie's a fool," Papa said tolerantly. "He'll get in with that crowd and do all their dirty work and when they have no more use for him they'll put him in the army and use him for target practice. Anyone who joins them's a villain or a fool, and little Willie's no villain. Most of them are like Willie—fools. But we're getting out, whatever they are."

Debbie could tell that Willie's leaving, dressed in his new storm troop uniform and wearing the red hooked-cross armband, had shaken them both more than anything before. And she felt that in some way the trip to Prague was related to Willie's sudden departure. They packed for themselves, telling neither Paula nor Hilda of their plans, at Papa's suggestion, which he made with all the heavy-handed casualness he could muster. Papa was her rock of self-confidence and courage. It was one of the wonderful ways in which Vic resembled him.

They were to leave on the morning train and in the excitement of anticipation, tinged with uneasiness, Debbie slept only fitfully. It must have been about four in the morning when she first heard the banging on the apartment entrance door. At first she could not be sure, but the sound grew louder in her ears. All the stories she had heard whispered about the nocturnal visits of Brownshirts came rolling over her mind like a wave of nausea. She felt weak and sick, but somehow forced herself into her robe and ran downstairs as quietly and quickly as she could. In the foyer she listened for the voices of the men she knew were waiting in the outer hall, but all she heard was the sound of sobbing, a kind of strange gasping, punctuated by the knocking of the great brass knocker. She turned the light on and opened the door to let in a wild-eyed girl clutching an overcoat over a nightgown and hoarsely inarticulate. It was Gussie Goldenberg, crying hysterically and for the moment beyond reach.

Debbie had an immediate feeling of tremendous relief. They were safe.

From the top of the stairs Mama and Papa, robed and sleepy-eyed, called down hoarsely to know the trouble.

In no time Mama was cooking hot milk and honey for Gussie, and Papa and Debbie in the drawing room were simultaneously soothing her and listening to her incoherent account of the arrival of storm troops at the Goldenberg house at about eleven and the arrest of her father. Gussie had no mother. After a while she calmed herself enough to make sense, but Debbie noticed that she blinked harder than ever, her little nervous habit accentuated.

"We didn't know what to do, what to think. They said there were irregularities in Daddy's contracting business, at least that's what I think one of them said, there were three of them, and he had to get his things right away. It was really so funny. He had no idea what to pack. You know, Daddy hasn't packed a bag for himself for years. The maid was asleep, so I had to help him, and it was really funny. He took three ties and left his toothbrush and razor. You just don't know what to pack, you know, how can you decide what to take on such short notice? You don't even know whether you'll be indoors or outdoors. Really. And we didn't expect anything like this. It was so funny. He told me not to worry, of course Daddy would, but I could see he was worried himself. I've never seen him so white. Just white. Two of them were polite, I'll say that, but one of them kept saying he should hurry, they couldn't wait all night. After they left, I just didn't know what to do. I couldn't stay there any more. I know from my uncle in Hamburg, that's Daddy's brother, you know, the one who had the department store, once they start on the family, they take everyone, sooner or later. And what could *I* tell them about Daddy's old business books? Then I thought of Debbie and you all. I just couldn't bear to stay home another minute. I was just so *scared*."

She ran herself out, like a phonograph record running overspeed, and no one tried to interrupt her until she paused for a slight coughing spasm.

Mama was kind and calm. "But how did you get here, child? Here, have a few cookies with the milk."

"I walked," Gussie gulped. "I don't know how I did it, but I just ran and walked, I just had to get here somehow. I think I never ran so far—or so fast. And I lost my way. The streets are so difficult at this hour without lights, without people. What time is it now?"

"Quarter to five," Papa said.

"Why, it's over ten kilometers out to your place!" Mama said. "Out in Döbling, aren't you? You poor thing!"

"But what else could I do? Where could I go? I'm so worried about Daddy, I don't know what to do. I hope I'm not causing you any trouble. Do you think I will? I wouldn't want to make any trouble for anyone. If you think I ought to go somewhere else—"

"Don't be silly," Papa said impatiently as though he were angry.

"You can sleep in with Debbie," Mama said. "And don't worry about your father. I'm sure it's only some misunderstanding with these stupid officials. Bureaucrats. You know how things are today—all mixed up. Mr. Pretsch will make inquiries about him. We'll get a good attorney. Mr. Jarcho is a very clever lawyer, dear, isn't he?" She turned to Papa. "He always gets his clients off, doesn't he, dear?"

"Don't go up just yet," Papa said. "Not yet. Who could sleep now anyhow?" He lit one of his cigars.

Paula the cook appeared from the dining room clutching her old-fashioned kimono to her throat. "Is there any trouble?" she inquired, and her normally small eyes were enormous.

"No," Papa said. "Go back to sleep. Everything's fine."

Paula retreated, but when she saw Gussie her eyes were, if anything, larger.

Papa sat on the edge of one of the wing chairs, rubbing his bald head with his characteristic gesture of brushing the hair out of his eyes.

"Did these storm troopers say what kind of irregularities there were in the books?"

"Oh, no." Gussie shook her head as though she were scarcely thinking of Papa's question, as if she almost had not heard him. "I didn't understand what they were driving at. One of the men just kept telling Daddy to hurry, and said not to ask questions, he would get plenty of time to figure things out later. He said there will be figures and figures from Daddy's own books, that's the way he put it, figures and figures, which he could explain to the District Leader, who could not make head or tail of them. The other men were polite and kept telling this one trooper to take it easy and not say so much. I really don't know what it was all about. Everyone knows how honest Daddy is. Why, he never cheated anyone in his life."

"Yes, of course," Papa said, and now he seemed not to be listening either. "Of course, your father was really an exceptional man."

His past tense hung in the air like a foul word, and Gussie took off her thick glasses and cleaned them carefully.

Mama pulled Papa aside to the study, and while Debbie brought a robe for Gussie to replace her topcoat, which was all she had over her nightgown, her parents were in animated conversation.

"Didn't you bring *any* clothes, Gus? Not a single dress?"

"Just this coat, and my purse. I just ran out the way I was. I have five thousand marks Daddy gave me while we were packing. That's quite a bit. It ought to last quite a while. He just gave me the money and whispered, 'Escape, Gussie. Escape.' And the last thing I took before I left was a picture of my mother that we always kept on the piano, you know, and—and this picture of Daddy." She bit her lip. "Isn't that a good one of him?" She unfolded a portrait photograph of her father; a little gray man with a sharp silver mustache and pince-nez glasses.

"Yes," Debbie said, "I always liked it. He looks so distinguished. Like a professor."

"I'm never going back to that house!" Gussie said suddenly and with unexpected vehemence. "Never. I don't know what I'll do, I'll hide somewhere, I'll think of something. But I'll never go back there and I'll never wear a yellow star no matter what. Never! No one can make me!"

Papa and Mama returned to the living room, and Gussie jammed the photo back into her purse and closed it quickly, batting her eyes more furiously than ever.

Papa said, "Who's your father's lawyer?"

"I don't know. Mr. Pfizer, I guess. At least I'm pretty sure."

"Is he Aryan?" Papa said.

"Yes, I think so. I only met him once."

Papa went to the phone and called a number.

"Mr. Jarcho. Oscar? It's David. David Pretsch. I know, but nowadays it's always the middle of the night. Listen, Oscar. Listen carefully. A friend's been arrested. Selig Goldenberg. A building contractor. Of course, a Jew . . . I don't know. His daughter's here with us now. His lawyer's an Aryan, name is Pfizer. You know him? Good. So much the better. Work with him. Do whatever you have to. Whatever it costs. I don't care. I'll take care of it. I want him out . . . His temple?"

"Temple Israel," Gussie said. "We're members."

"Temple Israel," Papa said. "But Oscar, take my advice, don't get help from the rabbi. It won't do any good and it might do plenty of harm. Nah! They wouldn't care if he were the pope. They wouldn't care if he were Jesus Christ himself. Don't you understand, Oscar, they don't like God? They're against Him. Leave God out of it and do it like a plain lawyer, will you? Use what's-his-name, Pfizer. Good. And, Oscar, I'll be out of town for a week. Yes, Prague. I'll be at the Ambassador. Let me know. And I'm sorry, Oscar, to wake you. Good. Thanks."

He hung up, exuberant. "Was that telling him? Nothing to it. Have him out in a few days. A wonder, that fellow Jarcho. You ought to hear him in court. Absolutely has them eating out of his hand. Really Reinhardt should hire him. The man's a consummate actor."

Mama was relieved, and Gussie smiled wanly.

Papa said to Gussie, "We're leaving for Prague in three hours, to visit Mrs. Pretsch's cousins."

"He just insisted that we come," Debbie said. "*You* remember Victor."

"Of course," Gussie said, "the one at Puchberg who taught us to swim." She looked at Papa searchingly. "But how will you get across? The borders are closed. They're not letting Jews—"

"We'll get across," Papa said sharply. "Don't worry."

Gussie blinked. "But then where can I . . . ?"

"We want you to come with us," Mama said softly. "We've been talking about it."

"Me? But how? I could never. I have no papers, no passport, no visa . . ."

"Everything'll be arranged," Papa said. "I have a few friends."

"And in Prague, Victor has lots of friends," Debbie said proudly.

"I hear Prague is a beautiful city." Gussie spoke oddly; she seemed far away and vague again. "What if we are caught?"

She looked at Papa and at Mama, and then at Debbie. No one answered her.

"I suppose I might as well come with you," Gussie said. "What can I do for Daddy by staying here? I'm a girl. I'm only seventeen. What can I do?" She was crying but ignored it.

"Of course," Mama said. "You must try to be sensible. The first thing to do is to get away for a while."

"Oh, I'm sure I'll have a wonderful time in Prague. They say it's a beautiful city. Daddy was always promising to take me there some day for a holiday."

She was sobbing hopelessly.

How would Papa manage to get them all to Prague? Debbie wondered whether Mama and Gussie were as frightened as she. Papa, as always outwardly confident, made several phone calls while they dressed and gathered the baggage, and Mama scribbled a hurried line to Paula saying they would be home next Monday. By eight o'clock they were at North Station, where Papa hustled them into a first-class compartment. During the train journey to Gmünd, where they were to cross the border, he left them from time to time to see the conductor or one of the officials—there seemed to be a thousand uniformed men on the train—and on two occasions, shortly after he returned, he pulled the compartment shade down, took off his right shoe, removed part of the sole and drew out a thick stack of German hundred- and thousand-mark notes, took off the rubber band, counted carefully, put two or three bills in his pocket, and after rubberbanding the stack again, returned it to the compartment in his sole. Only after he had replaced his shoe, did he ask Debbie to raise the shade. Mama read her magazine, pretending not to notice, but, of course, in such close quarters it was silly even to pretend. Debbie had heard the new currency regulations; they could hang Papa for what he was doing. He always carried a big roll of bills with him, but it was a family joke that he could never in a million years guess how much there was in the roll, within five thousand schillings. Counting his money this way, it was positively creepy.

The girls and Mama talked with overlively interest about the snow-dipped mountain peaks, crystalline in the spring sun, and the farms and hills timidly streaked with new foliage, innocently green. Papa was not much for scenery; he muttered and dozed over the script of a new play that had been submitted to him for backing several weeks ago, looking up from time to time at Gussie with a glance so searching that Debbie wondered about it. Gussie was wearing one of Debbie's gayest new print dresses and looked much better than she ever had in her own unbecoming things. More Aryan, somehow, but not Aryan enough. Perhaps they had made a mistake bringing Gussie. But what else could they have done? If only she were not so obvious—that prominent bulbous nose, her black kinky hair, the plump figure.

At Gmünd Papa left the compartment and when he returned said, "We have to get out here. There'll probably be an examination, just routine. I'll take care of the currency declaration and baggage. Gussie, now you remember who you are—Augusta Pretsch—it's very important because you're traveling on my passport."

They were separated from Papa for the first time in the station, and with six other women undressed and searched by two uniformed matrons, wearing the ubiquitous swastika, who went sullenly from one shivering woman to another, ran their hands through their clothing and viewed their bodies with the impersonal interest of cattle dealers. Sullenly and deliberately one of them drew a rubber glove on to her right hand and called Gussie into a cubicle. In a few moments Gussie reappeared, red and furious, the matron following her, still expressionless. Debbie found the entire episode fiercely embarrassing and kept her eyes off Mama, whom she never remembered seeing naked in her life. Mama surprised her by taking the entire matter with indifference, as though she did this sort of thing every day. "Aryan?" the matron asked, even though their papers so attested.

"Yes, naturally."

She stamped the exit permits and they dressed hurriedly and returned to the compartment. Papa, who was already there, said with restrained buoyancy, "Everything okay? In a few minutes we'll be across."

Mama was shivering, and quite suddenly she turned on Papa, her eyes blazing furiously. "They undressed us!" she whispered. "They stripped us!" Debbie realized she was trembling not with cold, but with fury. Papa tried to calm her, but she brushed him aside. "What kind of people do they think we are? They stripped us as if we were dogs," she said, and there was wild hate in her voice. "Dogs!" She crouched in the corner of the compartment. "One of them took my watch and wedding ring."

"Are you sure?" Papa said.

"Of course I'm sure."

"I'll go get it," Papa said grimly and started out.

"David!" Mama cried out, and pulled him back into the compartment. "You stay right here!"

Papa shrugged and grinned. "Don't worry, Bertha dear, we'll get a new wedding ring in Prague."

An official looked in perfunctorily to see Papa's passport again and ducked out.

Soon the train started and they all looked at each other in disbelief. Papa grinned mischievously, took his shoe off, removed his money, and put it in his pocket.

Vic and his father met them at the station and helped them through Czechoslovak Customs and Immigration. Dr. Jan looked older and tireder, his hair nearly white now. His step was still youthful, but he was trying harder. Vic looked more wonderful than ever.

At the hotel Vic was able, by charming the desk clerk with a smile and a hundred crowns, to change their accommodations to two connecting double rooms. Gussie and Debbie shared a large high-ceilinged chamber that looked out on the traffic of Wenceslas Square four floors below.

Vic and his father left after inviting them to supper at their flat.

Debbie lay on her bed exhausted from the tension of the trip, waiting for their dinner dresses to smooth out in the steamy bathroom. Her heart was hammering with the excitement of Vic, but she found herself unable to concentrate on dreaming of him. She looked at Gussie who lay with her eyes closed and mouth open, breathing evenly, and wondered what ever would become of her now. It was too hard to think about. Some other time. What about Mr. Goldenberg, that kind little man who used to give her chocolates on her visits to Gussie's, when she was a child? What they must be doing to him now! He would never be able to stand it. After all, he was not Papa. Papa would never be afraid. Papa would spit right back at them. Something about Papa now made him seem twice the size of other men. What would she and Mama ever do if anything happened to him? She got out of bed and spent a few moments combing her hair furiously. She could hear Papa talking softly in the next room, and she felt better and went comfortably to sleep.

Matters of the greatest moment were treated in the most casual fashion at dinner, as indeed Debbie found they usually were. They were mixed in with the weather, the scenery, a cold in the head and the rising price of silk stockings.

While coffee was being served, Papa lit one of Dr. Jan's cigars, tipped his chair back characteristically and blew a large puff of smoke over their heads into the barren, sparsely furnished room. He was in an expansive mood.

"I've been thinking, Jan, of moving to Prague—with the family, of course." Debbie was stunned; no one else said anything; Mama coughed gently, and Papa continued. "Theater conditions are difficult in Vienna now you know, very difficult. It's not only the Jewish business—" He lowered his voice and they all turned slightly toward the kitchen door—"but also business conditions in general. The Nazis are giving such good shows, and all free—parades, meetings, shopwindow smashings and all the rest, really there are plenty of rather interesting shows, without going to the theater. The box office is way off, way off."

He looked carefully at his cigar. "Excellent cigar." He meant it was awful, and Debbie smiled at him and he back to her. "Of course, I wouldn't have to go into the theater business here. I'll have capital. I'm liquidating—everything—the theaters, even Lindenhouse. Might as well look facts in the face. You have no idea how many friends have been in my office the last few days and tried to make a deal for my theaters. Of course they want them for peanuts. But what can you expect? You'd be surprised if I told you who they were, too. All of them doing me favors too, anything to help me out. They want to kill me with kindness. I threw 'em out of my office. For a few weeks I'll be the maddest man in Vienna and then—" He smiled slyly and shrugged, "I'll make a deal. And I expect to do pretty well. Meanwhile I thought I'd take a week to look around this town. Nice place, Prague. The way I see it, there's always room for a gambler with capital."

"I suppose it's damn selfish of me," Vic said, "but I'm tickled you're coming. And I know Dad is. I was half afraid you might decide on Palestine."

Papa snorted, "Not me."

Vic raised a glass of sherry and drank it. "Welcome, neighbors." Then he leaned forward and addressed Papa with more purpose than Debbie had observed previously.

"Before you make up your mind about investments, Cousin David, I'd like to take you to Kolin. The town's not far from here, about half an hour's drive. In fact, why doesn't the whole family go next Sunday, we can make it a sort of holiday. It's a lovely trip this time of the year, and I'll show you a proposition that'll really interest you. It's a lighting-fixture company, a perfect setup, absolutely no real risk. Two principals, and they need cash and they need it now. It's just ripe, like a plum. And there are no brokers involved."

Papa smiled cynically. "Of course, who knows what Mr. Hitler will do next? There could be war. He seems to be thinking seriously of Czechoslovakia, but I have it on high authority that he'll settle for the Sudetenland. This outfit's not in the Sudetenland?"

"No," Vic said, "Kolin is just east of here."

Papa laughed. "What am I doing, talking seriously about a lighting company? What do I know about lighting fixtures?"

Vic said, "You don't have to. I know as much about them as anyone."

So it was arranged for everyone to make the trip Sunday, the day before they were scheduled to return to Vienna. It would be a holiday and a business trip together.

"A holiday!" Gussie said quite unexpectedly and her words seemed to choke in her throat. "A holiday! What a lovely idea!" She put both her hands over her face, rose quickly from the table and ran to the bathroom. They could hear the door slam.

In the bleak silence, Debbie rose and followed her friend.

Nine

When Gussie said next morning that she was going to look for a job and a room, Debbie was shocked. "Oh, Gus, you don't even know your way about town. You don't know a soul, you can't speak a word of Czech. You have no papers . . ."

"You're all going back to Vienna and I'll never go back."

"But what about your father? How can you just—I don't know, Gus—how can you do it?"

"Oh, Debbie," she said morosely, "don't preach to me. I've tried and tried. I've called myself everything I could think of. Coward, traitor, worse. I promised myself to go back, I'd knock on doors, I'd stand in lines, I'd wait in offices, I'd ask and ask and ask and insist and stamp my feet and cry or scream or threaten. Oh, I'd make a terrible nuisance of myself. I'd never rest until they let Papa go. I was Brunhilde and Esther and Joan of Arc rolled into one. Rolled, that's really good. But I can't, Debbie, I can't. I'm afraid.

"I'll tell you something I've never told anyone before, not even my own father. I used to have a dream, over and over the same dream. Oh, long before the Nazis came to Vienna. I used to dream I was arrested by storm troops. They screamed at me, beat me, pulled my hair, but I would stand up to them. I'd laugh and shout at them and stamp my feet. I'd scream, 'You'll suffer for this! You'll see. I'll go to the courts, and justice will be done. I'm innocent. I've done nothing. You're only a bunch of gangsters. I'll go higher, if I have to go to Schuschnigg himself. The Palace of Justice will hear of it. I'll make them listen, the judges will be fair and justice will be done.'

"And one of the SS men would laugh at me, slap me or kick me and say, 'You fool, there's no Palace of Justice any more. There's no Schuschnigg any more, only us.'

"And I would never believe them, because that seemed much too terrible. You see, what they were doing to me was bad enough, but that there was no one to go to, that high up on the very top, above everything, there was no place where justice would be done, no appeal, no last, last place to go, when I finally believed that, it was the end of God, that was when I would cry in my sleep and cry and cry until I woke myself, all wet from sweat, calling for help, praying to God to come back. Oh, it was awful. Then I felt the truncheons on my back that day the boys chased us outside school. That day I was glad I could run. But to think if someday I couldn't even run, to be trapped in a room with no place to run. And to have no one even to cry out to, to know that the highest men in the land have announced that to torture Gussie Goldenberg is true justice, to grind me under is good, wonderful, the finest type of activity. Who cares if I've done nothing wrong? My father did nothing. Oh, I hope they'll get him out, but what can I do for him? 'Run away,' he told me. 'Run away, don't worry about me,' he said, 'don't take any chances.' I'm sure that's what he said. That's what he wanted for me. The lawyers will do everything that can be done. Your father will try. We're only girls, Debbie. I'm terrible I know, but I'm only seventeen, I don't know anything, I don't know what to do. What can I do?"

Debbie said, "Mr. Jarcho's a very clever man, Gus, I've heard Papa say so many times. He'll get your father out. I know he will."

"I have to get a job," Gussie said glumly, "I've got to have something to do. I have to make some money. I need a place to live."

"You're so brave about it," Debbie said. "I can't stand it, Gus. Heavens, I can't imagine what I'd do if ever I . . ."

Gussie was annoyed with her.

"Of course you do. You'd probably become a woman of the streets."

"Gussie!"

"Don't be childish. I thought of it for myself," Gussie said. Poor Gus, that would be the day! "But I'd starve at it, I'm much too ugly and sullen. I don't fool myself. I suffer from the blight. But you! What a success you'd make!—you're gay, pretty, young, not a care in the world, the brain of a sparrow in your head."

Debbie felt too sad for Gussie even to pretend to take offense.

The next days were filled with furious activity. Gussie, with help from Vic, hunted for a job in the factories and for a rooming house in the alleys of Prague, riding trams and busses, walking her feet off.

Mama found a charming real estate broker who, Debbie was positive, was a retired jewel thief. He drove Mama and Debbie about to show them luxurious apartments, and one enormous villa, thoroughly run down at the heels, but which, in a happier day, would have put even Lindenhouse to shame. "Just a little paint here and there, a bit of stucco here and there, a little imagination here and there," said the smooth real estate agent, "and presto." Mama had just enough imagination to believe him and not enough to be nervous about it. "I think we can make it lovely," she said to Debbie. "And very simple. So close to town, too, we won't even need an apartment. Heavens, we could be so comfortable here. I must get Papa out here to see it."

"They're asking a million two," the broker said casually.

"I can't make head or tail out of your Czech money," Mama said. "You'll have to figure it out with my husband."

Papa meanwhile made the rounds of the brokerage houses and examined theaters and office buildings. Each night they would gather round the dinner table at the hotel or in the Marmorek flat and tell each other their adventures. In all these days Debbie and Victor had not found an hour together without the families. She was counting heavily on Sunday's outing to Kolin.

On Friday Gussie had incredibly good luck. She landed a job and found an inexpensive flat the same day. She was as happy as if she had suddenly turned beautiful. The job was in a textile plant, laying up goods at a machine, and paid four hundred crowns a week. The manager of the plant was a patient of Dr. Jan's, and had received her cordially. The room, which was in an old building on a narrow street off Na Prikope, had its own sink and coal stove and running cold water, and cost a hundred ten crowns a week. She couldn't move out of the hotel fast enough. Before she left, Papa and Mama said good-bye, and if she ever needed help or money she was not to hesitate to call on them. Papa would let her know the moment he heard from Mr. Jarcho.

"I think," Gussie said to Papa, "I have everything I need—except my passport. If I could get a passport, I would feel better."

"I'll do my best," Papa said confidently. "In fact, consider it done. Get me a photograph of yourself and next time I come from Vienna, I'll have it."

Debbie felt the same chill each time Papa mentioned going back; yet she supposed they had to. There were her aunts, if nothing else. Papa would never do anything foolish. She pushed the prospect of Vienna into one of her secret recesses, out of consciousness. Time enough to worry about going home.

Gussie said, "Keep on trying about my dad." Her voice was flat and dry and hopeless. One might have thought she didn't care.

Mama kissed her gently before she entered the lift, carrying the valise Debbie had lent her. "We must see each other often, dear. As soon as we get back."

"Don't worry about me," Gussie said, "I have five thousand marks." She looked remarkably unforlorn, almost defiant.

Debbie was surprised that Gussie hadn't once said thank you. And she sensed that, like herself, neither Mama nor Papa was really sorry to see her go. What she faced was terrible indeed, but what more were they to do? Mama kept murmuring, "That poor girl! Whatever will become of that poor girl?"

Sunday was beautiful and even the manufacturing plant they visited in Kolin was moderately interesting. There was no doubt that Vic was at home with the great hum of activity in the neat brick building, even the oil smelling almost clean. He tried to share his pleasure in it with Debbie, but for her it was all a mysterious riddle. When Vic described the operation of the plant he spoke as women talk of a beautiful child. She saw now what she had hardly imagined before—he was really in love with light, this throbbing power that could be sent over hundreds of kilometers, move trains, turn a thousand shafts, do hard labor or intricate and delicate work of a hundred kinds, brighten a lonely street or a cozy bedroom. This power was real to him, his love was real, and he took no pains to conceal it; he was at ease with it. If he would only think of *her* sometime as he did of a generator!

But when they had got back in the car he said to Papa, "I love these plant fellows, pure production men. So naïve. This fellow Malewist loves his fixtures, but talk to him about profits and you draw a blank. The stockholder? Poor Malewist probably never heard of him. Oh, these engineers! I think they're wonderful!"

Papa looked at Vic quizzically, and the two men smiled.

On the way back Mama asked Vic to drive to the villa so Papa could judge for himself. Mama had made up her mind about it—Papa would certainly like it.

While Papa groused through the old house with Dr. Jan and Mama, counting the cost of renovation, Vic and Debbie strolled over the neglected grounds, picking their way through the weeds of what had been a formal garden. As it grew late, Debbie felt the chill of a fresh wind starting from the east.

Vic said, "When your folks fix the place up it'll be as nice as Lindenhouse. Nicer. You'll go on as though nothing had changed."

"Not quite, I think," Debbie said. "Golly, I guess I couldn't help missing Vienna. And still I'm worried about going back tomorrow. Isn't that silly?"

"I'm sure everything'll be all right there."

"I'll miss the old apartment, and Lindenhouse. And I'll miss my friends especially," she went on. "And, of course, the Prater. Remember the Prater?"

"How could I forget?" Vic said gently. He was half serious, half teasing.

"That was a lovely evening," Debbie sighed, "one of my nicest."

"One of mine too," Vic said, "but try not to miss Vienna too much. We have music all over Prague also and nice restaurants and all the rest. You just have to look a little harder for them. And won't this villa be lovely?" He paused studying her. "As for friends, you'll have all the friends you want. I tell you what, I'll give you mine."

"Thanks," she laughed, "such a touching gift!" She looked about and lowered her voice. "Of course I worry more about Mama and Papa. They don't say much, but it's harder for them."

"I know, but it won't be nearly so bad as you think. You'll see. I know it's selfish of me, but they did so much for me at Lindenhouse every summer, helping me with the university, I'm glad now I can do something for them and for you. You know, when you take and take from friends, no matter how much you're sure they love you, there's something incomplete about never being able to pay back. Not in money. I don't mean that. But in kindness, in thoughts, in little things. You know what I mean?"

"I think so," she said.

He held her off by one shoulder and looked at her a long time and she was certain he was going to kiss her, but he only put his arms about her shoulders.

"You're so cold," he said. "You're shivering. Why didn't you say something? Here, take my coat and let's go in."

"It's really not that cold," she said as they entered the vaulted foyer. "I get this way thinking about going back home. I suppose there's nothing to be afraid of, not really."

"Why do you have to go back?" he said suddenly, wheeling her about to face him. "Why not stay here? Your father'll return in a few weeks."

"Oh, I could never," she said. "Mama and Papa have had it out once and for all. Heavens to Methuselah, you should have heard it, it was one wing-ding mess—Papa wouldn't hear of Mama's going back. But she says where he goes she goes and that's that. She may look soft, but she's got a stubborn streak too, you know. Really stiff and stubborn. I think Papa was secretly proud of her. And if Mama can do it, why can't I?"

"But it seems a little extreme to me," Vic said. "Just too sentimental to be sensible."

"Perhaps we're not very sensible people," Debbie said sharply. "Perhaps not as sensible as you—might like."

"Don't be angry," Vic said. "All I meant . . ."

"I know what you meant." She spun about and bobbed her head in distress. "Let Papa take all the chances! That's what you meant. Well, we won't. We're going with him and whatever happens will happen to all of us!"

Papa, Mama and Dr. Jan were coming through the dining hall, Papa in animated dissertation. "Of course, who said it would be easy? But we're going to do it, that's all. Luckily we have a little money and the right spirit in the family. We'll make a new place for ourselves right here." He saw Debbie and Victor and grinned. "First thing we'll do when we get back from Vienna is make an offer on this place and pick up the stock of that electric-fixture company, Vic, my boy. I have great confidence in you, great hopes for you, and that's not just snap judgment. Probably I shouldn't even tell you, but after all, why not? I've made inquiries about you. Yes, sir, all week. Talked to a dozen people. I've been to your boss, to the university, to the Sokol offices; it's too embarrassing to tell you what I heard everywhere I went. It'd make you too stuck-up, which you are already." Papa slapped Vic on the back, in a half embrace.

"I'm an insufferable egotist when it comes to power," Vic said, laughing aloud. "I admit it. Guilty. Guilty."

They were to have their last late supper at the Marmoreks' before starting for Vienna in the morning. Just as they sat down to table the Marmorek phone rang, and while this was routine in the doctor's home, where calls came at all hours, the maid came in, her face flushed and her eyes wide with disbelief. "You better come to the phone, Doctor, I think it's someone trying to tease me. The lady, she says it's Jerusalem calling."

"It's Karl!" Mama shrieked. "It's Karl! Isn't that wonderful! Leave it to Karl to be thinking of us!"

The cook looked dubiously from Mama to Papa to Debbie. "Is it really Jerusalem?" she cried, great wonder in her voice. "Jerusalem on the telephone?" She crossed herself and muttered piously, "Mother of Jesus!"

Mama was at the extension in the living room and Vic ran into his father's office to listen there.

"Hello!" Mama cried. "Karl? Karl?" She listened intently and turned to Papa in exasperation. "It's the operator, she's talking Czech. Shh—Vic's saying something."

Vic was back in an instant. "It's Karl all right. The operator says the call will come through about eleven our time. They have to be sure someone will be here."

Papa said, "Karl must be a rich young fellow to be calling from Jerusalem. The fortune that kid has made from driving a bus. He must be simply pocketing all the fares. In business for himself. Amazing, that boy. Takes after his father."

At supper the conversation was all Karl. Mama was so excited she ate scarcely a mouthful and grew more and more flushed as the evening wore on.

"I hope he's not worried over us," she said. "You did send the wire, David, didn't you?"

Papa grunted, "A hundred times I've told you I sent the wire."

Debbie was thinking of Karl so far away, worrying over them. An hour and she would talk to Karl—the first time in almost eight years. How time had flown! And yet how much had been crowded into it.

After demitasse Vic, who had been unusually quiet, said, "I think I'll run down to the post office. I've a few letters that really ought to go out tonight." He turned to Debbie. "Would you like to come?"

Debbie hesitated. "I wouldn't want to miss Karl's call."

"We'll be back in plenty of time," Vic said. "Come on, I want to talk to you."

Papa said, "Buy me six cigars, Vic. Debbie knows the kind. Partagas. The large size. Here's the money."

They walked for a long time in silence, hearing the measured sound of their own shoes on the sidewalk. Debbie found the streets crowded, but more subdued than the crowds on the Ring. People out for an evening stroll, unspectacular, along the broad walks of Wenceslas Square. It was not Vienna. There was no sound of music. People were not as rich, not as poor. The eager heartbreaking teenagers always soliciting in Stadt Park were not in evidence here. There was sobriety, decorousness, but not gaiety. She'd bet there was no Prater in Prague. No music gardens, only the bookshops, newsstands, and the museum; for a fleeting moment she began to feel homesick again. Then she noticed several times that they passed men in gray chauffeurs' uniforms, walking usually in twos or threes.

"Where do all the chauffeurs come from?" she said. "There are more chauffeurs than autos."

"Sudetenlanders," Vic said grimly. "The government forbids them political uniforms so we have an army of chauffeurs. But these Nazis will get nowhere with us. Mostly crackpots."

On the way to the post box they stopped at the newsstand to read the headlines of the Prague papers and those from all over Europe, neatly stacked according to language, and she saw the Berlin and Vienna headlines in red block letters. VIENNA GREETS THE LEADER. Vic studied the papers distractedly and bought one which he tucked under his arm.

After he had mailed his letters he spoke hesitantly. "You have no idea why I asked you to come with me?"

"I thought you wanted company." She felt coquettish, even though she knew it was outrageous to behave so.

"It's come to me quite clearly that I can't let you go back. Not tomorrow or ever. I've been stupid and dense and insensitive to my own feelings. You know I'm always sitting on my feelings, but they just wouldn't stay sat on any longer."

"What feelings, Vic?" She could hear her own voice quaver. He took her hand and they walked together in silence until he said, "I love you, Debbie, and not like a little girl or a cousin, but like a woman. Stay here with me, Debbie. Marry me."

It was as if someone had struck her suddenly in the pit of her stomach and she felt she would have to stop walking, sit down, get her breath. But she went on looking straight ahead, not daring to turn toward him. "If you'd like it, I'd like it very much," she said in a voice that sounded small and far off, as if someone else were saying the words.

"Really?" he said. He had stopped walking and had turned to look down at her.

"Did you think I wouldn't?" she said.

"I didn't know." He was grinning.

"I think we may have a lot to tell each other," she said wisely. "I'll tell you my secrets if you'll tell me yours."

"*All* your secrets?" Vic teased. "God forbid."

They were standing under the street lamp, looking at each other as if for the first time. Adults smiled and two little pigtailed girls giggled as they hurried by. Debbie felt almost nearer to them than to Vic. She missed her pigtails.

"Where can we go?" Debbie said. "I feel so silly here this way."

"Why, where do you want to go?"

"Some place, private, any place."

Vic laughed. "I'm afraid we'll have to put it off," he said. "I wouldn't want you to miss Karl's call. But hello for now." He held her off by the shoulders and looked at her and pulled her close to kiss her as he had never done before, in the full light of the street lamp, and her knees trembled and she felt dizzy and weak. What a queer feeling! "Oh," she said, "oh Vic, not here. Not like that here in the street. What will people think? Why, we'll be arrested!" She leaned her hand weakly against one of the stunted saplings that lined the square.

As they walked now he had his arm about her waist and she could feel his fingers tracing a delicate pattern as they talked. "Shall we be married tomorrow? Tuesday? Wednesday?" he asked as he led her along a narrow street just behind the museum.

"Whatever you say. But soon, please. I suppose I'm too bold and immodest."

"Can you help it if you're a Girl Scout? The truth, Scout's honor."

He took her into a tobacconist's near the museum. "Six Partagas cigars," Vic ordered. Under no circumstances would he have forgotten Papa's cigars!

Back at the apartment, nothing had changed. Incredible they should all not see at once what had happened, but no one even bothered to turn the radio off. They had hardly taken their coats off before the phone rang and it was Karl. Mama took one phone with Papa standing by and Vic the other with Debbie behind him. Cousin Jan lit one of Papa's good cigars and sat calmly on the great sofa listening.

"Hello," Vic called. "Yes, yes, this is Victor. How are you? Good. Yes, of course, I understand. No, because as a matter of fact they're right here. Didn't you get your father's wire? Yes, here in Prague. Here in the house with us. They've been paying us a visit. Of course, and Debbie too. Your mother's listening on the other extension."

Debbie, after gesticulating impatiently, got the receiver from Vic.

"Thank God," she heard Karl saying and she could hear his voice tremble over two thousand kilometers of wire. "Thank God! Mama, are you there? It's Karl, Mama!"

"Karl darling, how are you? Can you hear me all right?"

They heard him call to someone apparently with him, "They're right there in Prague. They're safe. I'm talking to my mother right now. Isn't that wonderful?" Now his voice came in clear and slowly faded out again, and in, like the roaring and fading of the seas across which it traveled. "Mama, are you really all right, Mama?"

"Yes, of course, Karl. We came for a visit and it's been lovely. What's the trouble, Karl?"

"Trouble?" He laughed wildly. "Mama, I've been going crazy. It took me eight days to reach Vienna. Everyone in Jerusalem is trying to call Vienna, but everyone. I finally got Paula. She was so vague. All she said was you left suddenly and she hoped you'd be back soon, but she couldn't say when. She said she woke up one morning and you were all gone. You can imagine how I felt! Then it took five more days to get Prague. I've been going crazy. Mama, I'm so glad to hear you, you have no idea."

"How are you, Karl? Are you happy there, Karl?"

"Of course, it's wonderful here!"

"And Lilith?"

"Also. She sends her love. Is Papa there?"

"Yes. He wants to talk to you. Didn't you get his wire? Don't pull the phone out of my hand, David. It's wonderful to hear you, Karl. Don't worry about us. Everything in the newspapers is exaggerated, you know. God bless you, dear."

"Good-bye, Mama."

Papa was on the wire. Debbie wanted to call, It's Debbie, it's me, Karl. Hello in Jerusalem: I touch you out there.

But Papa and Karl were talking together. "Don't get so excited, Karl. Calm down. It's just as Mama says. Everything's exaggerated. How come you didn't get my wire?"

"But how can you even dream of going back?" Karl shouted. "You'll be arrested! You'll never get out again."

"Don't be silly, Karl. Everything we have in the world is in Vienna. Not to mention your mother's sisters. I *must* go back. Don't worry, I have no intention to stay there long and I won't have to. Just a couple of weeks to close a few deals. I have to try to save as much as I can."

"But why go back? Can't you get the lawyers to do it?"

"What about your aunts, boy? Be sensible. Who can we trust today, Karl?" Now Papa was shouting. "Only ourselves!"

"It'll never do any good, Papa. Please listen!"

"Karl," Debbie broke in at last. "Karl, it's Debbie!"

"Debbie, little Debbie!"

"Not so little, Karl. I'm going to be married—to Victor." There was silence for an instant. Then Karl's voice. "Really? It's not possible! Little Debbie! Are you big enough?"

"I'm eighteen," she said, "and I'm a meter and a half tall and I weigh forty-five kilos."

"Congratulations! I'll bet you're pretty as a picture. And congratulate Victor."

Behind her she was conscious of Mama's fluttering into the room and talking excitedly to Vic.

"Are you planning to go back to Vienna too, with Mama and Papa?"

"I—I don't think so. We're going to be married right away. As soon as we can."

"Good. Can I say something? Papa's absolutely mad, isn't he? What's got into him? Why don't you stop him?"

"How can I?"

"Talk to him. Tie him up. They'll kill him! They'll never let him go."

"They already did let me go!" Papa shouted angrily. "Do you take me for an idiot?"

"Only luck. Listen, Papa, please listen to me! Make him stay in Prague, Debbie. Do what you can. Let me talk to Vic again."

The operator said something in Czech and she heard a click as if they had been disconnected. "Are you there, Karl?"

"Yes, yes, put Vic on. I've only a minute more. Come see us soon, Debbie, you and Vic."

"Good-bye, Karl." She handed the receiver to Vic and Mama was waiting to embrace her.

"Everything's happening at once," Mama wailed, "I can't keep track."

Through Mama's embrace she heard Vic saying, "Karl, I agree with you. I'll try again, but you know him. We'll do our best. No, Debbie won't go back, I promise you. Don't worry. Thanks, thanks, Karl. No, I don't think so. But I appreciate your asking us. I guess I'm just not cut out to be a pioneer. Thanks, you flatter me. But this is *my* home, boy. Yes, of course I do. I know—I know—Good-bye, Karl."

"Good-bye!" she could hear Papa call from the next room, "and don't worry about us!"

After the call everyone talked at once.

"I heard him so clearly," Mama said over and over, "as if he were here in the next room. But he talks German with a funny accent now. Did you notice?"

Papa said, "I don't understand why he didn't get my wire. He's still a pretty fresh young fellow if you ask me, talking to his old papa like that. But it was nice he called. Very damn nice."

Mama said, "And you, Debbie, what a secret you've been keeping from us! You naughty children!" She embraced Vic again and dabbed at her eyes.

"I just found out about it myself," Debbie protested.

Dr. Jan said, "So it seems I'm coming into a new daughter and you're getting a son. I think I've the best of the bargain. No offense, Vic. It's just that I'm partial to girls." He shook Victor's hand and kissed Debbie gently. His mustache tickled her cheek.

"So," Papa said, "can a bald old man get into the act?" He embraced Vic. "Debbie, promise me you'll be happy. Of course, you realize I'm highly insulted. Vic should have stood about hemming and hawing and left in a state of suspense. After all, I had to do it twenty-eight years ago, and the only comfort I had that night was that someday I'd be in the father's seat and could be stern and forbidding and snarl and humph around the room. Bertha, imagine your father if I hadn't gone formally to him for a little chat? Well, times have changed. Thank God I don't have to make another such decision. Once in a lifetime is enough."

Dr. Jan brought out special bottles of Vouvray and they drank and talked about the wedding and about Karl until very late. Dr. Jan said he would get the Mayor to marry them—Dr. Klapka, a fine man with a permanent case of acid indigestion since he became Mayor. Mama and Papa decided to postpone their trip home until the wedding later in the week. But nothing Vic and Debbie said would persuade Papa to cancel it altogether and Mama could not consider staying in Prague if Papa went.

Dr. Jan made no effort to influence them. "They're going home," he said to Vic and Debbie in the kitchen. "It's not for the money, believe me. That's just an excuse. They actually have no choice. Your mother's two sisters are in Vienna. How can they forsake their own? Haven't they always depended on David and Bertha Pretsch? I think those poor souls must be terrorized tonight. They're waiting. And David wants to save as much as he can."

"I know," Debbie said miserably. She had been trying not to think of all their friends and her aunts. "It's hopeless to try to stop them, I suppose."

Nevertheless they tried again, but Papa was unmoved.

"Whom shall we have to the wedding?" Mama asked brightly, trying as always to change the subject. "I always planned such a big wedding for you, Debbie. Something to show your aunts. I thought you'd have the most wonderful wedding gown with a long train, and flower girls and all the rest." She shrugged helplessly. "Your aunts won't be able to come, so we'll do the best we can. Whom shall we have?"

"We must have Gussie," Debbie said and everyone fell silent and sipped their wine thoughtfully.

Ten

The wedding was a simple ceremony at the Mayor's office, in the presence of their parents, Gussie, and a dozen of Vic's relatives and friends, including Martin Schroeder, who acted as best man. Mayor Klapka, a friendly wizened little man, spoke Czech to Vic and German to Debbie, putting his questions in a babyish high-pitched voice, his spectacles bobbing at the end of his nose, and no sooner was the brief ceremony over than he shook hands hurriedly all around and said, "Please excuse me, but the Sanitation Commissioner is waiting. Lucky I was able to squeeze you in between Public Works and Sanitation. Good luck." Vic laughed and translated for Debbie. "Good luck," the Mayor piped again in German.

After the wedding they walked to the Ambassador, where Mama had arranged for a wedding breakfast. There was champagne, wedding cake, toasts to the bride, the groom, their future children. Vic rose and said to his friends, "I propose a toast to my wife's mother and father, two of the nicest young people I know. They're moving to

Prague. Happiness in their new home from their new neighbors." Vic was the kindest, nicest, most lovable man ever invented.

Debbie had never been kissed so often by so many people she'd barely met. Martin Schroeder was especially gay and bold on three glasses of champagne and kissed her as if he were the groom.

"Congratulations," he grinned thickly, "and I'm very sorry Vic saw you first. Very very very sorry. It will be the tragedy of my life. Did I mention, congratulations?" And he kissed her again.

She was giddy from the drinks and the smoke, the piano music and singing, the jokes, half heard and never understood. She kept reaching for Vic's hand to make it real. And then they were at the station and Mama and Papa were getting on the train. Mama was crying and laughing all at once, but the mood of their departure was a cheerful one. Everyone was happy, and Hitler was forgotten. Just before he left, Papa gave Debbie an envelope with money. Three thousand marks. She scarcely noticed it at the time.

With two valises and their skis, Debbie's brand new, gleaming on the roof of the car, they set out from the station for the Giant Mountain of the Krknos. The snow was deep by the time Vic turned into a narrow winding road up a treacherous hillside, bouncing into sun and more snow.

When they stopped it was not at the hotel where they had stayed when she was a child, but at a smaller inn, set quietly in the infinite stretch of untouched snow and sky. Inside, laid out neatly in amateurish display beside the registry desk, were ash trays, belt buckles, post cards, knives, toys and miniature figures. An old gentleman wearing bifocals and smoking a long curved meerschaum greeted Vic pleasantly.

"The room's ready, Mr. Marmorek. We hope you'll find everything satisfactory."

"How's the skiing?"

"Fine. Not much of a crowd, though. Too much politics these days, and not enough pleasure, but we manage."

The man behind the bifocals stared at Debbie. "We hope you'll be comfortable, Madam."

"Thank you," she said, trying to sound like Mama. "It's charming." She'd never been called anything but Miss before. She was aging fast.

"I'm looking forward to getting out on the slopes," she said. "My husband taught me to ski when I was a little girl."

"That so?" The man carried their bags up one flight to a warm, paneled bedroom; a fire crackled in the corner hearth. A massive bed jutted out from one wall, and a great oak table and three chairs completed the furnishings. Through the window the snow-reflected twilight gave the room an eerie quality.

"So," Bifocals said, "if you want anything, just call." He dropped the valises and closed the door on them, and they stood still—for ages she thought.

"Well," Vic said.

"Well," she said, "this looks nice."

Here she was in this moment that she had been wishing for as long as she could remember. All that hoping and now, impossible as it seemed, she was living the moment. And she was surely not ready for it. She was so puzzled because she had only the faintest idea what to do with it. She was glad she knew Vic so well, for so many years. How awful to find yourself locked up like this with a perfect stranger! Someone you'd known only a year or two! She was the luckiest of girls.

Yet she was not prepared. Mama had said nothing—she hadn't really had time to think herself, except foolish imaginings, and everything had happened so suddenly. What was supposed to happen now? Was she supposed to take all her clothes off? Or what?

Would she see Vic naked? Would he be wild and rough and like some kind of animal? Surely not Vic, her lovely loving Vic. After all, millions of people were married and had babies, and seemed to get along afterwards.

"Well," Vic said gently, "how do you like it?" He took in the room in a gesture.

"It's beautiful," she said warily. "The whole place is beautiful—all that endless snow. It's something to feed on." She pulled the curtains aside and watched the shadows the trees were weaving in their windy patterns on the whiteness.

"I think it's all rather plain," Vic said, "compared to the bride. The bride's the diamond of the piece. Flawless, see?" He turned her profile and examined her like an artist. "The setting may be changed a thousand times."

"Oh, Vic! What a pretty thought. And so untruthful."

"A certain amount of untruthfulness is essential." He was behind her, speaking softly, trying to reassure her with chatter. "Are you all right, honey?" His arms were about her waist and he was kissing the back of her neck gently and tracing light flutters along her side.

"I'm nervous about myself, Vic," she whispered, telling him her greatest secret. What words she said were between kisses and she was beginning to feel a little heady from them. "But I do love you, darling. With all my heart." That was what she would hold onto for support.

She could almost hear the smile in his voice as he said, "Turn around, Girl Scout. You wanted to go some place. Well, now we're some place, and you're nervous as a pussy cat!"

He embraced her, and began to kiss her lips, at first still gently, then more and more insistently, deeply, until she could not say whether she was standing or floating. She was dizzy. She heard his words from time to time as he caressed her, but they came from further and further away.

"No one can find us now except that little man below and he's already forgotten us." He spoke as if he were lulling her into security. His hands passed up and down her spine, over her shoulders, as if he were trying to memorize her. "You know, you're nothing like the girl I used to know. You're all grown up and I find it better."

"Please, Vic, we're not unpacked yet." She could hear the unreasonable panic in her voice; she sounded ludicrous to herself.

Vic laughed compassionately. "Let's not unpack just yet," he said quietly, "we've waited long enough."

"I suppose you think I don't know the first thing about it!" she wailed defensively. "I suppose you think I'm a mere child. I suppose you think I'm scared!"

"I think no such thing, Madame Pompadour."

"Oh, Vic. I am. I just don't know a thing. Be nice, don't tease."

He had unzippered her dress and carried her to the mammoth bed.

"It's so light," she said. "Shouldn't it be dark? I'm so embarrassed really. I shouldn't be, should I?"

Gently, but oh so gently he had removed her clothes, with her help where it was necessary. For a long time he looked at her and his eyes were eager, anticipating, devouring, but soft and considerate of her. Slowly her alarm faded.

"You like me?" she asked at last. "I'm not too painfully skinny?"

"Mmmmm," he said. "I'm not looking at your body, honey, I'm looking at your heart. You can't keep anything from me now, can you, any hurt or pleasure? Any sweet or lovely thing when you're like that?"

"Oh, Vic, I love you so, really, I guess I have from the day I saw you looking at me in the pool, and I was trying so hard and you yelled, Kick your feet up and you'll get along. Remember? You taught me to swim and I was so proud of myself. And I thought you were so wonderful."

He was on his knees beside her, kissing her eyes, her ears, her eager mouth, ignoring her silly chatter as she hoped he would and his fingers laced along her side, almost soothing her. He was cuddling her, like some new pet he had discovered, a Persian kitten.

At last she said, when she had grown bold and astonishingly curious, "Aren't you ever going to take your own clothes off?"

"You hussy," he said abruptly. But she could see he was pleased. "I'm much more bashful than you and not so beautiful." But in a little while he was standing naked beside her, and he was, too, beautiful. Massive and overpowering and brutal.

She watched him curiously, fascinated, but not daring to touch him, afraid she might break the spell. Perhaps some day later she might have the courage. When they knew each other better.

"I'm glad it's light," she said. "Aren't I awful? Because now you can't keep any secrets from me, any hurt or pleasure."

He knelt, then stretched beside her and embraced her, stroking the back of her neck, kissing her softly, patiently. She knew that from time to time he searched her face, kissing her kindly, intently and he whispered, "All right?" and she could only murmur. She couldn't remember what, but he knew it was all right. Sometimes they lay almost motionless for long stretches.

But slowly the flames which started in his fingertips grew brighter and more unbearable and finally unquenchable until she could feel them soaring and crashing and roaring and at last she had no weight, no body, and she was able to contain all that brutality and make it her own, consume it. There was pain and pleasure, but she was nothing, only air and flame, and scarcely aware, and then after a little while Vic was there again with her and they lay silent.

"Why did you look at me?" she asked timidly. "You kept watching me."

"I don't know," he said. "I suppose to see that everything was all right. After all I'm not only your husband, I'm your teacher."

"I suppose you must have learned about all this *somewhere*," she said, "but I don't really mind. Isn't that strange?"

"I read it in books," Vic teased and she giggled. "Now that we're ready to go skiing, it's dark out. If we had any brains we'd have used the daylight to ski and saved the night."

"Golly you're so nice," she whispered. "So so nice."

"We'll ski tomorrow if we ever get up. Maybe next week we'll ski when we're old and married a long time. Then we'll manage our time better. I'll try to get Old Bifocals to bring some food up."

"Whatever you say, Vic. Always, whatever you say."

He pulled the bell and soon fell to kissing her, cool fresh kisses and they murmured to each other words and half words that meant nothing.

She said idly, "I hope Mama and Papa will be all right. I'll be so relieved when they get back. Two weeks seems so long to have to wait." But in truth she was scarcely thinking of Mama and Papa. She was thinking of two weeks with Vic alone in this great bed.

Eleven

In two weeks Mama and Papa didn't come back to Prague. They were not aboard their train nor the later trains that day or any day.

Debbie could not reach them in Vienna. The phone was out of order. Mail went unanswered. At last Vic was able to find someone going to Vienna, an aunt of one of the men in his crew. Vic gave her a letter to deliver to Mama and Papa, and Debbie could scarcely wait the three days for the woman's return. Vic promised to call as soon as she came to the office. Debbie waited till four o'clock on the third day and finally could contain herself no longer and called Vic at the office.

"No," Vic said, "not a word, she hasn't come in yet. I really don't know when to expect her."

He sounded evasive, worried.

Within the hour he was home from work. She knew at once from the look on his face. Drawn and tired. "It's bad," he said simply.

"No," she said, "it can't be. Is it Papa?"

"Here," he said, "it's a letter from Paula." He handed her the envelope; she held it, crumpled tight in her fist for a long time, unwilling to open it, for she thought she knew. At last she braced herself and read. It was worse than her wildest fears.

Dear Miss Debbie,

I decided to take the chance to give this kind lady a note so that you know the sad news about your father and mother. I have almost not the heart to write it. Three days after they came home, on Saturday in the middle of the afternoon about three o'clock, four SS men came with Willie. Willie is now a group leader in the SS. They searched the house and said they must arrest your father. Willie spoke very rudely to your mother. I never expected him to talk so disrespectfully. There is no reason for it. Your mother was always a very nice woman, always kind to Willie, but when he called her those terrible names she became more angry than I ever saw her. She slapped Willie's face and he tried to strike her with the back of his revolver, but she kicked him and I don't know what happened next. The gun went off and your mother was shot. She died right away. Willie was like crazy and swung the gun around, screaming and your father who all along was trying to get your mother to leave Willie alone, now he became wild too and he started to choke Willie. The other SS men tried to pull him off and beat him and one of the guns went off again and your father was hurt. He was shot in the stomach, but they would not let me call a doctor. He was in pain, but they wouldn't give him anything. They stood around letting him bleed until he was very weak and fainted because the bleeding didn't stop, but he said to me, "Paula, Karl was right—tell Miss Debbie." I can't imagine what has got into Willie. He says to me he is unhappy, that he is only following orders. But I believe he feels absolutely nothing. He even threatens me. He is so different and your father was so good to him and his son Fritz. It's all those politics. I can't understand it. Why shouldn't everyone be friends like Jesus says and love God together? Everyone is afraid to say anything against them. Your mother and father were very brave. I'm sorry. I am ashamed to write this. I'm thinking of you. I liked your mother and father. They were good to me and all the help.

PAULA

There was no funeral as there had been for Aunt Erika, no services in the temple, no official notice, nothing but this unreal penciled note from Paula. She couldn't believe, much less accept it.

Many months passed before she could realize it, and the realization would have been unendurable, to lose not only Mama and Papa, but all her armor, except that Victor was taking care of her now. She had her new shield.

When the rantings from Berlin grew louder and the chauffeurs' uniforms on the streets of Prague were always more in evidence and even during the days when Victor was called up and shipped off to the little Maginot line and war was in the air, she was saved by the comfort that Vic was there for her. But always somewhere in a tiny recess of her mind she held safe what Papa had said to Paula. Karl was right. Tell Miss Debbie.

Twelve

Victor always seemed to know useful Christians in the right places, and he had an uncanny sense of timing about moving on. There were unpleasant, rather frightening moments, but he managed to get them out of Prague on the last day of March. Martin Schroeder, who was then an economics instructor at the University of Prague, also had a part-time job in the passport division under the new Nazi-Protectorate Government. He got them a passport and an Italian visa, which was the only kind available. But he did it grudgingly and it cost Vic every crown he had. Martin seemed to know the precise amount of Victor's bank balance. Actually the money business seemed pure spite. Martin's family had plenty; he certainly didn't need it.

But Martin resented Vic's leaving. She remembered that day vividly—good-natured, fat Martin talking grimly, slowly. "Now that the Nazis are here, every decent Czech is needed *here,* Vic. Not in Rome. *How can you think of going?* How can you *think* of it?"

"I've told you," Vic said. "I have a better job there. Fellow's got to get ahead. This town's all politics."

"Seems to me," Martin said coldly, "you've never been interested enough in politics. You never joined a party in the old days. Any party." He plunged ahead. "Why deceive yourself? You're only running out. And if you ask me, sweetheart, from the frying pan into the fire. You know those fascist bastards down there are as bad as the Nazis. Worse, because they're more haphazard."

Vic snorted, "Be honest, Martin. Six months ago when we were mobilized, I was willing to fight, as much as you. I don't pretend I was eager, but I was willing. You can't expect more than that from anyone these days. I didn't relish leaving Debbie here, in a strange city with air raids coming, but I did it. How d'you think I felt knowing that fifteen minutes after war started they'd be dropping bombs on Prague? But I went out with the rest of the boys to sit in those Goddamn concrete bunkers until I was bored out of my wits and betrayed. We were all ready to do what we could then, weren't we? It was in the air, you could feel it. Syrovy was inspiring. Our finest time in a way, I suppose, but then what happened? *We* were willing, where were Benes and Syrovy? Making phone calls to Mr. Chamberlain and Mr. Daladier. Please, Mr. Chamberlain! Send help. We were ready then. I was, you were. But all the big boys flew the coop nicely and left us with this midget Hacha. Well, what good are we doing here now? What can any of us do? With no army, without leadership?"

"I can tell you, Vic, we have leadership. Good leadership, the kind we haven't had before. There are tasks to be done. But it's not a game of pat-a-cake. I can tell you whom to see. Think about it."

Vic was unimpressed. "The people are hypnotized, Martin, like frogs being devoured by a snake. What can a few of us do?"

"We'll do what we can do." Martin was suddenly almost shouting. "Of course it isn't comfortable, sure, it's not easy. You have Debbie, I have Maria. Some of us have children, but we're not going to let that maniac make chopped meat of us. Not Hitler himself, nor the hangmen he's sent here, nor anyone else. In plain words, we'll make it tough for him. We'll fight our guts out. He'll find Czechs aren't Germans. Nor Jews either." He cast it out on a long-shot and watched Vic's face carefully. None of their crowd was sure whether or not Victor Marmorek was a Jew, and until now most of them had made a studied effort not to care.

Vic's face was composed, he wouldn't be provoked. "I'm going," he said, "and if you'll help me, I'll be much obliged. If not, just say so. But for Christ's sake, don't lecture me."

Debbie knew then that Martin had got under his skin.

"If you've made up your mind to take off," Martin said, "sure I suppose I'll help. You'd be no damn good to us anyway. But it'll cost you a lot of money."

Vic's fists clenched, but he controlled himself. "How much?"

"How would I know? Depends on how many people I have to get to help me. It's at least a hundred thousand crowns. Your papers will be Aryan."

Vic swallowed. "A hundred thousand? I have only forty thousand to my name."

"A hundred thousand's minimum."

"Include my father, and somehow I'll get the money."

"Your father?" There was a flicker of having nailed down the suspicion in Martin's mind, almost a self-satisfied smile. "Agreed. Bring me passport photos of you and Debbie and your father by Wednesday the latest."

Dr. Marmorek was visibly upset when he heard their plan and grew agitated almost beyond control when they asked him to go with them. His hands trembled as he tried to keep his voice calm. "Since I'm a small boy I've lived in this house, with my parents, on this street, with this old furniture, and you expect me to move to Rome now? Why, my father died in that chair. I was married here. Victor was born in that room, in that bed. I have my hospital here, my patients, they need me, and to tell the truth, I need them. We belong together. Prague is my city just as my mother was my mother. You say 'new home'? For me the two words contradict each other out of existence. And Vic, how can you think of it for yourself?" His unsteady hand clenched on Vic's shoulder seemed to be trying to divert Vic physically from the course he had chosen.

"But, Father," Debbie said, "even after we know the awful things that happened to my poor Mama and Papa?"

He shook his head. "That was in Vienna, my child, among the German barbarians. Here we are Czechs, civilized beings. Oh, I hear what they say in the streets. I see the uniforms. I know what they intend. But we are Czechs, after all. Nothing will happen here. We'll never permit it. Not in a thousand years."

Dr. Jan Marmorek was a physician, a deep thinker, and as easily fooled as most people. Nothing could persuade him to come with them. Poor, loyal, foolish Father Marmorek. In all the years after war and peace they never heard of him again.

Debbie wondered what would become of Gussie Goldenberg alone in Prague. She had no Vic, no money, no shield. But when she spoke to Vic about taking Gus he shook his head. "I know it sounds terrible and cruel," he said, "but she looks too Jewish. It's too big a gamble."

"But what will become of her, Vic?"

"What will become of my Dad? What will become of any of us?" He changed the subject abruptly.

Before they left, Debbie visited Gussie in her sparse one-room cold water flat. "Write to my brother, Gus. Maybe he'll help you get into

Palestine. You've always thought of going. I'll write him about you myself."

Gussie was pitifully grateful. She'd lost her job and was reaching a state of desperate exhaustion. She looked terrible.

Debbie tried not to think of the meaning of leaving Gussie; after all, she did look so Jewish.

When Martin came to the flat one night to bring the passports and get the money, he could not resist flinging his last taunt at Vic. "When are you people going to have the backbone to stand and fight? It's no wonder no one wants you!" He turned, about to leave without shaking hands, without even a farewell nod to Debbie, whom he had always liked. But at the last minute, he stood in the doorway, rather forlorn, and said, hopelessly, to himself as much as to Vic, "Don't you think *someplace, sometime,* a man's got to make a stand, even if it's hopeless?" He left quietly, not bothering to hear Vic's answer.

Debbie never questioned Vic's decision. She knew that he would see that she was protected as he always had. She would be taken care of, kept comfortable, loved. They were to leave Prague as she had left Vienna, just in time, with a passport, a valise and Debbie's money from Papa, three thousand marks.

After Martin had left, Vic said, "Poor old Martin's scared, whistling in the wind. So he lectures me. What he won't admit is that there's a time to fight and a time to retreat. The poor guy's world is full of villains and heroes. In a way he reminds me of your brother Karl, except that Karl had an excuse. He was only seventeen. What army commits suicide, after all? Didn't Benes himself go into exile?"

When Angelo di Sabatino, who had gone to electrical engineering school with Vic, wrote the second time that he had made final arrangements for the job in Rome, it seemed more wonderful than they had dared hope. His letter said:

> Of course, it's no job to suit a man of your talents, perhaps I should say genius, dear Victor, but it's after all in the primary Rome power plant with plenty of chance for promotion, and I think I know what you want. I can't forget how you and your father treated me when I came to Prague to study, how you took in a homesick kid with electricity on the brain and not a friend in all Czechoslovakia.
>
> Another thing. Don't think my getting you this job is all one-sided. We need men like you down here—and desperately. Can't get the help, at least not with brains and training. Only one thing. My boss has asked me about your politics. You know how important that is these days. Drop me a note on this, so that there'll be no questions.

Vic wrote him, "My politics have been to stay out of politics at all costs. I promise you my philosophy has always been, When in Rome do as the Romans. I expect to support whatever is good for Italy and I would imagine no one knows better what Italy needs than the King and Mussolini. Tell your boss he has no worry on that subject."

When they posted the letter, Vic said cheerfully, "I think you'll like Angelo. We got along wonderfully at school. Lucky fellow's got a short left leg, which kept him out of the army. He always said it was his most useful piece of equipment."

"Is he married? It would be nice to know another girl in Rome."

"Angelo married? I sure as the devil doubt it."

Across the Ostmark and through northern Italy to Milan they had a first-class compartment all to themselves, and he talked to her as he never had before, almost grimly. "Of course, Angelo is right about my job. I'll be a glorified maintenance man, a cog in the turbine room, but a fellow like me has to be patient." He leaned forward and they huddled together. In an undertone he said, "It's not our fault, honey, all this. The world's gone off its head, something we can't do anything about, like a typhoon or a hurricane. We have to be sensible. We have to try to stay afloat. It's that simple, be alive, get through it. Maybe we can get visas to France or Switzerland or even America. We'll try. But meanwhile hold on. We'll do what we have to do to hold on. All right?"

Her stomach had become hollow and weak, for Vic was saying something she never thought to hear him articulate. "I suppose it's all right, Vic," she whispered. "Are you sure?" He looked at her in surprise and nodded. Even she was shocked by her own impudent doubt.

Then he blurted the ugly thing that troubled him, half mumbling. "No matter what we have to do or say from now on, honey, don't worry and don't let's be surprised at each other. And if there's any question whether this or that is necessary, we'd better lean over backwards and be on the safe side. Better too much than too little, because one little mistake—well, when you're dead it's for more than a weekend. Remember that, Girl Scout. Dignity's okay, but not when it costs your life. So let's not be heroes. Not this week anyhow. We'll leave that for Martin. And no matter what happens some fine day it will *never* have happened. You see, we mustn't let this time do anything to *us*—to what's so nice between you and me." She could feel Vic's hand trembling as he stroked her cheek. "While we're in Rome, we'll play Romans, shall we? Remember, we're good Catholics, we're German-type Czechs, we love Hitler and Mussolini and don't care for Jews." In spite of everything that had happened already Victor's words chilled her.

Angelo di Sabatino met them at the terminal in Rome. He was of medium height, walked with a marked limp, and when she first saw him she thought him ugly, with his sharp oversensitive nose, his nostrils fairly bristling, shining black eyes and a great shock of black curly hair just thinning at the temples and dome. No wonder he wasn't married. He laughed hard with head thrown back and slapped Victor on the shoulders, embraced him, and finally had even his guest infused with his enthusiasm. Vic seemed to be so easily inspired by the people he was with that before long he usually became an unconscious mimic anyhow. In Rome as time went on, he seemed to grow more and more carefree, more open, somehow almost more simple. His Italian was soon fluent. His emotions seemed to come clear to the surface. He cried easily with pleasure or pity. Then later, in Palestine, he had become so proper and rather—what could she say?—British. Yes, tea at four, casual, lower the voice, push the emotions way way back. Really it was like being married to three or four men. Then from the day he had made up his mind to join Haganah, he was quickly less English and more Jewish, less restrained, more pointed and bitter and emotional, his manner positive. Even his accents were changing lately. His English was more guttural, his Hebrew purer.

But Angelo had always been the same, probably still was. Active, eager, helpful, he enjoyed being the patron. No doubt it gave him a sense of importance. The more he did for them, the more expansive and generous he became. From the first moment after he had gallantly kissed her hand he insisted on carrying both valises, limping along the long platform into the street, four blocks to the bus stop. She was astonished at the number of nuns, soldiers, priests, and pushcarts on the street. Angelo took them to the apartment he had rented for them and introduced the landlady, a fat jolly woman, who grinned and bowed, but said very little.

"See, not a palace, but it's nice and the rent is cheap." He spoke a schoolish German.

"It was nice of you to go to so much trouble, Signor di Sabatino."

"Ho—ho! Listen, charming lady, I'm Angelo to Vic, I think I can be Angelo to you also, please." He smiled the smile of the courtier.

Vic put his arm around Angelo's shoulder. "You've gone to so much trouble, boy, how can I repay you?"

"You've forgotten, *I'm* repaying *you*. Here, I've brought you two bottles to celebrate the new flat. One of red wine. The other of white paint, and one moment! Puff! With these two bottles home will be beautiful!"

He even helped them paint the room a few days later.

"Does your friend Angelo know that we are—what we are?" she asked Vic one day. "Non-Aryans?"

"I don't know. Puzzles me. He met my father in Prague many times, but you know Dad isn't much for Jewishness, any more than your family."

Nevertheless that night, prodded by her question, he came home with a surprise. "Honey, look. Want to see something I've got for you?"

Solemnly he was hanging something round her neck, the way she had seen Papa hang an expensive pearl necklace around Mama's with love for the neck, but with proper respect for the jewel also. "It's becoming too. Makes you shine." He had bought her a crucifix, a silver filigreed cross. "It's been blessed by the Pope himself, no less. The man at the shop claims to be a commissioned agent of the Vatican and he says he has had it blessed by the Pope. Wear it in good health."

And on the wall a few days later he hung a cheaply framed picture of Jesus with a huge bleeding heart. It was gory and gaudy, but conclusively Catholic.

Debbie knew he was casting about for means to get them to Nice or Chiasso, but he was cautious. Having failed after days of trying and waiting to get visas at the French and Swiss Embassies, or even to Holland or Belgium, he was fearful of everyone and hypersensitive to the slightest doubt, or inflection or sign that could signify doubt, in his fellow-workers. At the plant he was cultivating one man whose brother had a job at the foreign ministry, but was proceeding cautiously with him. Someday soon he planned to have him over to the flat.

Then they discovered Debbie was pregnant. She was afraid for a while to tell him, but Vic took it without a flicker of dismay, and after the first shock became jubilant. It was odd how pleased he was. He would bring her little special gifts of fruits or flowers which he bought at the market on his way home. The baby would make no difference in their plans, he said. There was no hurry. It was going to take a little time anyhow to find the right person to get them visas. Meanwhile it would be better for them to settle down a while and let Debbie have the baby before making any moves. The suspicion flashed through Debbie's mind that Vic might think border authorities would be more sympathetic to a girl carrying a new baby in her arms. She suppressed the thought. It was really unfair to Vic, although he usually considered everything.

* * * * * *

It was Angelo who had located the midwife when the time came. What a way to have a baby! She thought now of the Maternity Section of Hadassah on the Scopus where she had worked for so many months, and had helped deliver babies herself—the immaculate beds, the delivery rooms, the sympathetic nurses, so civilized. She remembered the hospital Mama had pointed out where she and Karl had been born, an impressive building out beyond the university, where she had planned as a girl to have her own babies, five or six of them. And how David had come!

"Bite on this, Signora." Her own palms blistered and bleeding from wringing them. And Vic gone. Where in heaven's name was Victor? Why did Angelo stand there like that? And what was that rat doing on the kitchen sink? Perhaps he'd learn a thing or two. Go away, rat. Oh, let the rat stay, but Angelo, make Angelo go away.

I'm going to die. Of course I'll die. How could anyone have a baby like this? Nothing's clean. Nothing's sterile. Roaches on the floor, insects in bed. And the midwife so unconcerned—the pain, O the pain —Up, up, up and down, down—better. One could have the pain and bear it for a baby, for life. But just to die, one could die some easier way. . . . Don't make me suffer. Give me something, something for the pain . . . Smoke . . . Steam . . . yes, steam. Ah . . . Clink . . . Metal on metal. The woman had instruments.

The ugly midwife so sharp and knowing. Signore this and Signore that, to Angelo. Take it easy. No need to hurry. Yes, plenty of time.

Make Angelo go away. He hardly knows me. Oh, I'll never be able to face him! Stop staring down at my nakedness. My huge ugly belly. I'm not like that really. Deborah is flat and small and handsome and not all swollen up like a fat pig. Go away, stranger.

"Don't worry, honey." It was Vic. "Everything is fine, fine, everything is just the way it should be. Absolutely normal. The baby is coming now and the midwife says you're in perfect condition."

Oh, thank you, thank you, how can I thank you? I can stand it, anything, only not the worry. Oh, the tearing, tearing. No, no, please, Lord —Make it go away. But Vic's here and Vic said not to worry. He'll take care of everything . . . So nice not to worry—

"Push now, Signora. Push like you go to the toilet. Hard."

What a revolting thing to say. Has she no delicacy? And she calls me Signora. Formal. Queens did it too, O Lord, push like you are going to the toilet, your majesty.

O Lord.

She wept and cried out. Her own moans seemed not even to come from her own throat or of her own free will. At last she was happy and relieved, exhausted and moved.

"It's a boy, a fine big boy, see."

"Take him away, please take him away." She turned away from the source of her pain.

"Signore," to Angelo, "help me here while I cut. Hold this." Another instrument, at least they'd boiled it. The midwife tied so quickly, expertly.

Vic said, "He's pretty. Looks just like his mother."

The baby was sweet. He was so small, red and helpless with a bush of light brown hair standing out of his head like a Fuzzy-Wuzzy, and he needed her so. It was like nothing ever before.

"I'm sorry, baby boy, to bring you out into this vile old world into this awful flat, but someday—someday—we're going on a big trip, far, far away until finally we reach our own home."

The circumcision was not much of a problem. Debbie mentioned it once and Vic dismissed it with a shrug. Dimly she remembered her Genesis: "Every man-child among you shall be circumcised . . . and the uncircumcised man-child whose flesh of his foreskin is not circumcised, that soul shall be cut off from his people; he hath broken my covenant."

Of course, Vic was right. After all, what was so all-fired particular about clinging to such a people? No doubt God had something rather special in mind when he mentioned the matter to Abraham, but since then the rewards of circumcision had become a little doubtful. A covenant after all is only a covenant, and in the year 1940, this little covenant was a passport to death. Yes, she'd heard all about circumcision being a sensible health measure too. Unreligious Jews liked to talk about how healthy it was. How sensible. Healthy! She could picture some unfortunate chap blindfolded against a wall, betrayed by circumcision, saying his last immortal words to a firing squad: "I thank God that due to circumcision I'm in perfect health."

The name was more of a problem. Vic insisted on calling the baby Angelo. Debbie wanted to call him David after her father, but Vic was firm.

"David's a fine name and I think it would be nice to name him after your Papa, but David was also a rather prominent Hebrew lad and it would be wiser not to raise any questions in anybody's mind."

For reasons that she could never satisfactorily explain to herself Debbie nevertheless called the baby David right from the beginning, at least to herself, and imagined sometimes he was Papa reincarnate—a childish concept, she knew, but one which gave her great comfort. It was too hard to believe that Papa was gone forever. In Victor's or Angelo's presence she avoided calling the baby by name and his birth was registered under the name Angelo Pretsch Marmorek. Angelo arranged for him to be baptized by Monsignor Rinaldi when he was six weeks old, at the church where they all usually went for mass. The baptism was on May 10, 1940, the same day that the Nazi Army swept across the French border. The dream which had never been more than a dream, of going to France or the Low Countries, faded. Only Switzerland remained, and there were thousands clamoring for Swiss visas.

Bringing up David in the one-room flat was no picnic and she soon began to be preoccupied with the danger of having another baby. Vic was so tired and depleted most of the time that their lovemaking was perfunctory and infrequent, but even these rare occasions became upsetting to her, until she insisted that he employ devices of prevention. "I love our little boy, but I just couldn't bear to have another one," she confessed. "Not here, not like this."

Vic had no idea where to buy such things, and was embarrassed to speak to Angelo about the matter, but she finally refused him entirely until he did.

"I just can't enjoy it, I'm too worried, I'm half out of my mind."

Reluctantly, Vic mentioned the matter to Angelo, almost as a ribaldry, to conceal his embarrassment. It was a hard, distasteful thing to do. Angelo shrugged and told him such devices were not easy to come by in this Catholic city especially at a time when large families were not only encouraged, but subsidized by government. But in a few days he did manage to find a supply of contraceptives in a shop in the Via Trionfale.

So Debbie's peace of mind was restored, although now when she and Angelo met, he took an appreciative, twinkling interest in her which, while not quite proprietary, represented a subtle change in a relationship which had already had to weather the birth day of her son.

Thirteen

There was much to do after the baby came: cooking, cleaning, and infant care; laundering, sewing, and trying to be a companion to a tired husband. Her domestic necessities were therapeutic, because since her Italian was poor Vic felt it was safer for her not to become involved with neighbors who might ask questions. So she only smiled and said, *"Buon giorno,"* and kept her distance from them all. It was lonely but safe. Vic's wages were barely enough for rent and food, but they managed. Money for entertainment was out of the question, although occasionally they bought a book or magazine. Neither was inclined to dip into the three thousand marks which Debbie kept safely in her now worn pocketbook. Most evenings they stayed home and read or went to bed soon after supper, a pattern that had been established when they first came to Rome. Only when Angelo came to visit was there any break in routine, and his visits came to be events for which she saved her food coupons and money to make little feasts. On these nights there would be more wine than usual. It was not that she felt anything special for Angelo, but after a year, he was still their only friend.

It was only natural that Angelo should notice her little kindnesses, although he said nothing except to compliment the food and cooking, in which he had a great interest. The truth was he was a better cook than she, and sometimes took pleasure in cooking his own tempting pastas or fish dishes with tasty sauces, which he ate with the unrestrained relish of a starving gourmet.

On the frequent festa days during the summer after David's birth he sometimes took half a day off—a luxury Vic could by no means attempt—and came for her on his motor scooter. In spite of the strict rations of gasoline, they would sometimes ride a short way into the country, David squashed docilely between them, and find a quiet place along the road where they could spread a blanket and have a bite. She got so she could ride the rear seat of a motor scooter with David in her arms almost as comfortably as she had sat in the great sedan behind Willie.

The little picnics were almost festive. Angelo brought his concertina which he played with zest, and taught her to sing Italian words which she scarcely understood. As the sun began to settle into the fields they would wrap up everything and put-put back to the flat. Angelo found it possible to take her hand on rare occasions, but she pretended not to notice, because she felt instinctively that things could become a great deal more complicated, without being any better.

Although she tried to avoid them, there were occasions when she found herself in the flat alone with Angelo, after David's bedtime or before dinner. She could feel Angelo's eyes on her then, his question, the unasked question which she was trying to avoid. Mentally she dodged and weaved away from it.

"You're looking almost radiant tonight. Have you had a good day?"

"Not really. Nothing happened. I went to market, but as usual not enough coupons and not enough money. I'm a little wilted."

"You look better wilted than other women do fresh. I think it comes from within, this glow. You must be inwardly celebrating."

"Angelo, are you trying to psychoanalyze me? Don't you dare!" She tried to laugh him out of his persistence.

"I wish I could. I wish I knew what you were thinking. I can only guess by examining myself. Look, I feel glowing too. Like fire. It is something to do with you. I can tell you that. I don't know what but something. Is your glow something to do with me?"

"Why, Angelo dear, I'm always happy when you come to dinner. Vic and I always love to see you."

When the baby was four months old he came one Sunday afternoon to call for them after mass to take them out to the great square in front of the Venezia Palace where Mussolini was scheduled to make an important speech. Everyone knew what it was to be, but Angelo insisted they come with him for the show. While Angelo admired Mussolini, he was almost ashamed to admit it. David, smart baby, slept through the entire proceedings, noisy as they were. The crowd was overwhelming, tremendous massed humanity shouting, Viva Duce! Duce! Duce! and milling about in holiday atmosphere, held in check by carabinieri and black-shirted Fascisti. She saw a flamboyant Mussolini, squat, but tremendously impressive, with a magnetism she could feel even from where she stood, a black-shirted figure surrounded by huge flag-bedecked photos and posters, gesticulating, screaming and chattering over the loudspeaker, his voice repeating and repeating itself in endless echoes over the imperfect public address system. The moment of decision was at hand. As of now Italy was at war with France and England. Italy had to defend her interests and her honor. The whole day had an aura of unreality, of bad play-acting. She was not even surprised to hear Vic's voice behind her, "Viva Duce! Viva, Viva!" There would be no trip to Chiasso now, until Lord knows when. She was too tired and bewildered to feel the impact of the terrible frustration of their plans. She would think it out some other time, when her mind was adjusted.

A week later Victor was transferred to the night shift. Actually it was a promotion in title and pay. He was to be night foreman in the turbine room, supervising a small crew. Nevertheless Angelo apologized obliquely, explaining that despite the slow pace after midnight he had to have a reliable man now that Italy was at war, someone he could really depend on at night, since attempts to sabotage had to be expected and even the night bombing of Rome was not impossible, and they had to have a man with his wits about him in event of emergency. Rather offhandedly he said, "This might do the trick and keep you out of the army too. You know they're taking foreigners now, but I think I can manage to keep you out."

Something about Angelo's explanation and his manner struck a chill in Debbie. He kept trying to catch her eye, but she avoided his glance.

The evening Vic was to start on the late shift Angelo came to supper. He seemed subdued, and answered Vic's questions absently. When it was time for Vic to go, Angelo said he would stay just a minute more and help with the blackout blankets and the dishes. She could feel the beginning of the strain of his intent.

They said almost nothing, just hung the blankets over the two small windows, and started the dishes, she washing and Angelo drying. The only sounds were the click of the dishes and the cold water running from the tap. Where do we go from here? Not this young lady, Angelo. Find a plump Italian lass.

Angelo cleared his throat. He spoke in his careful German. "I feel sorry for the Jews here in Rome. Honestly, it's quite frightful. The Nazis have issued an order, they are really running everything now, you know. Italians must identify any Jews they know. Turn them in. Over two thousand were carted off yesterday to Regina Coeli. I saw them in the trucks, really quite awful. Two boys I went to school with were taken. Luckily for me they were turned in by someone else. I simply couldn't have done it. They don't keep them at Regina Coeli long. Two or three days and then they take them to the catacombs and shoot them. I've a friend at Regina Coeli and he is quite sick about it."

Debbie tried hard to be uninterested. She put the dishes on the shelf.

"I understand even the children. It's really quite shocking when you think how hard it is to have a baby and how easy it is to shoot one. The Vatican is trying to help a few, but how much can the priests do?"

He dried a black pot in silence and lit a cigarette. "Sometimes," he said, "I envy Victor really. He's so much more brilliant than I. And not only brighter, but luckier. See what a nice wife he has and a cute baby. Everything."

"Perhaps you should find a nice girl, Angelo. Some nice faithful young lady like me. Settle down." She must be cautious. Angelo was no simpleton. He laughed bitterly.

"Look at me. Be honest. Crippled. Not clever, not witty. The only thing I know anything about at all is electricity. And of what interest is that to a nice girl?"

"Oh, there are girls who would be delighted with you, electricity and all."

He ignored her. "Besides, the Germans have taken all the nice girls. They have the cigarettes and candy to give away, even if it is ersatz, and so naturally they have the girls. But I wouldn't want a girl for a price. I could only like a girl if she liked me. For myself." He held the cigarette carefully under the leaking faucet, let one or two drops extinguish it, and put the butt into his breast pocket.

"I think you underestimate yourself."

"You think so? Perhaps people underestimate themselves generally. I've seen men behave like heroes and never think of themselves as anything special. You have to give them credit. Even if they conceal a Jew today, they can be sentenced too. Not tortured, of course, the way the Nazis amuse themselves with Jews, but still to be shot is not pleasant and I know some fellows who are concealing Jews. I think they're rather brave, don't you?"

She couldn't answer, couldn't free a word through her throat.

"Don't you?"

"Yes, I do."

Her answer was almost a whisper. Her flippancy was swallowed down deep; the flat had become chilly, terribly cold for June, and she put a shawl around her shoulders to keep from shivering.

"They don't have to do it, perhaps they are really foolish to do it," he said.

"No, I think they're rather brave," she said as offhandedly as she could. "There should be some kind of reward for it."

"In this world or the next?" he asked.

"Oh, a medal or something that can be hung around the neck," she said.

"Something like this?" He fingered her crucifix, her filigreed key to survival. "This is so pretty. It's not something you brought from Prague, is it? It's rather new, isn't it?"

"Oh, I've had it some time now."

"Yes, but it looks Roman; isn't it?"

"Yes, it's been blessed by His Holiness."

His hand was on her shoulder and she said nothing. O Victor, David. Little baby, David. Mama, Papa. I'm not even twenty yet, I'm only little Debbie Pretsch. I'm not ready for this—I have to think—to think, and I must be clever. Is he guessing? Vic dear, if only I could ask you—what to do—What was it you said? We'd better do what we have to. And better too much than too little—lean over backward—O Lord, that's literally what he wants me to do—who'll I share that vulgar little joke with? O Vic, see how it is? In a way he may be trying to be nice, yes, trying to offer me my life, my husband's life, my baby's life. Really it's the height of reasonableness, Vic. It is. He couldn't ask less.

He looked at her solemnly. She would need time to think. Time, more time. She could see how he was staring at her now. Why deceive herself? "You feel sure you can keep Vic out of the army?" she said.

"I'm sure. Don't worry."

She leaned upward and kissed Angelo's cheek. "You're kind, aren't you?"

His fingers gripped her shoulders hard, almost viciously. "You're so tantalizing," he murmured. "Do you mean to be or am I teasing myself?"

She let him kiss her.

"I don't know," she whispered. "Is it possible for a girl to love two men at the same time?"

His arm about her grew bolder, stronger. "Of course, darling. When someone is bursting with love as you are. Of course. You know how I feel. I have been thinking of nothing but kissing you for months."

She let him kiss her again, and this time responded, in spite of herself. What he said had worked upon her.

"You must give me time, time to think, time to figure things out, time to feel. Dear Angelo. Please."

He held her close and tight and she could feel the strain and tension of his body. "All right," he said. "But you know how I feel. And I know how you feel, that's enough for me."

He left abruptly, but he came soon again and stayed.

Angelo had the faintest smell of garlic about him and his body had a pungent sweaty odor which during the months that followed really came to stir her. It was amazing what could be done with scarcely a word.

The first night when Angelo lay back on the bed afterwards and smoked his cigarette she made him give her a drag; he taught her to inhale and as she felt the irritation of the smoke in her throat and lungs, she felt mightily depraved. A girl picked up all kinds of bad habits these days. And in the years afterwards when she smoked, she associated a peculiar depravity with the sensation of smoke in her lungs. That night was always with her.

When Angelo left after the first time, she was sure she would need to weep for release or toss in agonized confusion, but she slept soundly till David's morning murmurings wakened her.

Still, though the relationship subsisted on a comparatively wordless diet, their silences had their own secret meanings. She was pleased and thrilled, glad that whatever he did was done with compassion and enough tenderness to make it less difficult. Difficult? Why should a girl pry into every corner of her slumbering mind. Not now, not ever. Yes, it was difficult, God forgive her. It was her cross to bear, the unspeakable past so many of her friends in Jerusalem had, and never mentioned. It made her part of these people. One had only to assume the far-off hurt and blank look that said, I just can't bear to think of it. It was nothing to be pleased with.

After it started, once or twice a month, Angelo sent particularly luscious bunches of purple grapes to the flat as a gift, and although the symbolism was obscure, Debbie rather enjoyed it. Otherwise there was no word. Not before an encounter, nor during, nor after. When they were with Victor, Angelo spoke as always about the plant, the war or the food so that there was no dissembling before Victor. There were no assignations, no plans, no elaborate deceptions. It became routine: supper and after Victor's departure, the ritual, so much the same, but always rich with variations on the theme. As they became practiced with each other she realized he was not wholly inarticulate in his tenderness. He conveyed his emotions in action. His body, his hands, his lips were his language and they were often tender and full of love and she could not choose but respond.

Only once, when David was past three, he awakened as Angelo was leaving. He was frightened by the thunder of a stormy night and began to whimper in the dampness that never left the flat. He complained that the bed scratched, as it so often did. In the dark Angelo must have seemed a strange figure. Angelo had bought a hand puppet for David that evening, a beautiful blond doll of a puppet, but David had gone to bed early, slept all through supper's noise and confusion. Now in the hush of three in the morning he woke. In the dark he must have heard whispering voices in the room.

"Mommy!" His own voice was a frightened whisper too. "Mommy!" Louder. "Mommy!"

"Shhh! What is it, dear?"

"Someone's in the room."

Debbie giggled softly to Angelo beside her.

"Who is it, Mommy?"

"No one, dear, go to sleep."

"Maybe God's in the room!" That made her laugh too, louder.

"Of course, dear. God is everywhere, you know that." Her voice was soothing now.

"Tell Him to get out. I can't sleep with anyone in the room."

Then there was a match and light from the kerosene lamp, and it was Angelo. He loved his Uncle Angelo because he always brought toys and fruit and he knew how to cook and make attractive cooking smells. Angelo had no shirt on, and David asked if he was going to take a bath. Angelo put his shirt on.

"Hush up, little fellow. Uncle Angelo has a present for you. When I got here you were fast asleep. So I saved it. And here it is."

The wrappings were newspaper and the excitement of opening it, wondering what it was, made him tremble. Uncle Angelo always brought such wonderful things—once a balloon, once a small whip, once a funny paper hat. But this was different from any of them. This was beautiful. It was a girl in a bright red dress and Uncle Angelo could put his hand inside her head and make her wave her hands and bow her head. Angelo said to the puppet girl, "Give my little friend a kiss," and she flew right to David and bowed down and kissed him and he said, "Give me, give me!"

Angelo took her off his hand and gave her over solemnly and David said, "What's her name?"

"See if you can guess," Angelo said.

"Nina," he said promptly. The pretty lady upstairs who occasionally smiled to him, but to whom he had never talked, was called Nina.

"Absolutely right!" Angelo cried. "On the first guess!"

This Nina was pretty, and although she was cut off in the middle, David loved her, because he could put his hand into her head and he could help her to say anything she wanted to, and he was sure she liked him too, for he confessed she told him so many times.

Uncle Angelo kissed him and on tiptoe, it seemed, he waved goodbye to Debbie. She said, "Now be a good boy and go back to sleep." So he hugged Nina to him and comforted her, and soon slept, and after that Nina went everywhere with him. For a while he was a little embarrassed to tell anyone about Nina, somehow he thought they might laugh, but soon he was bolder and thought it natural that everyone should understand how Nina could be his wife and why he talked to her as he did, only, of course, she never answered anyone else, only him.

Yes, Angelo could be tender. Sometimes when he failed to come for a week or even longer, she missed him. He brought his little gifts not for her, but for David. After the early rattles and teething rings, the balloons and tin horns, there was Nina and finally when David was four the beautiful concertina, which from the beginning gave him so much pleasure, and apparently gave Angelo a thrill teaching him. He was so quick to catch on, the little devil.

Would Angelo ever have gone to the police about them if she had not made matters absolutely fascinating—? He was so nice. She hoped it was necessary.

What choice had there been? Poor Mama, she would have died of shame; but Mama was dead and Papa too. How carefully Debbie and her girl friends, people like Gussie, had been prepared for the lives of their mothers instead of their own. A proper education—Goethe, von Hofmannsthal, Heine, Schiller, Beethoven, Brahms and Strauss, good manners, dear fräulein and curtsey when you meet an older person, and no thank you and yes please. Speak when spoken to and be pleasant with young men, but never bold. Skate and ski, swim and sail, piano lessons and French, algebra and horsemanship, waltzes and ballet. It might have been a quiet pleasant life. As it happened these high-born girls became the best-mannered whores, field hands, and corpses in Europe. Poor Mama!

Had Vic guessed? She mustn't think about that, it's silly to brood. Wasn't it Victor who had decided for her? She depended on his wisdom so. "If there's a question of what's necessary we'd better do it. Lean over backwards." She had to smile to herself. Words were such a comfort. And it was comforting to place it all on Victor.

What had he meant the morning he came home after Angelo had sent a particularly luscious bunch of grapes, "Angelo's been very thoughtful. I must remember to thank him for the grapes." He popped one of them into his mouth and cupped the seeds in his palms, "Delicious too, thank goodness; I loathe sour grapes." He was cryptic; he said nothing more, he asked no questions, not then, not since. Vic was not one to break a bargain, even if the bargain had not been clearly laid on the table. If during those months he noticed a shyness, a reserve in her which was partly shame, partly withdrawal, he made no observation. Had she succeeded in deceiving him or had he deceived her? Why dwell upon it?

In spite of Angelo, or perhaps because of him, she needed Victor more than ever and she felt he needed her too, more than he admitted. In the early darkness of the mornings he would come home and crawl into bed and they talked in whispers to keep from waking David. He was always glued to the war news, to the papers, to the radio. Mussolini's first fall was a tonic for him although the Germans were still in Rome. The slow failure of the Nazi Armies meant so much to them, they sometimes talked of nothing else. Really, when you thought of it, it was quite comical. Victor slipping into bed in his underwear like a secret lover one morning, holding her tenderly in his arms, saying, "I wouldn't tell this to anyone else in the world, darling. It's our secret." He looked deeply into her eyes. "I must confess I love someone else—

General Eisenhower. I love all Americans. Tonight they have landed at Anzio." He chuckled a little even then and spoke with relief.

"When they come, my little Girl Scout, we'll be free! We can walk the streets like people; you see, our patience has paid off. I can tell you now, sweet, I've been scared, but really scared these last few months. There's a guy at the plant, one of my assistants, Giuseppe Ritucci, been watching me, suspicious as hell. Always rather distant, and you never know what goes on in his dim little mind. Every time he looked at me cross-eyed, I'd die. He made a few vague cracks, nothing definite. But tonight he was a little friendlier, guess he heard about Anzio too."

"Vic dear," she whispered, "don't ever tell me you're afraid, you're my backbone!"

"Well, we're coming to the end of this nightmare and then we'll go back home again. I can get my old job back in Prague. We can get Lindenhouse back, and the theaters. We'll be rich again. You'll be beautiful again—not that you aren't now, only you can bring it out into the open more. We'll go skiing in the Krknos or at Snow Mountain again, only this time you'll be careful and not break any bones, and summers we'll swim in the pool at Lindenhouse, or go riding—we'll have a whole stableful of wonderful horses, just like the old days."

It was no time to argue seriously, to tell him she'd never go back, so she joined his daydream. "I'll cook fancy French dishes to taste like ambrosia."

They murmured and kissed and lay quite still.

"I'm glad the Americans and English are coming soon. I'm glad for us, but I'm happier still for David's sake."

"Yes," he said drowsily, "he's a lucky little monkey, he won't remember anything of all this, thank God. But don't go about calling him David yet. Let's wait till the last Nazi has gone north to the great Götterdämmerung, the bastards."

Almost before he finished the sentence he was asleep.

She scarcely realized it at the time, but she needed David even more than Vic during those days. Victor thought the baby was cute too, but ten minutes at a stretch was his limit. He tickled the baby, made him scream with laughter, tossed him about, alternately scaring the wits out of him, and pleasing him to death, and then put him down, patted him on the head, and said, "Now go find Mommy."

She had to rig up a screen to shield Victor from the worst of the mayhem, because Victor had to sleep during a good part of the day and David was a menace to sleep. But to Debbie the baby was pure joy. They played together and giggled together and she loved to hear him try his first words.

"*Tisch,*" he would shriek and pound the leg of the table. She would say, "Shh! Daddy's sleeping." Then he would wobble about the room, touching everything and calling it a *Tisch*. If Debbie disappeared behind a piece of furniture and he became conscious of her absence he shrieked in panic. Later she made a game of it and taught him to cry, "Where's Mommy?" When she would pop out, he would cry, "There she is!"

Later he learned recitations which he insisted on saying in a loud clear voice that was so much larger than he. Vic picked him up to hug him. "Show-off," he cried. "A born show-off like his mother."

Debbie pouted and said, "It's his theatrical blood. He comes from a long line of exhibitionists."

She enjoyed making David's clothes and she became expert at cutting his hair. And she thought he looked rather fetching. By doing everything herself she kept contacts with other people at a minimum and made Victor's thousand lire a month go further than she had thought possible.

David liked to shop with her. She herself would have found shopping a terrible chore without him. For many months it was the only chance either of them had to see other people and David found the barren markets a wonderland.

After he was about two and a half she took him most days by bus to the park at Villa Borghese and let him play with the other children while she read and watched, and soon he spoke as fluent Italian as German. He liked to teach his mother Italian words. It made him feel quite grown although they always spoke together in German. He made no regular friends, but occasionally he would see the same child for several days running; then if it lasted too long Debbie chose another spot in the park. It was safer not to let friendships develop; the other mothers tended to get gossipy.

One day after David and three other boys had tormented and chased a little girl in the park screaming into her mother's arms, Debbie scolded him as they were coming home on the bus.

"Why were you chasing that nice little girl?"

"She's no good. Pietro says she's a Jew," David said to her. "Jews are no good, you know. Someday I'd like to kill one."

She was aghast, but the bus was jammed with people. Still she couldn't let it go entirely by default. "Where did you hear such a thing?" she whispered to him.

"Pietro, the boy in the park, told me."

"You mustn't say such things."

"What are Jews, Mommy?"

"They're people—just people. God made all of us and it's very naughty to say you'll kill anyone."

He looked at her in surprise. He had meant his remark merely as a pleasantry and was contrite to have displeased her.

"The boy in the park who told you that is a very bad boy."

David's brows knitted and he concentrated in thought for a spell. "He's no good," David agreed seriously. "Probably he's a Jew."

A mustached man sitting opposite her broke into a stifled guffaw; she smiled a little too, in spite of herself.

She never mentioned the incident to Victor. Sometimes she thought it was a mistake to tell Vic too much.

Like that occasion when David was older. They frequently went shopping on Viale Giulio Cesare, near Mazzini Square, where she bought food, choosing from one or another of the many stalls where different merchandise was sold. One insignificant stall attended by an old crone was stocked with ersatz candy, and while she was buying vegetables and cheese and spaghetti and olive oil, David used to watch the candy counter, and he discovered two things of importance. The first was there was always a small knot of people who liked to gossip with the old lady, and the second was that a stock of white, pasty candy was piled at the edge of a counter he could reach. Most of the purchasers were German soldiers, and they frequently ate their purchases on the spot with such evident satisfaction that David was bound to have some. Debbie refused to buy any because she had to conserve money. He found that so long as he was quick about it and took only one or two small pieces, no one seemed to mind, perhaps because they had not noticed. On the way home he would jam one into his mouth and they were really delicious, but he never mentioned the matter to Debbie, and she found out about it only on the morning the old woman caught him. Oh, Debbie would never forget *that* day. David had come to think of the candy lady as such a nice old woman, the guardian of such a store of wonders, that he was sure she was kind and sweet. But suddenly she became terrible and began to scream and point at him, and caught him when he tried to run, and she dragged him roughly to the street by his shoulder and called the first carabiniere, a wicked uniformed man with huge yellow teeth. Debbie arrived instantly, looking terribly upset, and the policeman began to ask her questions, while several German soldiers laughed and made jokes about them as they walked by. All the while she was fishing in her pocket for the lire to pay for the candy, and at last she paid the old woman, who sullenly counted out her change.

But the carabiniere began to ask her more questions and she drew out her passport at last and showed it, and when the policeman did not seem satisfied, she turned on David, furious beyond reason, and slapped him in the face and about the shoulders as she never had, so hard he would never forget it, and at last, while she was beating him the policeman left and the crowd thinned out, and they went home, walking stiffly, neither saying a word.

When they arrived at the flat, he said, "I got a piece for you too," and handed it to her from the depths of his pocket. She took and ate it slowly, chewing hard and regularly, and suddenly, she did not quite know how, she was holding him close to her and kissing him and she could tell from her own wet cheeks that she was crying.

When she told Vic he became white with rage, even though she tried to minimize it. She said, "I'm sure he won't forget it, Vic. I'm sure I've done all that's necessary." But Vic took his son roughly by both shoulders and said to him, "You'll never, never, never do anything like that again. We don't want policemen, we don't want questions." He lifted him like a sack and laid him face down on the bed deliberately, even gently, so that David almost didn't know what to expect; and the terrible crash came like unexpected fire across his backside, and again, and again.

And then Vic too was holding him in his arms, as she had, a bitter little boy crying fiercely, wronged, shouting, hysterical, trying to soothe him, but saying firmly, "I'm sorry, but you are to behave yourself. You're not to forget it."

She stood by pale but not interfering, because Vic knew what was needed, and perhaps David tried to understand that some purpose was being served, because his parents had always been kind to him. No doubt he thought adults were unpredictable, especially his father. So much anger over a piece of candy! And such terrible blows on his small backside. His Daddy was so strong.

After that whenever he saw soldiers or police, he clung tightly to his mother's skirt, making himself as small as possible, and hurried past to match his mother's quickened steps.

David's frequent earaches too, always accompanied by high fevers, were devastating to Debbie. Several times they became abscesses, which finally burst. The elderly doctor Angelo sent prescribed sulfa drugs and heat applications to the ear, but where could one find sulfa drugs? A bundle of heated salt was the best device, but David wept softly and after a while lay still, like a morose injured animal, clutching Angelo's girl-puppet, his wife Nina.

If the pain were not too great, he pretended Nina had earaches herself and he comforted her as he always did when he was worried by anything strange, painful or frightful. But during the worst of his earaches even Nina was no help. He would lie still, his eyes wide, pushing away the wooden toys Victor had made him and refusing food and crying softly to his unseen pain, "Don't hurt me, don't hurt me." He was underweight, sallow and scrawny even when he was not actually sick, so that when he was ill sometimes it was more than Debbie could bear. Her own resistance was not great and once or twice after being awake all day and night she couldn't keep from weeping herself. Nothing must happen to her baby. O God, not after all this. At these bleak moments she would cuddle him in her arms and comfort him; he'd speak in a weary voice, but brave, "Make it go away, Mommy. Sing a song, Mommy."

"All right, lovey. What song shall I sing?"

"Sing about David's friends."

"All right, put your head on my shoulder . . . Someday, Daddy and Mommy and David will all go home together on a big—"

"Ship."

"And home is a place that is very very—"

"Warm."

"Because the sun shines all day long and everyone there is very—"

"Happy."

"Because everyone is—"

"*Friends.*"

This delighted him and he smiled at her triumphantly even when she could see the grievous pain his ear caused him.

* * * * * *

At last she felt she should talk to Victor about Palestine. They could get in touch with Karl, and he could help get them there. She had lived with it a long time. Papa's words were etched in her mind:— "Karl was right. Tell Miss Debbie." It was her little corner of comfort, the promise of a sunrise behind the bleak gray horizon, but soon she really had to talk to Victor. Of course, he would be disturbed to be reminded of her brother Karl.

Early one March evening before dinner she was on the verge of it, but at the last minute she thought, I'll wait for the Americans and English. I'll think of some clever way to go about it then. Something that will make him take it seriously; I won't be treated like a child this time.

Fourteen

The wild night when the last of the German trucks and half tracks, cars and mobile guns roared north through the Via Trionfale, and distant guns crashed closer and closer in an endless succession of explosions, was enough to scare the wits out of anyone; David had to reassure Nina with all the phrases Debbie and Vic were using on him: Nothing to be afraid of, the guns will stop soon, the bad men are going. The English will come, and the Americans. They're the good men, it will be better. Then in the middle of the darkest part of the night they had come and she and Vic and David had run into the street with the crowds, holding each other tight to keep together, David clutching Nina. He found it impossible to tell the difference between the good men and the bad. Vic pointed out how these men had stars painted on their tanks and trucks, while the others had the crooked cross. But David saw only that they all wore the same iron hats. Still he helped throw flowers at these new soldiers and they danced with others about the streets and everyone drank wine from the flasks. Vic gave him a small bottle of wine for his own and said, "Remember tonight, David." Vic had never called him by that name before, and David was pleased. He whispered to Nina, "It's a party," and Nina behaved as bravely as he. It was a great beginning for them.

As an American Captain of Engineers entered Rome early in the evening the first day of the Allied occupation, he was surprised when his driver stopped the jeep on the Via Trionfale and a pretty, slight young woman dressed in shabby black pushed a small boy through the crowd and into the jeep to shake hands. She spoke excitedly in German, half laughing, half crying. "Captain, you beautiful Captain from America, I'm so glad to see you. You'll never know what it means to us. I love you, my husband loves you, my son loves you." Debbie had not been so emotionally stirred for a long time as she was by the sight of American khaki. The American could understand not a word, but he understood her kiss. The driver motioned that he would like a kiss too, so she gave it to him. The driver said in halting German, "The Captain thanks you and I thank you, lady." They laughed and the Captain gave her a pack of cigarettes. David insisted on kissing the driver too. The driver said, "I have a girl his size in Minneapolis, girl named Laura," and he gave David a chocolate bar.

David chased the jeep clutching the chocolate bar, with Debbie after him, both waving at the Americans until they disappeared around a corner.

David was jubilant. "A policeman kissed me," he told his father proudly. "He gave me candy. I'm not afraid of policemen any more." It was a small defiance to his father.

Debbie spoke to Vic that night. "I think we ought to write Karl now, I'm sure he can help us."

"Karl? What would we write Karl? What could he do for us?"

"He could help us," she said.

"My God," he said, "you're not thinking of going to Palestine, are you?"

"I think we ought to write Karl," she said. "He doesn't even know we're alive."

"Not tonight," Vic said. "I'm too exhausted tonight."

"Darling, we've simply got to get away as soon as we can!" She was thinking of David and of Angelo—and of Papa—"In Palestine we can make a brand new life!"

"We can go back to Vienna or perhaps Prague. At least there we have Lindenhouse. I think now we'll be able to get it back. My friends can help me get a job."

"Vic, how could you think of it? Never mind us, but for David!"

"Silly, why not? Those filthy people will be finished. They'll crawl back into the crevices they came out of."

"Vic, darling, darling, are you teasing? Go back to them? How can you forget them? We saw it with our own eyes. They knew what was happening to us, and what did they do?"

"How about Paula? How about Mayor Klapka?"

"Vic, I can't argue. I just couldn't go back. Maybe if we'd stayed and fought, like Martin, like Mayor Klapka, like your father—maybe then—we'd have had the right. But we ran away, Vic."

"We're alive and they're not. Martin, Klapka, my father and the rest, heroes, but dead ones."

"Well I couldn't, I just couldn't live with those who are still there. I couldn't stand to see them on the streets. I'd wonder does this one wish me killed or that one? They were perfectly willing to see us killed, Vic—us and our children, kids like David. Oh, not personally to do it, but to see it, to have it done. I believe they were secretly happy, lots of them. Not indifferent, no, that would have been bad enough, but happy. Glad. Tickled. Blood, blood and more blood. I couldn't go back to them, Vic, never, never, not as long as I live."

Vic turned away from her tirade. She was tense and overwrought and he put his hand on her shoulders as if to soothe her. "Don't try to pet me like a cat," she cried sharply.

"Those people were afraid," Vic said. "They couldn't help themselves."

"Yes, I know, like we were with Gussie. May God forgive us. We were as bad as the rest, that's another reason I could never go back."

"I don't understand you, Debbie, so help me. I've never seen you so overwrought. Think of all the good things that have been done for Jews and at such personal risk!"

"Sure," Debbie said. "Men who are shielding Jewish girls to use them for whores! I know *that* kind. Nice friends like Martin Schroeder who got passports at a hundred thousand crowns apiece, sweet women like Paula who took all the trouble to write, both your parents were killed. 'I'm sorry,' she wrote. I know about them too. I can't stand to look at them either. I suppose there are nice ones, decent ones, but they're dead or scarce or resentful at us because we didn't stay and fight. The others made their arrangement to live in peace with murder and evil. Who's there to go back to? Where do we fit?"

Vic turned away, but during dinner he said what must have been on his mind for a long time. "America must be a great place. My mother had a cousin who lived in Cleveland, I think, I'm not sure, Selma Goulder, I think her name was. Think of America—opportunities everywhere to be a big man. How do you think our son would like to be an American?"

Debbie said, "David's a stateless Jew, Vic. Only on your side and mine, of course."

"Americans," he said, "are made, not born." He shut his eyes, holding them closed with his fingertips as though he had a headache. He had no appetite. The dried fish offended him. She had upset him, but she couldn't help being as stubborn as Papa or Karl.

Vic lowered his voice and spoke almost as though he were ruminating. "We'll get no certificates for Palestine, there just aren't any, that's certain. And if we're caught by the British trying to break the blockade, Lord knows what they'll do to us. Coop us up in some filthy camp, no doubt. Give us slops to eat. We'll never get out, no future at all. Look at what they're doing to the poor fools they've caught already."

He turned on Debbie. "I can't understand you, Deb. We'll have our full legal rights in Austria. We'll get everything back. We'll be somebody. In Palestine we'll be outlaws, even if we manage to get in. Hiding. Worrying at night, lying. Just to keep from being tossed into some new hellhole. I wouldn't mind taking the risks so much for myself. But what about David? Are we being fair to him?"

"David is willing," she said grimly. "You have it on the authority of his mother, who loves him more than herself."

She could have written Karl herself, but it wouldn't do. During the next weeks Vic was busy, exploring ways and means to get to America. There was nothing she could do to stop him. He would leave the flat at two each afternoon and return in time for supper, whistling and mysterious, as though she hadn't the faintest idea what he was up to. After a month he looked so thin and tired, she felt sorry for him.

"I guess perhaps you'd better write Karl," he said quietly one evening.

But she was firm. "*You* write, Vic. You know how Karl admired you, even though you may have disagreed." It was a difficult letter for him to write.

Dear Karl:

Hello from Debbie and myself from Rome. As you can see we're making a tour of the continent. You may have thought us dead with the rest, but we're still very much alive here, and we have a son now—David—named after your Dad, and we're all in good health. We've been lucky.

Of course it's been hard, but why write of such things now? We're happy to be able to write at last and to say straight out—you were right from the beginning and all of us who stayed were wrong, totally wrong. Believe me, it's hard for me to write these words. Those who put their trust in the goodness of men were disappointed.

Debbie and I would like to go to Palestine. Can you help us? Can you write us the best thing to do? We hesitate to go to anyone else as we understand certificates are scarcer than hen's teeth. Meanwhile, don't worry about us. The Americans and English are in Rome now and we're safe. I've a job at one of the big Rome powerhouses. We hope you and Lilith are in the best of health.

Our most cordial affectionate regards to you both.

VICTOR

She made him rewrite the letter and take out the reference to those who put their trust in the goodness of men.

"Vic, my darling, will it hurt too much to say, Karl, you were right and we were wrong? It's enough and it's true." She added a few words of her own.

Karl, remember the day you left Vienna and I promised to come to see you in Palestine some day with my husband? Who'd have thought I'd turn out to be a Cassandra? Certainly not I. Soon, Karl, I pray it's soon! With all my heart!

After she posted the letter she felt for the first time in her life almost like a full-grown woman. She had made the decision, not Vic's, but her own, and although she was satisfied with it, she was frightened of it too. She was still only a young girl and she needed Vic to take care of her. Perhaps she had done the wrong thing. Perhaps America. Maybe they should have waited a little longer. She must not be so sure she was right. For how terrible it would be to grow up and not need Vic any longer!

Angelo continued to come for dinner occasionally after the Germans had left Rome, but Debbie was skillful at avoiding an encounter. She managed to keep David awake, or be ill or tired.

"Have you been running away from me?" he said one night.

"I?" she said. "Why, no." They sat together a little while listening to music she tuned in softly on the radio and while they smoked, she smiled at him comfortably. "Do you know," she said, "Vic tells me the English have been investigating the men at the plant, looking for Fascists, party members I understand, putting them out of the important jobs."

"It's all a comedy," Angelo remarked wryly. "The English have no idea what they're doing."

"All the same they're doing it. Men are losing their jobs."

"And who do they put in their places? Fools, incompetents, children, Communists! It's ridiculous. Rome will fall apart in three months. Take our plant. Suppose they arrest me and Lionetti and

Donato and put strangers in charge? In six months there wouldn't be a light in Rome. Not a tram would move. Nothing would work." He ground out his cigarette violently.

"But why should they have to bring in a stranger? Vic could run that plant, you know he could. And he would have no trouble proving he's anti-fascist, after all he's a Jew."

Angelo frowned, but said nothing, only watched her suspiciously.

"Of course, he has no intention of taking your job. If there's any trouble about you he intends to go straight to them and tell them how for all these years you've protected us, how you saved our lives. Three lives to your credit, Angelo. That must make you feel good."

"I did what I could." He shrugged, elaborately modest. He rose and walked to her slowly, hesitantly, knelt beside her chair, took her hand gently and studied the back of it, the painfully thin fingers, the light blue pattern of her veins. "Debbie, darling," he said, his voice husky and charged with feeling, "one last time. Please, now it would mean so much more." He looked at her so pleadingly, wide-eyed, the way Axel, her collie, had looked when he'd been bad and wanted forgiveness. She stroked his cheek softly and he buried his head in her lap.

"No," she said.

"You're sure?" His words were muffled against her.

She nodded quickly, "I'm sure."

He rose and started out.

"I'm sorry, Angelo," she called, but he did not reply. The radio was still playing softly.

A tall man with sparse sandy hair, gaunt and dressed in British Army fatigues, came to their flat about supper time one August evening with a letter from Karl. The familiar handwriting had not changed.

> Greetings!–Vic and dear little Debbie alive! Your letter has just reached me and I'm still crying–real tears from a man over thirty. It's a letter one prays for and I've prayed for five long years. In all that time we never gave up hope. I don't know why. Tonight I'll be in the synagogue giving thanks to the Almighty. Who cares who was right and who was wrong? My heart is pounding with excitement. My sister, my brother! If you knew what that meant! I can't wait to see you and the baby. Such a precious thing, a baby. And named David! It brings to mind poor Papa!
>
> As you've surely read, the British these days have become more pro-Arab than the Arabs. They stop at nothing to keep our people out. The coast of Palestine is blockaded by British warships. Thousands are being caught offshore and turned back, or sent wandering over the oceans on unseaworthy ships. Certificates for legal entry are not to be had at any price. Still, many brave or desperate people are get-

ting through the blockade. There *are* ways to do it. If you're willing to take the chances, the man who gives you this letter will tell you what to do—We will be praying. . . .

On the first of October, a night filled with lightning and thunder, but luckily no rain, the lorry came for them. David was in the midst of one of his fierce earaches, an abscess just reaching the breaking point, his body hot with fever, but they bundled him up as warmly as they could, packed everything in the old brown torn valise she had always kept under her bed, and joined the huddled figures on the truck, so tightly crushed, almost lying on each other. Three Allied soldiers were waiting to help them, speaking German, Italian, Polish and Yiddish. The people in the truck all spoke different languages too. But she could only think of David and the agony of his ear. "It will break open soon now, soon." The night seemed to grow colder by the minute and she wrapped his head round with a scarf and kept his face inside her coat. It was not until the motor started that he realized they were leaving Nina behind. They had the concertina, but they had left Nina. At first he screamed so hysterically that she could not make it out and she said, "Hush, David sweet, the ear will be better soon."

After the truck started down Via Otranto she finally understood and called for the driver to stop, she and David making a terrible spectacle, calling out, while Vic tried to tell her to forget it. He was disgusted that they should inconvenience so many people for a puppet. The other faceless people who squeezed so tightly together in the van muttered and cursed, and when the driver finally stopped and doubled back to the house, even the soldiers were upset. She said only that she had to get something important. She had Vic hold David and David called after her, "In the bed, Mommy, she's in the bed."

When she came back he could see she had Nina inside her coat, hidden just where he had been himself only a few minutes before. It was always the trivial things that seemed to make excitement.

At last the truck was on its way. The breath of the people was making frost smoke in the night air and next to them one of the women was holding her baby tight to her; intermittently it cried and squealed. After a few minutes she pulled down her sweater, undid her blouse and began to nurse the infant in the frozen night. The woman looked at least forty-five, but was surely younger, and she cooed to the infant in her arms. David moved right up close to watch, even in his pain, because it was a sight he'd never seen before. In the flash of lightning for the first time Debbie saw the woman's face smile at her own baby and at David for his curiosity, and while she was old and her hair was stringy and one side of her mouth smiled more than the other so that her face was twisted almost into a grimace, Debbie found the smile of this strange woman quite beautiful in the blue lightning.

"*Shalom*," the woman said, "next year Jerusalem." They were going home!

As they rode, the abscess in David's ear broke. She could hear it break herself and she knew he would now have some blessed relief.

"Look, Mommy," he said, "Nina's hungry." He had put her against his breast and was trying to nurse her. He had so nearly lost her.

The woman opposite them laughed dryly.

"Mommy," he said, still whimpering from the bursting ear drum, "where are we going?"

"Home, dear."

"Like our song?"

"Yes, dear."

"Nina wants Uncle Angelo to come too."

"I know, dear. But Uncle Angelo lives here. His Mommy is here, his friends are here. We're going home, David, to *our* friends."

It must have been a puzzle for so small a boy. The cellar flat on the Via Silla had always been home to him, the only place he had known, and now she was saying home was elsewhere.

He turned to the nursing woman and spoke with bravado. "I'm going to see my friends, aren't I, Mommy? They're waiting for me. Sing about David's friends, Mommy."

She put his head on her bosom and they comforted each other.

"Tonight Daddy and Mommy and David are all going home together on a big—"

"*Ship*."

"And home is a place that is very, very—"

"*Warm*."

"Because the sun shines—"

When she had finished her home-made song, a white-haired man forward in the truck started softly to sing, a melodic wailing song—now she knew it was "Hatikvah"—and soon the whole truckload of men and women was singing softly, the strange melancholy music with words that were not really words of language, and singing so you could feel a mysterious wonder in them. No word could tell it like that music softly jarred in the bumpy night. She had never seen or heard anything like it, but after a few minutes the driver stopped the truck and his companion called back to scold everyone for singing.

Everyone was quiet for a long time and the truck bounced along the rutted road in a monotonous, hurtling ride to the unknown. Twice they were stuck in the mud and eight or nine men including Vic had to get out to push, while the motor roared. Several times they were stopped in the glare of a great searchlight and the soldiers answered questions before they started on again. They rode all night and many slept.

Fifteen

The harbor in the pale dawn was eerie under the hills of Naples, cluttered everywhere with the ghastly remains of so many ships and small craft of several navies, lopsided remnants, half submerged, but somber in battle gray. Most of the buildings at the waterfront were indistinct piles of rubble. The driver and his companions seemed to have a plan for their passengers, for when the truck stopped abruptly, they signaled to a man who sat idly smoking in a small boat offshore, a boat like the ones they had seen floating downstream under the Tiber bridges.

It wasn't possible for so many to crowd, bag, baggage and bric-a-brac along with themselves into the tiny craft—the entire truckload of them; but they did it. To the chaos the Marmoreks contributed the old valise, which Vic carried, the concertina, which Debbie took, while David clutched Nina. The water line was so high on the tender's hull that David could reach out and let the gentle wavelets run through his fingers. As they plowed outward into the open bay, the cold spray was neither friendly nor reassuring.

The ship toward which they were heading was larger, uglier, and no more reassuring than the tender. *Petah Tiqva,* she read on the ship's hull, an unfamiliar name. The woman with the twisted mouth said, "Petah Tiqva's a town near Tel Aviv, a small city, one of the first." Even as she lay at anchor, they could hear the ship creaking weirdly as if she were breaking apart. Old men and women were lifted aloft by their companions and the soldiers, to the ship's ladder; Vic carried David aboard under one arm, like a sack.

It took time before their eyes accustomed themselves to the dimness of the hold, which had the familiar stench of the flat in Rome. There were wood bunks—small, one close above the other; and lying in the bunks (they were too shallow to sit in) or sitting erect on the floor, or standing wherever there was a square foot of room was so much seamy humanity, clogged into such small space that Debbie had a real sense of calamity. Where had they all come from, these huddled figures peering through blank eyes and moving in listless shuffles? A few watched with some flicker of interest as the new load of refugees arrived from the tender. Some were reading; two old men, one cadaverous, the other round and short, both wearing black skullcaps, sat cross-legged on the floor playing chess. Several women had infants strapped to their backs and one wizened man sitting on the floor, doubled over with a bellyache, held a huge yellow cat, which he stroked with great affection. When the newcomers were aboard, one of the young soldiers stopped in to show each passenger where to put his things and where to sleep. David was too fascinated with the cat to listen to the soldier, but Vic called, "Keep away from that cat. He's probably full of germs."

The man stopped stroking the animal to cast at Vic a long evil squint, which grew into a belligerent glare, maintained with incredible ferocity for an amazingly long time. Vic paid him no attention whatever. At last the man said in German, "Never you mind, pussy, you have to forgive them, many of them have suffered terribly, you know, and it's affected their manners. Some are—" and he made a whirling motion alongside his temple and shrugged. They could hear the cat's purr, almost like a motor, across the room.

She wanted David to try to get some sleep because his ear still bothered him. It was not too difficult for him to doze; the only light was from the kerosene lamps. And the canvas bunk was in many ways better than the mattress at home. At least it had no sharp black elusive bugs, so hard to catch. David had always been covered with red blotches at home after he'd been sick in bed for some days. These ship's bunks were better.

No one bothered to dress or undress for sleeping. They curled themselves into balls in their bunks. From time to time new people came aboard and crowded the facilities still further, until she, Vic, and David were all sleeping in the same bunk, sometimes together, sometimes successively.

Two meals a day were served at long tables in an adjoining room, and everyone ate standing up. Eating was in four shifts of two or three hundred. The mess room was jammed eight or nine hours a day. Each person had a card to be punched for every meal and each was required to wash his own tin dish and cup.

The bank of toilets which everyone used, men, women, and children alike and simultaneously, were curtained affairs just off the large sleeping room. There was a constant queue waiting to use them.

Throughout the waiting period Debbie remained cheerful as much for David's sake as for any other reason. She said to Vic, "This is the life! I've always promised myself a Mediterranean cruise. But think of the poor beggars traveling steerage!"

After what seemed like days, the engines started up, they could feel the ship tremble and shake and hum; the passengers, squeezed together as they were, looked to each other for comfort, a few smiled and some mumbled prayerfully.

The Mediterranean can be mountainously rough in November. Debbie had not expected anything like it. On deck when they were at last permitted to go, she could look up and see the sky, and the next moment, still looking up, she saw the sea, then alternately the sky again and the sea. She turned a pale green color, and went below to lie motionless in her bunk, and when David lurched his way to her side, she rolled and put her back to him; she felt at death's door.

"Mommy."

No answer.

"Mommy!"

"Yes, dear?" Weak, almost a whisper.

"My friend wants to look at you, Mommy. Turn around." He was tugging at her.

"David—Mommy doesn't feel well."

"Meyer has a dog. Look."

She heard a second child's voice speaking German with a slight Dutch accent. "She's sick all right. You want to help me with the funeral? That's my business."

"What business?" David said.

"The funeral business. We make funerals, we dig the holes."

"Isn't it hard?"

"No, and we're very rich."

She forced herself to roll over to get a look at this enterprising youngster. He was taller and thinner than David with a mournfully vacant face. Under one arm he had the remnants of a toy dog.

"What's your name?" she managed to ask.

"Meyer Van Bern," he said cheerfully. "O994436."

"Where's *your* mother, dear?"

"Upstairs. But not my father. He couldn't come. He's in Amsterdam, living in a cemetery. You feel bad?"

She nodded, and he continued with genuine pity, "Why don't you kill yourself? You'll feel better."

In spite of herself she had to laugh. It hurt her to do it, and the sound came out more like a gasp.

Meyer, taken aback by her reaction, searched for the joke. "Sure," he said, "that's right. You're so sick you'll probably die anyway." He laughed right with her.

"Please, won't you boys go upstairs to play? I'm just not feeling—" She had to stop.

"I guess she will, all right," Meyer said laconically. "Come on, let's play doctor. You lie down. Open your mouth. Now say Ahhhh!"

The passengers argued and squabbled. Many were singularly morose; some boarded the *Petah Tiqva* ill and others took sick after they were one or two days at sea, and everyone hated the food. They complained of their quarters, of the cold and the heat. In the sleeping section in the hold pale men or women would abruptly sit half up in the bunks, turn miserably and vomit on the floor before rolling back numbly with a low moan to face the wall or to stare vacantly at the bunk above.

These occurrences had a tendency to make David nauseous and nervous; so he spent most of his time on deck. But Debbie, after she recovered from her first attack of seasickness, was undisturbed and so was Vic; they found themselves leaders among the passengers and crew in mopping-up operations, in nursing sick people, in bringing tin cups of water and tea, and in encouraging them as best they could with small jokes. Several of the passengers announced they were doctors, and two of them spent a good deal of time examining patients, but while they seemed to know precisely what was the matter, there was not much they could do without medicine.

David was impressed with his father's solicitous care of the skinny little man with the luxurious cat; on the second day this man, who had been a strange sallow color to begin with, took to his bunk, holding his precious cat to his bosom all the while. Vic helped feed the man through a glass tube and dropped medicines in his eyes, but when he tried to take the animal away, the man put up such a howl that Vic let him keep his cat. In spite of all help, the patient grew steadily weaker, until at last he lay motionless on his back. He was the first passenger to die, and his funeral was a rather impressive affair.

All the passengers, healthy and half-healthy, the ancients and children, men and women, gathered on deck; the cat, who seemed never friskier or more playful, was there. The corpse had been sewn into a canvas sack, obviously along with heavy weights, because it took six men including Vic to lift him. The sack was placed on deck and the passengers gathered round, while one of the lanky chess players with the skullcap conducted the service in German and Hebrew. Everyone wore hats, and Debbie tied a kerchief over David's head. The rabbi said first of all this man had not died for nothing, that he had stood for something, just as they all stood for something at last. He said this man had the will to survive just as they all had the will to survive. But simply to survive personally, that was nothing special. That was instinct. This man had the will to survive as part of a great people. This man had wanted not only to live but also to live in a land of his own, proudly, with his head high, and not a slave to cruel masters. But to do this a man had to dare bravely, and this he had done; this they had all done. Debbie failed to see that pride was the great common denominator aboard. These folks looked a little mangy to her.

And, continued the rabbi, for someone to die seeking the goal of a new life in a new land, just as a man named Moses had died, was as good a way to go as any. It was much better than to be carted off and slaughtered like a pig. He said no one is going to look through this man's teeth for gold. He said this man leaves us in dignity; he has friends; even his cat is permitted to come to say farewell. The fact is, Debbie thought, the only one here who is a personal friend of this man *is* the cat. He has, the rabbi continued, touched us and we have touched him. Friends have nursed him in his bed and brought him comfort. Hands have been stretched out to him. This man is not a number, even though on his arm there is a number. He has a name, and his name is Hyman Shapiro, Citizen of Palestine. Let us pray.

Many wept. They were not weeping for Hyman Shapiro. They were weeping for themselves or for reasons not known. Debbie herself stood with her head bowed and tears rolled down her cheeks, although she had no sensation that she was crying.

Vic and five other men, including Meyer Van Bern's uncle, lifted the canvas bag which sagged and rustled, and carried it to the rail. In a low voice, Vic said, "Ready, one, two, over!" David looked through the rail and watched the sack fall sternward, twisting and turning, and disappear before it struck the water, behind the ship's hull. Then he saw it again. He waved a last farewell to Mr. Shapiro, whose canvas sack he could see swirling in the wake for several bobbing instants before its final disappearance. David was deeply disturbed.

When Debbie looked around, one of the pallbearers had lifted the huge, germ-laden yellow cat by the scruff of its neck and was in the act of tossing it overboard. The cat made no sound until the moment after it struck the water and found itself in this unfriendliest of elements; over the drone of the ship's engines and the creaking of the timbers, they heard a piercing yowl, almost human, that was a protest by the cat both for himself and for Hyman Shapiro. Vic was furious.

"I don't like disease any better than you," he growled, "but we could have chloroformed it first. Don't you know cats hate water?"

There were two other deaths, both old women, but each funeral was less flourishing and less well attended than the previous one. Debbie kept David away; the funerals he and Meyer pretended were much gayer affairs and more ornate. The coffins were usually gold, and the corpse was always dressed in a red suit.

The third evening, after the last dinner shift, three members of the crew, two Canadians and a Swiss boy, visited the sleeping quarters with some formality, and one man called Si with kinky hair and pocked skin spoke clearly in Yiddish. He asked everyone to be quiet and listen carefully. Then he said the same thing in German, and his first companion followed him in Italian and French, followed by the second companion who did the honors in Polish. No other sound could be heard now except the coughing of the sick passengers.

"Tomorrow night we shall approach the coast of Palestine. We'll enter the harbor of Haifa. Directly ahead and to the right you'll see Mount Carmel and you may be able to make out the lights in the windows of the buildings which is the city of Haifa itself. I'm sorry we cannot enter by day, because it is a pretty sight and I'm sure you'd enjoy it. To the left as we enter the harbor is the town of Acre, and between Acre and Haifa on the left is a beach called the Haifa Bay region. The *Petah Tiqva* will approach as near to the Haifa Bay beach as possible without running aground, and then passengers will be taken to the beach in small boats. The boats will travel back and forth until everyone is ashore. Please try to cooperate with the crew, and be patient while waiting.

"The British police are reported to have patrols in the harbor, and that's why we must enter at night, and without lights. Everything and everyone must be on deck at eight o'clock, and families will please keep together. No matter what the police do, keep calm, and follow instructions from the crew. Hold your belongings with you at all times. Absolutely no lights of any kind from now on. Is that clear? If you have questions, please wait until we finish all the translations, and we'll try to answer you all."

It took quite some time to complete all versions. At last the questions poured forth, great formless questions in every language, questions which were the fears and hopes and doubts of a fragmented generation of people. The crewmen answered them patiently, for they had heard them before.

"When we reach the beach, then what?"

"There will be people on the beach. Friends."

"And if we are caught by the British?"

"You'll be sent back where you came from. It's much better if you don't get caught." A shrug and timid half-smiles all around, half-smiles of conspiracy.

"Are these people glad to have us? The other Jews? They don't resent us? After they worked so hard, why should they want to share?"

"They worked so you would be able to come. That's the meaning of the work. Later you'll work to take in others. Then your work will mean something."

"Where will we find work? Where will we sleep? Where will we eat?"

"My husband still has a fever. Where will we find a real doctor?"

"How are the Arabs? Are they very unfriendly?"

The answers were reassuring. Too reassuring.

"Everyone will be on deck. Eight o'clock tomorrow night. The bell will ring as a signal. Bring all your belongings. Families keep together."

Tension pervaded everything from the moment of this alert. Even Debbie and Vic had a violent argument when Debbie half-jokingly suggested they leave their valise full of old clothing aboard.

"I hate these old rags. Truly I do. If I bring them, no doubt I'll have to wear them, and I swear I'd rather go stark naked."

Vic threw up his hands in disgust. "I've dragged this Goddamn valise halfway around the world. I could've left it in Rome, or dumped it in the Naples harbor. Here, I've been standing day and night watch over it! I've got a hell of an investment in that bag."

She said, "All right, dear, all right."

"Look at the way you drag that damned concertina about! But clothes! Throw 'em in the sea!"

"All right, honey!" she cried. "I'm childish, I'm scatterbrained!"

They weren't real fights, and they weren't about anything, but everyone seemed to be having them. Meyer's mother gave him a terrible licking over losing his family's cake of soap, which had been carefully hoarded for months. Meyer was outraged at his gentle mother, especially since it wasn't he who lost the soap, but he didn't cry.

During the daylight hours of that last day, passengers tugged and pulled their baggage on deck and families repeated to each other, and especially to the children, at least a thousand times, exactly where they would stand. The sky grew threateningly dark, the sea became rougher, and rain threatened. The evening air was chilly, and everyone said it would grow colder during the night.

By the time the last shift from the evening meal had come up on deck, they were traveling in complete darkness. After a short interval there was great excitement on deck and everyone rushed to the port rail, as if responding to some signal, pointing, calling. Even Vic, jumping up and standing on his toes, became agitated and said, "There, Debbie, there! Look! Lights!" He took her by the waist and lifted her aloft as if she were a flag of victory and he was raising her for all to see. She hadn't seen him so excited in a long time but as suddenly as it had come, it went. He put her down.

"I want to see," David shrieked, jumping up and down. "Let me see, lift me up!"

Vic turned and said, "It's nothing. Only a few lights."

But she lifted him high over her head and pointed and said, "Can you see the lights? That's Acre. That's Palestine. That's home."

In truth it was nothing much in the way of a sight—the dim fluttering lights. Nothing unusual, simply a distant flicker. Nothing to get excited about.

In only a few minutes then the motors strained in reverse, and stopped. High up on the right and ahead of them were lights, still barely visible in the foggy air, but so many thousands of them, flickering and fading as though someone were shaking out a blanket of weak stars.

The crewmen were busy on deck, and in their determined hustle completely ignored the passengers.

The only illumination was provided by two hand flashlights held by crewmen. A number of people had disappeared down the rope ladder into the blackness, lugging bags and bundles and each other. When their turn came, Vic lifted David and they were making their way down. It was impossible for them to see each other or just what they were doing. She lunged downward, holding the concertina box on her head like the farmer women she had seen in the Roman markets balancing baskets of bread. The jerky motion of the ship made the descent hazardous, and her heart pounded to the discordant churning and whooshing of the choppy waters of Haifa Bay. The rains had begun, a typical Middle East December rain, a release of the heavens. Everyone was quickly wet to the skin, and a substantial quantity of water swished inside the small boat they were now in, as they bobbed in the unsteady sea. The sudden streaks of jagged lightning and the tumultuous thunderclaps terrified her, but she said nothing.

She became aware of babbling and occasional squeals of surprise or fear in the small boat and from the deck of the *Petah Tiqva* or from the ladder; an old man lost his footing and fell almost the full height of the *Petah Tiqva's* hull into the water with a wild, unearthly scream. How he was fished out she was not sure; but there was sudden activity and clearly shouted orders by the crewmen and by Vic, and soon the old man, his white beard matted and dismal in the uncanny blue light of the storm flashes, lay soaked and breathing heavily, his head in Vic's lap, uttering sounds of gratitude and kissing Vic's hands like a child.

This boat, which was even smaller than the tender in Naples, was not quite so crowded. But the trip in Naples Bay which had made her uneasy, she now recalled with nostalgia. This one was horrible. The black night was blacker than any of her life; the splash of water had the force of wet towels slapping her face and body; and each flash of lightning and following thunderclap set her teeth on edge. Only Vic gave her and David courage—how easily he had saved that old man!

David shouted, "Daddy, I'm getting all wet. Nina's getting all wet too."

The spell of fear was dissipated for a moment. "Isn't it exciting!" she called to David. In the lightning they both looked comical, with their hair plastered all about their heads. To Vic she shouted over the roaring of the water and the motor, "I haven't had so much fun since the Prater. Remember?" Vic nodded and put a protective arm about her. "The Ride with the Devil, I think it was called, wasn't it?" She was shouting over the roar.

Vic nodded. "Of course. And I was the devil."

"I'm so happy," she said suddenly, but Vic couldn't hear.

"What?" he shouted.

"Nothing! I only said I was never happier in my life than right now," she shrieked with every ounce of her strength. "That's all."

"I won't exaggerate," Vic said. "I've been happier and also more comfortable."

"This is my last sea voyage," Debbie said. "I'm through traveling, I swear it."

All about them people sat stolid or sullen or calling to each other, when one of the men passengers stood up precipitately and pointed toward the Carmel. "Look! Look!"

A great finger of light, no not one—three, five, an uncountable series of piercing, probing lights was being thrown toward them from the foot of Haifa's great sheer bluff, fingers reaching and feeling and swinging back and forth across the surface of the water. All at once one of the lights caught the *Petah Tiqva.* Their little tender chugged onward, but everyone in it was looking back through the storm at the ship which had brought them to this place. There was a sharp report, not so loud as the thunder, but more purposeful, from the shore. She knew it at once; it was the sound they had heard in Rome during the days when the Americans had come. Cannon fire.

The other tentacles of light continued to ride the surface of the water, seeking, reaching, until two of the small boats were caught in them. There were more shots and over all the roaring of the elements they could hear the excited shouts of the passengers. And then their own little boat was in a blaze of light too.

"Overboard, overboard!" the crewman shouted. He shut off the motor. "Everyone overboard, swim, it's not far! It's your best chance!" Someone in the boat moaned, she couldn't tell whether it was a man or woman, and a woman screeched, "Isaac! Isaac!"

Vic jumped over the side and called to them, "Jump here, both of you! Look, I can stand! Nothing to be afraid of, only hurry!" David jumped without hesitation despite the salt water in his mouth and ears; and his father was holding him about the middle again, above the water for the most part, so that he was able to breathe again. Debbie still had the concertina poised on her head, holding Vic's hand, and quickly they waded their way back into the dark. She could see now the dark was not something to fear; the dark was a blessed refuge.

She was gasping and she said as she strode through the waist-high water, "You see, I told you there was no use taking along that ridiculous valise full of old rags. I'm glad we're rid of it."

Vic said, "We have nothing at all now. Nothing."

And she cried as they neared the beach, "Good! Vic, I don't know why, but I feel like a free woman for the first time!"

There was a crash of gunfire, closer, much closer, and when they looked about, there was another vessel, a gray ship of war, about the size of the *Petah Tiqva,* almost alongside her, with lights trained on her. They could see uniformed men clambering up the ladder, and people jumping into the churning water. David said he hoped Meyer Van Bern was not still aboard.

At last Vic set David down and took his hand. There were people on the beach, not only passengers from the ship, but others, baggy in raincoats and sluggish in rubber boots, pulling people from the chill water. She saw the old man Vic had saved on his knees, and for a moment thought he was ill. Then she saw he was kissing the sand on the beach. There were others doing the same.

"Here," a man called in German, "no time for that. Come with me."

Sixteen

They followed the voice away from the water's edge to a rickety donkey cart. Behind them they could still hear the rifle fire over the surf's recurring wash.

As the incredibly small donkey pulled the wagon and its burden of seven adults and a child along the black road, the unmerciful rain beat them with wicked insistence until the moment they were instructed to follow the driver single file into one of the doors of a long low building, squat and sprawling in the night.

The furniture in the sweet-smelling ground floor apartment was fresher and cleaner than any she had seen in a long time, the lights were bright, and even the confusing noise of the people arriving failed to diminish the first glowing impression of shining immaculateness. Everyone was talking at once, but more cheerfully now, and several were even grinning happily. It was a change for the better.

They were all drenched to the skin except the hostess, who had evidently been waiting in the kitchen for them all evening. She was plump and jovial, with a large hooked nose and jet-black eyes, framed in a fringe of black ringleted hair, which flew straight out from her scalp at right angles. David took to her instantly, ludicrous as she looked. She stood before her stove like a sentry guarding four black steaming kettles. Hastily she wiped her reddened hand on a cloth to greet each of the persons from the ship and to each she smiled so warmly and said the word which had so many different meanings: Peace. She not only shook David's hand, but also patted him on the head, almost as if for luck, and inquired kindly about Nina. Her husband, who was even fatter, and every inch her equal in handsomeness, removed his boots in the kitchen, just as they heard the entrance door open again. The hostess' beaming rosy face became bloodless for an instant, until her husband, at first paralyzed and then galvanized into sudden action, darted back to the door and, after an instant, boomed a loud "Welcome, welcome!" in German. "You're from the *Petah Tiqva,* aren't you?"

They heard the mumbled voice of an adult in the hall and the sharp piping of a child, speaking Dutch.

In the hall, dripping wet, stood Meyer Van Bern, holding his white toy dog about the neck in a one-handed vise-like grip as though he were choking him without noticing it. The stuffed animal was soaked even more than his master. Meyer's mother kept one hand on his shoulder as if she were afraid of losing physical contact with him.

David said, "Hello, Meyer. I think your dog is dead. You choked him."

But Meyer replied, "He's only sleeping. He'll be all right in the morning."

David said, "Where's your uncle? The man said families should keep together."

Meyer shrugged and said, "I guess we lost him. But he'll be all right."

Meyer's rather pretty mother, usually undemonstrative, was excited and said, "In the little boat we lost him. I called his name, but it was so dark, the water was so rough, we couldn't see anything."

The host led Vic and the three other men into one room and the hostess took the women to another. The children followed their mothers, and there on the bed, laid out almost like living people, were dry clothes and shoes. The hostess went about lifting the dresses and holding them against each of the women, selecting the closest fits, and then urged the women to get out of their wet things. "Then," she said as though she were speaking to children, "we'll all have nice fresh coffee, and we'll play a little cards."

For David and Meyer she had shorts, five or six pairs to choose from, and colored shirts—Meyer's blue and David's gay yellow, and shoes which were too big for them both, and short socks, and even white cotton underpants, which David had never seen before.

The women threw their wet clothes into a corner of the room, the hostess assuring them they would all be returned, and for a few moments the presence of five naked women and two small naked boys filled the room. Debbie noticed during that naked moment that three of the women and Meyer had brownish printing on their forearms, tattooed numbers written into their skin. "Mommy, what's that?" David pointed to Jacinta Van Bern, who was calm again, Debbie noticed, and a comfort to everyone.

"Hush, it's nothing, dear."

But Meyer broke in proudly. "The Nazis put the numbers there. Everyone gets his own number."

"Does it hurt?" David asked.

"Not much," Meyer said.

"Why did they do it?"

Meyer shrugged. "Everyone gets his own."

Debbie's clothes were limply long on her, but she scarcely minded; and in no time she had David completely redressed in his bright new clothes. His shoes were so loose he was afraid to lift his feet off the ground.

When they returned to the large room, the men had already gathered there; Vic was dressed in a black suit with coat and trousers matching, and an open-collared brown shirt. He looked gloomier than ever, like an angry nun, and she could not keep from laughing at the sight of him.

After they had gathered, the host addressed them in the hushed tones of a conspirator, first in Hebrew, then in English, and finally in German. "The British soldiers or constables may come searching. If they do, don't worry about it. You are simply neighbors who have come for a party. It's my wife's birthday—thirty-seven today, and we celebrate."

One of the women interrupted to say, "Congratulations," and they all smiled.

"We have taken your clothes out to be dried, and hidden your luggage, and my wife will give you an address to say. Meanwhile we eat and later we play cards, so it looks like a party. The children would like to nap?"

"No, no!" David jumped in protest and Meyer followed his lead. "I want to stay up. Just a little longer."

The host shrugged. "The children must be quiet. If anybody comes, you'll let the grownups talk, all right?" He turned to the others. "The W.C. is right there. Don't stand on ceremony. And the washbasin is there. This door."

In a few minutes the hostess brought in a tray, with twelve steaming cups of coffee and a cake with bright green icing, which she placed carefully on a card table her husband opened. David trailed after the hostess, openly fascinated, as she plied between rooms, to the gleaming white box in the kitchen, out of which she drew cold meats and potatoes and fish.

"Gefüllte fish," she said proudly to her guests, as if this were a great word, and they responded with little cries of pleasure: even Vic smiled. "It's not so much," she said, "but we must make it look like a party." Coffee, cakes, stuffed fish, cold meats, fruit. Not much! It was all delicious, and the coffee warmed their bones. Even Meyer stopped shivering after the coffee.

"See," the hostess said. "We grow the oranges here in Palestine. Also the bananas, although they're small. But we like them because they're ours. Here, little fellow, have one—what's his name?" She looked for her answer unerringly to Debbie.

David tried to eat his banana, skin and all, but she showed them how to peel it, while the host brought forth a deck of cards and put two boxes of cigarettes on the card table. "Help yourselves!" Some of the men drew in long breaths of smoke, as if they were drinking their first glass of water on a blistering day. Debbie, too, drew in the smoke and seemed to relax as if someone were stroking and soothing her.

"My name," said the host, "is Schlomo Moskowitz. My wife is Helena. Please be good enough to tell your names, and try to remember each other's names, it may be important for you."

Each gave his name, Vic for the three of them as Schlomo Moskowitz had done, and everyone continued to eat hungrily.

"Now it is necessary," Schlomo Moskowitz continued, "to tell me the names of your friends or relatives here, so that we may notify them."

He went from one to the other, taking these names and addresses with notebook and pencil and she heard Vic mumble in a low voice, "Karl Pretsch, Beth Hakerem, Jerusalem."

The fat host smiled and said, "Now, that's a nice neighborhood, Beth Hakerem. Oh, wait till you see the forest they made there! Out of rocks, believe me, out of bare rocks they grew it. A regular miracle, a real forest from nothing." He looked toward the ceiling with an expression of knowing more than he could ever say. "Still, I'm a Haifa man myself. Give me the Carmel every time for mountain beauty."

For each he had some such word.

The hostess had discovered the concertina, which Debbie had placed in the hall. "Look," she called, "look what I found. Who plays this?"

David was uneasy and clutched Nina tightly, but Vic said, "Our son David."

"David!" The hostess seemed delighted and her hair stood up straighter than ever. "Play us something, David. You know, King David used to play music on the harp. Come, I'd love to hear. Wouldn't you love to hear, Schlomo?"

Schlomo shrugged. "Why not? King David and his concertina."

David looked to his mother, who smiled and said, "Of course, dear. If you'd like to."

Vic appeared disconcerted, but he said, "For a five-year-old he's really remarkable. An Italian friend taught him."

It was ridiculous for David to play at such a time. The rain beating on the windows and on the roof pounded echoes in their hearts. Everyone was looking at David. He had his audience, and he shone.

"But what should I play, Mommy?"

"Anything, dear."

Vic said, "He loves a chance to perform."

David played his favorite, "Holy Night, Quiet Night." The German hymn was not only his favorite, but also his easiest, and he knew he would make the fewest mistakes.

Some of the adults hummed, and they all smiled to each other. A hymn to celebrate the birth of Jesus in nearby Nazareth.

While David played and the host was still making the rounds, talking in low conspiratorial tones to an emaciated man who could eat more between any two words than most people manage in a meal, there was a sharp rap on the door, and sharper words which followed.

"Englishmen," someone whispered in panic. David stopped playing, and the host in his heartiest boom called, "Welcome, gentlemen, welcome. Come in."

Two soldiers entered. Everyone tried not to be terrified; they continued to eat and tried to act as if these were the most desirable visitors in the world. The host addressed the soldiers, now in English, a hearty, smiling, cordial English, as if he were inviting them to join the party.

Debbie remembered the night of the British and Americans coming into Rome, how they'd danced in the street, kissing strangers, because the British had come, and now they were trembling before other Englishmen.

The soldiers neither reciprocated nor rejected the hospitality. They behaved cautiously and one of them turned to one of the men and asked a question in English.

"They speak only German and Yiddish," the host said in German.

"Yiddish Nazis, eh?" one soldier said with a slight grin. "Who are you?" he asked Vic in German.

"Marmorek," Vic said, "Victor Marmorek, 15 Pevsner Street. Also, I speak English."

"And you?"

"Sarah Lefkowitz, 12 Bezalel."

"You," the second British soldier barked impolitely at the wizened little man, who looked even skinnier than usual because he stood beside the well-fed host.

"Me?" the little man asked obsequiously. "If it's a girl friend's birthday, I can't come to celebrate? It's against the law?" He rose and approached the hostess and put his shriveled arm familiarly about her luxurious waist. "Helena, dear girl, it will be necessary hereafter to eliminate your birthday. The British Army has some objection." David was delighted and laughed.

"That'll be enough of that," one of the soldiers said sternly. "What're the kids doing here? Isn't it past your bedtime, boy?"

Everyone was looking at David. Debbie started to say something, then changed her mind.

"Speak up!"

"Tell the soldier what you're doing here," the host said in German.

"I play the concertina for the party," David said boldly.

"Amazing, too," the host said. "Show him, David."

He played a few bars from a little Italian folk song Angelo had taught him.

"Five years old," the skinny little man said.

"I'll be damned," one of the Britishers said. "By God these people are balmy, even the kids. Plays that thing like a bloody Eyetalian."

One of the soldiers poured himself a cup of coffee and drank it black, then came up to Debbie and felt her shoulder with his palm and fingers. "Bone dry, Sergeant. Couldn't be," he said, and the two left by the front door. After they had been gone a few moments, Debbie pulled David to her and embraced and kissed him, just as one of the soldiers put his head back through the door. "Happy birthday," he called, "and thanks for the coffee."

That night all the guests slept on the terrazzo floor in the living room between coats and blankets and scatter rugs, David holding Nina tight under his chin between his parents. Meyer lay wrapped in his mother's arms. Even more than on the boat, Debbie was conscious of all the different kinds of breathing and snoring and burping, and the sudden noises of this night were special to her, so many people together in great trust in this strange apartment.

Next morning the hostess gave them all a breakfast of fruit and real eggs, fried and delicious, and after they had changed back into their own clothes, Mr. Moskowitz accompanied most of them to the city in a large blue bus, up the hills to Herzl Street, where he let the Marmorek family off, pointing out a particular bookshop to Vic. As they got off, he waved a cheerful good-bye. Vic waved and called, "Many thanks," and the bus drove away with the other guests, including the Van Berns—mother and son. Would they meet again, any of the people who had shared the ship?

Vic said they had a little time to look about until the hour when Karl would come. The wet streets were hills, much steeper than Rome's, and extraordinary creatures roamed them. David took his father's hand and never stopped asking questions. Is that a man, Daddy? Why does he wear a skirt? What kind of hat is he wearing? What for? Look, that boy needs a haircut! Why is that lady wearing a black rag over her face? They were streets of mystery and wonder, and the most surprising circumstances were that Vic, who had rejected the thought of Palestine, knew the answers to all the questions, and explained each mystery patiently; but he often grew disgusted with what they saw and sometimes sad or angry. The women in veils enraged him. "To read about it is quite colorful," he told Debbie, "but to see them really living this way, not play-acting, it's revolting. They treat their women like cattle, you know. And the kids—look at that one—running sores, look at those eyes. He'll be blind before he's fifteen. And we're supposed to be the disinherited, we're the dispossessed. What are these benighted Arabs then? Debbie, the human race is an enigma—it reaches the highest peaks of wonder, and it can go so low, I'd call it subhuman. Would we let David run through the street like that—half-naked, half-dead? Would we? Stealing, starving!"

"I suppose they have parents," she said. "I suppose they're very poor."

They saw many of these dark children covered in sores and rags, their eyes blazing dark and deep in their sallow unfriendly faces.

"They're Arabs," Vic said, "and remember they're people, too, and remember they need help."

The Jews, for the most part, looked fine.

David said, "You know, Daddy, I'm glad we're Jews."

But Debbie suspected it was still a dangerous thing to be.

Seventeen

Without warning Karl was there, getting off a bus. Karl was shorter than she remembered, and he looked just like her, even to the freckles and the pug nose and blue eyes. They embraced each other on the street, she crying and laughing, and Karl saying, "I've got my sister back, I've got my sister back."

Vic was more sensible. He shook Karl's hand and smiled and said they were all well and the trip had been uneventful.

"They threw the man with the cat in the sea. He was dead and they threw the cat in too, but he wasn't dead," David said.

"We had a few typhus cases," Vic said.

"But the cat's all dead now, I bet," David concluded.

"Getting ashore there was a little trouble," Vic said.

"Shh," Karl whispered. "It's all over town. We'd better be moving; the British have eyes and ears everywhere. Please be careful what you say and where you say it. How's your English?"

"Pretty good," Vic said. "Debbie's is only so-so. David knows only German and Italian."

"We'll use English if you can," Karl said. "It's safer. English or Hebrew."

Karl saved the last greeting for David and lifted him to carry him as they walked. Debbie said, "Haven't you a kiss for Uncle Karl?" and of course, David had.

Karl said, "He looks like Papa, and Mama too, a little, doesn't he?" And they walked in silence.

The bus journey to Jerusalem seemed interminable. After the monotony of endless stretches of barren desert, and a twisting nerve-wracking ride over a sinuous mountain road, that went up and round, they rolled through a half-flooded Jaffa Road into the New City of Jerusalem. David was sound asleep, and never knew quite how he got into his Uncle Karl's apartment in Beth Hakerem.

Lilith was waiting in the flat still dressed in her nurse's white which made her seem taller, although she was as small as Debbie. Debbie embraced her at once, and while David was too dazed from his recent sleep and too confused by the excitement to say a word, he never took his eyes off her. Her dark, pointed face seemed distorted for an instant when she shook hands with Vic, as she said in faltering German, "People come back to us from the dead so often we don't think much about it, but when it happens in the family . . ." She shook her head almost like a shudder, and closed her eyes tight, as if something hurt her deeply. Tears rolled down her cheeks; she wiped them with her kerchief and blew her nose. "And this is David. Welcome home, David." Her voice was piercing, harsh. Now she was laughing over something Debbie said, a raw cacophony, but her eyes were never off David. "Such a quiet little man," she said loudly.

"He's never seen a nurse before," Debbie said. "I guess the uniform fascinates him."

"I just adore children," Lilith said. "My pets at the hospital are all children, and I always feel they're really mine. Isn't that always the way? Of course, it's not exactly the same as one of your own, but Karl and I haven't given up hope. We've been at it ten years, and we keep trying, don't we, Karl?"

Karl shrugged. "Anyway it's a good excuse." He and Lilith laughed uneasily, and there was an embarrassing little silence, until Karl said with unexpected vigor, "Well, Vic, the first step is to do something about a decent job for you, I'd say. Have you given it any thought?"

Vic said, "Well, only in a general way of course. My real training's been mostly in the electrical field. In Rome . . ."

"Can I say something?" Karl broke in rapidly. "I think I have a good lead for you. There's an opening a friend of mine has in the Telephone Office. You know the government runs the telephone system here. For most things, of course, you'd need Hebrew, but working in the Mandate Administration, you can always get by with your English. Most of the British make a studied effort not to learn Hebrew. And you can pick it up later without too much trouble. Of course, working with the English is no picnic, but it's not really so bad."

"Why, that's fine," Vic said cautiously. "What kind of job is it? Not that it makes a hell of a lot of difference. I'd be damn glad to dig ditches at the beginning."

"It's quite a good job, in fact, and pays well too. That's why I'm so pleased. You'll be wire chief. Assistant to the fellow who runs the entire field staff in Jerusalem. The whole works. Ben Kronstein. He's an old friend. A little prissy, but intelligent, and hard working. They're short of good technicians. Of course Ben wants to talk to you and you have to be okayed by a couple of Englishmen. Pays forty-five pounds a month."

Lilith broke in, "It's a marvelous salary for a newcomer, Victor, you know. Poor Karl has worked like a dog to get the job too. You should have heard how he built you up! Honestly, going from one man to another, as if *he* needed the job. Out sometimes all night. But after all, how often does such an opportunity come? I said 'Go ahead, Karl. A little extra effort won't hurt you. I don't mind a few evenings alone, it's the least we can do.' "

"Can I say something?" Karl protested. "It wasn't that bad." He lit a cigarette for Lilith, and one for Debbie and offered Vic one of his cigars. Karl's cigars smelled stronger than Papa's but more pleasant. "I was lucky. Besides I told Lilith it's not only for a sister, but also for a fifth cousin, and a brother-in-law, which is a hell of a lot of relatives."

Vic said hesitantly and solemnly, "I appreciate your making a joke of it, Karl, but—my God—I just don't know what to say. It's terrific. I can't tell you how unexpected it is. More than I ever hoped for. Not in my wildest dreams. A job like that—and the salary—working for a telephone company, that shouldn't be so different from power work . . ." His hands were more expressive than anything he said. She had rarely seen Vic so touched.

Karl shrugged it off. "You'd have done the same for me."

Vic said, "I wish I could be sure of *that*."

Lilith broke in stridently to destroy the moment. "I told Karl of course you could live here with us for a while, but it would be better not to make it a permanent arrangement. You know how it is, it's hard even for the best friends to live in the same house, especially two women, believe me, I know from experience. Don't you agree, Deborah?"

Debbie shrugged. "I just hadn't thought about it," she said.

"Well, Karl found you a beautiful apartment in a new house that's nearly finished in Rehavia—a four family. And if you only knew how hard it is to get an apartment these days. But really beautiful, wait till you see it. A gorgeous balcony and such a big kitchen, and overlooking the whole city. It's right at the end of Gaza Road, near a marvelous school for David, you see we've tried to think of everything. Ten pounds a month, which isn't too bad, is it? And only a hundred pounds key money. Of course, Rehavia isn't Beth Hakerem, but it's much more convenient, oh, absolutely—near Vic's job, and really quite nice for being right in town. I like it much better than Katamon or the German Colony. Anyway, who'd want to live with all those Nazis?"

Nobody could get a word in edgewise, Lil talked with such speed and clamor.

"I'm hungry," David managed to say in a low voice, "and my pants are wet."

"You poor child," Lilith cried, "how we've neglected you!" She knelt to embrace him, but he drew back at her vigor. "Don't be afraid, little David!" Then rising and turning to the adults, "It must be the white dress. I just got in a few seconds ahead of you. Elsa Schumacher gave me a lift from the Scopus, it's such a long drive, you know, I didn't even get a chance to change. I was so afraid of not getting here before you. Now you just be patient, David, while I change my clothes, and we'll have cookies and milk and I'll find you some new pants to wear."

She went swiftly into the next room.

"Is she my real aunt?" David asked, trying not to sound worried.

"She is," Karl said, "and I'm your real uncle too."

He knelt beside David, who, she saw, resembled his uncle, too. "And you, David, you're our real nephew, and more, so much more, you'll never know. Because of you, we believe in miracles."

Karl's arm went around David, and David looked at Debbie.

"Are they part of my parents?"

Debbie had to laugh. "I suppose in a way they are."

"Then I have a real aunt and uncle," David said. "I have relatives."

The first night David was put to sleep in a separate room in a separate bed, the softness and luxuriousness of which put him into a trance of disbelief. He lay back and felt the pillow's softness with the back of his head, and pounded his fists into the resilient mattress with an abandon he had never known. The unfamiliar sheets were smooth and soothing. He asked his new Aunt Lilith all sorts of questions. "What's this?" of the pillow, and "What's it for?" and of the sheets, "What's that?" Lilith seemed quieter when he asked her these questions, and she explained all about the feather stuffing of mattresses, about sheets, pillows, and springs.

When David understood, he took to jumping on the bed, higher and higher, making the springs creak, until he was flying, flying from head to foot of the bed, and back, wilder and wilder, losing all control of himself. His face was red and his eyes bright, until he was exhausted. When they had said good night and turned out the lights, he lay with Nina, his puppet, in the dark which he had come to respect as a refuge, and they heard him say to Nina, "We're home at last."

Eighteen

Those first days in Jerusalem were full of perplexity and wonderment. Debbie was a tourist who had to see everything. She was fascinated by all the priests and nuns, monks and rabbis, inscrutable and solemn in every street and alley; speeding military and civilian vehicles and decrepit blue and gray busses; soldiers, constables and keffiyahed Arabs, veiled women, small boys and girls, dressed only from the middle up to save underpants; men, bearded or clean shaven, with the inevitable briefcases. They visited the lobby and gardens of the King David Hotel and the Eden, the spectacular YMCA and its football stadium; they traveled the broad avenues and the narrowest scraggliest streets in the Old City, with its open sewage running foully down the ancient central gutters, alongside some of the holiest landmarks of the Western and Moslem worlds. They beheld the churches and the missions, the less opulent synagogues, and the seatless mosques. They visited the Church of the Holy Sepulchre, the Mosque of Omar, where Solomon's temple once stood, and Mt. Zion, where in an unprepossessing room Jesus ate His Last Supper above King David's tomb. The somber cellar room of King David's burial interested David especially, because he apparently identified himself with the ancient king of Israel; they had, after all, much in common: they loved to play music and they liked to have people listen to them and in general they liked to be king. "King David was a show-off like me," he said to Debbie with satisfaction.

Vic also took them to visit the great building on Julian's Way, which was the post office and telephone office where he worked. There they saw the central room where men and women manipulated the switchboards. And there they met the people Vic worked with: Esther Schamel, a sallow girl with tight clothes who sat in the outer office to deal with customers and subscribers. Debbie recalled that she seemed pathetically undernourished, and almost obsequiously pleasant to them, happily permitting David to peck away at her typewriter. In a small private office inside they met Karl's friend Ben Kronstein, the chief engineer and Vic's immediate supervisor. Ben, in his early fifties, was a precise, meticulous man with pince-nez and a few gold teeth. He spoke gingerly, as if each syllable hurt slightly. Ben made a proper fuss over Debbie and David, and said flattering things about Karl and Lil, then asked, as if he were being daring beyond belief, "Would you care to meet the big boss?"

"Why—uh—" She had no idea how Vic might like that.

"I'm sure he'll be delighted," Ben said. "He has an eye for beauty, you know. A pretty young lady is his dish of tea." And he wheezed as if he were choking and placed his hand over his mouth, so that she became alarmed, until she realized he was only laughing at what he had just said.

Vic had no objection; so they went in to meet Redge Walker. Redge was about the same age as Vic, and almost as tall, but physically flabbier. No doubt he watched his weight. The roundness of his pleasant face was accentuated by his hair being parted in the middle and his rimless round spectacles. He was, at the moment they walked in, talking to his administrative assistant, John Halliwell, a younger and handsomer man, more nearly Debbie's age. She could see him looking mentally down at her, and she took an instant dislike to him. But Redge was pleasant. In the few words they exchanged after Halliwell excused himself, she found him friendly and anxious to put her at ease. He struggled with Hebrew words and German to tell her her husband was already a tremendous asset. Vic looked pleased himself.

"You must come see us at our hotel, the two of us. We'll have drinks together, shall we? I'll have Enid call you. And how do you like Jerusalem, young fellow?" He slapped David on the back. "I have a lad about your age. You must get together."

When they had left his office, Ben Kronstein whistled wisely. "The boss was smitten. I'd advise you, Marmorek, to keep an eye on Mr. Walker."

Debbie laughed. "He looks harmless."

During the short time they lived with Lilith and Karl before the new house was finished, David liked the routine of early breakfasts, with Lilith doing the cooking, and then the men and his Aunt Lilith going off together; but Debbie, left alone with David for the day, felt in some way that she was not pulling her own weight. She was anxious to get into her own home. And perhaps her feeling of restlessness was heightened by their visit to Hadassah Hospital.

Not long after their arrival, they went to the hospital at Lilith's urging. She arranged for them to go when Dr. Alpert was on duty. He was a friend of Karl's who had come from Breslau when his Aryan wife divorced him in the days of the Nuremberg laws.

Their bus wound slowly up the Scopus and they alighted before an endless building of Jerusalem stone, inlaid with endless rows of windows. The halls were filled with the smell of ether and a ghostly hush was made more ghostly by women in white and blue walking through the halls. In the rooms off the hall, they could see patients pale in white sheets. In one room they saw several undersized, shriveled children, but they hurried by. David clutched his mother's hand in terror as they followed Vic down the mysterious corridor.

At the end of the long hall they entered the out-patient department, where a dozen men and women were already waiting, one of them an Arab gentleman colorfully dressed in long white galbieh and fez, with a brief smile for David, and the others more somber in European dress. From an inner room an aide called the patients singly or in groups, and later they emerged and left. There was no telling from their expressions what had befallen them. At last the Arab was summoned inside. In a few moments there was the sound of shouting in anger, and then an unearthly shriek, followed by silence. At length the Arab came out, smiling broadly, and without looking to right or left, passed into the corridor, proud and sure.

When the aide signaled to Debbie, their family group entered the inner office, which smelled violently of antiseptics and anesthesia. The nurse, she saw, was a heavy woman in her fifties, formidable, impersonal, but not unkind. This was Debbie's first look at Elsa Schumacher.

Dr. Richard Alpert, whom Lilith was always raving about, was an attractive, light-complexioned, sandy-haired man in his early forties. When the Marmorek family entered his office, he was still smiling at the antics of the Arab who had just departed.

"Like Jerusalem?" he asked Vic.

"Quite well," Vic said. "We've only been here a few weeks." Elsa drew from the sterilizer a long hypodermic syringe, which must have seemed like a dagger to David.

"Too rocky for me," Dr. Alpert said to David. "Ever seen so much rock? I miss grass."

As he spoke he gave Debbie an anti-typhus injection. His technique was lightning-fast and effortless, but David watched with growing horror.

"Where you from?" the doctor asked David, as he refilled his syringe for Vic.

"Rome," David said nervously, never taking his eye off the needle. "But Mommy's from Vienna."

"Now that's a new technique for bringing mothers into the world," Dr. Alpert said. "Very sensible. Keep 'em in a different town altogether. Have less trouble with 'em."

He vaccinated Debbie and Vic for smallpox. David turned away, too horrified to watch. His poor parents!

But when Elsa started to roll *his* sleeve up and he knew Dr. Alpert intended to give him the same treatment, in a sudden movement he twisted himself free, and ran through the open door and outer office, down the hall screaming with terror. "I came to *see* the hospital." Vic caught him. "Let me go! Let go!" He cast about wildly to express himself. "I wish I was in Rome! I'm sorry I ever came here. I hate it here! I wish I was back on the ship. It was better on the ship. I wish they caught us and sent us back!"

Vic dragged him back through the hall crying, protesting, kicking in futile agony to be sacrificed to an unfathomable ritual. Elsa was grim-faced. Debbie began to explain patiently what they were doing and why Mommy and Daddy had submitted, that it was to keep sickness away, like his earaches. But David heard very little of what Debbie was saying because his own shrieks drowned her out.

Dr. Alpert dropped the syringe with a deliberate clatter and put his hand on David's shoulder.

"Ah," he said with mock disgust, "who needs these injections anyway! Let's you and me go look at something I've got back here." He led David into the next room. "Ever see tropical fish?"

He pointed to a tank in which a score of tiny vari-colored fish swam about peacefully. A white light in the center made them iridescent and David stared, fascinated, slowly relaxing.

"You probably won't believe this," Dr. Alpert said, "but I injected every one of these fish." He tapped the tank and a fish scooted. "In the arm." David sniffed himself quiet and smiled. "Of course they weren't fish *then.* They were boys. Except that black one there. She was a girl. Had blond hair, too. Don't know what turned her black like that. Know what their trouble was?"

David stared at the tank.

"Cried. Kicked. Screamed. And zingo! Changed right into fish. Matter of fact, you're pretty lucky you're not in there yourself."

"I wish I was," David was able to say at last. "What kind of fish are they?"

"Just told you," Dr. Alpert said, dryly. "Jewish fish." He led David back to the examining room, and his parents followed. "Isn't that the best fish story you ever heard?"

"They aren't *really* children," David mumbled to himself for reassurance. Elsa was rolling his sleeve up again, and he blinked tight as the needle darted into his arm.

"There we are," Dr. Alpert said with exaggerated apathy. "Another life saved."

Elsa was shaking her head in disapproval. "I'm afraid he hasn't been very brave, doctor."

"Lot braver than that Arab who was here," Dr. Alpert said. "Oh, what a huge fish *he* is going to make!"

David giggled. It was over.

"Nice guy," Vic said, when they were back in the hall.

It was difficult to recall all the details of the rest of the hospital visit —the eye, nose and throat examination; the dark room where a radiologist, attired in goggles and great clumsy mittens, held the cold fluoroscope plate to their chests; more needles to extract blood. And David now much more relaxed. Debbie was grateful for Dr. Alpert and his tropical fish.

As they were leaving the hospital grounds, Debbie said to Vic, "I just can't explain how I feel, seeing all this. Look, I'm just trembling! Don't you think it's wonderful?"

"Very nice. Not quite Vienna of course, but really complete."

"I wonder," Debbie said as they walked toward the university grounds nearby, "if I could take the nursing course without living here at the hospital? After we get set, of course, and David's in school."

"Whatever gave you that idea?"

"I just feel," Debbie said as if she were only dreaming of it, "I'd like to *do* something like this. I'd feel better. And I think your father would approve."

Vic spoke softly. "Remember, sweetie, you still have a husband and son. A nursing course is no part-time job, and we'd hate to feel neglected. Before you do anything impetuous, think about us, won't you?"

Debbie put one arm around Vic's waist and the other about David's shoulder, as she said, "Goose. Of course I will, but just think . . ." She never finished, but went swinging along the path, pulling them with her, feeling she had discovered some nice new secret.

While on the Scopus they visited the university. David was soon so fascinated with the great open amphitheater that he began to forget the hospital. They watched young men and women walking together in friendly groups, talking and laughing and waving, as they made their way from one class to another. And the view—all Jerusalem was spread before them, like a dish for dinner—was breathtaking.

"Someday," Debbie said, "perhaps you'll study here, David."

"I want to act in that theater. Before everyone."

"The little show-off," Vic laughed.

Moving into the new house was exhausting, too, but in its way exhilarating. She and Vic bickered but it was mostly a cheerful kind of arguing, loud and unrestrained, and they felt much younger, setting up house like newlyweds. She took to wearing her hair youthfully loose, instead of under a black kerchief, and she seemed to bloom like all the fresh flowers that were making the countryside gay in April; it was even fun to argue.

The apartment was finished, in spite of the heat and their tempers, and although either she or Vic had at one time or another expressed himself as unalterably opposed to every separate piece of furniture in the house, they all thought it was quite elegant.

It was not long after they were settled that they were invited by the Walkers to join them for tea at the officers' club. Vic was cautiously elated.

"It's only a first step, of course, but a tremendously important one. Inner circle people, that's us. I have no desire to be one of those fellows on the fringes of decent life, and never getting in the front door. Like

Kronstein. Fine engineer, but an utterly different kind of human being. No sports, no art, no books, no music. Not even a decent vice. Just the telephone office business and the Jew business. It's no wonder Redge Walker can't warm up to him. One of these intense fellows. The British pace themselves better."

There were many people at the officers' club out of uniform, but except for three Arabs having tea with a colonel, they were all English. Even the few Jews were English. Redge presided at their table, easy-going and friendly, clearly proud of his wife Enid, who was a pretty woman, six or seven years older than Debbie, taller and fairer, with her blond hair braided and worn in a coronet. She was breezy and warm to them both, and drank her Scotch whisky without water or soda. Also at their table were the Halliwells, John and Margaret. She was a large woman, much less handsome than her stalwart husband. Neither of them could unfreeze, and their conversation for the most part was vacuous and aimless, as if they were doing their best to get through the hour. Debbie felt a little more vulnerability in Margaret, who seemed awkward partly, perhaps, because of her size—Debbie heard she had been a champion swimmer in her late teens—and partly because she was terrified that something she might say would annoy her husband.

Debbie imagined that John Halliwell was there at tea under duress from Redge, and Margaret was bound to come where her husband was ordered to bring her.

It was only when Redge got on the subject of tennis that the afternoon thawed somewhat.

"Do you play?" John Halliwell turned to Vic as if to dispose of him.

"Yes," Vic said. "Yes, I have in my time."

Debbie couldn't resist the temptation to jump in. "He was on the Davis Cup team for Czechoslovakia," she said brightly. "Weren't you on the doubles team, dear?"

"Yes," Vic said. "We beat everyone that year but England in the European division."

"I remember!" said Redge excitedly. "Saw you at Wimbledon myself. Thirty-two, wasn't it? Or thirty-three?"

"Thirty-two," Vic said. "I was just a kid, and I had to give that sort of thing up."

"Well, think of that, John."

John Halliwell blushed, and she could see his mind bend a little. He said, "We've got ourselves some real competition, Redge. We must have a go at a game soon, old chap."

Redge poured new drinks all around, chuckling to himself. "Never had a chance to beat a Davis Cup player before. I'd better watch my p's and q's, eh, Vic?"

* * * * * *

By unrelenting advertising in the *Post* for two weeks running they found a man who was willing to give David lessons on the concertina at eighty piastres for a half-hour, once a week, Wednesdays at three. His name was Sam Pearlman, but his friends called him Maestro Sam.

He had seen the ads, he said, right from the beginning, but it had taken him two weeks to make up his mind. Maestro Sam played with the Palestine Symphony Orchestra on the bass viol, but he earned additional money from his music lessons. Although he played the piano and the saxophone as well as the bass viol, he was certainly no expert on the concertina, surely not as good as Angelo, but he was willing to come to the apartment for lessons, and was absolutely the only man in Jerusalem qualified for the job. He was comically lanky, like a willowy scarecrow, and usually came to the lesson with not only a lollipop, but also some special treat like a mechanical mouse or a toy that made the noise of a cricket. Maestro Sam, with his lollipops and gadgets, delighted David—who practiced faithfully to please him. David, he told them, had a flair for music, really a talent you might say. Vic immediately took to the man, though she never quite fathomed why. They were nothing alike.

In July she hired Tani and in September when she started her nursing course, David began kindergarten at the Rehavia School.

Miss Even was the first teacher they saw the day she brought him to school—a solemn boy all tight inside, a stranger in a school for other children, not for him, clutching Nina, his puppet, in one arm and clinging to Debbie's slacks with his free hand. Miss Even had met them in the hall. Her smile was startling, and she did her best to reassure David.

In the building across the sunfilled courtyard, they had found the kindergarten, where the children were already assembled. He watched, but from outside the inner circle. He was a strange intruder. Suddenly he began to call Debbie, pulling at her desperately when she tried to detach herself.

A large fat boy—it had turned out to be René Blum—approached David and pointed to the puppet. "What's that?" he said ominously.

David hesitated.

"Give it to me!"

"No."

While he argued with the fat boy, Debbie stole out of the room.

He told her later that he could scarcely distinguish the children one from another. When she asked if he had made any friends, he said morosely, "They were all taken." The only one he knew at all was René, the fat boy, of whom he was terrified. They found out later that René was a Moroccan with a fierce father, who once killed an Englishman with a knife.

On the second day of school David tried to be sick and avoid going back, but Vic gave him a lecture.

"Why do you think we came here?" he shouted across the table to David perched high on his pillow. "So you could have friends! So you would be happy! Your mother wanted you to be happy. Now you've got a wonderful school, wonderful teachers. Be happy you have them!"

"I like school," David said. "Only my wife doesn't like it."

But back he went.

And soon the school courtyard with its varied plants, the rock-strewn playground and gymnasium, teachers, children and all came to be as familiar to David as his new flat. The sparkling newness and shine which he first looked upon with surprise and awe, Miss Even the beautiful, Miss Baruch and the others became almost but never quite commonplace. The difficult Hebrew started to come more easily, until he was thinking in it.

It was only the other children of whom he continued to be wary, and at times frightened. He hated the constant wild fighting, and he was terrified of René, who saw to it that no one at all played with him.

It was Meyer Van Bern's arrival that wrought the first great change in David's status. He instantly had one friend, Meyer was his friend from the boat, something each flaunted before the others.

The second change came about later. Once a month the class had Parents' Visiting Day, and one of the activities was "Show and Tell," during which two or three children volunteered to tell some interesting experience, or exhibit prized new possessions—butterflies or photos of trips to Bethlehem or Nazareth. Debbie was able to arrange at the hospital to take two hours off for these monthly visits, and she came slowly to know Jacinta Van Bern better; she found herself attracted to this pleasant but unexciting woman.

Several months after the Van Berns arrived, Meyer volunteered for his first Show and Tell. "I'll tell how my mother and I came to Palestine," he began without ceremony. "The night was dark. Because we weren't supposed to come in, they didn't want us, but we came anyhow. And my sister from camp, that was in Buchenwald, she couldn't come, but they made her go on a trip ahead of me. My mother didn't like it, but after she was happy again. That was all right. There was nothing wrong with that, they said she was a bad girl, my sister, and she was. She used to pull my hair. But maybe she'll come here too, I hope so. My mother says so. Then it started to rain in the boat. Bang, bang, and we fell in the water, and a man took us to a house to go in there. But there were storm troops, they were looking for us and we had to hide. The fat lady said it was her birthday and David was there, weren't you, David?"

David said, "Of course, you know I was there."

"So when these storm troops came, *someone* had to *do* something.

So David played the thing, the black box, you know, David." His hands went in and out. "Music came out . . . from the black box, not a round box, not a square box. A sort of round square box, and music came out. And the storm troops liked it, and they didn't make us go back on the boat, did they? They said Happy Birthday. And the man said, it was like King David and his harp."

Usually the children were bored by Show and Tell; they rarely listened; but on this occasion they sat on the edges of their seats. They looked first at Meyer, then at David, and at their mothers; and Shari, the pretty Syrian girl, said, "I came in an aeroplane from Damascus. I flew in the sky. Zoom, zoom." And her hands became an aeroplane and her body the motor as she raced gracefully about the room. There was a babbling of voices and almost everyone seemed to want to talk and tell how he'd come, as though someone had opened a dike. René said loudly, "I came in my mother's stomach in the Hospital on the Scopus."

Miss Baruch said, "Hush, children. You'll all get your chance. Can you really play music, David? What is it you play?"

David said, "I don't know what you call it in Hebrew. It's a *concertina.*"

"Will you bring it?" she said. "You must play it for the children tomorrow, will you?"

David looked about doubtfully. The faces of the children were expectant, and he spoke tentatively. "I'll try to bring it."

That night he said to his parents, "Meyer Van Bern is my best friend." He practiced on the concertina for almost two hours, and sleeping for him was not easy that night. It was a terrible risk; but, as always, he was excited with the promise of an audience.

Just as David began to doze at last, there was a sudden explosion which seemed to come from the center of town, a violent jarring roar that shook the windows and jarred the furniture. David came into the living room, white as a ghost. Debbie was shaken, but Vic said it was nothing, David was to go back to bed. Soon the phone rang; it was Karl to say the explosion was at the newspaper building, and casualties were heavy. The Epsteins came over from across the hall to talk in somber tones, and they all gathered close to the radio to listen to the Voice of the Defenders newscast. David kept reappearing at the door, worried and pale, until she warmed him some milk and made him go back to bed, where finally he slept, while the adults tried to decide what the British could have in mind to bomb the newspaper office. The phone rang again, this time the hospital. Emergency cases were beginning to arrive, and even student nurses were needed.

Lilith came to pick up Debbie and they rode up to the Scopus together in one of the ambulances with three unconscious and bleeding men from the shattered newspaper office. For five hours they were busy receiving traumatic cases, and as the night wore on, an anger that had started hotly in her had grown cold and unreasoning. Gone was the sensation of fright she had felt in Prague when Paula wrote of Mama and Papa. But hate grew. One old man she could not forget. He was murmuring, "How will we ever get on the street? The place is a shambles," when he died. She got two hours of sleep at the hospital and worked all next day in the operating room with Lil and Dick Alpert until she was ready to drop.

* * * * * *

By the time she arrived home she could think of nothing but a bath and sleep. David, however, was waiting eagerly to tell her of his day's wonderful triumph. His eyes shone, and he danced about and tugged at her to get her attention. But she was too exhausted to be able to respond.

Vic, too, was morose and unapproachable, gloomily reading a mimeographed account of the explosion.

Debbie kissed David and Vic mechanically and sprawled in the armchair.

"I played the concertina in school today," David cried.

"Yes, dear? How was it?"

"Wonderful! Just wonderful. I did 'Tzena.' "

"That's nice, dear, and it's such a hard piece. I'm glad. You see it pays to practice. Now get ready for dinner, honey."

She turned to Vic who began to speak glumly. "I can't believe it of the British. I was talking to Redge Walker this afternoon. He believes the Etzel may have done it themselves, just to stir up the people. Or the Sternists."

That made her angry. "Oh, Vic, how can you even listen to such, I hardly know what to call it, wishful stupidity. Either Redge Walker's an awful ass or he's clever as clever. He's been friendly and nice to us, and yet—never quite lets the bars down all the way, does he? He's always so fair, only he's fairer to the British. He knows perfectly well even the Etzel isn't going about blowing up buildings and killing Jews. Really it's too ridiculous. You know as well as I who planted the bombs. Only you just won't say so out loud."

"Miss Even said it was beautiful!" David shouted. "Even René liked it. And Tamar came home with me. She wants me to marry her."

"That's fine, dear, now wash up, dear. Hurry. Mommy's exhausted."

Without warning David began to whimper. He was deflated, defeated. "I left Nina at school," he whined. "I want Nina." And before long he was in full tears.

Vic and Debbie were not sympathetic; it was his own fault for forgetting her; and Vic thought it silly for him still to be carrying a doll. Vic's patience was at the breaking point. "Last night," he stormed, "a hundred people were killed and hurt. There was something to cry about. And all you're worried about is your Goddamn puppet!"

Debbie tried hopelessly to hush Vic. "Sure," Vic said excitedly, "sure, we've always kept him good and protected, wrapped around in cotton batting. He might as well find out what the world is, it's never too early, and it's never too late. He may as well know what goes on!" David screamed on. "Everybody likes me," he screeched, "except my own father and mother!"

In the ensuing weeks David found increasing comfort in Tamar. Sometimes he went to her house and sometimes he brought her home. Debbie overheard enough of their conversation to realize that it was a serious matter. "What do you think of René?" David asked one day.

"He's fat," she said.

"He's a big fat slob," David confirmed.

"He's a big fat ugly terrible slob," she said, "he's a big old jerk of a fat dirty awful slob."

"Yes," David said, "he's my best friend too."

"I thought Meyer was your best friend," Tamar said in some surprise.

"Oh, that was last week." David was developing *sangfroid*.

"How about friends that are girls?" Tamar asked boldly.

"Oh, I don't like girls," David said. "I guess you're the only one I have for a friend."

"Then I'm your best girl friend. Would you like to get married?"

"Sure. Then I'll have a real wife." Nina was through.

Nineteen

The summer the Marmoreks became friendly with the Walkers was a tense one in Jerusalem. The leaders of the Jewish community had been imprisoned at Latrun by British authorities; Tommies patrolled the streets in squads; and boys and girls carrying knives and pistols were sullen and restive. Immigration was at a standstill and the community fumed with impatience. There was loose talk of violence.

Nevertheless David and his school friends played in the streets from dawn to dusk, as if everything were normal, or went riding up into the hills on the handlebars of Noah Mendoza's bicycle.

Debbie was on her feet all day at the hospital, tired when she came home, but she always made the special effort to read David his bedtime story or listen with both ears to his day's adventure.

Vic was busy and happy at the office, and the Scotches and tennis he shared with Redge Walker led to bonds between the families that both men nourished, in spite of the politics of the day, or perhaps as a defiance to something both men considered nonsense.

They dined with each other frequently, sometimes at the King David, but usually at one of the less obvious places in town. The Walkers came frequently to the Marmoreks' for bridge, and they went to concerts or movies together. Enid took David along with Lloyd occasionally to see a soccer game or to visit the traveling fair in town.

Since Debbie found it difficult to have enough time for David, Vic filled in the gaps. Father and son grew closer together that summer. On the weekends, while she was at the hospital, they would walk about town together, dressed in their finest, to see soccer at the "Y" or to visit the Walkers, Karl and Lil, or Ben Kronstein and his wife Willie, who always had milk and cookies for David.

Vic would buy him a pack of sunflower seeds, which if they didn't furnish nourishment, at least kept their teeth busy; and once in a blue moon, for a special treat, Vic let David have falaffel in pitah, an unleavened Arab bread formed like a hollow pie crust and filled with highly seasoned vegetables which were delicious to David, but which Vic called pure poison.

These small diversions were sandwiched between news broadcasts. Vic, like most people, was usually glued to a radio or newspaper. Then in July there was the most disastrous explosion in the history of Palestine, at the King David Hotel. Debbie was at the hospital when casualties began to arrive. But David and Vic were visiting Lil on her day off in Beth Hakerem, three kilometers from town. They heard the explosion as they were playing in Lilith's garden with Yehuda, Karl's poodle.

When they heard the distant thunder of the bomb, they went at once to the radio. After only a few minutes the music broke off, and the voice of the announcer, speaking hesitantly, said, "We bring you a special news notice at this time. The headquarters of the Administration at the King David Hotel have been severely damaged by an explosion, the source of which is not known at this time. Loss of life is feared to be heavy, but is not known. Keep tuned in for further notices."

The music resumed; Vic gathered David up and started instantly for the bus. He was deeply shaken. "Those crazy kids. Those crazy little wild bastards. The Walkers live at the King David," he said to Lilith. "I think I'd feel personally responsible if anything's happened to them, just for being what I am."

Lilith said, "Oh, I think that's ridiculous, absolutely ridiculous, Victor, you of all people. I hope nothing's happened to them, of course, but—"

"They have a little boy—David's age."

"Yes," Lilith said, "I know. But on the other hand don't those bloody British have it coming, really, absolutely don't they? And mind you, I'm not one to condone this sort of thing, I hate it. We've spent too much time building up to start tearing down. But really now, don't you think there's a limit? All our leaders in prison. Tommies everywhere. I mean, really."

"This sort of thing never did any good for anybody," Vic said. "Look at Europe."

"Of course, you're absolutely right," Lilith said in her loudest, most positive voice.

They caught the bus from Deir Yassein, and everyone in it—Arab, Jew and Englishman—was talking about the explosion. Agitated arguments were taking place in loud, unrestrained voices, sometimes between perfect strangers. Others sat silent and morose, as if they were waiting for some inevitable blow to fall.

David was only moderately interested in the proceedings until he saw the King David Hotel. The destruction was worse than anything he'd believed possible. The King David Hotel, the massive fortress, now half shambles. He saw bits of clothing amongst the rubble. The place was filled with dust and smoke and they still heard cries and shouts and saw the feverish activity everywhere. Military and other vehicles jammed Julian's Way. Men were being loaded on stretchers.

The exterior walls had collapsed, and bereted troops picked their way through the frightful destruction looking for more survivors. Police and the military restrained the crowds across the street in rough unpleasant fashion, as if this act of violence had been perpetrated personally upon each of the Englishmen, police and soldiers alike, by each person in the curious crowd. Only the Arabs were treated with politeness. For the rest there was derision, barked commands, pushes and once even blows. David was frightened and wanted to leave at once, but Vic insisted upon talking to one of the soldiers.

"You wouldn't know, would you, whether Mr. Reginald Walker and his family are all right, would you?"

"Now 'ow would I be likely to know?" the young English soldier snapped. "I'm only workin' 'ere. I s'pose if this 'ere Walker bloke was dead 'n' buried in the bloomin' mess, you'd say good riddance, now, wouldn't ya?"

As it turned out, the Walkers had all been out of the hotel at the time, and none of the other victims, English, Arab, or Jew, was known to the Marmoreks personally, though rather a large number were friends of the Walkers.

If anything, the explosion at the King David brought the Walkers and Marmoreks closer. Vic's real abhorrence of these methods of violence and his denunciation of Jews who used them were too eloquent not to touch Redge, who was equally horrified when the English used them.

The only way in which their friendship for the Walkers became a problem for Debbie was that now they insisted on giving them embarrassingly large and elaborate gifts, which she felt they could neither accept nor reciprocate. The first one was a refrigerator, which came for her twenty-seventh birthday. She insisted Vic make arrangements to return it, and he spoke to Redge about it.

"Redge says we're to keep it. That's an order, he says. And we're to think no more about it."

Karl and Lil lifted eyebrows slightly when she told them about the gift during her little birthday party.

"They're practically strangers," Karl said seriously.

"Yes, absolutely," Lil said. "I feel like a piker, with this bracelet for you."

The Kronsteins, especially Ben, were horrified, although he obviously didn't know what to say.

At Christmas, Redge and Enid gave Vic a Parker 51 gold pen, which Vic wore and used thereafter as if it were an insignia of rank.

And for Vic's birthday there was a washing machine, which it took Tani weeks to learn to operate, and of which she was afraid to this day. Debbie never knew just how much of Tani's protest was technical and how much disapproval of the Walkers. But she overheard her mutter, as she glared at the kitchen full of new white machines, "They don't need a maid here—they need an engineer!" For Debbie's part she was too overwhelmed by the Walkers' generosity to keep on protesting indefinitely.

Twenty

During the next term David came into his own. In first grade he grew physically powerful. He gained weight and shot up almost two inches.

When Tuvia, an emaciated lad from Persia, entered the class after the middle of the term, and René Blum, with his customary directness, decided to obliterate him in a single attack during recess, David was outraged, and his anger became the making of him.

When he saw René sitting astride skinny old Tuvia and pounding mud into his face he lost all reason. "Stop it," he shrieked, "stop it, you stupid Bevin!" He pushed René off Tuvia and they began to wrestle. René locked David's head inside the crook of his elbow and twisted him to the ground. Suddenly he became aware of the cries of the other children, encouraging him, urging him up; but René's grip was deadly tight, he felt as though he were beginning to choke. Tamar was screaming, "David, David! Get up!"

With all his effort he jerked himself loose, avoided René's hand grasping for his clothing, and twisted free. René, just on the threshold of victory, came quickly after him. It was pointless to try to wrestle. David drew his arm quickly back, clenched his fist and crashed a quick blow at René's unguarded face. Happily he felt his knuckles pound into René's nose. There was a grunt of surprise from René as his hand flew to his nose. David waited for the next onslaught, gratified but worried.

René's hand came away from his nose bloody and he gave an unearthly scream. "Blood! Look, I'm bleeding! I'm bleeding!" He broke into horrible weeping, his face distorted and craven, as he backed away from David, pointing to him and calling for the teacher. "Mrs. Jacobinsky, David wounded me! Look!" His wails and outcries could be heard in every classroom in the school. His defeat was definite.

On the way home from school that afternoon, David led a parade of first graders, who insisted that he lead the way through the streets playing the new march he had learned on the concertina. Even René joined the parade. This was really the way to be secure. It was a curious sight Debbie saw, the weaving, squirming little bodies of eighteen seven-year-olds following a small boy playing a sprightly march on the concertina. When they came to the house, David called, "I have to go upstairs. My mother has cookies for me. Come on, Tamar. And Meyer." The others all waved, even René. "Peace, René."

René responded not unenthusiastically. "You see," Debbie heard David say to Tamar and Meyer in the vestibule, "René and I are friends."

Now David felt as though all things were possible. His boasts were not really boasts, they were hopes. They were not lies or bragging, just dreams. And it was surprising how some of these matters turned out. Like the affair of the bicycle. When he told everyone at school that he was going to get a brand-new shining two-wheeler, it was simply the result of seeing another boy with one.

But the more he considered the matter the more it appealed to him; and at supper he said to Vic, "Do you think when a boy is seven he needs a two-wheel bicycle?"

"Desperately," Vic said.

"Well," David said with a hand flourish that had recently become a mannerism, "I'm seven."

"Well, isn't that a coincidence?"

Debbie interrupted to say, "What's all this?"

"Of course," David said, and he was debating with accompanying hand gesticulations, "I don't absolutely *need* a bike, but then in a way I do."

"What way is that, dear?"

"I told some kids I was getting one, and I don't like to be a liar; a liar is bad, don't you think?"

Vic said, "They need him in the British Cabinet," and Debbie laughed.

A week later a brand-new bicycle was delivered. Debbie scolded Vic on spoiling David, but Vic hadn't bought it, and there was a mystery which for several days remained unsolved.

Then one night Vic came home, with a look which meant he knew something, and as soon as David arrived he told them both.

"Guess who sent the bicycle," he said solemnly. "None other than my boss, Mr. Reginald Walker, bless his English soul. You know what happened? I told the boys about what David said at the office. About not being a liar. Just a small item of amusement, I meant, you know. And Redge's reaction was typical. 'Damn clever chap,' he said in that ridiculously decisive way he has. Well, I forgot all about it. Then today he poked his head in the door and called out, 'How's the lad doing—can he go it with no hands yet?' grinning from ear to ear, the old son of a gun."

Debbie said lightly, "Well, let's give it back, shall we?"

And Vic said, "But why?"

"Well," she said and her voice was so high it squealed like a small girl's, "we can't go over the same ground again and again, can we? It's so monotonous."

She went to the mirror, studied herself carefully, and took to combing her hair, pulling the comb angrily through the knots.

"Karl tells me you're in a very special position at the Telephone Office. Karl's always using phrases like that—'special position.' He says you could give Haganah a lot of help if you wanted. Or you could do a lot of harm. He's awfully mysterious about it, I must say, but he's concerned over you. I am too. You're being careful, aren't you?"

"That's a silly question, Debbie. I do my job. I keep my nose out of everything but my job."

"Karl says you could just be unaware. You *are* politically so unaware, darling, too. I know that about you, that's why I worry. Men like John Halliwell or even Redge could be using you without your ever knowing it. Doing things like this bicycle thing to keep you off guard. Karl says you have certain information. That's the way he talks—'certain information' and John could be pumping you. Just by being chummy. Even Redge might, though I'll admit it's hard for me to believe it of Redge."

Vic was heavily sarcastic.

"Has it occurred to your worrisome brother or you that the game works both ways? Why make John Halliwell and Redge so clever and me so stupid?"

"Only unaware, Vic, not stupid. A bicycle, a refrigerator . . ."

"Oh, what Goddamn rot," Vic said in a rising rage. "Sure I'm in a position to help Haganah and I guess if I were idiotic enough I could help the Arabs. Does Karl take me for an imbecile?"

"But, darling, where does Redge get all the money for these presents? I can't fathom it. He's on salary and his isn't much more than yours."

"Oh, Lord, so *that's* it," Vic said with triumphant relief. "That's how all these half rumors start. My darling Debbie, Redge is quite a rich man. His family has shares in Anglo-Iranian, matter of fact. Of course, he doesn't like it noised about, told me in the strictest confidence, the time I tried to send back the refrigerator. After all I'm really not so naïve myself."

She shrugged. "Okay, I'll hate myself in the morning for badgering you so. And I think I'm losing a popularity contest here." She ruffled David's hair. "We'll say no more about the bicycle, shall we?"

"Good," David cried, relieved. He felt he had to show his gratitude to his father for his defense of the bicycle. "René Blum said you were a spy," he offered helpfully. "That dumb Moroccan dope. I had to beat his brains in." This was probably a slight exaggeration, all around.

Vic grinned at David. "That's fine, old chap. You protect your Pop's honor against all detractors." He turned to Debbie and grinned, "I wouldn't give you a phony piastre for Redge's chances of corrupting me. But that Enid now. She might lead me into temptation and she wouldn't need a bicycle."

"Oh, you cad," Debbie laughed. "Can't you see you'd have only to crook your little finger at Enid? She has her eye on you."

"Now," Vic said, "who're you kidding?"

"I didn't mean it," Debbie cried, "I take it back, please strike it from your mind. Oh, I must learn to keep my childish mouth shut."

"I'll have to look into this," Vic laughed. "As a matter of fact I've invited the Walkers and Halliwells to dinner this Tuesday."

"Fine. Oh, damn. But I'm sure I told you we've already asked Lilith and Karl for Tuesday. And Dick Alpert. It's in the book."

"Now isn't that stupid of me? You did tell me and I completely forgot."

"Well, I guess we can have them together. Oh golly, we only have settings for six. Well, I'll have to ask Rose for silver. I guess we can wedge them all in together."

Vic looked horrified. "Dick Alpert's okay. But how can you have Enid Walker and Lilith at the same dinner table? That's impossible, honey. Your poor mother would have passed out at the thought. She had such a delicate sense for that sort of thing."

"It was Mama's career, but I've another career, remember? What do you suggest?"

"Why, Lilith will eat both those poor girls whole! And raw!"

She turned stubborn. "Well," she said, "if you feel so strongly, I guess you'd better call Redge and make it for another night."

"Now, you know I couldn't. What the hell would I say?"

"Say I'd already made another date you didn't know about, dear." She knew she was being too sweet.

"Well, why don't *you* call Lilith and tell *her* that?"

"Coward!" she mocked. "At least *you'd* be telling the truth."

"But, Debbie, how could I, right after the damn bike? They've made all their plans for Tuesday. Redge called both girls from my office."

The argument was incredibly trivial, but she had herself worked up over it. With effort she calmed down.

She was pensive and spoke slowly. "I guess in many ways the Walkers and Halliwells *are* more important to you than Karl and Lilith."

"Now that's damned childish."

"I see."

"If you'd asked anyone but Lilith—that little tigress never stops pouring out her Zionist propaganda. It's repetitious and boring. In that rasping voice of hers—she has the most exasperating voice I know, so damn positive about everything. And, if *I* can't stand her, imagine how she'll strike the Walkers. Everything's crisis to her. Life and death. Black and white. No room in her soul for trivia, no. Tell her it's a nice day and she unleashes a lecture on how too much sun is bad for the crops and how we Zionists have overcome all the handicaps of climatic conditions. From there it's only a step to the Life of Herzl. I certainly don't want Redge Walker to tie us up with her."

"Why, Vic, when you're with Lilith, you're nice as pie to her."

"Well, I have manners," Vic said.

"I know all about Lilith," she said bitterly, "I spend part of every day with her. And I know about her loud voice and irritating mannerisms. But she knows what she is and wants, which is more than I can say for us."

"She has no choice," Vic said. "Neither has Karl."

"Well, Karl means a great deal to me," she said. "Much more than the fact that he's my brother. And I won't slight him for Redge or even Enid. Let the Walkers come, and the Halliwells too. I really can't think of anyone I'd rather see Lilith eat alive than Margaret Halliwell. She's vapid, inconsequential, not a grain of humor—the soul of a moron in a Viking body. She'd like to be friends, Enid says, but she's afraid of her husband. I understand she was a great long-distance swimmer. Always trying to cross the Channel." She was snapping, her eyes flashing and her cheeks flushed.

Vic said, "Very well, I'll call Karl myself."

She lit a cigarette. "It's not very different from Prague," she said, "or Vienna. You haven't changed a bit—after everything that's happened.

The right people are always there to be pampered, aren't they?" She was surprised at her own boldness.

"Margaret and Enid certainly seem to rub you the wrong way," Vic said. "I just don't understand you. You can be as sweet as a kitten if you want to. Purring all over Dick Alpert or Elsa, gay as a bluebird, but sometimes you're so stiff with these girls. All the fun seems to go out of you."

"Can't snap it on and off like a light," she said. "I confess I rather like Enid. But I don't like most women, you know that. Elsa's different. She's so cosmically gloomy. I love to tease her and she can, at least, laugh at herself. As for Redge I don't think I can warm up to a man unless somewhere way down in my subconscious I could have a yen for him. Oh, not only animal attraction, but some kind of special yen. I need to feel sorry for him or be anxious to please him or want to break him down or *something*. Like some patients. I've a terrific yen for some of my patients and none for others. I want to mother Dick Alpert. I have a soft spot for him somehow. But Redge doesn't do anything to me. He leaves me blah. Honestly. And I'm sorry about that because I think he likes me."

"Maybe you can't warm up to him just because he's an Englishman. It couldn't be that?"

She thought a moment. "I doubt it. I think I'm pretty liberal that way. But maybe being an Englishman has made him what he is. I just think he's a proper fish. I don't believe you'd give a hoot for him yourself if he weren't one of the right people."

Vic picked up the phone and dialed, holding his hand over the mouthpiece as he talked in a low voice, angry too. "Where would we be if it weren't for the right people? Martin Schroeder. Sure, I know, he had his price. But where would we be if it weren't for him? And Angelo, and the bloke, whoever he was, who helped your father get out of Vienna? Where would you and I and David be? You know." He hung up. "No answer at Karl's. Anyhow the whole discussion's stupid. It's a question of a dinner invitation and I don't feel like being psychoanalyzed over it. Very well, we're alive. We have a few English friends. Therefore, I'm not the perfect Jew. Well, let's leave it at that and be friends ourselves."

"I haven't said a word, dear."

"We just ought to get it settled once and for all. What's wrong with our English friends? The time may come when we may be damn glad to have them, and in any case Redge is my boss."

"Of course, darling, you may be right. But I can't help thinking. This isn't Vienna—or Prague. Something's in the wind. All these investigations, committees, and now America coming into it. People are having to choose sides. Ordinary people like us."

"That'll be the day," Vic said. "When we have a side. Sure, the British are on one side and on the other there'll be ten sides, maybe twenty. Socialists and rabbis, kibbutzniks and Zionists, Christian Arabs and Moslems, the fellaheen and the Grand Mufti, the Etzel and Haganah, not to mention the Communists, bums, anarchists, Sternists and what not. How can anyone speak of sides? There are no sides. Only the British and fragments."

Debbie said, "There's a Jewish side. You're not ashamed to be on it, are you, Vic? Even in Jerusalem?" She jabbed her cigarette into the ash tray and got a drink from the cupboard. "One for you?" Vic nodded.

"I wouldn't say ashamed," Vic said deliberately. "I'd say I was—self-conscious. As if I'd been born with one eye, or one leg. A man with an infirmity through no fault of his own, but glad to be friends with healthy people. Even in Jerusalem. People without defect. People without self-consciousness. Glad to be taken in by them. Glad to shake their hands. Glad they give us a little dignity."

"Well," she said, "if that's dignity, I couldn't care less for it."

He raised his glass. "I give you the High Commissioner," he teased. Debbie raised hers. "I have nothing against the High Commissioner. I wish him only bon voyage."

They drank, she almost gulping hers. Vic said after a wait, "Do we have to go on like this?"

She said in a low voice, "No, I suppose not. I'll hate myself in the morning. I really will."

Vic sat beside her and put an arm behind her shoulders and ran his hands through the hair at her nape the way she liked. "Let's have the damn dinner party," he said brusquely. "I'll just pray none of our new furniture gets smashed in the melee."

Her voice sounded like a small girl's as she said, "I suppose I could call Lilith. It's just that I keep dreaming this is home for us, that someday it'll be ours and the English will go home and leave us alone. And there'll be an end to all the killing. It's just a dream I keep having and you keep waking me with your realism."

Vic kissed her gently. "You've been listening to voices of illusion. The English'll never leave. Remember there are fifty million Arabs and a hundred million barrels of oil and history. We're only two people . . . trying to get along. We have our own lives to lead." He kissed her again and she put her hands on the back of his head, gripping him hard as if she were trying to swallow him altogether. Nothing like any other kisses were Vic's. His hand slid gently to her breast and she sat up suddenly and looked at David. "Honey!" Vic looked at David too.

David said, "Can I go out and ride my bike?"

"Yes," Vic said. "Yes, of course." His voice was uneven.

"Be careful of the cars, David," she called after him, but her voice didn't sound authoritative. He ran down the stairs quickly, embarrassed.

Twenty-one

More than almost anything, Debbie would have loved to give and go to gay parties. But for Hitler, she'd have grown up in Vienna, perhaps to outdo Mama.

As it was these days, there were only rare occasions when Debbie could indulge her latent talent; in fact it was unprecedented to have even nine for dinner at the Marmoreks'. Tani, who usually took things stoically and in stride, behaved quite badly. She grumbled about the chores, muttered her disapproval of the guest list and grunted that it was just like Debbie to run off to the hospital and leave the dirty work to her. When Dick Alpert called to say he couldn't come because of a sick little girl, she said one guest less was at least a small blessing.

Debbie came home early, to check on Tani's progress, and brought last-minute things, ice cream, cigarettes, and an armload of sweet-smelling lilacs, still rare in Jerusalem. In spite of Vic's apprehensions, she was optimistic about the party. She dressed and spruced David, then went to work on herself. She enjoyed bathing, dressing in a new cartwheel cotton, fussing over eyelashes and hair, mouth and nails. She powdered, whirled, patted, and combed, looked at herself in all three mirrors, this way and that. Still pretty nice. She snatched a cigarette, poured a drink, and waited like an actress for her cue.

Karl and Lil arrived first. Karl kissed her and Lil twisted her mouth to offer a cheek.

"When do the members of the Occupying Power get here?" Karl grinned.

"Oh, Karl," Debbie said, "you be good now."

"Hope you have plenty to drink," Karl said. "Mama would've, you know."

"What'll you have?" Debbie asked. "Bourbon? Rishon wine?"

"Scotch and water," Karl said, and Debbie poured. "I've decided to give the English no quarter tonight. I plan to uphold our honor." He drank half the tall drink.

"Be sensible, Karl," Lil said irritably. "With your stomach. I don't look forward to being up all night with you."

"Do behave, Karl," Debbie said. "Lil?"

"Nothing, thanks," Lil said. Nonetheless Debbie poured a stiff bourbon drink, and Lil went to work on it without protest. Fortified with his highball, Karl sat at the spinet, gobbling the jelly beans Debbie gave him and rippling his fingers easily over the keys in Palestinian folk songs. Lilith stood behind him swaying and singing in her loud gusty voice so that Debbie's small voice was all but drowned out. Lilith was graceful as a cat and, almost motionless beside the piano, she seemed to be doing a whole composition in dance. Her hands and arms barely stirred but the music seemed to take hold of her body.

"Get the concertina, David!" Karl called. "We'll try a duet."

David loved to accompany Karl, who made even so small a boy feel himself bursting with the swell of a melody. As usual, Karl let David call the songs; they all sang together and the house was full of music.

They were going strong when Vic came barging in with Redge Walker and John Halliwell and the music stopped abruptly.

Redge said, "Now, don't stop for us. We could hear you as we came up. Have you ever heard anything like it, Johnny? It's got something that's quite different. Not Arab, and yet not European either. Don't you agree? Don't stop for us, please."

John Halliwell said indifferently, "Yes, do go on."

But Karl had left the piano and was fingering his drink. "Later, perhaps," he said.

"We've been out there playing tennis," Vic said. "It's a wonderful day. Reminds me of late spring in Prague. And the courts are in excellent shape."

Vic sounded strange, as if he were reciting.

"You know, Debbie," Redge said, "Vic's too tough for us. Johnny and I aren't in his class, actually. But we have him at our mercy. We're the only competition in town."

"I'm absolutely sorry for you, Vic," Lilith said cheerfully, "being at their mercy that way."

"Drinks, boys?" Debbie said. "What'll you have?"

David ran out to tell Tani to bring the platter of hors d'oeuvres while he passed the olives and sardines himself.

Vic was still pouring drinks and everyone was chatting when the two English ladies arrived. Neither woman kissed her husband, but both smiled cordially at them as if they were meeting old friends.

Enid drank half a glass of Scotch and water before she made her way across to Vic. There was something sinuous about the way she walked tonight.

"I've often wondered why the telephone service here isn't up to London's," Enid said, smiling, "and now I know. All the executives are off playing tennis during working hours."

"Don't they in England?" Vic said, smiling.

"Only in July and August and no one cares then because everyone's in the country."

"Well thanks for putting me in the executive class," Vic said. "I'm really only a technician, you know."

Debbie heard Karl mutter "Oh, God!" under his breath, and she hissed "Shh!" into his ear.

Enid took another gulp of highball. "I think you're as executive as the rest. Tell me, Vic, do you think you could give Lloyd tennis lessons? Or is he too young to start? Only seven."

"Oh, not at all," Vic said, "I've been meaning to start David, and he's just seven. Perhaps I can take the two boys out together. Weekends, of course." Vic *had* mentioned several times that he ought to give David a few lessons.

"That would be splendid," Enid said. "I'll come and watch. Perhaps you can give me a lesson or two, as well. I'm not too old to start, am I?"

"Not if you take it slowly," Vic was saying.

"I'm really not bad at games," Enid said, "I was quite a creditable golfer at home and the principle's usually the same, I always say. You have to have the desire to play and lots of practice and follow through. But above all I think you have to have a love of sport. Some do and some don't. I have it. I think you do too." She was lighting a cigarette for Vic and one for herself and looking at him provocatively. Vic turned to David and smiled weakly.

"We'll plan to get the boys together then, shall we?"

By dinnertime everyone was high; even Lil had lost the chip on her shoulder, and dinner went better than Debbie had thought possible. Vic told several stories which struck everyone as much funnier than they were, and started from the others a stream of stories and jokes, which more and more easily had them all laughing. Everyone thought the food was delicious, the wine excellent, the conversation gay. Vic and his groundless fears!

After dinner Margaret Halliwell sat at the spinet and, in her alcoholic condition, romped through "Country Gardens" as simply as a schoolgirl. The song and Margaret went together, and everyone applauded vigorously.

"How about bridge?" Debbie asked.

"Excellent idea," John Halliwell said. "I feel clairvoyant tonight."

"Who doesn't?" Lil said. "Bourbon makes me feel like the Delphic Oracle."

"Before we start," Redge said, "we ought to make Karl finish the piece we interrupted. Do that thing for us, Karl. You should hear him play, darling," he called to Enid. "We heard him when we came up and he promised to play for us after dinner. He's magnificent."

Karl, who swayed slightly from his drinks, set his highball on the piano, and sat down without argument. He slipped into a complicated Mozart study and after a little while spoke over the music. "I used to be able to play this thing. Now my fingers won't do what I tell them any more. I had a teacher in Vienna, his name was Ludwig Bachman, I remember, he used to tell me, 'Karl, you have the fingers of Paderewski.' Now if I only had the soul for such fingers." He tinkled a few bars easily. "And the last thing I remember my mother's saying just before my train left for Trieste was 'Practice, Karl. Be a good boy and practice.' "

"You certainly can play that thing," Redge said. "I don't see how you dared give it up with such talent. Vic, you never told me your brother-in-law was a genius."

"You think I'm a genius?" Karl laughed. "The real genius in my family is Lil. She could've been the greatest ballerina since Pavlova."

"That's how Karl and I met at the kibbutz," Lilith said. "A few of us used to dance in the evening and Karl came to play for us. Remember that beat-up old piano, Karl, all out of tune? I was eighteen. Karl was nineteen. Those days were fun, weren't they, Karl? But, you see, we decided we'd like to be first-class citizens first. When I was back in Budapest, my mother used to promise me that if I worked very hard, someday I would dance before the crowned heads of Europe. Oh, my poor mother was a dreamer; she didn't know that soon there would be no heads with crowns. She taught me everything. She was a prima ballerina herself in Budapest. You may have heard of her, Marta Hessels?"

"Yes, of *course*," Margaret said, excitedly. "I *saw* her! Didn't she dance in London?"

"Yes, several times."

"Marta Hessels, your mother, imagine! She was quite exquisite, John. You'd have loved her. John appreciates grace and rhythm, no matter whose, but he was in India then. Where is your mother now, dear?"

There was an appalled silence and John Halliwell glared at his wife.

"We don't really know. You see, she was a first-class dancer but a second-class person. She was killed in some non-specified way. Probably the usual—gas . . ."

The faces of the other women were blank as though they hadn't heard, and Lilith continued. "I remember watching her dance one night when I was seven. She seemed like a fairy to me—like—"

"What a shame," Margaret Halliwell said. She might have said more but for the renewed glare from her husband. She smiled nervously.

Karl, who had been playing idly through the talk, pounded heavily into the *William Tell* "Overture." The music was so impressive that all conversation stopped and Karl played on, heavily. When he finished, Margaret Halliwell spoke wistfully.

"I'd give anything to play like that," she said.

"Anything?" Lilith said sharply. "I wonder if you really mean that."

"I *think* I do," Margaret Halliwell said, and Debbie saw her shrink and look across at her husband.

"Would you give up being an Englishwoman, and become—shall we say, a second-class citizen?"

"Why—uh, I don't know what you mean. I should think it a worthwhile sacrifice."

"You're only saying it," Lilith laughed. "You don't mean it."

"Perhaps," Vic said with an embarrassed laugh, "Margaret's more broadminded about that sort of thing than you are, Lil."

"I just don't believe she realizes what she's saying," Lilith said.

Enid spoke mildly. "Aren't the refinements—oh, perhaps they are not entirely useful or functional—but aren't the beautiful, lovely things hard to give up?"

"There hasn't been time for us," Lilith spoke abruptly. "We've been working." She threw a dried apricot into her mouth and chewed hard.

"Perhaps," said Vic, and Debbie could see the voice of moderation about to assert itself, "perhaps there's something to what Enid says. Life can't be all tractors and pioneering. Existence isn't all fertilizer."

"Maybe Lil will have a chance to get back to her ballet work soon," Debbie said lamely. "All she needs is a little time."

"Oh, really," Lilith snapped. "I'm thirty-three."

"You see," Debbie said, trying to smooth things over as best she could, "Lilith's been busy at the hospital and it's first things first, I suppose. There's a price one pays for being a pioneer."

Karl had risen from the piano and now swallowed half his highball. "It's not too great a price to pay, is it? No pioneer ever had good manners, but look what we've done. Look at our farms, our forests, our factories!"

John Halliwell's grimace was barely noticeable but Debbie could see the wheels going round in his head. Pioneers! Forests and factories! Every three trees to these grubby people was a new forest. Every little weaver's a new factory, and the settlement of each new kibbutz a military victory! Exaggeration. Sell, sell, sell! That was John's big complaint about Ben Kronstein.

"If it's the last thing we do," Lilith snapped, "we're going to build this country and be first-class people. Otherwise you just never know when your friends might take it into their heads to gas you. It's enough to make a girl like me nervous! Perfectly lovely friends, too, whom you might have had to dinner. Some of my mother's best friends were simply delighted to see her go."

"D'you know," Halliwell said suddenly, "it's not actually that the Hebrews lack culture. They have it in great measure. And it's not that they haven't done fine work in their little settlements. What they've never developed is a satisfactory relationship with the rest of the world.

Energetic fellows, and yet no matter how much they accomplish—and I'm the first to admit it's satisfactory—almost nobody gets on with them—as a race, of course. Perhaps that's why they *are* second-class citizens. Personalities aside, I trust I'm not offending anyone."

Karl snorted loudly as if he were trying to prove Halliwell's point, and walked away from the piano. "Nothing personal, I assume," Karl said.

"You know," John said, "Mr. Balfour and his magnificent gesture to the Jews of the world is probably the most colossally unappreciated generosity in history. The Lord knows, we've tried."

"You 'spect us to be *grateful?*" Karl leered. "Or polite? Or patient?"

Halliwell blinked, and in the silence that followed, he walked close to Karl and brushed a small piece of lint off Karl's lapel. "Don't you ever blush, Mr. Pretsch?"

Karl backed away, waved his hand in dismissal. "No manners! There's a criterion for greatness. Keep the pinkie up at tea, no matter what happens. All the world loves the good old upraised pinkie."

"Politeness *is* rather an asset," Halliwell said, "when one is a guest. I might even say a necessity. And of course, the Hebrew is here in Palestine as a guest of the Arab. A guest does not take possession of his host's living room, you know. It's not done."

"We're just too damn busy to learn the rules," Karl snapped.

"More's the pity," John Halliwell said icily. "It's made the job we have to do that much more difficult. Quite serious for the Administration, this lack of courtesy. Now you take the Arab. That chap Moustapha over in Katamon, Redge—the fellow who owns all those houses there—you know him, Redge. Just the opposite. Devilish nice chap. Never a word against the Hebrew. Not a word of propaganda. Just polite and nice as could be. To the manner born, so to speak. Hospitable and charming and all that. I had dinner at his place last week. Right on the floor. Absolutely charming. Never impatient or rude. Never pushing."

"You see?" Lil said, and her face was beet red. "From here it's only one step to the gas chamber."

"Now, now," Enid said. "We'd better get on with the bridge, hadn't we? It's getting late."

Tani had cleared and was setting up the two bridge tables.

"I'm afraid I'm not quite up to bridge tonight," John Halliwell said offhandedly. He yawned and patted his hand over his mouth elaborately. "After all that tennis and such a heavy meal. I think we'd better run along. I really feel I'd like to get some sleep."

"Yes, I think we'd better," Margaret said nervously. "But please don't let us break up the party. Please."

Vic blinked across the room at Debbie, shaking his head dolefully, but Debbie only shrugged, and was about to say mechanically, "But it's only nine. You don't really have to go so early. Won't you stay a little longer?" But it never came out. The Halliwells put on their coats, shook hands and left. They said they'd had a lovely time, that the meal was charming, and Debbie said she was so glad they could come.

As soon as the Halliwells left, Debbie got David to bed, and by the time she returned the card game was started.

"Poor Johnny," Redge said in a lull. "He ought to be back in Bombay. Things were simpler there. Never had much of a telephone service and nobody gave a damn. He's a young chap really. Inexperienced. Five years younger than I, and yet . . ."

"Oh, I'd never have thought that," Debbie said. She was purring as she knew Vic would like. "He looks older and he *acts* much older."

"That's the point," Redge said, very pleased, "the precise point I was going to make. He's young, but he has such old-fashioned ideas. Typical fellow out here. Lower middle class. Never went to a decent school, poor fellow. He still believes in there being only two kinds of people in the world—Englishmen and colonials. It's kind of a religion with him. He's a character who might have stepped out of W. S. Gilbert. He thinks you've got to give him credit, for he is an Englishman. Plays a terrible game of tennis too, doesn't he, Vic?"

"Oh, I don't know," Vic said, "with a little practice—"

"Come off it, Vic. You don't have to be cautious about Johnny Halliwell with me. That's one of the nice things about Vic and me. We don't have to be forever stuffing each other full of nonsense. We work together for the team, and as the captain of the team I'm saying John Halliwell never should have come out here. I feel I can be that frank."

There was a pause and only the snap of cards and then Karl's voice, thickly. "Good ol' Vic, good ol' teammate, ol' boy, ol' boy."

Karl swallowed his drink between words. "This—intrigues me—this business of everyone working on the same ol' team, Redge. What team's that?"

There was an uncomfortable little silence in the room.

"Why, the Telephone Department, old man," Redge said. "We're trying to give old Jerusalem the best telephone service in this part of the world. And we'll do it too. We've got quite an expansion program. Vic and I are working on the project together, hand in glove so to speak. Of course, everyone's trying to get new phones, but at the moment there's just not enough material and equipment to go round. We're working on a preferential system for the time being. We give new service to the most essential places first. That's one of Vic's big jobs now. He gets the phones in, processes all the applications and I have to dig up the material for him somehow. I've absolute confidence in him and I hope he has in me."

"Of course I have," Vic said.

"Why, Vic," Karl said, "you're a better man t'know than a policeman. Could you get me a phone 'f I were to ask?"

"You have a phone."

"But 'f I didn't."

"I suppose I could, but you wouldn't rate one."

"Oh, Vic's conscientious. That's why I never need to worry about him," Redge said. "We've got it all worked out. The way the Ministry sees it if there should be any trouble—street fighting, that sort of thing, the places that need service are hospitals, schools, places of public assembly, doctors' offices and such spots. Very sound, I think. It's all worked out. We're getting service to the right places."

"So Vic decides who gets service and who doesn't?" Karl said. "Well how a-bout *that!*" He shook his head as though he were highly impressed.

"Well," Redge said, "within the limits of our directives. And I see that he gets the stuff to do the job. That's a chore in itself. Scrounge and scrape."

"Big job," Karl said. "Didn't know you were such a big wheel."

"Oh, I have my lines out," Vic said vaguely.

"So I imagine," Karl said just as vaguely, then added, "This better be our last rubber, Lil. We have to be running along."

"But Karl! You can't. It's not even ten yet."

"Sorry," Karl said, "I have to be out at six. My bus is calling."

"Karl, don't ruin my nice party."

There was silence again and Karl said lightly, "I'm not ruining it, Debbie. Not a-tall. If things get dull, you can talk 'bout us, and that should be fascinating. Because you're all on the same team."

"Karl!" Debbie was pleading.

"May I say something?" Karl said thickly. "I prob'ly sound stupid an' I 'pologize. But I wouldn't swear you people right here aren't the only hope of this funny li'l country, and th' poor li'l world too, f'that matter. Folks who can get along. Music lovers. Civilized human beings. Me, I'm not interested in bein' polite 'r telephones 'r music 'r ballet. You know what I am? Deep down? I'm a Moses man myself. That's it. I'm a Moses man. Out of the wilderness to the Promised Land. This nice li'l Promised Land. Pretty stupid, I guess, eh? You folks here, the Marmoreks and the Walkers, maybe you're the big fat hope of the future—you and your teamwork. But I'm damn' if I think so!" He was passing the piano and smashed a terrifying chord.

"Be careful going home, Karl," Vic said. "You've had quite a bit to drink."

"May I say something, Vic, kid?" Karl said. "G'night, ol' teammate!"

The Walkers and the Marmoreks played bridge until eleven o'clock, and the evening ended in hushed good-byes to keep from waking David.

Debbie and Vic undressed quietly for bed.

"At least no one broke furniture," Vic said. He didn't say he had told her so, nor did she expect him to.

"It was like a military formation," Debbie said laughing. "Each couple marched out on schedule. Margaret backs John Halliwell to the hilt. Terrified of him, of course. Yes, dear, let's go. Hup! Enid and Redge see so eye to eye on everything and so do Karl and Lilith. Do you think living together does that to people?"

"I'm sure to them we seem to agree with each other on everything," Vic said.

"Yes, of course, I see what you mean," Debbie said, "they probably don't see things any more alike than we do. They're just too lazy and too polite to fight each other. Like us."

"At least before strangers," Vic said.

"I feel pretty lazy and polite myself tonight," Debbie said, "but may I make a suggestion?" Vic said nothing and she continued. "Get out of the Telephone Office, Vic. Get some other job."

"I can't," he said, "not any more."

Twenty-two

As time went on, Vic's work became more and more demanding; he was often at the office or on field missions all night. When he did get home, he was fidgety, preoccupied or exhausted. But to David's intense pleasure, in spite of all his work Vic now for some reason took a great interest in David's progress on the concertina, and made it a point always to be at home during his lessons on Wednesday afternoons. After each lesson Maestro Sam Pearlman stayed for a cigarette and brandy with Vic and they talked, Vic said, about music and politics.

On several occasions, before full-scale war started, Vic took David down to the "Y" for tennis lessons, together with Enid and Lloyd.

In Debbie's own work she developed a new intensity. The little ceremony at which she was capped by Elsa Schumacher gave her satisfaction and fulfillment. Although she spent most of her time at the hospital, when she was off duty she felt entitled to flightiness. Now in her spare time she loved playing the new spinet on which she learned all the latest French and American tunes. She bought gay cottons which she wore jauntily, and made Vic take her dancing. She was barely able to manage a politely cheerful interest in David's and Vic's affairs, any more than they could be absorbed with what was happening at the hospital. Each member of the family had his own focal center; in a sense the family was flying off in fragments.

There were, however, compensations for this fragmentation. The Marmoreks had achieved a new and undeniable prestige, gratifying to Vic, pleasant to David, and nostalgic to Debbie—it reminded her of Mama, Papa and Lindenhouse. Vic was known by the neighbors and shopkeepers as an influential technician with the Administration; she was the pretty nurse at Hadassah; everyone knew they had a washing machine, a spinet and a console radio; even David had a reputation as an expert on his concertina and the two-wheel bike. In short they were an Important Family in Gaza Road.

One February evening Debbie came home after an exhausting day of nursing Elsa, who had come down with a bad case of virus pneumonia. "Come back, come back soon, Deborah," Elsa had whispered. "I'll die without you." And because Dick Alpert said Elsa had only a fifty-fifty chance, she promised to come back after dinner.

Vic and David were sitting at the piano, Vic picking out "Du, Du, Liebst Mir im Herzen" with one finger and both of them singing full blast.

She hugged David, and gave Vic a quick kiss. "You taste like whisky and soda," she said, her words tumbling over each other, "or are you cultivating bourbon and plain water?"

"Today," Vic said deliberately, in an entirely contrasting tempo, "today I had three Scotches and I needed them all. I not only needed them, but I was entitled to them."

"Good," she said. "Excuse me, honey, but I really do have to brighten myself up. I'm a mess. I have to rush through dinner, isn't that bad luck? I'm terribly sorry, hon, but I have to go back tonight. Tani! Tani!" She was in the bathroom, washing and calling toward the kitchen.

Vic followed and wheeled her round, her hands and face dripping, and looked at her almost sternly, but his voice was pleading. "Not tonight, Deb, any other night, but not tonight. We've got big news, David and I, don't we, old chap?"

"Really?" She slowed down to catch her breath, and dried her hands. "Well, that sounds fascinating. Tell me!"

"We'll start with David," Vic said, and he put an arm over David's shoulder and stood beside him as if they were having their picture taken. "Today you're the proud mother not only of a great scholar, a great soccer player, a great bicycle rider, and a great musician, you are also the mother of the President of the Second Grade of the Rehavia School!"

She was delighted. "How wonderful! Class president! It was always my secret ambition, but I could never be elected . . . Why, I'm so glad, I'm so proud! Remember, dear, how we used to sing—'When David grows up he can become . . .' "

"Chancellor or king," they sang out together. David laughed sheepishly at the babyishness of the chant and decided to show his new grownup attitude. "Well, I'll start off as president," he said. "That's a good beginning anyway."

"A sensible approach," Vic said. "Start at the top and work your way up. Which reminds me of me. Not that I'm class president, but I thought that you'd be interested to know that Ben Kronstein is being transferred to Tel Aviv. Personally I suspect he's being kicked out of Jerusalem. Tossed upstairs. Typical British technique, y'know."

He was being casual, but Debbie sat down abruptly. "Not really, but poor Ben! Why, what'll he do? That's an awful thing for him. Awful! His friends are all here. And what will Wilhelmina do? Both their daughters are here, grandchildren and all. And you always said how hard he worked. Whatever happened?"

"I guess he just wasn't the kind of chap that could get along with Halliwell and Redge Walker. If you ask me, he was driving them mad, nothing more. He can be quite a nag, you know, and the way he's been carrying on, you'd think Redge blew up the newspaper building with his own private stick of dynamite. Ben's all principle and no heart. You can smell his terrorist's mind—like a damned old schoolmaster, without human frailty. An inflexible old fussbudget, that's Ben."

"But how can they do it? Why, they could do the same thing to you! And just as easily. It's really creepy; it's frightening, Vic!"

"They could, but of course they won't. I just had a little old talk with little old Redge before I left the office. Matter of fact we went down to the little old King David together. That's why I needed the drink. Who do you think's moving into Ben's spot?"

"Don't tell me," Debbie said, now mocking bitterly. "Make me guess."

"You really could have blown me over, most unexpected thing!" Vic was ignoring her attitude. "So you see why I thought it was kind of a special night. Thought maybe we'd go out on the town. Have supper at the King David. After all, how often do we get such a fine excuse for a party? And David ought to come along. He's the real celebrity!"

"Vic, I'd love to, but not tonight. I really have to go back to the hospital. Maybe tomorrow, if Elsa's better. Or why don't you and David go out together? Tani can fix me a sandwich. You two men ought to . . ."

Vic's eyes flashed in anger. "By God, you don't really give a damn, do you? Doesn't mean a thing to you. You realize this gives us over six hundred pounds a year more and a hell of a lot more prestige? And for your information I'll do a damn sight better job than Kronstein ever did. I can give Jerusalem a telephone system like Zurich's or New York's for that matter. I can get the appropriations where Ben couldn't. It's got so I can twist Redge Walker around my finger. With me nudging him, he'll come back with a capital budget that'll give us a chance to do a decent job. I can do a job, Deb."

"I'm sure you will, dear, and I'd love to celebrate with you tonight, but Elsa's a sick woman. Dick Alpert's worried about her, and I promised her I'd come back."

Vic and David went alone to the King David. There they ran into Enid having supper with Lloyd, and joined them. Redge was off to Tel Aviv on Telephone Office business, so the four of them celebrated Vic's promotion as best they could.

David and Lloyd went off to the movies together and on their way back they saw a man shot on Jaffa Road, not fifty feet away, by a sniper from the Old City. They ran the entire distance to the hotel, Lloyd screaming hysterically all the way, and David flushed with worry.

Debbie was furious when she heard about it. The man who was shot had been brought into the hospital dead on arrival. "You worry so about my going up to the Scopus and you let David run about the streets at night alone. Whatever could you have been thinking?"

"It's such a short walk," Vic apologized. "I never gave it a thought. And after all Enid let Lloyd go. They pestered the life out of us."

She was silent for a while to let her anger subside. A drink made her feel better.

"Whatever in the world did you and Enid find to do all evening?" she asked amiably.

"Danced," Vic said. "Listened to that awful four-piece orchestra. Had a few drinks. Enid's not a bad dancer."

"She's pretty good at almost everything, isn't she?" Debbie said in her highest voice, and Vic laughed.

"You're not kidding," Vic agreed. "With a man less iron willed than I she could be dangerous."

"My hero," she said, and pounded his chest with harmless little blows. "That's just for thinking." And she kissed him hard; she was a little more uncertain about him than she could admit. And Vic was everything. She mustn't forget it. She was even sorry that she had snapped at him about David. She had to learn to control even justifiable outbursts.

Twenty-three

Only five days after the sniping incident there was a new outrage in the city—an explosion in the Officers' Club. All of downtown Jerusalem was cordoned off and people were arrested in large groups and at random; Debbie kept David home from school and let him play only in the courtyard. She herself needed a special pass to get to the Scopus. And for two days there was no sign of Vic. He was tight lipped and serious when at last he trudged home. "By God," he stormed, "you'd think *I* threw the damn bomb. Couldn't even ring you up."

Debbie had been anxious as a cat but she said, "We weren't worried. Anyone who was anybody was arrested at least once and we knew phone service was cut off. I had trouble getting to the hospital myself. I assumed you'd have Redge get you out of the local pokey."

Vic was annoyed. "I can't figure that man. I sent him half a dozen messages, gave his name to the lieutenant. I'm sure they must have got in touch with him. Just letting me sit in that Godforsaken trap—not more than a hundred yards from my own office. Sitting and waiting and waiting. I got damn fed up with it and sent a note over to Enid at the hotel and that finally got some action. Redge apologized like mad, swore he hadn't got any of my messages, said he'd been wondering where I was." Vic shrugged. "Maybe."

He pulled his clothes off angrily. "I itch all over. I've really gone soft, you know. Need a bath every day or I itch. Sometimes when I think how we lived in Rome I can't believe it. You know, these British chaps here are behaving rather poorly the last couple of days. Great Britain—cricket—fair play. Ha, who're they ribbing?"

Debbie said, "It's your team, love, remember?"

Vic scowled and turned on the bath, standing in his shorts and undershirt, shouting over the running water. "Now, Deb, let's not, shall we? I guess it's pretty hard on them, after all, hard on even their top brass to restrain themselves. Some of their own buddies killed in cold blood for no damn good reason."

"Perhaps you're right," she said, calling above the bath water. She'd just left a Tommy on the Scopus, who'd died—Timothy Cunningham, a younger version of Vic. Reminded her of Vic in so many ways. Cursed the Jews up and down for a couple of hours, bleeding from the mouth all the while. Then he said well, maybe they aren't all such terrible bastards if they include a nice girl like you. Now wasn't that a pretty compliment? And he made her promise to have a drink with him when he got well. About midnight his fever had run way up, over a hundred and five. They gave him five transfusions. He became garrulous, talked about the place near the square in his home town, where the children still go for pony rides and it sounded a bit like old Stadt Park. And how his mother used to give him a shilling every Sunday afternoon for candy and a pony ride there. He'd told her about his sister and a baby brother almost ten years younger, and the house he'd left, part of a row, but with flowers behind it, and he'd said, "What the devil am I doing in this hospital? I'm from *Manchester*. I could almost understand it during the war, living in the bloody desert, in and out of Tobruk, Benghazi, and those blooming tramp towns. There were great villains abroad in those days. Herr Hitler, Limited. His blokes were out to get us, okay, I could get that through my poor nut. But we're not fighting here and we're not having any fun, just sitting around getting killed and killing. Scared to death and taking it out on blokes who're more scared than we are. Nobody likes us and they don't even really hate us." Well he was entitled to that illusion. "So tell me, sweet nurse, what am I doing up here in this Jew hospital on Mt. Scopus? *What the bloody hell am I doing here?* I'm from *Manchester*. And don't tell me about Richard the Lion-Hearted. Because I'm Timothy Cunningham, the chicken-hearted. I wish to God I was back on dear old Roseberry Road." He took her hand as if he were going somewhere and needed someone to walk with him and he asked her where she was from. She told him and he said, "Don't you wish to God you were back in Vienna right now?" and she said, "No, I'm glad I'm right here. I don't want to go back to Vienna again." He just lay back for a little while, very weak by that time. Must have been an awful strain for him to talk. But he said, "How stupid of me. I keep forgetting you're a bloody Jew. Still why *shouldn't* you go back to Vienna? That's where you were a kid, isn't it, that's where you remember the wonderful days when you were a kid. Don't you have as much right there as anyone? Don't you have more right *there* than I have *here*? Or even than *you* have here?" Oh, he was keen, his brain was as sharp as a razor. And he went on like that to the moment he died, arguing and making reasoned debates, that's why he reminded her so of Vic.

She was shaking her head from side to side with eyes closed, trying to rid her memory of that English boy. She was out of breath and swallowed hard as if to clear her throat for further use.

"The British'll never leave, never leave, never," Vic was saying. "Not UNO, not America, not anyone will get 'em to pack up. Bevin'll talk pretty but they'll never go."

Debbie answered, and she was shocked by her own words, and by her voice, which was set and harsh. "They'll leave when we've killed enough Tim Cunninghams."

Vic said, "It's not decent, by God. Suppose there were an explosion in an officers' club in Devonshire, sure they'd arrest suspects, they'd search, but damn it, they wouldn't haul people off the streets indiscriminately and they wouldn't declare martial law and cut off all the telephones and stop the mails in all of England and put the whole place to sleep, would they? They're trying to outdo the Nazis. Reprisals, hostages. Someone ought to point it out to 'em."

Debbie said, "Are you really as surprised as you look?"

"At the British, yes I am. It's wrong, all wrong. If there's an explosion, let 'em find the guilty men who caused it. This sort of thing's a stinking crime against us and it's a crime against themselves." Vic looked funny declaiming above the roar of the running water, now stark naked, with one foot tentatively in the water, feeling its temperature.

She swung her small hand and smacked Victor square on the backside with a resounding sharp crack and said, "Honey! *You* said it this time, not me. Bless your heart!"

"Get out, and don't dare come back here, wench!" Vic cried. "You've destroyed me."

He kicked water from the tub at her and she screeched and dashed out of the bathroom, and the spray hit David full in the face. The force of it made him gasp and Vic laughed. "David, old chap, tell me, what would you do if your old man became a soldier?"

"Could you get killed?" David looked down on his father lying comfortably in the tub. He wanted to get things straight.

"God, I hope not, that wouldn't be my plan. But I guess that's what I'll have to think over."

"Also it depends on which army," David said. "If you went in our army it would be fine, as long as you didn't get killed. But if, say, you got just an arm off or a leg off, that wouldn't be so bad." He noted the incredulous look on his father's face. "Would it?" he asked doubtfully. "It wouldn't be *too* bad, would it? Of course it wouldn't be good." Vic laughed.

"What army are you going in?" David persisted.

"Why, you little devil. So that's what you think of me. Do I look like an Englishman?"

"Well," David said solemnly, "my best friend in school, Tuvia Aleman, says you're an English stooge. I have to smack a lot of people lately. After all he's my best friend."

"I thought René Blum and Meyer Van Bern were your best friends."

"Well, now that I smacked Tuvia he's my best friend, too," David said solemnly.

"I see," Vic said. "Well, if it makes you feel any better I'm not joining the British Army, not even as a stooge. And if anyone says so you keep right on smacking 'em."

David felt better.

"But if I were to join Haganah, you think it would be okay as long as I lost only an arm or a leg? I must say, you're quite a sport with my arms or legs."

"Well," David said judiciously, "it could be worse."

"I'll think it over," Vic said.

Twenty-four

For seventeen days the city stood still and most people left their homes for only three hours a day. When martial law was lifted, the calm was dangerous. Trouble stirred the streets; even children were beginning to look over their shoulders. Barbed wire and sandbags were everywhere. The *Palestine Post* not only reported recurrent shootings and stabbings, skirmishes and explosions which rocked the city and which all Jerusalemites could plainly see or hear for themselves; but also made quite a hubbub over an impending visit by a number of gentlemen from the other side of the world—from a place optimistically called Lake Success, headquarters of the UNO. They were coming to settle the matter of Jerusalem and Palestine once and for all. Skeptics, including Vic, said nothing would be settled, but all, including the skeptics, were expectant and nervous.

When in June the men from Lake Success arrived, the police and military were in greater evidence than usual; and each evening the family, including Tani who now considered herself a member, listened avidly while the radio's Voice of the Defender reported the testimony, the pleas and lies, the eloquence and filth which were being aimed each day at the eardrums of the men of the UN. Debbie and David walked down to the "Y" one evening to see these men for themselves and watched with great satisfaction as the shining enormous black Chrysler flying the blue banner of the United Nations drove through the curious crowd to the entrance; but they were let down when four unusually ordinary mortal men, each carrying his own ordinary briefcase, came slumping down the steps in the afternoon heat and crawled into the great car. Could these really be the men? She didn't know what she could have expected, of course. Giants, probably. Purple robes, scepters, shining swords. She was as childish as David.

June and July were over and the committee went home to Lake Success, leaving behind bitter Arabs and Englishmen, disgruntled Jews, Moslems and Christians. The men of the Mufti broadcast wild appeals, calling down the curses of Allah upon the Jews, and followed with fights and riots in the streets, resulting always more frequently in bloodshed; tight-mouthed Jews torn with worry, and without illusions, went grimly about their daily business.

Huddled Arabs, optimistic but uncommunicative, drew more to themselves, and a truculent British soldiery scowled and, to cover uneasiness, made preparations, but precisely what for even their officers could not tell them.

It was in December that Vic made his final decision. In November, Vic, like everyone in Palestine, stayed close to the radio to hear what was happening and what final judgments were being made six thousand miles west by the men who had sat in the YMCA. Vic said nothing. He sat and listened passively with the others, but he was gloomy.

The living room was full; not only Tani and Karl and Lilith were there, but also Sam Pearlman, the Epsteins from across the way, Dr. Alpert and Elsa Schumacher from the hospital; an American friend of Dr. Alpert, Ben Kronstein (who had not gone to Tel Aviv after all, but had taken a position with the Electric corporation) and his wife Willie, who had brought her inevitable cookies for David.

The radio was static ridden, but most of it could be heard clearly over the shortwave, despite the sudden increases and decreases in volume, the roar of ocean over which the words were flying. It was very late, but no one suggested to David that he go to bed. Speeches were being made by spokesmen for Arab states. Speeches of threats and violence. At every word, the looks of hatred and fear on the faces in the room grew more intense. Only Vic looked calm. At last a voice spoke in English. "The chair now calls for the vote." This was the world speaking. The world was settling the matter of Palestine.

"Argentina . . . Yes . . . Australia . . . Yes . . . China . . . Yes . . . Egypt . . . No . . . France . . . Yes . . . Lebanon . . . No . . . Union of Soviet Socialist Republics . . . Yes . . . United Kingdom . . . Abstain . . . United States of America . . . Yes . . ."

It was a tedious, monotonous business, but to this assemblage it was the edge of a razor. Lilith had a pad and wrote as each name and vote was called. The world voted; and the vote was Yes. Thirty-three Yeses. The Jews will have a country. This was the meaning of the vote. The Jews will have a country—without British soldiers, without a landlord; they were to have a country of their own. This was the decree of the world.

Willie Kronstein broke down and wept. Her ample body shook with sobs. David was distraught to see a middle-aged woman racked over words the radio had spoken. Lilith and Karl took hands and then embraced and kissed solemnly. Ben Kronstein repeated over and over, "Two thousand years I waited for this." Debbie danced about like a moth filling everyone's glass with liquor and kissing nearly everyone, even embracing Tani. When she came to David she was mock angry.

"David, look at the time! You devil, you've just been quiet so I wouldn't notice you."

David grinned. "Will the British go away now, Mom? Will the Arabs stop shooting now?"

She poured soda into a glass and a few drops of whisky and handed it solemnly to David. "This is a night to celebrate!" As she had said the night the British came to Rome.

Vic said morosely to the assemblage, "You can make a child with love, can't you, that's the recommended method, but you can also conceive one by cold-blooded rape and sin. Do you suppose countries are conceived by the same methods?" He snapped off the radio over which the announcer was still babbling excitedly. "From what I heard, there was mighty little loving in the proceedings tonight. But the seed's been planted, and did you hear those Arabs screaming rape? Well, it should take nine months for the baby to come to term; that would make it . . ." he counted on his fingers . . . "August. I hope we live to see it."

He turned to David. "Come along, old chap, put on your coat. You and I are going down to the Agency and see how people behave when they've been given a cup of hemlock to drink and think it's a cherry fizz."

Lilith said, "Oh, you're horrid, absolutely, Vic, but then in a way I see what you mean, of course. And you're absolutely right. It's going to be tough, but we can take it, can't we, Karl? And you can too, Vic, only you're too stubborn to admit it. Personally I think you have more courage than most of us."

Vic bowed to Lilith elaborately. "Thank you."

"He has," Sam Pearlman said quietly, and Debbie looked sharply at him, trying to fathom what he meant, but the music teacher was blank-faced.

Vic put an arm over Lil's shoulder. "I'm going down to the Agency with David. I think he should see this historic occasion. Anybody else want to join us?"

They all went and so did everyone else in Jerusalem. Outside the Agency Vic lifted David high above his head. "You see him? There he is! Ben-Gurion!" A cry went up from the crowd in the courtyard to their leader. He spoke briefly and waved, but they heard nothing over the tumult. There was the same wildness of the night in Rome, but with a difference. In Rome everyone had been relieved. In Jerusalem everyone was worried sick. As the crowd broke up and they all marched through the dark streets of the Rehavia quarter, David clung to his father as he had when they had left the ship.

Two weeks later Vic returned home ashen, his jaw set and his usually placid face strained and lined with anxiety. He was out of breath as if he had run all the way from the office, and when he came into the house he spoke barely a word to either Debbie or David. He washed in silence and ate in silence, preoccupied and not listening to the comments addressed to him. The strain at the table grew until she and David stopped talking altogether; only Tani's footsteps and the clicking of silver as they ate made sounds in the room. Debbie said again, "What is it, honey? What's the trouble?"

Vic's sarcasm was not directed at her. "Trouble? Why I can't imagine what you mean. Of course, seven armies are getting ready to march on Jerusalem. People being shot in the streets. This morning some old guy came to the Post Office to mail a letter, and on his way out I saw six Arabs jump him and beat him into a bloody dead mess in less than ten seconds, and disappear into thin air behind Barclay's. When it was over a few Haganah boys came up on the double. They were arrested, of course, by two impartial constables. Saw it all from my office window. But is any of that trouble? Of course not. What's it got to do with us?"

"I know, it's awful."

"Awful," Vic said. "Awful. I'm glad to see you deplore the whole business. Too bad, life must go on. Stiff upper lip. Well, it's not my dish of tea. I'd prefer a little peace and quiet."

"Well, what's there to do? We can only hope for the best." She tried to sound soothing and hide her impatience.

"Listen to me," Vic said as though she were a child. "Have you ever looked at a map? Have you looked to see where Jerusalem really *is*? Do you know there's one little road between here and the rest of Palestine? A winding twisting path, round and up, like the red stripe on a barber pole? And all along that road are Arab towns—Ramle and Latrun, Ramallah, Kastel. All the other roads to Jerusalem are highways for Arab armies. Do you realize what the military situation is, in this God-forsaken city of peace?"

"Well," Debbie said, "what's there to do? We can only hope . . ."

"It's a ghetto!" Vic shouted. "But not just a little old local ghetto. This is the *world's* great big fat ghetto. At last they've got us all in one nice convenient place. And now they're getting the ax ready. Lovely. The Arabs know it's coming. They're leaving town. We're surrounded now, outnumbered fifty to one. They have tanks, divisions, generals. Artillery. Planes. And what have we got? Haganah! Etzel! The Stern Gang! All armed to the teeth with screw-drivers and kitchen knives."

"But everything may work out fine," Debbie pleaded, her insides quaking. "I don't think it'll ever come to that."

Vic turned angrily on her. "I looked out of my window this afternoon and what I saw in the street was an uncontrollable mob of Arabs. They were half-crazy. I never saw anything like it. It was like Vienna must have been, only worse, much worse. Because this mob was literally sick. Not just sick in the mind like the Nazis. But you know how they are, men with running sores and filthy galbiehs and keffiyahs, chewing that ghastly pitah—they've got pellagra and rickets, they're blind, lame, syphilitic and tubercular, and for all I know leprous, staggering around in rags and filth. Not a pair of shoes in ten. And what were they calling for? What did they want? Bread? Shoes? Medicine? Books? No ma'am, they were screaming for blood! And whose do you think they want? Well, mine would be satisfactory if it were handy. Or yours. They're not particular. They were spitting and screaming and shaking their fists up at the Generali Building like maniacs. And when these pitiful creatures get loose, they're going to find blood. Somehow. There'll be no way to stop them. Their need is just that great. Nothing's going to work out fine, Deb, believe me." He covered his face as if he were trying to rub everything out of his mind, and go to sleep. "When I saw that mob, I got out of my office. I went downstairs and left the building through the Jaffa Road side. And I did something I've never done before, not in Prague or Rome or anywhere. I ran." There was a distant explosion from the south to which none of them paid any attention. They were accustomed to the sounds.

"I ran all the way to the King David. I wanted to see Redge, just to talk to him—to reassure myself about the human race, to see if I'm still a member of it, after hearing those Arabs howl. Well, John Halliwell has gone. He and Margaret have left town, checked out, on the way to Haifa and home. Redge was up in Katamon, but I saw Enid. She's upset. She kept saying they had to think of Lloyd and themselves and they had no part in this mess."

He pushed his coffee away with a sudden gesture and rose from his seat to pace nervously back and forth beside the table. For several minutes he walked in silence. "By God," he said quietly but with a depth of feeling that was different from the ranting, "we have no part of it either."

He spoke without bravura, without expecting a response. "In all this world there must be some place where we can live in peace."

Vic was standing directly behind her, but she talked straight ahead. "During the blitz there were mighty few places for an Englishman to go. And even in Berlin the Germans stayed and crawled and bled because there was no place for them to go but home. So . . ." She shrugged expressively.

"Germans!" Vic snorted. "Nobody else'd have the scum. But plenty of Englishmen went to America or got out into the country. We'll have to go to Tel Aviv, Debbie. This town's about to be cut off one hundred per cent. You see how rarely food convoys are coming through now? They'll be serving rats in the restaurants, like Leningrad, you'll see . . ."

She cut him short. "They have their problems in Tel Aviv too."

"Well, I've arranged for an armored car to take us out, day after tomorrow. We leave at six in the morning. Cost me a hundred and fifty pounds, which is a lot less than Martin Schroeder's passports, thank heavens. Pack light, only what we need and don't tell anyone we're going." He turned to David. "You either."

"I don't want to go," David said.

"Never mind what you want," his father said.

"All my friends are here. I don't know anyone in Tel Aviv."

Debbie said, "Vic, you're not serious?"

Vic stared at her in surprise. "What else is there to do?"

"You think I'm silly, don't you? But there's your job here, Vic. If trouble comes, you'll be needed more than ever. Telephones, golly. They're about as essential as you can get."

"Debbie, Debbie, do you understand what's happening?"

"I think so, Vic, but we couldn't. We don't know a soul in Tel Aviv except Lil's sister. And we scarcely know her. Darling, listen . . . darling . . ." She could find no way to break through to him, to tell him how they were changed. "This flat's our city home and country home, Vic, winter and summer home. We have to take care of it. It's all we have."

He stood at the far end of the table and loomed large as his voice boomed like a cannon across the room. "I'll tell you all we have! I have you and you have me and we have David, and that's the beginning and the end. As far as I'm concerned it's the whole story. Our friends . . . the accidents of geography . . . how to be a good citizen . . . duty . . . Talk, talk, talk. I'm not interested. The time's come to do something. And whenever it's time to *do* something, to decide, who has to do it? Have you ever? Isn't it always 'Whatever you say, Vic'? Well, let me tell you, it's a Goddamn lonely thing to have to do. To be out front. Oh, how I'd love to have someone tell me, do this, do that! Printed instructions on how to behave in an air raid. Proceed to nearest shelter. All neatly printed. Walk, don't run. It's nice to be a child. Someone to take care of me, oh, what I'd give for that! Look at me like that all you want! After all, you're here. It's 1948 and you're alive. We've got David here, and we've had a little happy time. We've done all right, haven't we? *You* took the profits, too. So let's do what I say and not make it harder for everyone. Day after tomorrow, six in the morning, the sergeant guarantees a safe trip."

Vic was trembling when he finished and walked away into the bedroom.

She threw her napkin on the table and went after him. David stood in the doorway and Tani escaped into the kitchen.

She was in Vic's arms now and speaking against his shirt so that her voice was muffled and almost unintelligible. "We could stay a little longer, Vic, couldn't we? Please, darling. It's not so bad really. *This is our very last place in the whole entire world, Vic.* They need me at the hospital, they really do. And they need you. Even more than me. We owe that much, don't we? They've given us a home, Vic. I know how you've carried the whole load. Since way back when I was David's age. Hard to imagine, Vic, isn't it now? It seems like another century. I've always done what you said, and not even for someone else, the way you did, but only to save myself. Oh, I've been so much worse than you. You can't compare me to you in the same breath, darling, and you know it. I started running before you ever thought of it. But when I touched the beach in Haifa that horrible night I promised myself one thing: my running days were over. No more tourism. No more racing about. Golly, I must sound provincial and silly, and I wouldn't tell another soul, but do you know, Vic, I feel almost brave now? I'm nervous as a cat, of course, but I'd like to stay a speck longer. Elsa'd be cross as a stick if I left, and I think they'd *die* if you did. Especially with John gone and Redge thinking of it. Why, you're all the Telephone Office has, Vic!"

Vic's arms were warm and protective around her. She felt so small, but his voice was uncertain as he talked softly to her. "I've been all over the city. I know every Haganah headquarters and sub-headquarters. I know where they're making armored cars out of old taxis, with steel that's only plywood. I've been to the Brandeis School, where kids of fourteen are making rifle parts and repairing Sten guns. I was hoping there was a chance. Hoping to find courage. Hoping to find hope. But what *did* I find? Those damn few Sten guns and a handful of Molotov cocktails and home-made grenades and oh yes, pistols. There's a marvelous weapon of modern warfare in this atomic age. Pistols. I know everything Haganah has better than any man who's actually in it. Every place of the slightest importance has telephone service. And I'm the man who got it for them. I've been everywhere, and, believe me, Debbie, it's a hopeless mess. If there were a chance in a hundred, even a chance in a million."

She buried her head on his breast and shook her head stubbornly like an obstinate child. "They're so short of nurses at the hospital. Doctors, too. Most of the time I find myself doing a doctor's job. And the worse it gets the more they need me. Really I'm not trying to be a noble soul, Vic, but we're so short, how can we leave them?"

"Then perhaps I'd better take David to Tel Aviv."

"No."

Her face became horribly distorted and she tried to cry, but couldn't do it, it was physically impossible for her to cry. "Don't go, Vic, please Vic, don't." She found it hard to say any more. "Even if you do, I'm going to stay."

Vic turned on David. "And you want to stay here too?"

David, who was proud his father should ask him at all, said, "My friends are here, I have a girl. You know about Tamar."

There was a moment of indecision and then Vic seemed to give up quite suddenly. "Okay," he said. "That takes the cake. An eight-year-old's romance. I gave that Tommy a fifty-pound deposit and there's a fat chance of getting that back." He reached for the phone and lifted the receiver. "I'll get hold of Sam Pearlman."

"What for?"

"Maestro Sam," Vic said, "is a big man in some circles. I've been doing certain work for him—I'm in this deeper than you think, you see. Well, I told him this morning to make some other arrangements to continue the work. That I might be leaving. I'll have to tell him I'm staying now."

Suddenly he spoke into the phone. "Sam? Listen, I'm staying, Sam. I've made up my mind . . . I'm rather glad myself. Matter of fact, it's a kind of relief. Where? Yes I have it. Yes of course. I'll see you Wednesday."

So that was it. David, too, looked at his father in wonder for at this moment he knew his father had all this time been a fighter of Haganah. Soldier of the Jews. A defender of the people. He had not been mistaken, his father was a great man. He ran downstairs and took his bicycle from the hall and started down Gaza Road to the commercial center. He knew that he was strictly forbidden to do this, but something impelled him. He rode up Gaza Road toward the hills. The wind blew in his face, the cold December wind and thunder threatened and great streaks of lightning lit the road, but David rode faster than wind, ringing his handlebar bell so that everyone might hear him.

Twenty-five

The winter days in Jerusalem were cheerless ones for them all. Her own melancholia induced by the cold and rain, the continuous sniping and killing, and the endless work was aggravated by the fact that Vic seemed more than ordinarily wretched and disturbed. Many nights he was not home at all, working at the office, he said, until morning. She suspected he was doing something for Haganah. And on one occasion he came home fuming and furious at something Redge had given him to do at home: he had to spend two successive nights transcribing and typing on his portable, long lists from notes he had made at the office. "That man Redge," he muttered, "ought to think straight. If they're leaving, why don't they just go and leave us in peace instead of dreaming up these damn fool errands that kill time? Or maybe they're not going to leave. It's tough to know where you stand these days."

She never remembered seeing him so bitterly confused and troubled. Then for a week he was not home a single night. She wondered how he could go on without sleep.

And none of their spirits were helped by the endless funeral processions in the streets these days, rain or shine, heading from Bikur Holim Hospital to the Mount of Olives Cemetery, one crowd of mourners following another, winding through the streets on foot with bare coffins aloft on shoulders, each group spearheaded by old men, followed by stooped crones, who trudged stony-faced to the cemetery. Occasionally these processions were fired upon and fresh corpses created for new funerals.

One day in February Vic, after a two-day absence, returned with a briefcase bulging strangely. Debbie had arrived only a few minutes earlier and turned now from her frenzied hello to David to an even more frantic embrace with Vic. She felt her nerves at her fingertips, from overwork and anxiety. Everything she said or did was with tremendous, exaggerated emotion. Tonight she was trying hard to be gayer than usual. They had caviar for dinner, and wine out of the tall, fancy rock crystal glasses, and the meal proceeded in a state of high ceremony, as if it were some kind of celebration. She had no idea why she had arranged it that way, but the mood had taken her.

After dinner they sat and talked; she played the piano and Vic sang—old German songs, Italian and English songs, and wild Hebrew ballads that had such a different quality of melancholy abandon. David must have been speculating upon the methods of driving himself into the arena of this sudden warmth, and decided to attempt a handstand, which he had recently learned to do in school. "Ma, want to see me walk on my hands? Watch!"

Before his mother could answer he had somersaulted onto his hands and begun to navigate wildly across the living room from the piano toward the hall. With an uncontrolled swoop he tumbled against the table, and Vic's overloaded briefcase slipped off it toward the floor. Vic's voice was hoarse as he cried, "Look out!" and sprang forward to catch the briefcase before it hit the floor. He was white.

He opened the leather case and removed five grenades, which he examined carefully, and a pistol. "Of course," he said deliberately, "the pins are intact so nothing could have happened anyway." He was perspiring. "You must be careful, David, you'd look silly with your head off."

"Can I see your gun?" David shouted with great excitement, then remembered suddenly it had to be secret. He barely whispered, "Please can I just look at it for a minute. I won't shoot anyone."

Debbie smiled. She was shaken too, but she thought that was funny; Vic was as stern as ever. "You're not to touch it," he said. "Do you hear? And don't tell anyone I have it."

Vic said more lightly, "Eight years old is entirely too young for pistols. You'll have to wait till you're at least eleven."

Then he turned to her and in an aside which pushed David out of the inner circle again he said, "You should see some of the kids in my group. Some aren't fourteen. And they'll do anything. Boys and girls both."

Debbie said, "When I was fourteen my mother still wouldn't let me play with matches. She forbade me to go in the kitchen, I remember. The kitchen was for Paula. I remember it as if it were yesterday."

At the sudden and unexpected knock on the door David darted to the window and in the rain-washed street saw an armored car of the British Army parked at the front door. "Daddy," he called in a hoarse whisper. "Don't open the door. Look."

Vic gathered up the grenades deftly and carefully locked the brief-case before placing it on the floor of the guest closet. The revolver went behind three volumes on the book shelf. When the knock on the door was repeated, Debbie called, "Just a minute, I'm coming." Tani came out from the kitchen to answer the door, but Debbie motioned her back. After the last of the books had been replaced, she opened the door. But it was only Enid and Lloyd.

Enid said quickly, "I might as well tell you both, Debbie, I'm deso-late. I really don't know what to say. We're leaving. Lloyd and I, that is. Redge is staying a little longer. He's got to clean things up, he says. I haven't even been allowed to tell anyone. Honestly, I feel so awful about it too. Faithless in some way. We're to join a convoy in twenty minutes and get off for Haifa and day after tomorrow we sail for home."

Debbie sat down clumsily and abruptly. "Of course," she said. "I can understand."

Vic, who was paler than usual, shrugged as though the most normal thing in the world were happening. "Well," he said, "when a chap like me starts carrying around a revolver and grenades, it's time for sensible people to leave. I'm a terrible shot and I'm not the only one. No won-der the streets are dangerous."

Enid was not amused. "Vic, you're not!"

Debbie looked quickly at Lloyd and back to David. "Not actually, he's simply bragging."

"Of course, Redge carries one of those horrible things, but it really gives me the shudders." Enid walked to the closet and poured herself a drink. "Do you mind?" She took a long series of swallows as though she were quite thirsty. "Of course, Redge can do it, but you, Vic. If you were to be caught. They're so harsh these days. Especially with—well, you know. Really, it's not right, but then what can they do? They're trying so hard to bring people to their senses."

She was pacing back and forth now holding her glass before her with both hands as if she were studying it. "All our friends have gone mad.

Actually, quite mad. You. Moustapha. You've heard us talk about him. Nicest man, really, but *now*, honestly. Oh, the Arabs are really worse than you. And all that talk you hear in the lobby of the King David. People just seem determined on bloodshed and it's so senseless. Haven't we learned that?"

"Well, Enid dear," Debbie said kindly, "you'll soon be out of it."

"But that's just the trouble," Enid said, gulping the last of her drink and setting the glass down; perhaps too carefully. "I don't want to be out of it. I've friends here. Friends I adore. Like both of you and David. What will happen to you?"

"We'll manage," Debbie said. Enid sounded so sincere, but she could not quite believe her.

"Of course," Enid said. "Of course you'll manage. That isn't the point. Perhaps it's just that I feel like a coward running off. Really I don't want to, you know. Redge and I had a terrible row. He kept telling me I had to think of Lloyd and I suppose he's right. See here, would you let me take David to England with me? We'd take good care of him."

Everyone tried to adjust their minds to what Enid had said. For the moment they were too astonished to answer.

"Are you serious?"

"Yes, of course, Debbie. Of course I'm serious. I've thought about it a long time. During the blitz when Lloyd was less than two we sent him to America, some people we didn't know at all—relatives of friends of Redge in Boston and it was a blessing to us to know that he at least was safe. I've never forgot that blessing."

She sounded so eager David looked worried. Matters about him were being decided too quickly. Debbie could see a surge of protest rising in his throat.

"That would be so much trouble . . . How would he get along in England?"

"Oh," Enid said, "don't fuss about that. He and Lloyd get along and my neighbor at home has twin boys about their age. They'd get on splendidly."

"It's a thought," Vic said meditatively.

"But really," Debbie said. "How could we? He's so happy at the Rehavia School, all his friends . . ."

"In a way I'm being selfish," Enid said. "I don't want you to think it's a favor. I'm doing it for myself actually. David will be my sure link to you both. You *couldn't* throw me over if I had David and we'd have to come together as soon as everything's settled here. You see I'm afraid of losing you—both. I'm thirty-four years old. I've learned not to give up good friends lightly—wherever you find them."

Debbie was nonplused. David was confused and Lloyd was smiling rather foolishly. "Come along, Dave. It'll be great fun."

"Think it over. You mustn't decide now. I know it's a terribly difficult thing to do. Especially on such short notice. But—well, we do what we can these days. He can leave almost at once if you wish—tomorrow morning if possible. They have a convoy going through, before dawn. It's entirely irregular of course. But you can go see this man at the hotel. He'll make all the arrangements for you. They'll be leaving before six." She took a card from her purse. "Whittemore, very nice chap. Redge will introduce you. He knows all about it."

"I just don't know what to say. I—I'm overwhelmed."

"Would you like to come to England with us?" Enid said, finally addressing David. Quite obviously she expected no more than a polite answer.

"No," David blurted. "I don't think so. Thank you very much for asking me," David added quickly in the uneasy silence, remembering his manners.

"But why not?" Vic said impatiently.

"I just wouldn't go away. I just wouldn't."

He saw the hurt look in Enid's face and a sense of remorse overcame him. "I like Aunt Enid, but I have all my best friends here."

"You talk to him later," Enid said in a low voice to Vic. She belted her coat.

There was more fussing with clothing and finally from the street below the horn sounded impatiently.

"Bye-bye," Enid said abruptly. "Good luck." She embraced Debbie and kissed David and turned to Victor. "Good-bye, Vic," she said softly. Vic put his hands on her shoulders and looked at her for what seemed an embarrassingly long time. At last he kissed her. Perhaps the time seemed longer than it was. " 'Bye," she whispered. She gathered her purse and gloves, waved now to the three of them, and Debbie saw she was crying. She turned away quickly.

Karl and Lilith came over later; they argued long into the night over whether David should go. Debbie was torn, turning this way and that. She was so busy at the hospital, she had so little time to take care of him herself. Perhaps it would be better. After all, Enid could probably do more for him than Tani, which was the actual alternative. On the other hand, why was he any different from all the other boys in Jerusalem?

Vic felt he ought to go. In a way, he said, it was the greatest break they could have been given. It was wonderful of Enid to have thought of it. Really wonderful. There was nothing David could do to help in Jerusalem. He and Debbie had jobs to do and worrying about David would only make their jobs tougher. He reduced their efficiency. Karl's remarks were not helpful. He merely repeated, It's hard to tell other people what they ought to do. Even a sister. If he and Lilith had children perhaps they would understand the problem better. He must have said the same thing, almost the same words, a dozen times. And Lilith said that each of them was right, oh, absolutely right, absolutely. Slowly, reluctantly, they decided, almost without deciding, that he ought to go. At four-thirty she and Vic woke him and in the eerie morning took him to the King David. Vic carried the concertina and Debbie took a canvas overnight bag and David saw what they intended. "I don't want to go away," he pleaded.

Vic was kind, but firm. "England's beautiful. Everything's green. Gentle, smooth lawns and farms all through the countryside. I was there myself when I was on the Davis Cup team." Their steps echoed in the semi-darkness.

"I like it here," David maintained. "Who cares about lawns? I hate lawns, especially green lawns!"

Debbie said, "Don't you see, David, sweet, there's going to be trouble here. Maybe fighting, like war time. It'll be hard to get food. Maybe there won't be much water to drink. Just as soon as the trouble's over, you'll come home."

David retired to frustrated silence, afraid to say anything because he knew the effort of talking would lead him to tears and tears were not for him, not at his age. "I talk English with a terrible accent," he blurted out at last. "English people laugh at me. But I speak perfect Hebrew, as good as any *sabra*." Debbie felt herself crumbling, but Vic said, "That's nonsense. You'll speak perfect English in no time."

They were at the hotel and Redge and Mr. Whittemore were in the lobby. There were details of papers to sign and addresses to be exchanged as if they were enrolling him at school.

For so early an hour the lobby was remarkably crowded with officers and civilians. The wait seemed endless. She reminded David not to ask for gifts or favors, to remember his manners, his thank yous and pleases. At last the bellhop approached to speak in undertones to Mr. Whittemore and then motioned to Redge and to the Marmoreks.

In the carriageway at the hotel entrance there was an armored car like the one that had carried Lloyd away, but to David this khaki, graceless contraption in the early light must have seemed hateful, a rolling prison, without mother, without father, without friends (what would *they* say when they discovered he had fled, and to England of all places?), without Miss Even the beautiful. They were handing the concertina to the driver and Vic was putting the canvas overnight bag into the back seat. David knew, standing beside the armored car, how completely he was betrayed. He had waded through a cold sea in the darkest part of a November night, narrowly escaping drowning and bullets to get here, to reach this world, which during his babyhood was only the dream of a hopeful mother. "Someday, someday . . . we'll come home . . ." Well, he had got here, and nobody was driving off with him.

Abruptly he twisted loose from his father and darted across Julian's Way up the twisting path along the "Y" playing field, like a frightened animal, blinking wildly in the certain knowledge that he must be caught. But he was running for his life, like a boy about to be put to death—unwilling and with nothing to lose, since everything was about to be taken by force. He had summoned an unsuspected reservoir of speed and endurance to break this bondage and to escape this last most hateful fate of banishment. Vic started after him, huge footsteps after small ones, along the rocky path, and called his name, angrily, peremptorily; and Debbie followed pleading, in a sad almost tearful way. "David, honey, wait. Wait, please wait. I only want to talk to you!" He turned as if he were about to heed his mother's appeal, but he was too frightened to stop. Up the steep hill he went, his feet slipping and his breath beginning to come hard. Before he had reached King George Avenue and Mamillah Road they had caught him. It was Vic who reached him first and behind him were Redge and Debbie.

Vic was furious. With his open palm he struck David a stunning blow on his right cheek. It fell with unanticipated rage and begot a greater rage in David. The two succeeding slaps, although they probably stung with all the fury of a whiplash, had little further effect on him. But until Debbie physically held him back, Vic seemed unable to stop. He was distracted, wild, as if something strange had got into him. She'd noticed it for several weeks, but could not fathom it.

Vic's voice was low, almost inaudible. "You've behaved like a child of the gutter. I never thought I'd be chasing you through alleys like some savage! You take my hand now and your mother's and march back to the hotel with us like a gentleman! March!" He tried to take David's hand, but the boy squirmed free again and clung to his mother.

"What'll they think of you?" Vic hissed as Mr. Whittemore approached the family group at a snappy gait, his smile gone now. He was frowning sternly.

"Now, now," he said petulantly. "What have we here?"

He turned on the parents with barely a show of irritation. "We really must be going back," he said. "I realize how difficult it must be. But there are others going through on this convoy, you know—English people—I hate to rush you, of course, but then you must know how it is."

"I won't go, I won't, I won't!" David screamed. The veins stood out on his neck as if the blood vessels were about to burst.

Vic took him by the back of his collar. "By God," he said and his voice was ominous, "you listen to me. We're doing this only for your own good, do you hear? We want you to go some place where you'll be safe. We're doing it for you!" He practically lifted David off the ground.

At last David was helpless. There was nothing more he could do.

"I don't want to go. I don't want to go," he repeated softly, more as a catechism than an argument. "I want to stay here with Mommy and you." He turned on Redge and Mr. Whittemore and said sniffling, "I think if you're a boy Jew you should stay in the Jew's country. I don't want to be an Englishman!" He wiped his sleeve across his tear-smeared face.

Debbie turned to the men, all of whom were watching her. But she said nothing to them. She turned back to her son and put out a hand. "Come along, honey." He took her hand reluctantly, but with faith. "Let's go home. We'll talk about it later." She turned to Redge and Mr. Whittemore. "Thanks for everything. I'm sorry we put you to so much trouble, really I am." She blew her nose and wiped her eyes, trying to compose herself. "Redge, we'll pick up the bag and concertina tonight. See you then."

Vic threw up his hands as though he had no further connection with the whole mess. "I hope you know what you're doing, Debbie," he said as she put her arm through his. Mr. Whittemore shrugged and they went back to the hotel. The first gold of a new day's sun blazed fiercely from behind a distant hill.

"Come along, old chap," Vic said ruefully to his son at last. "Come along." He put his free arm over his shoulders and pulled him tight. There was love in his rough embrace. "Somehow," Vic said as they reached King George Park a few minutes later. "Somehow, I think we're doing the wrong thing, but I feel better about it."

"Maybe we've done the right thing once too often," Debbie said cheerfully. "Too much of a good thing."

Along the border of the park, Haganah men had erected a ten-foot security, concrete rampart against sniping from the Old City and it was safest to hug the wall as you walked. They were still a block from Ben Yehuda Street, beyond the Agency, when a series of terrific blasts shook the whole city. One terrifying shock followed another in a matter of seconds. The air filled with debris and the ground shook as though a giant were shaking the earth by the scruff of its neck. Vic shouted, "Down, get down." He pulled David and Debbie roughly to the ground, pushed their faces to the base of the rampart wall and covered them with his own body. In spite of the protection of Vic and the wall, stones struck them and they hugged the earth desperately. Even as they lay quiet, there were additional blasts with greater force, shattering windows in the houses about them. Screaming, bleeding men and women in nightclothes poured into the bleak and frenzied air, and from Bezalel Street and Rafaeli Street men came running out of apartments toward Ben Yehuda. Smoke billowed up over the roofs of the buildings on Bezalel.

Vic was brushing the grit from his trousers when the next blast came and David went down. She knew at once he was hit. Her heart was filled with terror as she called his name. "David, where is it? Where is it, honey? Where does it hurt?"

When he was able to breathe again after the shock, he tried to cry out, but he knew that he must make a special effort and although the pain must have been sharp and intense he tried to be reassuring. "I'm not dead yet," he whispered, "don't worry," and he pointed to his shoulder.

She tore his shirt and looked at the place. "We have to get him to the hospital." Vic held him like a baby and could feel the wetness of his son's blood on his shoulder. Debbie said, "It's nothing, dear. I know it hurts, but it's nothing. Only a little tiny piece of metal. It's really nothing." And he was reassured as Vic carried him toward the center of town and the temporary hospital which Hadassah had established, now that the Scopus was cut off by Arab bands. It was good to lie back in his father's strong arms and be still. He kept saying he was tired . . . so tired. As they approached Ben Yehuda Street she could scarcely believe what she saw. Nothing remained. As far as she could see there was rubble, stone and rubbish. Here and there a person sitting dazed in the middle of the street or standing befuddled, and occasionally men scurrying up and down trying to help. One man, his face a bloody mass, ran crying up the street shouting in some language she could not understand. They hurried across Jaffa Road, amid the greatest confusion. Not only were enraged and stricken people scurrying back and forth and ambulances screeching to the scene, but a food convoy had arrived from Tel Aviv and people who were not normally in the streets were there with an impulse to rejoice, for it was the first supply convoy to have arrived in Jerusalem in ten days. The ambulances and the food trucks were hopelessly mixed. She turned to Vic. "What are we supposed to do," she said, "cheer or cry?"

At the hospital the rumor was that a group of men in British uniform had parked a lorry containing explosives in Ben Yehuda Street at four that morning. Scores of emergency patients were clamoring for help; but everyone on the staff knew Debbie, and David was taken immediately to a ward where he was undressed. Dick Alpert was there to examine him.

"You mean to tell me a little thing like that hurts?"

"A little," David gasped, somewhat encouraged.

"I'm surprised," Dick Alpert said, looking up from the wound. "Let's see your tongue."

David poked his tongue out. "Yup," Dick Alpert said. "Just what I suspected. Chicken pox."

David blinked foggily. "But I'm wounded," he insisted.

"I'm the doctor," Dick Alpert said, "and I say it's chicken pox."

Even through his pain David tried to smile.

In less time than Debbie had thought possible David was in the bare concrete dungeon with its great glaring lights, one of the inadequate operating rooms. She had to scrub and change quickly to be there, and tried to reassure him, but with her mask he didn't recognize her. Lilith was there to apply the anesthetic.

Just before Lil began to pour the ether, Dick Alpert stood over David and smiled. "Hey, did I tell you about my fish?"

David shook his head.

"All turned back into boys and girls again, what d'you think of that? Just in time, too. We ran out of water."

"Lucky," David said weakly, as Lilith began to let the ether drip.

Three small pieces of shrapnel were removed from his shoulder by Dr. Alpert. "Well, another life saved," he said lightly, and she knew he considered the wound negligible. Still she felt sick in an operating room for the first time.

In the ward, when David awoke he was nauseous and threw up. He must have seen the look of concern on his parents' faces, because he said weakly, "I guess I should have gone to Haifa with Mr. Whittemore." She felt the sting.

"Don't worry about it," she said. "It was a poor idea."

"Very poor," Vic said. "You wouldn't have liked England. It's so foggy there."

"Of course," David said emphatically. "What good are green lawns if you can't see them in the fog?"

Shortly after David went to the hospital Vic was sent out on the Road for Haganah, where he worked full time after Redge left Jerusalem. Ben Kronstein took over at the Telephone Office, although it was never quite clear to Debbie why this had come about. Debbie took to sleeping at the hospital, for the streets were dangerous. Only once in a blue moon she would scurry back to the apartment. New casualties were brought in every day. There were many dead now—dead to be piled in the courtyard and carried away for burial only at night. You could smell them. Elsa's flat was wrecked by a bomb, and she asked if she could move in with them at Gaza Road. Then in April a medical convoy to Mt. Scopus was attacked by Arabs and Dick Alpert was on the last bus, one of half a dozen who survived. Everyone was bitter over it. Jerusalem's leading doctors and nurses were massacred wholesale. It was that kind of war.

Near the end of David's stay he saw Tamar for the last time. She came to visit him with her mother, Meyer Van Bern, and Tuvia. David never knew how she got them, but Tamar brought him a bunch of anemones, which in these April days covered the hills, although no one would dare venture up to pick them. The sight of the flowers in Tamar's arms made him feel quite wonderful, as if the war were over. Meyer and Tuvia stood by, taciturn and boylike.

"Hi!"

"You feel okay?"
"What d'you think? Miss Even's got a fella."
"Yeah? I don't believe it."
"Sure. How d'you feel?"
"Fine."
"So long."

The conversation wasn't the important thing about the visit. As he said to Debbie later, if he got wounded in England, who would have come to see him?

Perhaps because he had actually been hit, once they moved back to the flat with Elsa, David didn't worry so much about the mortar blasts. She thought he would be more frightened than ever, but through the grimmest days of the siege, when others were terrified, he was perhaps the least afraid.

Twenty-six

Debbie stirred in her camp chair in the courtyard seeking a more comfortable position and smiled to herself. The mortars had stopped and there was so much to be grateful for. One scarcely knew where to begin. They had dignity first, and comfort. It wasn't Lindenhouse, but they had the sunny apartment, the piano, David's concertina and the Rehavia School. They had a refrigerator and washing machine, theaters that would have surprised Papa, and David had his bike. She was busy—she was needed as she would never have been in Vienna—and Vic would have his work again, just as important, at the Telephone Office, once the Road was finished. They had shared a tremendous adventure. Why, the eyes of the world were on them! The world's radios spoke of them each day. Statesmen debated their fate at Lake Success. In America, in England, in Prague and Vienna they were heard. And who had done it? They had done it themselves. She and Vic; Karl and Lilith; Dick Alpert, Elsa, and tall, skinny Sam Pearlman; Noah Mendoza, and Miss Even, and the Epsteins across the hall, with their son in the Valley, even loyal old Tani; and David and his little friends—they had done it too, for it was for them it was done. And now here was the truce and Vic would be coming home to stay . . .

"Mrs. Marmorek!" Debbie opened her eyes and the bright sunlight blinded her for a moment. A soldier stood opposite her in full uniform. As her eyes accustomed themselves to the light she thought he looked stuffed, so formal and even comical. An orthodox religious soldier, a black-bearded character with long sausage-curled side locks, the left one hanging down and the other tucked neatly inside his tam, giving him the unsymmetrical look of a sporty rabbi. Startled as she was, she had difficulty restraining her smile.

"You want me?"

"Are you Mrs. Marmorek?"

"Yes, you gave me such a start!"

"Come with me, please."

"What for?" She had a weak and watery sensation in the pit of her stomach. "Nothing's happened to Victor?"

"Who's Victor?"

She could actually feel her heart slow its thumping to normal.

"Really I have to catch my breath. My husband is working on the Burma Road and I thought . . ."

"I have a jeep out front."

"Yes, of course, but where are you taking me? What's it all about?"

The soldier shrugged. "Colonel Horowitz wants to see you at the Agency."

"Do you have any idea what for?"

The soldier shrugged again. It seemed to be his favorite gesture. "Since when do colonels tell privates? In Haganah it was different. We had equality. But last week Ben-Gurion makes an edict. From now on it's an army. All of a sudden the officers make like they are officers. Saluting. Yes sir, no sir. So now we have privates and we have officers. It's a step, but I don't say in the right direction."

"Who's this man Horowitz? I never heard of him."

"That's a good question. You think maybe I heard of him? He comes from Haifa. Runs a gift shop, so naturally this is perfect training for a colonel. Probably robbed people for years. Last week the little plane arrives from Haifa and who steps out? Horowitz. Ah, you should see him, such a fancy uniform. Braids, things here, medals, like the movies. But why should I tell you? You'll see for yourself. So this morning he says to me, 'You!' That's the way he thinks of me—Private You—like a number, well, what can you expect? He says bring me this woman. You shouldn't come back without her. Deborah Marmorek. Thirty-two Gaza Road. So all morning I'm looking for you. Nobody in the neighborhood knows where you are. Up and down, in every store, to the school, and meanwhile Horowitz—excuse me, Colonel Horowitz—is chewing his nails up to here. So what can I do? Is it my fault?"

His elaborate protestations of ignorance worried and irritated her. Oh sure, you innocent cherub, lying in your teeth. No doubt you told Baumerstock the whole story, whatever it is. Well, why worry? Perhaps Colonel Horowitz will be more informative. She noticed her hand was still bleeding.

"I cut my hand a little while ago. I'll have to dress it. Wait just a moment for me. I'll be right down."

"I'd better go up with you," he said stolidly. "I waited all morning already." She tried not to look surprised.

"It wouldn't look nice if you escaped. Be bad for my record, no?"

"Escape!" She watched his stolid expression, and determined to suppress her curiosity. He followed her upstairs.

"Elsa!" she called.

"The substantial lady left," the soldier said.

"She's my boss at the hospital—at Hadassah. This is our first day off in three months. A whole day off. It really doesn't seem possible. She probably went looking for food tins. She's a wonder at finding food."

Why was she gossiping with this idiot?

"She packed her valise and left," the soldier said doggedly. "Where she went, I don't know, but not to buy food. Maybe to find another apartment."

It was true. Elsa's bags were gone.

"Tani!"

"The little black one? Gone also."

When she tried to lap a bandage around her palm she saw her hand was shaking. The soldier helped her and although his fingers were clumsy, he was able to do a better job than she. She dampened a cloth and cleaned her smeared face, combed her hair, and put the bottle of water in the refrigerator—how silly, a refrigerator without electricity! There was a dish full of olives. Bruised olives but edible and she took half a dozen. "I've had nothing to eat all day," she said. He helped himself to one.

"Who eats nowadays?"

"What have you been telling people about me?" She wheeled on him with sudden impatience.

"I look like a man who tells people about people? I'm a messenger boy. I don't say a word. Colonel Horowitz, he does the talking. He'll tell you plenty."

She held her breath all the way to the Agency. He drove like a demon, narrowly missing two pedestrians at the turn into King George Avenue, and in a few minutes the jeep whirled by the sentries into the Agency courtyard and came to a screeching stop.

The courtyard was in blossom, but the damage of March's explosion was an ugly blotch on the graceful building, made uglier by the scaffolding of the repair crews.

Civilians with their inevitable briefcases and men and women in many kinds of uniform bristling with sidearms and rifles scurried in and out of the two usable entrances in feverish haste. An American limousine flying the small blue and white standard of the UN was parked before the main entrance, its driver in gleaming uniform, sitting in majestic indifference at the wheel.

In the reception hall behind the long wood counter two young men and a chunky girl, their khaki shirtsleeves rolled and collars open, perspiring continuously from the *hamseen*, examined passes and papers in the desultory way in which papers and passes are examined everywhere.

Debbie's escort said to one of the young men, "This is the Marmorek woman." His attitude, even while he spoke, seemed to change; he had turned subtly hostile.

The soldier behind the counter eyed her with frank curiosity and the other two turned to look at her. There was the barest hush in the hall, then after a few seconds the hum of conversation resumed. The other two receptionists turned away, and the young man said into a phone, "Tell Colonel Horowitz the Marmorek woman is here."

He turned to her escort, ignoring her as if she were inanimate. "Room forty-four," he said.

She had to lean heavily on the highly-polished wood banister to help herself up the broad graceful terrazzo stairway. Her knees were playing her tricks, or perhaps she was weak from hunger. There was nothing to be nervous about. If anything had happened to Vic they would never choose this way of telling her. Casualties were routine enough, sometimes there was no notification at all. Surely nothing so formal, not in Jerusalem today.

The Marmorek woman! They all seemed to expect her. What nonsense, what imaginary nonsense! In the wide anteroom on the second floor she saw Yehuda Epstein's vivid oil painting of the Maccabeans slaughtering Greeks on the steps of the Temple. Heads were smashed against the stone steps and the blood was flowing so profusely that all the carnage seemed to have been pleasure to the artist.

When they reached room forty-four, halfway down the bare semicircular hall, panic seized her—an unreasoning panic she hadn't known since the day David was born. She felt sucked under by it, drowning. She *must* stop this trembling!

Her bearded companion knocked, received no answer, and opened the door.

"Wait here," he said, holding the door open for her and closing it after her. She was alone in the room, facing a desk and an empty chair.

Twenty-seven

The footsteps in the hall were for her; they had direction and purpose and when the door opened she had a sense of relief.

The man who came in was gentle looking, tall and angular with a slight stoop, and from time to time his hands twitched as though he were trying unsuccessfully to snap his fingers. He wore horn-rimmed glasses, which seemed an affectation, like his glittering British-type uniform, complete with tie. His thinning hair helped make his face softer, almost humorous, but it was a thoughtful face. This was Colonel Horowitz.

She rose when he came in, out of uneasiness, and he motioned her to sit, pleasantly, but without a smile. His motions were almost jerky as he placed an open folder containing a thick sheaf of closely typed pages on the desk near his right hand. He caressed the papers, as though to reassure himself of their contents. He placed a package of English cigarettes on the desk and slid them toward her. Her fingers trembled as she took one—stupid to let him see her so nervous! He reached across to hold a light for her and she inhaled a long breath of smoke, so soothing, even if it made her a little dizzy.

He opened the larger drawer in the desk and removed a sealed fifth of brandy and two tumblers which he proceeded to fill—mammoth drinks! This was certainly a ridiculous way to begin an interview or a conference or Lord knows what it was to be. Whatever did the good colonel intend?

"Mrs. Marmorek," he said in English, "I'm Colonel Horowitz of Military Intelligence. Unfortunately my Hebrew is utterly ragged, y'know, and I understand you speak English rather well (however did he know that?), so if you don't mind, we'll proceed in English, shall we?"

"If you wish. I'm terribly curious."

He patted the neat pile of typed sheets with his right hand and spoke softly. "Yes, I s'pose you are. Have a drink."

"Thanks, but I haven't eaten a thing all day, only a few olives. I'm afraid I'd be quite a disgrace to you and myself." She smiled hopefully, but there was no response.

"You don't mind if I do?" He took in half the tumbler in a single gulp. "I'd really suggest you do the same. Come along, girl, do as I say."

She drank from her glass slowly while he watched her. It was like drinking fire at first, burning and choking in her throat and then it spread, a gentle warmth until she felt glowing.

After a few minutes the colonel was remote. So far away and so nice. Wasn't it thoughtful of him to have brandy for her? Such a nice colonel, nice colonel. Colonel what? Oh, yes, Horowitz, of course. He was really sweet. She smiled more boldly and though there was still no response she felt he liked her. He was bashful, that was all. Bashful Colonel Horowitz. He *must* like her. After all he was a man and men liked her. She'd washed her face, hadn't she, and combed her hair, hadn't she? Oho! What would Victor say to this! I spent the most delightful afternoon with Colonel Horowitz. This was an important man in the new state. Wouldn't Victor be impressed! What was he saying?

He had drunk the second half of his glass. "I hope you'll forgive the unusual refreshments, but in a case like this I think we ought to fortify ourselves, don't y'know."

She saw him in a haze, a kind of majestic glow. My, he was pretty in a scholarly way. Quite different from Vic.

"I really don't know where to begin. I thought I ought to see you myself. Psychological compulsion you might say. Could've delegated it, I s'pose, but somehow couldn't bring myself to do it. My responsibility after all, and in my job you have to take the bad with the good." He took a strand of his hair and twisted it slowly between his thumb and forefinger, until it stood erect, like a small horn on the right side of his head, and for what seemed an incredibly long time was silent.

The colonel looked at her carefully, spunky girl all right. This was going to be worse than he imagined. So much pride there, maybe he'd made a mistake to undertake this himself. He should have let Ben Kepelow do it. Ben Kepelow would come right to the point and get it over with. But this sort of thing gave him the jitters.

"Jerusalem's been a hellhole," he said. "I thought Haifa was bad, and Jaffa, I've seen 'em all, but nothing like Jerusalem. I couldn't believe it when I first came here. Close quarters, my God, and no fooling, y'know. Never saw anything like it in North Africa. Or Greece. More like Leningrad I s'pose. Arabs here, Jews there. Fifty feet apart with stabilized lines. Well, under the circumstances it's only natural to find a great deal of sabotage, looting, spying. Travel between lines. Clever fellow can always cross lines. War, y'know, you expect these things."

" 'F *course*."

"Spies, good God, there were spies everywhere, when I got here. Still are, matter of fact. Damned difficult problem, don't y'know. In a besieged city, any sentry can be a traitor. We've caught a few, but small potatoes. Few girls who've lived with Arab men, not much in the way of Jews anyway, just a grade above common prostitutes, you might say. Sell anything for a shilling. Fortunately for us they didn't have much to sell. Then there were a few English, whom we haven't caught, most of 'em 've left, matter of fact, gone back home. Rather clever. Have to hand it to my fellow Britishers, even if they're Gentile, they're not stupid. They didn't like us, but they were rather clever about it. Handed the Arab Legion all sorts of information they couldn't have got for themselves."

What was he driving at?

"Got it from a few Jews, it seems, and passed the good word along to Glubb Pasha. Your husband's name came to our attention, of course. Had English friends, never been a Zionist, lived as an assimilationist in Prague and Vienna, even Rome you might say. You are a Jew, I take it? I only ask because—well I don't want to seem indelicate, but this is hardly the time for delicacy. I understand you have a son."

"David?"

"And that he's never been circumcised."

"Of course not, we were in Italy."

"It's unusual. You've lived here three years. I'm sure you realize that. Well I won't dwell on it. But I don't personally know any Jew, man or boy, who's not. Though I s'pose there are some."

"Victor is." What kind of nonsensical defense was that?

"Well you'd know that better than I." She flushed. Oh, she hated this man.

"In any case he worked for the Administration, position of responsibility, and so forth. We'd had reports on him which didn't look quite right from chaps we trust. So we picked him up last week."

She was confused. The brandy confused her. What was this man saying? "Why Colonel, Victor's on the Burma Road. He's been working twenty hours a day. He hasn't been home for weeks. How could he . . . ?"

"Yes, of course, that's where we picked him up. The Road."

She had to be careful of what she said. Mustn't make a fool of herself, mustn't say anything to hurt Victor. She didn't trust this man. Must say something to show him how ridiculous, how absurd . . . speak clearly, keep her head.

"But don't you think it's fantastic for him to be in Haganah and at the same time to . . . don't you see how absolutely, utterly fantastic . . ."

She took another sip of brandy as if she were having cocktails with this man.

"Certain human beings are strange animals and they behave in ways that are, shall we say, unpredictable, not always consistent . . . possibly there's some explanation. Perhaps a psychiatrist could explain it. But the Army of Israel can't afford psychiatrists for such matters, m'dear. At least not yet. Perhaps it'll come about. But to get on about your husband. We made a thorough inquiry, as thorough as it could be under the circumstances, with due regard for military security and all that. Glubb's Arab devils had got hold of a mass of terribly damaging information. A list of every point of military importance in the city. Every important post, every headquarters, every command post, every machine shop. They're not awfully good shots, y'know, but their mortar fire here in Jerusalem was devilish accurate. Can't reveal much about it under present circumstances. Only a thirty-day truce, so far, highly secret, and all that, y'know, can't tell when the blasted thing's liable to break loose again, but believe me, m'dear, it was bad. Brandeis Institute, only decent machine tool shop in Jerusalem—had our rifles repaired there. Smashed to bits. Same sort of thing going on all over town. Nothing but mortars, but too damned accurate. They had this list. With exact addresses. Killed hundreds of our most useful people. Made it difficult to hold on to parts of the New City, too. Might have lost it altogether."

Debbie had to watch this man carefully. He fascinated her.

"Everything pointed to Marmorek, your husband. I'd come over from Haifa, you know, to clean things up here. Well I talked to him myself. Pleasant chap, but not a very pretty picture I must say. Girl named Enid, I s'pose you know her, Enid Walker, seemed to have had something to do with it. She and her husband. You were rather chummy with them I take it."

Debbie was furious. Don't say anything, don't lose control of yourself. This man is being deliberately unpleasant. Enid? Never. Nor Victor either. She must be careful. She must be clever. Yes, she would have to see Victor. He would know who to go to. He had friends. Karl would find a good lawyer. It was so preposterous. "I'm sure you're completely mistaken. Victor would never—"

"It's not pleasant to tell you this, Mrs. Marmorek. On the basis of the facts I had no choice but to order an immediate general court-martial for your husband. We selected three of the most competent officers in this area. We provided him with the best advocate we could get on short notice. He was tried on two counts. Espionage—and treason."

The words sounded so dramatic, so unreal. She took out her handkerchief and blew her nose, as though she had not heard him. When she spoke it was with a great effort at composure. If only her mind weren't so terribly muddled, the brandy had mixed her up so . . . She must make some impression on this irritating man, before he said something even more terrible. She must forestall him.

"Victor—my husband—was hurt only a month ago on the Road. Burned. One of his men—Levin—Oh whatever is his name—Schmeul, that's it. Schmeul Levin. He'll tell you. Victor was fearless. He ran under this bulldozer with the fire simply raging, and brought out two boys . . ."

Horowitz twitched his fingers furiously. "I know everything I tell you may seem farfetched to you, Madam."

"Well, how soon is this trial to be? This court-martial or whatever it is?" She was impatient.

"It's over, I'm afraid. The court took testimony for two days. Naturally, we couldn't give it publicity. Since you weren't implicated in the matter in any way—the fact is you were cleared by several witnesses—we dared not notify even you. And your husband asked us not to tell you . . ."

That sounded like Victor.

"Don't you see, Colonel—he *couldn't* have! I'm his wife. Don't you think I'd know if he were doing anything like that? Why . . . what would he have to get out of it? This is the only place left for us. Jerusalem's our home, our only home on earth. Where else could we go? Why, when Ben-Gurion went on the wireless last month, he wept, Victor wept. He'd come a long way. You don't know what that means for Victor. He used to be quite a skeptic, and now he was so proud. The State of Israel. Our son is so happy now. You've no idea, he has so many friends already. He's so happy . . . You're an English Jew, so perhaps it's difficult for you to realize what it means for an Austrian . . ."

How could she stop him? How could she persuade him? Before he said something irrevocable.

He was twisting his hair into a left horn now to match the other, slowly, deliberately, while the quick drags on his cigarette had an element of hysteria. She could feel him stiffen as he struck.

"Your husband betrayed the State of Israel, its Army and people. He was found guilty on both counts. The verdict was unanimous. The court sentenced him to be shot."

She sagged in the chair as though a string which had been holding her together had snapped.

"No." Only a low moan escaped her. It wasn't true. "No, no, no." Karl would help them. She would find Karl. Poor Victor, what he must be going through! She must go to him right away. They would find a way. They would think of something. An appeal. A lawyer. Higher courts. They would go to Ben-Gurion himself.

"I'm afraid they've made a terrible mistake." She barely whispered.

"It's been my job to review the case before execution of the sentence." He tapped the file folder containing the typed sheafs before him. "This is a transcript of the trial. The evidence is here. One hundred and four pages of it. No question about it, the evidence is here. I've done nothing but review the testimony, word for word, for the past forty-eight hours. The case is airtight. We gave him every chance to defend himself we could, under the difficult circumstances. He denied the charges, of course. But he didn't deny the facts. I spoke to him at length myself."

"You did? How is he? Is he all right? Oh, it must be awful for him."

"When I saw him he was perfectly coherent. Believe me, it was the most unpleasant thing I ever had to do in my life. I'm not a religious man, but I spent many hours in the synagogue. To take a man's life is not a light thing. He was a fellow Jew, but I had no choice but to confirm the sentence."

Wildly Debbie sought a faint hope. "Nothing's been—done yet?" Karl would help. Oh, if only the Walkers were still here. Redge had influence. Oh, whatever was she thinking . . . ? The British were gone, of course. "It's an awful mistake, Colonel. An awful, awful mistake."

"There was no mistake. I deeply regret to tell you the sentence was carried out this morning."

"No!" She uttered a sharp unrestrained shriek. For a moment she sat motionless. Horowitz turned to look at the flowering courtyard. She shook her head from side to side incredulously.

"What could I do for a Jew who betrayed his fellows, you included? Too many dead chaps to make a row against it."

Debbie stood up. For some reason she felt steadier. "You crazy son of a bitch," she said and her voice rose shrilly. "Crazy, stupid son of a bitch, son of a . . ." She was acting badly; she must get hold of herself.

"You must get control of yourself, Mrs. Marmorek. Please, if there's anything I can do—"

Oh, Lord, now he was trying to be kind to her! This man, this foul man was trying to be kind. She turned away from him.

Colonel Horowitz removed his glasses and nervously ran his handkerchief over each lens.

"Mrs. Marmorek, believe me, I'll not try to persuade you about your husband. There'd be no point to it. I only ask you to remember that I'm responsible for the lives and security of a hundred thousand of our people in this city. It's not a light responsibility. I never prayed so hard." He spoke softly, but uneasily. "Your husband prepared a written statement which he asked us to give you. You can understand we've had to read it. Many of our officers have opposed my giving it to you. This is it."

She was not listening. He handed her an envelope and escorted her to the door. "You! Take Mrs. Marmorek home." The comical soldier with the beard was waiting.

"You can make arrangements to get your husband's body any time tomorrow," the Colonel said. "He'll be at Bikur Holim. Here are his personal effects." He handed her a large manila envelope, which she took without noticing what she was doing. He stood at the door of his office and watched the small underweight girl shuffle limply toward the stair landing, like a discarded child going no place in particular.

Somehow during the fighting yesterday with the shells crashing all about, bodies lying in the street, the shooting of one spy seemed almost a trivial affair. Today in the dawn of peace it seemed incredible that he could have done it. Still his conscience was clear. Bloody Arabs gave the man the jitters, and really what alternative had existed for a man of scruples? She'd recover in time. Perhaps find someone worthier of her. Reports of her were good. Of course, there was the boy. The son. Colonel Horowitz turned his mind away; he was relieved when Debbie disappeared around the curve in the hall. He put the folder on the Marmorek case into the drawer. "I thank God that's finished," he said aloud. "I really do in a most religious sense." But in his heart

Colonel Horowitz knew that the case of Victor Marmorek was anything but finished.

Twenty-eight

At the Rehavia School it was late in the day and no more children were expected. If they hadn't come yet they wouldn't come any more today. Except for David's concern over Tamar no one asked after anyone, because it was understood that they had not come either because it was inconvenient or because they were dead, and to ask was to open the door to the unbearable truth of a waste so great that even children were afraid to face it. It was easier to accept the pretense that no one was missing.

Nevertheless, as each new child came there was excitement and gossip and horseplay; they were veteran soldiers, greeting old buddies, thought to be lost through enemy action. Past frictions and feuds were forgotten. Gang divisions and loyalties had disappeared into a frivolous past and new loyalties, each to the other, even to well-known drips and jerks, formed at least for this day. No one was too insignificant or unpopular to miss his own personal ovation, although, to be sure, none had been as spontaneous as David's.

René Blum showed up when it was almost time to go home. Miss Even was inside with Miss Baruch and several of the upper grade teachers, and the children were scattered, the girls jumping rope or working in the planting beds in the courtyard, the boys in the playing field on the other side of the building in an improvised soccer game.

David saw René far across the field. A lone figure, leaner but with the same recognizable swagger, watching the game, but making no move to join it. For the first time René seemed a pathetic creature to David. He remembered hearing that René's father had been killed only a few weeks ago in Notre Dame.

"Hey," Tuvia was shouting. "It's René! Fellas! It's René! Hi!"

"Time out!" David screamed. "Hi, René!" He had decided to be nice to René, nicer than normal, for in addition to the loss of his father in recent days, the whole tragedy of René's fall from lofty estate in the class to near discard came suddenly into focus. René must have been very miserable his last months in school, his position of eminence usurped by David. How he must long for friends himself; there was a touch of magnanimity in David's attitude. He would make things up to him.

As he ran across the field he noticed that René's face looked different. It was not simply that he was thinner. All at once he saw that René had the most awful burn around his right eye. Raw, red, lacerated—and the eye itself was abnormal. A real pang, a physical sinking sensation hit David in the pit of his stomach.

The boys were crowding about René, ignoring the eye elaborately, not mentioning it, they were patting him on the back, shaking his hand, and Tuvia threw an arm about him, for everyone knew about René's father, whose name had become a symbol for the valor of Jerusalem's defenders. But René's responses were reserved. "Hi, hi." He waited for David, who came trotting up grinning and waving. David's trot was slowed up by what he saw in René's face. A new challenge and an old hate, almost the disdain of the kindergarten year, but with less swagger and more certainty. David saw that he was painfully thin. Everyone had lost some weight during the siege, but not so much.

René pushed the other boys aside, as if he were impatient with their greetings and prattle. Every motion revealed a sureness of purpose and a maturity which the other kids instinctively accepted, although they were not certain what it was or whence it sprang.

"You! Marmorek! What are you doing here at this school? Beat it before we kick you out!"

David was bewildered. "Okay," he said, "if you're looking for a fight."

"I don't want to fight! How can I fight? Traitor bastard! English lover, go on back to your Lloydy-woydy!" He was pushing David in the chest with his forefinger and David backed away at the unexpected onslaught.

"Take your hands off me," David cried. "Take your hands off." He twisted himself away and circled warily about his old antagonist, who puzzled him.

"After what happened to your father! How can you come to school?"

"My father?" David said. "What about my father?"

"He doesn't know!" René shouted and he laughed wildly. "He doesn't know." René ducked suddenly for a stone and threw it deliberately at David's head. David ducked just in time.

"What's happened to my father?" David screamed.

"He was killed, that's all. Filthy traitor of a whore!" René was saying anything that came into his head.

"Stinker of a liar!" David shouted. He could not imagine what had got into René to be saying such harebrained things. And he could not seem to tear his eyes away from the grotesque scar which gave René's screeching a bizarre quality.

"Bang, bang, bang!" René screamed. He was circling David now and the others stood by as puzzled as David. "They tied his hands and put a black rag over his face and shot him dead for a traitor!"

"Crazy!" David shouted. "He's working on the Road. You know he's a lieutenant in Haganah."

René bent to pick up a jagged piece of buff-colored rock about the size of his fist and held it threateningly. "My father was killed at Notre Dame," he shouted and his voice carried a hysterical pitch, "and Tuvia's brother and lots of others. But your father was a spy for the English, spy for the Arabs!"

Carried away by his own fury, he threw the stone. They were only six feet apart and although David dodged again, the stone struck him glancing on the cheek, and the blow rocked him. His hand went up to feel the raw cut.

He heard the other boys shouting now, but he was unable to distinguish the words. From the building he saw Miss Even come running. His instinct was to appeal to her for help, not to repel René, who, he saw, was no longer his physical equal, but to give this wild tale the lie. There was something in the way René shouted that gave his ranting a ring of credibility to the others; David felt René was taking advantage, in some clever and unanswerable way, of his own tragedies. David knew his own father was in Haganah, that to talk seriously of his father being a spy was fantastic; for his father was doing heroic work on the new Road. But he could think of nothing convincing to say.

When Miss Even came her face was flushed and she was out of breath, and calling "Boys! Boys!" Then turning to David she said, "Come along with me, David." There was something in her manner beside her appearance and breathlessness that made her peremptory.

"René says David's father was shot for a spy!" Tuvia piped.

"Isn't it so, Miss Even, isn't it so?" René was trotting alongside her but Miss Even walked quickly as though trying to ignore him and the question.

Miss Even had, by her silence, tipped the balance. Before David knew what had happened René and Loet had pounced on him, tearing at his clothes and pummeling. He felt the small hard fists on his face, his shoulders, his midriff. The shouting had become almost deafening, those high, shrill, piercing voices. It was difficult for David to make sense of what was happening to him. He twisted on the ground and rolled away and scrambled to his feet to run; he heard Tuvia screaming. "What's it his fault what his father did? What's it his fault?" Tuvia sounded puzzled and over his shoulder he saw Meyer trying to hold the others back, tugging at their arms and gesticulating, but no one was paying the slightest attention to his friends.

"If his father was, so's he!" René had the upper hand now, and he was directing operations like a general. "He's not even circumcised. You know that! Probably he's not even a Jew!"

David ran. What had happened to his father? He was terrorized now and had to get home. Mommy would be there or Elsa. But he stumbled as he reached the end of the playing field and before he could recover his balance the three boys in pursuit had pounced again. They were screaming and pummeling, and David, for a moment, found it impossible to breathe. He had the impression that Miss Even was calling to the children, pulling at them, barking orders, stern orders in her musical voice. David sat up and looked at the circle of faces around him. They were curious, a few were hostile. The girls had come from the courtyard, carrying their jump ropes. He looked for the friendly faces of Max and Tuvia and Meyer, but they were impassive, inscrutable as only the face of a confused boy can become. If only Tamar were here.

"Miss Even," he said hesitantly, "René says . . ."

Miss Even was pleasant, but her manner was robbed of its warmth. "Come along with me, David," she said. "Your mother is here for you."

She started to lead him toward the building entrance, but a stone came hurtling at David. He dodged and the missile struck Miss Even in the small of her back. She doubled up and her hand flew instinctively to the spot. Other stones flew. The same three boys.

"Children, children!" She did her best to stop it.

David saw his mother on the sidewalk at the entrance. Beside her was a bearded soldier and in the street was a jeep. Here was protection and he ran toward them, but the kids followed and the stones and the screaming made a terror for him that he had never known.

"Mommy, Mommy!" he cried.

He had not seen his mother like this since the days of the ship. Her face was streaked, her clothes disheveled, her hair wild. She looked slovenly, but very young, like a schoolgirl who had been in an accident, too shocked to care about herself. As the children came toward them she held her arms out to David and stood with a protective arm around him, her feet planted flatly, as if she were waiting for some blow.

"Go 'way," she shouted. "Go 'way, all of you!"

David knew that the children would be cowed by this voice of his mother's authority. Children didn't defy the parents of others, no matter what they might say of them behind their backs.

"Traitor!" It was René. "Bitch of a traitor! Whore!" He thumbed his nose at David's mother. René knew the most terrible words and was not afraid to use them. "Goy! Shiksa!"

"René!" Miss Even tried to pull him away. "Come inside." But René had stored small stones in his pocket and, twisting loose from Miss Even, he threw one at Deborah. Suddenly the other two were screeching and throwing anything they could lay their hands on, and two others joined the belligerents. The piping voices of the girls mingled with those of the boys and drowned out Miss Even's futile protests. David's mother looked wildly from Miss Even to the bearded soldier, who stood by passively.

Miss Even cried, "Go, for God's sake, hurry. Go home!"

The kids were literally closing in and Debbie took her son's hand and pulled him swiftly toward the jeep. "Come on," she called to the laconic soldier. The stones were flying and crashing spectacularly against the jeep body and one hit the windshield with the unfriendly but familiar splinter of glass. David saw his friend Tuvia, his face distorted, others screaming, shaking thin fists, and Meyer Van Bern, his old shipmate, slap the jeep as it started off, but after it had moved a few yards, he heard Meyer's shrill voice, "So long, David." He was waving in a sad and friendly fashion. "See you tomorrow."

David was shivering, as if he had malaria, and he felt hot and cold. His mother's arm was tight around him, trying to quiet him. As they drove through Rehavia, slowly, slowly his hysteria subsided.

"What happened to Daddy?" he asked at last in a small voice. "They said . . ."

"I know," his mother said. "Never mind what they said."

But David could see from his mother's face, the dull, apathetic, bewildered look on her face, that what René had said about his father was true. He understood the fact, but it didn't mean much to him. He felt he ought to cry, if his father was dead, somehow Daddy would expect him to cry, at least a little.

Twenty-nine

That his friends should have turned on him scarcely surprised David because he had always secretly half feared them, but that they had humiliated his mother and defied Miss Even stunned him. Adults were a world apart; the feuds of children were supposed to stop abruptly at the border of the child's realm. His head whirled at the awful fact that he had seen his mother helpless. She could be as defenseless as he. He was unprotected. He needed his Daddy.

Debbie was numb. Her mind could no longer absorb what she heard and saw. She had watched the children attack David as though he were not hers. Ordinarily his smallest unhappiness was a poison-tipped dart in her heart, but her heart had not responded now. The drinks she had taken from Colonel Horowitz had added to her haziness—all she could remember was that Miss Even had stood aside—Miss Even, who, she knew, loved David with all the fervor a natural child-worshiper lavishes on her favorite. This same sweet Miss Even had turned her back on David.

The new hate she had just seen was dimly familiar, but not in Jerusalem. Oh, everyone in town hated fiercely enough. They hated the Grand Mufti and the name of Ernest Bevin. They hated the Legionnaires of Glubb Pasha. But she had never heard anyone say a word against Mrs. Bevin or the polluted Arab children who roamed the streets. And when Etzel stormed Deir Yassein one bloody night and killed two hundred Arab men, women and children, even cynical old Baumerstock had been sick over it. These innocent people were not the enemy. The people of Jerusalem, racked by the starvation and fire of these weeks, had been remarkably clever about identifying the enemy, and sparing from the ever-widening circle of hate the enemy's helpless followers who had no choice but to travel with the enemy. But what she had seen today was a change. Miss Even had stood aside.

As the jeep rolled by Baumerstock's shop, she saw the black-hatted proprietor gossiping at the entrance with Mrs. Heller. She saw him point as they passed. Mrs. Heller's tongue must have been clucking fiercely all day.

The jeep skidded to a stop at their house and the soldier jerked his head. David made a gesture of helping his mother down and the soldier said in a low voice, "Good-bye."

For a moment they said nothing, until after an embarrassing silence Debbie said, "Thanks."

The soldier gave his comic salute. "That's okay," he said and whirled away on two wheels.

On the entrance door to their apartment there was a penciled note, scrawled on a torn piece of toilet paper and attached to the door with medical adhesive tape.

"Get out, traitors!"

The words looked so melodramatic, but the Hebrew scrawl was surreptitious and childlike. It put Debbie in mind of the taboo words scribbled on the lavatory walls at Fräulein Morgenstelle's.

Inside, the apartment was a shambles. Every drawer was out, clothing was strewn everywhere, much of it cut into shreds. The furniture was tumbled about, maliciously slashed, bedding pulled off and tied into knots. David looked to his mother for a reaction. How hard she had worked on this apartment and what hope they had poured into it! Even David could remember how they had walked from shop to shop, comparing, choosing, exulting, to make their first home. Debbie smiled weakly to her son, brushed her hair out of her eyes and started methodically but listlessly to straighten the living room. David gathered the clothes, folded them as best he could and restored them to their drawers. Folding his father's shirts and shorts gave him an odd sensation. His father would not wear these things again; it was difficult to really comprehend and he still felt nothing.

For half an hour they worked in silence, restoring, neatening.

On the bedroom bureau was a note from Elsa which she'd missed before. In a way it was kind.

> I've just heard about your trouble. I'm sure at a time like this you don't want to be bothered with boarders. Thank you for everything.

But no word of where she had gone. And no sign of Tani.

Debbie thought of something her mother used to say so often—"Everyone in town knows before the wife." Mama had been talking of ordinary human infidelity, but they were saying Victor's infidelity was on a monstrous scale, not only to his wife and child, but to a city and a people.

She could never believe it. If she could talk to Vic . . . to assure him . . . she felt he must need her, how he must need her now! If only she could go to him . . . but where? And for what? She had seen the corpses, stacked like grotesque potato sacks behind Hadassah A; she had watched relatives weep and wail over a body, tenderly kissing dead hands, embracing dead flesh, and it had always seemed an abomination to her. If there was no corporeal Victor, where he lay was no matter; he didn't really need her, not the body, the eager, protective body to which she had responded timidly and hopefully in the beginning, so eagerly and anxiously, and later with a sense of full partnership. It wasn't possible for that to be gone . . . tonight, this very night they were to have celebrated together, with wine and a little food and love . . . so much of it through their bodies. How people could prate about the soul, the spirit. But in the end one must have a body to enjoy them with. Love—love must be felt in the fingertips and on the lips and in the intimacy of passion. At least her kind of love. Freedom, even victory needs a body.

Vic, Vic . . . if you could tell me what's happened to you. Poor, poor darling . . . her imagination turned away from Victor's ordeal; she could not bear to share it with him and quite abruptly she became conscious of the package and letter Colonel Horowitz had given her.

The package contained Vic's watch and his Parker 51 pen.

The letter was in Hebrew, the first time she recalled Vic's ever having done that. All his other scribbled notes were in German and even this Hebrew was full of Germanisms.

> My heart's darling,
>
> It's good-bye, but not only good-bye, there is something more. Believe me, it's hard to go like this. It's all so sudden, without preparation, mental or physical, but I suppose the more preparation the worse. They've told me I could write you, in fact they told me I could

see you, but I couldn't bear it. It would only have hurt both of us and would have brought you in, and I did want to keep you clear of this horror. There's no use denying it, right now I'm more scared than I've ever been. It's my recurring nightmare come true. You know how it is, people who are in constant dread of cancer get it? And those who fear airplanes, crash. Well, I've lived with a terror of being killed blindly by bestial men who were a law to themselves, with no higher appeal and for no particular reason. Like Gussie Goldenberg's nightmare you once told me about. In a gas chamber, I thought, or by whipping or torture or maybe to be put out with a single bullet in the head, kneeling and blindfolded, the way the Chinese do, as though humans were roaches. As far back as I can remember this nightmare has tormented me and I suppose if I examine deeply enough into my subconscious mind many of the things I've done and made you do with me was to prevent such an end for both of us—and David. Poor David! What this will mean to him! Instinctively, I think, though I would never admit it to myself, I agreed to come to Palestine so that David at least would never have my torment, my fear, that I might someday be taken out for a Jew and be spit upon and reviled before being put to death.

And now look. It's not *as* a Jew I'm spit upon, but *by* them! Can my trial be called justice? Is my crime such a crime that to be cut off in the prime of life and put into a hole as dirt should be my penalty? Perhaps I made mistakes. I don't think so, but even if we admit it, in this confused little corner of the earth, aren't there many of us who've made mistakes like mine? But to call me traitor, to call me spy! I swear, although everything they say against me may be literally true, in the highest sense I'm innocent. Certainly I gave Redge the lists he asked for. I trusted Redge. I still don't think he could have betrayed me. I couldn't have been that wrong. Debbie, love, you know how during these past months I've been with Haganah, you know what I've been through. But I've been tried in this court for one mistake. I call it a mistake in judgment. At the worst. Things I did without seriously thinking. You see, these men didn't know Redge, and I did. Besides, in order to help Sam and Haganah I had to play along with Redge. What I did seemed so inconsequential at the time, so minor and now it looms so large, and here I am, living my old nightmare! Nothing I could say would move them, nothing my lawyer could say. The men from my outfit on the Road testified for me, but they seemed so determined, these three judges, that they would convict me. And the prosecutor. Ben Kepelow. A vicious man. The most diabolical man I have ever met, a dwarf of no character, with the soul of an ant, but with all the trickery and cleverness of our people. It's men like him, oily and sleazy, who have got the Jews hated the world over. Ami Ben Kepelow from Haifa. Remember him! And the worst witness against me, a man who knows how hard I've worked for him, Sam Pearlman. A man who plays five musical instruments! Wherever I turned, whatever my defense, there was always Sam Pearlman! Twisting and turning everything against me!

You should have heard my lawyer's plea. You'd have been proud of me. It was not the defense of a spy, it was a citation for patriotic awards. According to his speech to the court you'd think I was the first hero of Israel! A prince of a fellow. You must meet him. Boris Aronowitz, a Russian and a wonderful lawyer. So ironic, all of it. Then the verdict of the court! In less than an hour! And before I knew it, confirmation from Colonel Horowitz, an Englishman. So quickly. He came to talk to me three times. I'd never met him before. He seemed such a nervous uneasy man, so prejudiced in advance against me. I have the feeling I'm a pawn to his jitteriness. He was very unpleasant to me as though he wished I wouldn't present the facts to him. What a cold-blooded bastard he is! I told him I had a wife and son. He shrugged. Perhaps I'm to serve as an object lesson. Horowitz I blame above all the others.

Now he's offered me a rabbi! What nonsense—I, who have lived by science. And now there's not much more than an hour. Of course, Mr. Death doesn't come as such a surprise to me. I've lived with him these last few weeks on the Road. Any moment could have been the last one and now I wish to God one of them had been. I could have dispensed with these formal ceremonies.

I'll hope that something will turn up at the last minute. Some stay, some reprieve, some mercy, some good sense. If not, what can I do? I'm innocent. I'm devoted to this newborn land of Israel now. I commend her to you in spite of her little Colonel Horowitzes, in spite of her Sam Pearlman, in spite of her little judges and Ben Kepelow. I especially commend her to David. To Her, to Israel, I leave my treasures, my wife and my boy, both of whom I have loved, and in death whom I prize, to my own amazement, over everything, even life. Treat them well, Israel.

How I miss you! Both of you. I suppose it would have been easy for me to ask them to send for you, but I couldn't bear it, and this way seems to be better. If you don't agree, forgive me!

And for all that I have caused you, forgive me. Whatever you may hear about me, try not to believe. I've been only human in my frailties.

By the time Debbie had finished reading she was no longer conscious of David's presence, only the awful, hopeless, drained sensation that is grief possessed her and she began to sob. There was nothing to do, nowhere to turn, no last minute action of desperation. It was over, and the terrible finality was borne in on her mind and heart.

Karl came later in the day and embraced each of them without comment. Lilith was not with him, she had to stay at the hospital, he explained. "Of course, she's terribly upset, everyone I meet is so upset," he told Debbie gently.

"I just keep having the feeling I should go to him," Debbie said, not listening. "He must be lying somewhere, all alone, God only knows what state he's in."

"Debbie, please." Karl was trying to be firm as pleasantly as possible. "Think of David."

Oh, Lord, David! What's to become of him? she thought.

"This'll blow over," Karl said. "Everyone will forget. People here will have sympathy. They'll understand. If not them, who would understand? Give them a little time. Be patient."

"Even Lilith?"

Karl closed his eyes as though he had a sudden fleeting pain; his face was in repose again. "I told you. Lilith was at the hospital. She couldn't come tonight." His voice rose with some irritation. "Try to understand about Lil. She's upset. She's mixed up."

She wished she could send Karl back out into the night, to get rid of him. She closed her eyes—forget, forget everything.

"Would you like some caviar, Karl? I have a tin left, that I was saving . . ." She was talking without volition . . . nonsense . . .

Yet Karl sat contentedly and ate the caviar. Suddenly, it infuriated her. He was supposed to be her brother. If Vic were here, he'd throw him out. What could she do without Vic? Day after day?

"Everything we did, everywhere we had to go," she was babbling, "I counted on him to get me through. He took care of me. When I did something, good or bad, I always wanted to tell him. I meant to tell him sooner or later."

Karl looked at her sharply. She rose and walked unsteadily across the room to light two candles and change to a different seat. "I see a few things quite clearly now, even though I'm still quite drunk. You know that Colonel Horowitz gave me liquor? What do you think of the son of a bitch, he killed Vic!" Her voice had risen and she was shouting. "He could have saved him. But no! Worse than a Nazi. To hell with his family, we have to have an example. And then on top of it, tries to get me drunk. What kind of a man do you call that?"

She fished into her pocket and pulled out Vic's letter. "Here, read it." She tossed it to him. Karl read in silence and handed the note back to her.

She looked at him for some comment, but he said nothing.

"What should I do, Karl? You have to help me."

"Do? When?"

"Today. Tomorrow."

"Maybe we shouldn't go into certain details just now." Karl nodded significantly toward David.

"Why not?" Debbie was tired. "He's here. He may as well know what comes next and why and what has to be done."

Karl's shrug was of disapproval and washing his hands of responsibility.

"I'm pretty big, Uncle Karl," David said, "I'm over eight."

"You see," Debbie said. "He's over eight." She sighed. "I wanted him to be a boy as long as he could, the way I was a girl, protected and comfortable."

"May I say something? You're still a girl," Karl said.

"I try. Why not? I wanted it for David, not to have him a little old man like so many of the kids you meet today." She held her fingertips to her temples as though she were trying to steady herself. "Well, maybe he'll do better as a little old man."

"I'm not *that* old," David said.

She turned to Karl. "Tell me what's to be done. I can't think. One day at a time. Just tomorrow. What's to be done tomorrow?"

"We'll have to have a little service. I'll get a rabbi to come out to the cemetery. I'll try to arrange for a bus to take us all to the cemetery. They're using Sanhedria now. I'll arrange everything. I'm sure I can get a friend to drive the bus. You come to Bikur Holim tomorrow at one o'clock. We'll start from there."

"But what about David?"

"Better leave him with someone."

David broke in. "I want to go. It's my Daddy and if he's having a funeral, his own son ought to be able to go."

"Maybe," she said, "you won't even be able to get a rabbi to come . . . or a driver."

"Don't worry," he said. "I'll arrange everything somehow.

"Better lock up tonight. Don't let anyone in." He kissed David and Debbie. "Sleep well."

"Karl," her voice was pleading over the little nonsensical things which seemed so important at such moments. "Try to get a cheerful rabbi. I couldn't stand a breast-beater."

He ran downstairs as quickly as he could decently go.

Thirty

Debbie was sitting in the dark when a slight hesitant knocking startled her. It was not that she was brooding. Her mind was almost blank—wandering, moody, but she needed this undisturbed time by herself, needed it more than anything else. The knock was not only unwelcome, but roused her fears; besides she wanted nothing to waken David. Perhaps if she said nothing the caller would go.

But the rapping was repeated, not more loudly, but oftener, clearer.

"Mrs. Marmorek," a man's voice spoke softly in rather high-pitched English, but it was not a British voice. "Please, Mrs. Marmorek, let me come in."

Karl's warning was in her mind.

A long silence, and curiosity had its inevitable triumph. "Who is it?"

"Please, I can't talk standing in the hall this way. My name is George Stern. I'd like to come in."

She stood inches from the door and spoke in undertones. "Please speak quietly, my boy's asleep. What do you want?"

"I just want to talk to you. I'm an American."

It was difficult to know why the fact that he was an American persuaded her to open the door; perhaps it was that American captain she had kissed in the jeep on the Via Trionfale; perhaps it was Victor's theoretical cousin in Cleveland; America just seemed remote from everything real and harsh and what had happened to Vic.

The young man was in American khaki. He was light and thin, short of six feet by an inch or two, but his narrow face made him seem taller and thinner. Altogether he gave the impression of slightness; he looked to be seven or eight years older than she. She lit a candle. His eyes were deep set, blue they seemed in the half light, and his features were not handsome; they were rough but their configuration was not unpleasant, the full mouth, the large but well-shaped nose, high forehead, thin, light brown straight hair; his attitude seemed gentle enough not to cause her concern.

"Come in, please, we have to be quiet."

He slouched slightly and his arms swung easily; that was what characterized everything about him—easiness. He seemed to be in no hurry. "Would you like a cigarette?" It was an American brand, one she had not seen for months. Her hand was trembling when she took it.

"This morning," she said, "I thought to myself if only I had a cigarette now I'd be happy. But I wasn't able to get any. The grocer promised me a few yesterday, but he wouldn't sell them to me this morning. A man named Horowitz gave me one."

"Take the pack, I have more. Go ahead."

"That's very nice. The last American I met gave me a bar of chocolate for my son. He was very kind also."

"You speak English so well. I understood you were Austrian or Czech or something."

He had no desire to be disagreeable, it was only that the borders of middle Europe shifted too fast for him.

"I'm an Israeli. We've all had to learn several languages."

He lit both cigarettes, laced his fingers carefully together and spoke hesitantly. "I don't suppose you're going to like this, Mrs. Marmorek, but I'm a reporter for a Boston paper."

"Yes?" His statement made no impression. "A newspaper? Why should I dislike that?"

He was surprised with her indifference. "Good. Well maybe you would tell me your story your own way."

"My story?"

"Well, your husband's story."

"You mean for your newspaper?" So that was it. Naturally that was it. "Of what interest would his story be? He's dead. After that what do stories matter?"

"I must say most of my colleagues at the Pantilles agree with you. But the way I look at it, when a Christian Government executes a Jew that's monotonous, but when a Jewish Government executes a Jew it's news. First time it's happened in a couple of thousand years. Do I make sense?" His fingers laced and unlaced carefully.

"I hadn't thought of it," she said from the depth of her tiredness. "But I don't think a government did it. It was a little cockney named Horowitz, an antique dealer from Haifa. Why he did it I don't know." She felt exhausted beyond talking.

"Of course, you don't believe your husband was guilty."

She hesitated a moment. "They murdered him. A few little men did it. They can try to hide and blame the government, but I know who they are. Horowitz, Sam Pearlman, my boy's concertina teacher." She fumbled for Vic's letter. "Names I must remember." She was becoming overwrought, choking up again, unable to speak further.

"Look, Mrs. Marmorek. You don't have to talk to me if you don't want to. It's my job to find out as much as I can, and write about it. But if you'd rather I went away, I'll go. I happen to be interested, because—well because I'm an American and I have a legal background, and there are some tangled legal questions here. And human questions. I've participated in a few courts-martial myself in the American army. Been on both sides of the fence and even on the bench. I suppose this sounds phony, but I've a hankering to get the right answer. Not just a convenient answer or a simple answer, but the right answer. That's why I'm here instead of hanging around the police stations of Boston."

"I can tell you very little," she said doggedly. "My husband is no spy. He's no traitor. Go talk to Colonel Horowitz. Discuss it with him, he can be objective."

"I've talked to Horowitz."

"Did you ever meet such a nasty little man? I could tell you a thing or two about Colonel Horowitz."

"He seemed terribly overworked to me."

"Why not? He has to manage the killing of Jews while he thinks he's fighting Arabs. He works on two fronts! Too much for one man. Very hard on him. I think that's what makes him so nervous. He doesn't know which side he's on—half English, half Jew." She giggled harshly. "He has all the worst characteristics of both."

"I'm not a great believer in national characteristics myself," George Stern said.

"Can't you see the man is a cold-blooded fish with a Talmudic mentality? My husband was shot! And that man never even sent for me. My husband wanted to save me the misery, so Horowitz agreed with him. How can you let a condemned man make such a decision? What about me? I might have been some help, I think! I might have been able to save him. Perhaps not, but I might have. At least, I was free. I could go to people."

"Mmmmmm." It was a barely audible murmur that indicated simply that he'd heard her. He was disconcerting. Sympathetic, but not necessarily inclined to agree.

"It's not nice to complain to a stranger, I suppose. But I can't say these things to friends. My son was stoned by his schoolmates today. Do you have children, Mr. Stern?"

"A girl."

"Suppose she were stoned by her classmates? And you were there? And helpless? A little boy like that, such an eager, hopeful little boy. Our only son. And by his very best friends, children who've been here to the house hundreds of times. I tell you it was like the old days in Vienna, only worse. Worse for me because this was David and these were his friends."

"Look," George Stern said suddenly, "I've nothing else to do tonight. It isn't good for you to sit and brood all night. We've food and fresh milk at the Pantilles. Why don't you come over and have a bite with me? We can talk."

She smiled weakly. "I'm sorry you haven't been listening. My boy's sleeping in the next room. I couldn't leave him alone here."

He looked sheepish. "I just can't think of you as a mother."

"I'm twenty-eight," she said, "and he's eight. Nothing abnormal. And I really am sorry I can't come with you because in all my life I've never been so hungry. Just famished, honestly. You know, well-fed people lose their appetites at a time like this. But I'm too hungry."

"Wait here," he said. "I'll be back and we can talk right here."

"Will you bring something for my boy too?" she said. "Please."

She found herself waiting for his footsteps and the knock. He came with canned sardines and oranges, a loaf of bread and a tin of condensed milk. He talked sympathetically but very little and listened attentively. She talked too, like a torrent. She told him as best she could about Victor and Mama and Papa, about Vienna and Rome and the ship. She told him about Karl and Lilith and her work at the hospital and about Redge and Enid. He wanted to hear more. She told him about Mrs. Heller and the spilling of the water this morning and Baumerstock and Miss Even this afternoon after everyone knew about

Vic. When she talked of her visit to Horowitz she cried and although he was kind and patient he offered her no words of solace and waited until she left off crying to resume her story. He listened and, although she knew he could not picture what she said, she found calm in talking. Just letting it pour out, although she sometimes had the sense of being the fly on a needle for his inspection; even so it was a relief.

After her last long silence he rose, leaned against the wall beside the window and peered into the blackened street. "Eerie, all this quiet, isn't it? Disturbs me. Like a fellow who lives near railroad tracks. Can't sleep unless the trains go by."

Soon the sun was half up. Her face was tired and drawn and his sunbeaten face was tired too.

"Mrs. Marmorek, I sure hope I haven't imposed myself. I don't know how I can be of any real help, but if you want me, I'm always at the Pantilles. They'll know where to find me any time. Is there anything I can do?" She shrugged. "Anything you say. Just say the word."

"Bring my husband back to life." He looked hurt.

"I'm sorry for snapping at you. Thanks for the food. I'll tell David about you. I think he'd like you."

Thirty-one

The morgue at the Hospital Bikur Holim was off the street, the rear half of a dingy building behind a pretzel and sunflower seed shop and Le Bijou, dealers in silverware and costume jewelry, both now boarded and bare. But while the shops on the street were suffering lean days, the morgue behind them was doing a thriving business. In the alley which separated the morgue from the hospital, the families and friends of the dead attempted in vain to gather in solemnity; it was difficult to make anything solemn out of these helter-skelter improvisations, the continuous chatter, sudden shrieks of grief and cheerful greetings. Drawn up in businesslike array before the pretzel shop were four khaki-swabbed busses, dust-laden and battered by war's usage.

Debbie moved in a daze. As she, Karl and David crossed the street a corpse in a white shroud was carried on a canvas stretcher by four pallbearers to the first bus. Some mourners looked on in silence, others sniffed and some wept openly. "She was such a pretty girl," someone murmured.

The shrouded body was placed on the floor of the first bus and the mourners headed for the second, and the busses churned off.

Debbie was not certain when she became aware of it, but she realized that several of the people in the remaining cluster were staring at her and David. She saw an elderly man jerk a derogatory thumb toward them. Karl, Debbie and David stood close together in unacknowledged isolation.

"We're next, I think," Karl said.

"Did you get the rabbi?"

"Yes. He'll meet us at the cemetery. He had to go ahead, he has others before us."

"How about the driver?"

"I'm driving myself."

"Oh."

"We'll all have to go in the same bus."

"All? Who else is coming?"

"Victor."

A thin small man with dark glasses and false teeth, but white-gowned like a surgeon, stepped briefly outside the morgue door. "Marmorek!" he called. "Family of Marmorek?"

"Here!" Debbie raised her hand swiftly as if she were answering roll call. The murmur in the crowd was a confirmation of whispered suspicion.

"You?" The wizened man in the white gown and glasses had studied her for a moment. "Where are your pallbearers?"

"Pallbearers?"

With a certain professional patience the sorrowful man arched his brows. "Of course, Madam, pallbearers. Friends of the deceased. Or those gentlemen there can be hired for a reasonable fee." He pointed to the end of the alley where four black coated, bearded men appeared to be arguing.

Karl was impatient. "I've spoken to those men already. I'll carry the remains myself."

"Alone?" It was clear the mortician was not prepared for such nonsense.

"Of course. How far do you think it is to the bus?"

The man in white shrugged and disappeared shaking his head more gloomily than ever. In a few moments he reappeared at one end of a stretcher which carried a shrouded figure. At the other end was a plump little old man who handed his end of the stretcher to Karl. "Go, go," the morgue master commanded, "I'll help you to the bus."

The sight of the shroud had a sudden and violent effect on Debbie. She was nauseous.

"Is that Daddy?" David whispered in shocked disbelief.

Debbie could not answer.

Karl and the morgue master jockeyed the shrouded figure into the aisle of the bus toward the rear and lowered it to the floor. As he started back Karl handed the man fifty piastres and murmured his thanks. The man nodded funereally. "Return the stretcher, please. We're short."

Riding on the bus with Vic lying so, Debbie had a compulsion to tear the shroud off and see for herself, to touch Vic again, to reassure him, to comfort him, but it was impossible. There was David. She must act calmly, they would ride to the cemetery as though nothing and nobody were with them.

The bus lurched forward over some of the roughest terrain that has been called a road anywhere.

"Last night," Debbie said, "a man came to see me after you left. An American, George Stern." Karl was silent. "I'd never seen him before. He's a reporter. At least that's what he said."

"Did you tell him anything?"

"Well, we talked."

"May I say something? I think that was a mistake."

"But he was kind. He even brought us a little food."

"How can having anything in the papers do any good? The quieter the better. The sooner it'll blow over. The sooner we can return to normal. You, me, David, all of us."

"He won't write anything unless I tell him to. He's promised."

"Good. I hope he keeps his promise, but I doubt it."

"He even offered to help. Says he's a lawyer."

"A reporter *and* a lawyer? And how can a lawyer help? How can anyone help? What's there to help any more?"

"He only offered. I thought it very nice."

Karl was tight lipped. "May I say something? All I care about now is you and David. That you don't get hurt any more than you have to. The newspapers can't do you any good."

"But I really don't know what to do or where to turn."

"What's there to do? Time, Deb, time. There's nothing else to do but wait. It'll pass, believe me. Sooner or later."

The bus swerved suddenly to avoid an emaciated boy and his emaciated dog. "But I have to do something. What about David? He can't go back to that school. We'll have to find another school."

"Keep him out of school, Deb. The term's nearly over. In September it'll be all right."

"And what about my job?"

"Keep on with it. They need you!" She felt a little relieved at Karl's confidence.

"What'll I tell my landlord? This morning he left this charming little note under the door. Don't try to read it. Keep your eye on the road. He wants us to get out of the apartment. He puts it so considerately. He thinks it would be wise for *our* sakes to change neighborhoods."

Karl frowned. "I suppose there's something to that. You might go to Tel Aviv for a while."

They rode in silence. "Or you could go back to Vienna, I suppose. I told you we might have some rights to Lindenhouse."

As they started up the tortuous, rocky road that leads to the Sanhedria burial ground, she felt hemmed in by mistrust. "I only wish Vic could tell us what to do," she said dully.

Karl spoke with the greatest restraint he could summon. He said—and his face failed to mask the tremendous strain—"Let's try not to think about Vic any more." She could not believe he had said it.

The bus ground to a noisy stop. The previous funeral was under way, mourners gathered about an open grave, behind the rabbi who was intoning a prayer. Behind the crowd, four men leaned listlessly on shovels and waited with a boredom that was not wholly unfeeling.

Debbie had never been up to this burial ground before and the unexpectedness of the ugly barren site was a small added cruelty. She thought of the graceful cemetery in Vienna where Aunt Erika was buried, green and fresh and peaceful. This place looked like an abandoned city lot, strewn with stones and mounds of dirt. One half expected to see old tin cans and beer bottles. In one small area there were graves, perhaps six inches apart, each grave a six-by-two-foot rectangular plot bordered with concrete building blocks. A spike was driven into the ground at the foot of each grave and on each spike hung a rough cardboard lettered with the name of the dead and the dates. Most of the graves were fresh. It seemed impossible that such a site could have been selected by anyone with feeling as a final resting place for those who had escaped from the ignominy of the gas chambers. The mass graves of Poland, she thought bitterly, had more dignity than this.

Karl and one of the gravediggers had gone to the bus and were now moving Vic toward the grave as most of the mourners filed back into their bus. She was aware now of David. His hand which she had been holding tightly from the moment they had left the bus had turned cold. His face was white and his jaw was set as though he were preparing for physical onslaught.

"Mommy," he said softly. "I have to go to the bathroom."

"Can't you wait?"

"No."

"Well, come over here behind the bus."

She stood beside him in a spot half-concealed by the bus. "So many people are in the other funeral," he said.

The crowd was gone when they returned and the bus started down the hill in a lurching roar while three of the gravediggers covered the body of the unknown girl with efficient, unhurried dispatch.

The fourth gravedigger and Karl set Victor's shrouded body beside the second trench, and the rabbi who had officiated at the last funeral approached Karl and spoke to him for several moments. "Rabbi, this is my sister, Deborah, and David. This is Rabbi Simcha." The rabbi, a rotund, cherub-faced man in his fifties whose sparse gray hair could be seen beneath his black skullcap, nodded briefly. The gravediggers stopped their backfilling and one of them joined the group to take Karl's end of the stretcher. On a grunted signal from the chief, one side of the stretcher was raised and Victor's body rolled and thudded into the ditch. The gravediggers retired with the stretcher. Victor had fallen on his side and lay twisted in an angular position.

The rabbi read softly from his book, the prayer for the dead. He asked David to repeat it after him, but David was frightened into silence and Karl said nothing. Only the rabbi's voice was heard.

". . . and may God bring peace to all troubled souls and comfort the bereaved among us. Amen."

Turning directly to the trio he said, "In accordance with God's will we come from dust and return to dust and as a symbol of this coming and going I ask the bereaved family to join me in sprinkling a handful of earth into the grave."

He bent to pick up a few grains of clay and tossed it lightly into the trench and Debbie and Karl did the same. David, who had followed the ceremony with tight lips, bent down with his elders, but his hand found a rock, one of the yellow stones which littered the cemetery. His small fist was barely able to hold it. He peered into the ditch and with all the strength which sudden hate put into his eight-year-old body, he threw the stone at his father's corpse. It landed with a sickening, muffled thud and before anyone could say or do anything he had reached for another and thrown, and as Karl pulled him away he began to scream hysterically, uncontrollably. "I'll kill him. He took all my friends away! He took my friends away! I'll kill him!" After a few moments he stopped shouting and Karl heard a low peculiar moan. Then at last David was able to do all the crying he had intended, but it was for himself and not for his father.

The rabbi murmured a brief Amen.

Thirty-two

On the return from Sanhedria they rode wordless in the clanking bus, David jiggling, sullen, indifferent to Debbie's tentative caress; Karl pretending avid interest in the treacherous road; and Debbie unable to put the hysteria of David's denunciation out of her head. She had no idea what to do about him. She would try to think of something.

As they reached Jaffa Road Karl said slowly, "There was something about Vic in today's paper."

Everyone in town knew then. What must she do? She looked at David, his face still expressionless as he slumped in his seat like a tired old man.

"I itch," he mumbled. He retched and twisted in his seat.

At Bikur Holim Karl parked the bus, and returned the stretcher. Debbie murmured a word of thanks to Karl for having made the arrangements. She wished she could turn now and run home, run anywhere.

But Karl was walking home beside her.

They reached Jaffa Road just as a grimy caravan of trucks strained into town, coughing and gasping, Debbie thought, like their exhausted drivers.

"They're coming over from Tel Aviv," Karl said. "By the new road."

Vic's road, she thought, made by his hand, with his sweat, but it would mean nothing to Karl. It was only something for her. David looked up at her, and there was a flush of pride in his face.

"Daddy's road?" he said, then caught himself and retired to sullenness.

The City had changed. There was no dancing in the streets today, and people's steps were uncertain. The faces she passed were unfamiliar and frightened. Her head swam a little. How in the world did Fräulein Debbie Pretsch, of Lindenhouse, Snow Mountain, the girl with the brain of a sparrow, ever come to this street, in this ancient city to her husband's funeral? She felt like a rear echelon soldier who suddenly finds himself no longer safely behind the lines, but in the midst of combat, exposed, frightened, and amazed at being there. He has remained in the same place; it is the enemy who has advanced. It was no fun to be out front and see things as they were. Everything was squalid and grubby, squat yellowish buildings, matching the pallor of emaciated faces. What yesterday had been the ruins of heroic resistance was today the waste of a monstrously stupid enterprise. What effrontery, to believe these people were ready to become a nation! What is this Jerusalem, she thought, or all Israel, when you scratch below the surface, but a huge cesspool, the castoff refuse of other and happier lands? We tell ourselves the world cares. We scratch around the streets of this ugly old town which we call a holy city, telling ourselves what fancy heroes we are, fascinated by the sound of our own voices. But it's just as Vic says, we've trapped ourselves. The world has locked us in, and made us proud of it. There's a huge joke for you!

The old ghettos are out of fashion, gone from the streets of Warsaw and Berlin, of Moscow and Lwow and Minsk and Rome. The nice new, shiny, up-to-date type is a world ghetto. This one. Jerusalem.

The book stall on Julian's Way was open, and Debbie bought a copy of the one-page mimeographed newspaper and folded it carefully into her pocket.

On the steps to her apartment in the sudden shadow of the entryway they found a man asleep, head huddled into his arms. It was Noah Mendoza.

"Oh," Noah said, flustered from sleep, "I was afraid you'd never come." He spoke slowly in the deliberate, almost sluggish way he had, and reached automatically for his crutches.

Debbie was pleased to see him. "Noah, whatever are you doing here?"

"Waiting," Noah said sheepishly. "I thought maybe if there was something you needed—I figured you might . . ."

"This is my brother, Noah. Karl."

"Hi," David said. He was, as usual, troubled by his friend's stump and the new crutches.

"Noah was my favorite patient," Debbie said to her brother.

The two men shook hands solemnly. "We can't stand here in the hallway," Karl said. "Shall we go up?"

The clobbering of Noah's awkward crutches on the terrazzo treads shot through the house, and the door to the Epsteins' apartment opened tentatively as Debbie reached for her key. Rose Epstein peeked out, and on seeing Debbie her face suddenly contorted with pity and grief. She barely spoke.

"Oh, my dear poor Deborah. I'm so sorry!"

Dr. Epstein's loud raucous voice called, "Rose, get back in here!"

"Shut up, you! What are you, a monster?" She turned to scream back at him.

"Please, Rose," Debbie begged. "Don't fight with him. There's no point . . ."

"Come back here!" The dentist was at the door tugging at his wife, his red mustache bristling more fiercely than ever, although he avoided looking at Debbie.

The red-headed dentist yanked his wife unceremoniously inside, and after he closed the door firmly they could hear the couple's shouts until they were safely inside Debbie's apartment.

Noah had a package wrapped in old newspaper, which he began at once to pull open.

"Remarkable," Noah said cheerfully, "what a little thing like a missing leg will do for you. For example, Baumerstock, of all people. That old skinflint wouldn't give me the right time when I had both legs. Now he literally slobbers when he sees me. Disgusting. I can have anything in the shop. And you should see what he's hoarding in the back! I'm ashamed to take advantage of him, but just this once I thought why not? What good's all that slobbering if you can't cash it for emergencies?" He chuckled.

The package contained a can of American coffee and a loaf of bread.

"Free, imagine that!" Noah gloated. "On credit, which is the same thing. That man is a character." He hobbled with his newly-acquired agility toward the kitchen.

"Here," Debbie said. "Let me. You sit right down." She took the food into the kitchen, while Noah sat and trailed his crutches noiselessly to the floor. Karl followed her.

"Will you be all right?" Karl spoke tentatively. She wished he would get out, leave her alone. She wanted to say, "Yes, yes. I'll be fine if you'll only go away." Something about finding Noah on the steps had lifted her spirits a little. She had touched Noah at least. She suddenly felt that was the only important thing left to her. To touch someone, to have touched their trembling innermost being so that they could want to share even her bitterest hour.

"Why not stay for a little coffee with us, Karl?" She could hear the duty in her own voice.

"If you wish," Karl said uncertainly, "sure." He lowered his voice. "Is it going to be all right to leave you—" he jerked his head toward the living room—"with him?"

Debbie almost had to smile to herself. "Yes," she whispered. "He's very nice. Don't worry about me." She called, "David, open the window. It's so stuffy in there. Poor Noah will suffocate before he gets a sip of his own coffee."

The coffee and bread were eaten in polite silence, without a comment on the welcome aroma and taste after all the coffeeless weeks. Karl put his cup down after some moments and turned to Debbie hesitantly. "We're going to Tel Aviv for a few days, Deb—Lil and I. Lil's anxious to see her sister Clara—she's pregnant—you know how it is. And *they're* probably worried about *us*."

"I see," Debbie said.

"I was thinking," Karl continued, "maybe you and David would like to come along. You might be happier there for a while. Change of scene and all that."

Perhaps that was the thing to do. "But all my furniture, Karl, the house . . . David, dear, would *you* like to go to Tel Aviv for a little while?"

David shrugged dubiously. "If I could find Tamar," he said without enthusiasm.

It was impossible for her to think clearly about it. Later she would clear her mind for it. "When are you going?" she asked.

"Tomorrow morning, nine o'clock."

"Nine o'clock . . . I just don't know," Debbie said, her thoughts twisting this way and that. "They'll need me at the hospital." She wished Vic were there to tell her what to do. What would he have told her? She knew in her heart. Go! Get away from all the unpleasantness. But how, on such short notice? "I'll see," Debbie said. "If we want to go, we'll meet you at the Egged Station at nine."

"May I say something?" Karl said. "It would be a wise move. Even if people there find out—you know—what happened, well it would be more remote to them. They didn't have those mortars in Tel Aviv."

"I don't know," Debbie said. "I'll see. I need time to think."

Karl hesitated as if he were having difficulty in saying what he wanted. "Deb, I know it's hard for you to give a damn what other people feel right now, but I think you should try to understand because it may help you make the right decision. I don't want to hurt you, Deb, especially now, but you know how I feel. Papa's gone, and Mama. For me Palestine is mother and father. If someone hurts Palestine—it's something too bad to talk about. That's how *I* feel. So you can imagine the state of mind of other people. I think I know how you feel about Vic and I'm not trying to change you, but won't it be better if you understand how *we* feel? Because what's important to me is *you*, Deb."

"I know," Debbie said. Her whole being was outraged. She wanted to cry almost, to strike him, but she did nothing.

"You'll be all right meanwhile? Until tomorrow?" Karl looked from Debbie to David and back, uncertain and ashamed. "You're sure?"

"We'll be fine," Debbie said briefly. "Go ahead, go ahead."

"Don't worry about Mommy and me," David said with bravado.

Karl shook hands hurriedly with Noah, kissed Debbie on the cheek, handed her a few five-pound bills, and gave David a quick tight hug. "Take care of this boy," he said, "he's an old friend of mine," and ran downstairs. His going was a relief. She saw that Noah was studying her curiously.

"I never got a chance," Debbie said brightly, turning quickly to Noah, "to thank you for helping me yesterday. You know, I was so grateful for that little bottle of water, you have no idea. It was a lifesaver."

"My pleasure," Noah said.

"I guess that old battle-ax Mrs. Heller has plenty of company today," Debbie said. "She's on the side of the patriots today. I'm so glad you came, Noah. I just can't tell you, it's such a lift. Not everyone is doing it—you can see."

"Well," Noah said. "I can get away with it." He stared at his leg stump. "People don't dare scold me."

"That's what's nice about you, Noah. You actually don't feel sorry for yourself, do you?"

"Now, you know better than that."

"But you put on such a brave front, I mean. I wish I could."

"Don't fool yourself. Lots of times I get half crazy and frustrated and, if you only knew how I've lived over the minutes just before I was hit by that mortar and keep trying to decide if I couldn't have done something different to keep my leg. I *know* I could have. I know in my heart it was my own stupidity and it's hard to swallow."

"Ah, but you *don't* feel that way. I remember the talks we had in the hospital. I always thought you were the bravest of my boys. And how about your work, your painting, those wonderful charcoals? Don't they help?"

"I don't fool myself about them. I know people are only trying to cheer me up."

"No, Noah, no, your work is exceptional! Everyone says so, not just me. Miss Even was telling me just yesterday."

"You can all talk as if I were a kid because you all have both legs and none of you knows a damn thing about art. Still I try, I figure someday I may do better. I'm improving. But don't let me stop you from saying nice things to me. It helps. I think sometimes, if I could only be like you! No matter how bad things got or how hopeless they looked at the hospital you were always cheerful. Remember how you helped us slide or crawl under our beds during the shelling, and told us it was just practice for what to do when the husband comes home unexpectedly? We felt pretty helpless and silly, but you made it almost bearable. Don't go changing on me."

"Oh," Debbie said, "trouble isn't the same when it's your very own. How can you tease away something that's with you minute after minute and second after second? How do you *ever* forget it, Noah?"

Noah was silent and David whispered, "You know about my Daddy, don't you, Noah?"

Noah nodded.

"They killed him," David said, "because he was a traitor." When she heard that, something blind and cold took hold of her from her knees and the pit of her stomach and she saw nothing and knew nothing except that she must obliterate this horrible lie David had spoken aloud and she must protect Vic from it. She forgot it was David who had said it. She thought of Horowitz and Mrs. Heller and the children at school. She could hear her own voice now screaming, "David, you don't deserve to be his son! Don't you ever say that again, ever!" And she was flailing her arms at him, striking him as if he were an adult, wildly, blindly, she could feel her fists strike into his clothing and flesh. "How could you do such a terrible thing at the cemetery? Such an awful, awful thing? You're not an infant! You're a big boy! Your Daddy was a great man, and he loved you! Do you understand that? He loved us! Whatever he did he did for us! He loved us greatly and we loved him! He was always wonderful to us. You're never to say such things again! You hear? Oh, I'm so ashamed of you!"

She felt Noah pulling her away, she saw David cowering, crying with his hands protecting his face, huddled away from her.

"God, God, what's happening to us?" she moaned and fell into a chair and buried her face as she talked and cried. "You just don't know what to make of a child. Vic wasn't what they say, Noah, believe me, it's a lie. Oh, maybe he was weak or maybe he was cautious, or maybe he wanted to make things too safe and easy for David and me, but he never gave them any military things, Noah. That's nonsense. I'm sure, I'm as sure of it as I am—well—of God. Oh, Lord, I can't believe what's happening. What am I going to do, Noah? His own boy!"

"I'm sorry, Mommy!" David shouted, repeating and repeating the same phrase, trying to unsay what he had said. He was sobbing, from hurt and humiliation and the utter confusion of his emotions. Debbie sat trying to control her trembling and when at last she was able to calm herself she spoke in a frightened, distant voice, swallowing her words, talking almost entirely to herself. "I just don't know how to manage any more. Everything's got out of my hands. It's so trite and I suppose everyone thinks of it, but it would be so nice to lie down and call it a day. Just pull the blanket over my head and never wake up. We've worked so hard and tried so hard and been through so much and the only thing we had to go on was hope. We hoped someday, some fine day, we'd come out into light and now—instead—what was the use of all our trouble? I could have stayed in Vienna and died with my Papa. Or in Prague with Vic's Papa. Oh, I had so many good chances to die, wonderful chances that I missed. And now I'm too much of a coward to do it myself."

Noah said, "Of course everyone like us thinks of that. How many nights do you think I lie awake in the dark trying to feel all my toes? You can feel them, you know, each one separately, and I wished I could sleep away and forget them. I'd have visions of myself as a beggar rolling along on a little cart with a regular post on Zion Square, or put away in some horrible home to be forgotten."

"It's not the same, Noah. A leg can mean so little. I'd take Vic without either leg, blind, anything, just to have him back, I'd gladly nurse him the rest of my life! You're really lucky, Noah. You have no idea how lucky you are."

"Yes, I do," Noah said. "I'm glad to be living and painting. But you—you can be congratulated on having both legs, and this fine young fellow here." He slid his arm about David's shoulder and turned abruptly to him speaking cheerfully. "David, would you like to hear the amazing story of how I came to lose my leg?"

"Oh, please not, Noah." Debbie started to protest. It was gruesome and she'd heard it.

David's eyes were wide with anticipation.

"David's old enough to hear it, man to man," Noah said, and his manner was mockingly man to man. "Besides, I've never really told anyone before."

"You told me," Debbie said in a barely audible voice.

"What I told you wasn't true," he said almost cheerfully. "Not by a mile. A man never tells the truth to women, David, but I'll tell you the absolute truth. Because you'd know right away if I were kidding."

His voice was so bantering, Debbie was sure he was planning some fanciful yarn.

"Well, you know about the fight for Kastel. That's where it happened. Remember we were having trouble getting convoys through from Tel Aviv?"

David nodded solemnly. "One convoy got through the day I was wounded, Mom, didn't it?"

"Well," Noah continued, "a bunch of us were supposed to take over on Kastel. You know it's on a great hill and from Kastel you can see down to the Latrun Road and shoot up anything on it. That's where the Arabs were—on top of the hill, and our job was to get them off and get up there ourselves—otherwise . . ."

"No convoys, of course," David said as if he were playing a game.

"Right. The sergeant in my squad was an old buddy of mine, Josh Van Santen. Remember him?"

"Of course!" David said. "That was Tamar's brother, Mommy. Big Josh."

"Well," Noah said. "Josh was my best friend. You know what it's like to have a buddy like that, don't you?"

"Like me and Meyer," David said smugly.

"Right. We were great friends. Since we were ten or eleven. It was just an accident when we were put into the same unit, we'd each been working in Haganah separately without ever telling the other. Well, at Kastel, Josh was the sergeant in our squad and I was the machine gunner. I felt pretty good about my gun. The other guys had Stens and Brens and Molotov cocktails, but I had the heaviest weapon in the outfit. I was the powerhouse. That gun weighed a ton, but I was glad to lug it along."

"Give me a cigarette, Noah." Debbie spoke sharply. This was no fanciful yarn, this was the story he'd told her. "David's still really quite a little boy. Do you have to go on with it?"

Noah lit a cigarette for himself. "He's not so young. Weren't you pretty grownup at eight?"

Yes, she could remember being eight. The world was a place of happiness and mystery. People laughed and cried and were cruel unexpectedly and she never knew why, but to David the cruelty of the world was no mystery. She threw up her hands wearily. After today's events, what was she trying to protect David against?

"I have to tell it sooner or later," Noah said. "Could I have another cup of coffee?" He turned back to David. "We got out of the trucks before we reached the hill. That old fortress sat up on top like a crown, but it was no inspiring sight to us. In fact we took a dim view of it. We were scared, too. There we were in the pitch dark out on the Jerusalem Road and there was Kastel. The hill and us, that's all. There were maybe a hundred of us. And there I was lugging that bloody machine gun and whenever I looked up I had the funny feeling Arabs were watching me just for fun, and any minute, bang. Just to lug the gun up to the top is some job without Arabs taking pot shots at you. Forty kilos it weighed."

"Some job," David said sagely.

"That was a night. I dragged that gun all the way. When we got near the top the Arabs started shooting and screaming like a bunch of crazy animals, but they were lousy shots in the dark, and no one in my squad was hurt till we got to the top. I guess we got quite a few Arabs too and all through it Josh Van Santen and I were alongside each other."

"Did you really kill any Arabs?" David was following every word. "Did you see them?"

Noah stirred his coffee absently. "Well they threw these huge rocks down at us and popped off at us, and when we got up there we had to fight a couple of 'em with knives. They got one of our boys, a Yemenite kid named Asi. It was pretty rough, but by the time the sun began to come up, the Arabs were headed down in a hurry, and we were up there, snug as goats. We could see the whole road winding below us, that beautiful old road, and we knew that with us up there the road was ours.

"Josh and I were pretty scared, Asi was the first guy we'd lost, and we could hardly breathe from fighting and climbing so I set the gun down and we tried to dig a little cover for ourselves, because we figured the Arabs would be back. I remember that minute as if it were this morning. We were digging and my shovel hit a rock and we were trying to move it with our bare hands, our fingernails. Clawing away like, and our hands touched and we looked at each other. I don't know how I looked, but he looked worried. I don't know what made Josh say what he did, but he said it. He said, 'I'll keep an eye on you if you keep an eye on me.' I suppose all I did was grunt because it was ridiculous to be making private pacts right then. But I knew what he was thinking. Quite a few of our boys were hit in the convoy to Etzion and the Arabs made a mess of them. They weren't satisfied just to kill 'em. They cut 'em up and took pictures of 'em."

"What did the Arabs do exactly?" David said breathlessly.
"Never mind," Debbie said.
"Oh, they made a mess of those guys," Noah said. "And they seemed to get quite a boot out of it. Made a fortune on those pictures I guess, too. Well, that happened only a couple of days before Kastel and most of the guys had seen those snaps and were pretty sick over it. Even though it doesn't make a lot of difference what happens after you're dead, it bothered us. You figure they ought to draw the line somewhere. And one of those guys was a buddy of mine. I puked myself when I saw those pictures. I couldn't get 'em out of my head and neither could Josh—especially up there on Kastel, when we both knew what was coming next. No one was coming to relieve us, that was sure. We had Arab settlements all around us and it was just a question of time before they'd be coming back. At least I had the satisfaction of seeing one convoy go by around noon the next day. By then we were pretty tired and hungry."

Debbie had heard stories like Noah's from scores of boys, they told them like anecdotes the way Mama's friends had talked about their operations.

"When the Arabs came at us they had heavy mortar support and we took a beating. We lost two men. Josh and I had separated and kept calling to each other, but one hit real close. The whole hill shook where I was and Josh gave the most terrible scream I ever heard. Somehow I got over to him and his stomach was bleeding. At first I thought he was only hurt, but when I looked at him I could see the hole in his belly was so huge—half of it was gone—and the way he stared up at me I knew he was dead."

"Dead?" Debbie said, "but you told me at the hospital—"

"Just then I heard our leader call for us to abandon our position and get down to the road. The others started clawing their way down, doing the best they could, but I couldn't move, I just sat there with Josh. I felt like I was frozen. I don't know what got into me. Maybe just scared. I had one arm around my gun and the other around Josh and I thought of Josh's mother and father and those pictures and it just came to me that I'd be Goddamned if I'd let the Arabs cut Josh up, and humiliate his dead body. I guess it was the stupidest thing I ever did. Like a crazy fool I tried to drag him and the gun down that God-forsaken rock pile and I never had a chance. The hill was covered by mortar fire and the Arabs were on their way up. I might have made it okay alone, but I just dragged Josh along feeling my way and then I was hit. I don't remember much after that—just wondering how bad I was hurt, and whether I'd live. I guess I rolled a lot of the way and slipped and dragged myself. I lost the machine gun and Josh. I knew my leg was hurt pretty bad, but not how bad. Just couldn't bring myself to look at it or feel it and I never thought of Josh again, or the pictures or the Arabs—the pain wiped out everything. Well, I finally made the road."

"But you told me Josh was only hurt," Deborah said incredulously. "You said you were trying to save him."

"No, he was dead right from the start," Noah said quietly and rather slowly. "I've never told anyone that before, but he was dead and there wasn't a thing I could do for him. I just didn't want to see him humiliated because he was my friend. Isn't that about the dumbest way to lose a leg you can think of?"

David said, "Hey, that's too bad." Then suddenly comprehending all that Noah had said, he began to pace rapidly back and forth and gesticulate as he walked. "What's the good of saving him after he's dead?" he asked excitedly. "If they cut him up, whatever they do, it doesn't make any difference, does it, because they only have to throw him in a grave like they did with Daddy. So what's the good of saving him up?" He shook his finger at Noah and his treble voice shook with agitation and distress. "I'm sorry about your leg, but if you ask me, Noah, you didn't act too smart."

"David!" Debbie cried. "What's got into you?"

"He's right," Noah said softly and he buried his face in his hands wearily. "He's saying what I keep trying to forget." He shook his head, still covering his face so that his words came in a blur.

"Don't you agree with him?"

"I don't know," Debbie said softly. "Golly, pure reason doesn't prove anything. I can see where a friend might have to be defended even after he's dead."

"Can you?" Noah looked sharply into her eyes. "I wanted to tell you the truth about it today," Noah said, "not only because I had to tell someone sooner or later—you can't keep that kind of thing to yourself, and I don't even dare tell my mother—but I thought you might want to defend a friend too, even after—well, after death. You might decide to defend him from humiliation."

"I don't quite see how I could," Debbie said.

"I think you could try," Noah said.

Debbie said, "Perhaps I might, Noah, but it's so hard to do anything, isn't it?"

"It's not easy," Noah said.

"But *how*, Noah, how in the world will I fight for my friend?"

"I don't know. You'll have to find a way. Some way. Maybe that's what our whole fight's been for, this whole war, not for a piece of dried-up real estate—but to save us from humiliation, and especially our dead—all of us who were pushed like plucked chickens into ovens, or dug our own graves, all of us whose teeth were picked over for gold, or got melted into soap. Those are great humiliations. We had to wipe 'em out."

"I suppose," Debbie said uncertainly.

"Why do you think the Sternists made booby traps out of those two English sergeants, even after they were dead? Sure, they probably rationalized it, but in their subconscious it was to strike at arrogance with humiliation. We all suffer from it."

She thought of her own days of humiliation—the evening Vic lashed David for stealing a bit of trash candy in Rome; the station at Gmünd where she and Mama and Gussie were stripped; the day they decided to leave Gussie Goldenberg because of her face; the moment she passed two helpless women on their knees scrubbing Josefstadter Strasse. She could feel Fräulein Froelich's ruler across her knuckles. And she recalled her panic that Angelo would tire of her, the new ways she had to think of to make his pleasure greater.

"Do you think you'll be going to Tel Aviv with your brother?" Noah said.

"I suppose that's the sensible thing to do," Debbie said.

"It's probably sensible," Noah said.

"But I guess not," Debbie said. "It would be another humiliation, wouldn't it?"

Noah was silent.

"You know what Vic's father told us when we asked him to leave Prague and come to Rome with us? He was a doctor, you know. That was Grandpa Marmorek, David, I'll never forget it. His life depended on it, and I think he knew it. He said he wouldn't move even into the next block. His patients needed him and he needed them." She shook her head woefully. "Anyhow, I owe one pair of hands to the hospital, and it's the only pair I have." She paced up and down slowly. "What makes me so wild, is that all this was so unnecessary, it's so wrong. Some things you feel, well, they were inevitable, the people at Etzion or in the Old City—the boys who went in to save them. Well, it had to be done. If something happened to them you felt it was necessary. Even the gas chambers. You felt there was nothing those poor souls could do. But this is so wasteful and awful and stupid. This could have been prevented. That stupid Horowitz. I could kill him, I honestly could. And maybe I will." Debbie stopped her pacing. "Everyone in town seemed to know before I did, or do I just imagine that?"

Noah shrugged. "Jerusalem's a small town. No one's anonymous. It's not like Paris or Warsaw where you could hide. Of course, you hear stories and rumors every day; I figured it was just more loose talk until I saw it in the paper this morning. When I read that, I came over."

"Oh, yes, the paper." She fished the mimeographed sheet out of her pocket, searched a moment and found the heading in the lower right hand column:

TREASON IN OUR MIDST

No doubt during the past month a great deal of physical damage has been done our cause, our arms and our people by spies who have been giving information about the location of our ammunition depots, machine shops and other vital spots. It is now disclosed that a master list or lists of strategic posts was turned over to an enemy ring (via English Civil Service) to ensure the methodical destruction of those installations. The lists were given to the enemy by one Victor Marmorek, a Jew, an officer of Haganah, to whom the swift and classic punishment of the centuries for traitors has been meted out by the military. His is a name that will live in infamy. There may be a few here and there who will deplore the lack of mercy shown the guilty man. To them we say, in our fight for survival we cannot afford the luxury of mercy. Justice is our only criterion. We applaud Colonel Julian Horowitz for cutting out the evil cancer in our midst. Those who plot against our survival must know the fate which surely awaits them. Since the truce may last or fail, it is to be hoped that the military and the rest of us will continue to exercise vigilance to protect the people of Jerusalem from other spies and traitors, if such there be, in the trying days ahead.

Debbie crumpled the sheet. She'd find the fool who wrote it and strangle him. If only Vic could defend himself, tell them the truth, if only . . .

"Unless you do something," Noah said, "this is the final word. No one else is going to do anything. Ask yourself, who else in Jerusalem has a washing machine? How many have a new refrigerator? What other boy has a bike like David's?"

"Oh, Lord," Debbie said. "What am I to do?"

"I wish I could tell you," Noah said.

"What *is* there to do? And if there were something, when would I have time to do it? I have to get back to work, Noah. We're going to need every penny I can make now. I don't even know if we'll be able to afford this flat any more. Oh, I need time to think and work. I need time to feel. I should've been at the hospital hours ago, but I'm just not up to it; I can't leave David. He needs me too. Thank heaven someone needs me." She put her arm about David. "That's one thing I have, at least."

"That's all any of us have," Noah said, "isn't it? Would you feel any better if I slept here tonight?"

Debbie looked at him in surprise. "I think I would," she said after some thought. "That would be very nice for David and me. You can have Elsa's bed."

"And tomorrow," Noah said, "if you like I'll stay with David after school while you're at the hospital."

"I don't think David ought to go to school," Debbie said, "not tomorrow anyway."

"Oh, I could never go to school," David assured Noah solemnly. "That René Blum, he's crazy. He's wild and nuts, sort of. He'd kill me."

"Well, while you're at the hospital I'll stay with David. I'll get Baumerstock to loosen up with a little food, and I can show David how to draw."

"And I'll teach you to play the concertina," David said.

Thirty-three

In the morning on the way to the hospital Debbie stopped at the Egged Station to look for Karl and Lilith. The crowd milled in disorderly fashion, calling, screaming, pushing, for everyone was either going to Tel Aviv or saying good-bye to someone who was. She circulated in the crowd feeling more and more exhausted and only at the last moment saw Karl and Lilith as they climbed aboard a bus. Karl was standing on the step, peering out at the crowd.

"Karl!" she called. "Lil!"

They saw her. Karl waved and shouted, "Come on if you're coming! Where's David?"

"I'll have to stay here," Debbie said when she'd managed to reach them. "I couldn't go now."

"Well, I think you're making a mistake," Lilith said over the noise of the motor; she sounded annoyed, almost angry. "I absolutely do."

"I'm glad you two are getting a chance to get away," Debbie said. "I hope your sister's well, Lilith. I hope she has her baby without trouble. Give her my love."

"Will you be all right?" Karl said. "You're sure you don't want us to stay?"

She could see the quick cold glance Lilith gave him.

"I'll be fine," Debbie said. She kissed Karl; and Lilith, who usually jutted her cheek out to be kissed, quickly put her hand forward.

" 'Bye, Debbie, see you soon. Personally I think you're making a mistake, but it's up to you and I guess this won't be your first."

She turned to go to the hospital. But her legs did not take her there. Why was she heading home again? Especially when she knew how they needed her? She was tired, exhausted beyond feeling or thinking or knowing anything. She had to find rest, to blot out everything, to forget. She had to find a dark room with the shades drawn and pull the covers over her head and sleep. Oblivion was what she needed.

At the apartment David was working seriously on a charcoal drawing of a house. She said nothing to him or Noah but went into her bedroom, closed the blinds and lay down, in a kind of stupefaction. Oblivion was a long time coming, but it came. From time to time she woke and then dozed again. Noah brought her some soup and coffee and bread, once, twice, she couldn't remember.

Once David woke her to say Elsa was there. She had come with tins of food and a box of biscuits. Debbie was scarcely civil to her. She saw her through bleary eyes, unreal. Elsa left quickly after a muttered prayer.

There were dreams, hard to distinguish from the periods of wakefulness, but each time she awoke, she prayed to die, at least to sleep. Occasionally she looked into the living room. Sometimes David was there with Noah, sometimes the room was empty. From time to time she staggered to the water closet. Sometimes it was night, sometimes daylight.

At last she could lie still no longer. The stupor was gone, and she became acutely conscious of an ache, a dull steady weakness in the pit of her stomach, as though her insides were sinking, sinking. Her head was splitting. She had to get up, to see to David, to see what time it was. To get back to the hospital. She looked at herself in the mirror. She was ghastly, barely recognizable. She washed, scrubbed, combed her hair, put on a new khaki dress. Mentally she spurred herself. "What time is it, Noah?"

"Ten o'clock." He paused. "It's Thursday."

She'd been lying in that room for days. How many? Two, no three. Three days in a stupor!

"My God."

"You have to get hold of yourself, Miss Debbie."

"I know."

"Would you like to get back to work? I'll take care of David. We get along fine."

"Yes. I'd better get back to the hospital, hadn't I?"

"I suppose. You ought to keep busy. You'll die if you keep this up."

"That'd be nice."

"Go on," Noah said. "Get over to the hospital."

She found Elsa in the dingy right wing ward. There were still two patients in each bed and a large number of assorted visitors. Men calling for nurses were going unanswered because no staff member was there but Elsa. Visitors looked harried and helpless, and none stayed more than a few minutes. A young man, pallid and in evident discomfort, complained to Debbie of pain in his abdomen. His chart indicated abdominal infection from a small arms wound and called for penicillin shots; the last shot was already three hours overdue. She fetched the hypodermic needle and penicillin from a new girl who had graduated only last year and whom she knew only slightly, but who stared at her as if she had seen a ghost. As she gave the injection she was conscious of Elsa at her elbow. The men's faces, the voices calling Nurse or Sister or simply Miss, the hopeful calls and the groans formed the background to which she was accustomed. There was work to do. It was only rarely that she allowed herself the hazard of daring to let her mind dwell, without insulation, on these men and their pain and loneliness.

"Debbie," Elsa said and tugged at her shoulder. "Please." She led her through the tiny hall past the foot of the entrance stairs and outdoors into the front courtyard. "You shouldn't be here now." Her face was flushed. "I'm sorry about what's happened, Deborah. I'm sorry for you and I'm very sorry for David. That goes without saying."

"Thanks for coming to see me. The food tins are mighty handy."

Elsa waved her hand impatiently. "For your own good, Debbie dear, you shouldn't be here. You need rest. You're in a state of shock. Can't you see that?"

"Well, what choice do I have? What do you expect me to do?" Debbie's voice was rising. "I have to go on making a living. What do you think I'm made of?"

"Deborah dear, you know very well how I feel about you and David—"

"Oh, David was always a nuisance to you," she said sharply. "You know that."

"That's not so." Her eyes were wider than ever. "I grew to love that boy. I'm sorry for him, believe me. But you've never really believed in the Word of God, Debbie. It's something we cannot control. We can feel sorry, but we cannot change it. The sins of the fathers are visited upon the sons . . . That's the law of God. That's why—"

"No God would ever say such a thing! No sensible man would either. It's not fair. And his father committed no sin!" Debbie was shouting. "No more than your father or mine!"

But she saw Elsa had believed what they said. Vic's torture had not touched her, had not even occurred to her, to this woman who had lived in his house and eaten his food.

"You have to take into consideration what people will say," Elsa said placatingly. "Some say you are mixed up in it too. Well, of course, I've known you too long to believe that, I know it's nonsense, but they're saying it just the same. The nurses' room was buzzing with it last night. You should have heard—people were taking sides! How I had to defend you, you have no idea! Two girls started to fight, actually tearing at each other. Pulling hair, you never heard such shrieking and screaming. And how much worse would it be if you were here! You know I can't have my girls in that condition. What can I do? Things are hard enough as it is. And it's not good for the patients. So far, thank God, the patients haven't heard of it. Why, I don't know, but when they do, there'll be bad feeling. You know many say they were hit because their positions were given away. You know there's grumbling about spies, and if they ever thought Victor . . ."

I've tried so hard, Debbie thought, I've given myself and so have David and Vic, all our comforts. David could have gone to London. I've tried till I ache. Haven't I done a hard and conscientious job? O Lord, haven't I done everything I could?

"I don't care," she said trying to remain calm, "I've got to work here. I have David to think of. I need every penny I make here. Besides, if I don't keep busy I'll go crazy. I've always worked as hard as you or anyone else and I have my rights here." She could hardly believe she was saying such bold and desperate words. For, while she had scrapped a little with Vic on occasion, she had never stood on her hind legs and reared back to dispute the ultimate wisdom of others. Now there was no alternative. "How can I *not* work here? I'm needed and you know it. We need everyone we can get. What's the use of such a silly argument?"

"It's not silly!" Elsa's voice rose to semi-hysterical pitch. "You have plenty of problems to work out. You ought to move somewhere else—away from Jerusalem altogether—to Haifa or Tel Aviv. Nurses are needed there too. Get away. You have to hide yourself and study the Torah and pray! For your own good, my poor Deborah."

"Well, save your breath," Debbie snapped. "Don't be so good to me."

"I'm sorry," Elsa said and she grew calmer. There was a finality to her attitude. "I'm sorry, I wish I could change the decision, but I'm not the only one involved. It's not only me. They've decided you should take a leave of absence—for a while anyway, until all this—" she shrugged. "I'm sorry."

"But why?" Debbie heard her own voice rise almost to a scream. "What have I done? Elsa, listen to me, listen, Elsa, I need the money. I need the job now, don't you see? There's David. You've got to help me, Elsa . . . . I'll work in the lab, I'll find some place where no one will see me. Elsa, listen, please . . . I haven't done anything, you know that . . ."

Elsa turned to the front door and started back in. "Don't despise the chastening of the Lord," she muttered sadly, "for whom the Lord loves, he chastises."

"Oh, thanks. Thanks for your kind advice. You'd think they were doing me a favor to let me work here! You'd think it was some kind of privilege! Eighteen—twenty hours a day we're at it. You'd think it was some kind of pleasure!" She began to laugh.

"I'd better see Dick Alpert," she shouted almost hysterically. "At least he's human!"

"Leave Dr. Alpert alone!" Elsa flared. "He's had enough trouble with the Board already over you!" Elsa turned away. "There are some notes and letters for you at the desk," she said.

Debbie thought of going to the superintendent, insisting on her rights, but her soul cringed at the thought. O Lord! she thought, I've taken about all I can. When she had composed herself, she asked at the desk for her mail. The elderly attendant was surprisingly friendly and gave her a dozen envelopes at which she glanced quickly. They had all been opened and read.

Two of them started abusively, but several from old patients were sad and sympathetic. Two patients sent money and offered to help. Dick Alpert wrote, "Sorry, Deb. Someday this Board will come to its senses. I'm sure the army's blundered about Vic, who was my friend, and no more a spy than I. If you need me, call."

But the last letter was so exciting the others were forgotten. It came from Haifa, written in bold German script:—

Haifa—June 12th

Deborah dear!

I am hoping this will make the special plane to Jerusalem. I've heard this morning on the Tel Aviv radio the frightful thing which happened to Victor. I cannot believe it. To discover you and to discover it in this way! You will understand why so many impressions crowd in on me at once. I thought surely you were both long since dead. I'm sure you thought the same of me. However, somehow, here I am. I came in by the underground through the Balkans and Turkey. It seems a miracle to me. How I managed to do it is a long story, which I shall tell you when I see you. I arrived only two months ago but of course never suspected you were here. I wrote your brother from Prague as you suggested, in 1938, but I guess he never got my letters. So I had to manage for myself.

How is your brother? Is he still married to that nurse? I can picture her photograph, and I'll always remember her name—it always seemed such a pretty one to me—Lilith.

I have a job now in a textile plant, and a room here in Haifa in the Carmel—lovely—and—you'll never believe it—a boyfriend. Debbie dear, I can never forget what you and your family and Victor did for me in getting me out of Vienna and helping me find a job in Prague. I cannot believe Victor did what they say. Please, if there is anything I can do to help, I will be grateful for a chance to repay you no matter what anyone says. I will come to Jerusalem for a weekend if you want, or you can come here for as long as you please. I have room for you.

Your ever grateful,

GUSSIE GOLDENBERG

P. S. I was so surprised to hear you have a son! Though I suppose I shouldn't be. How sad this must be for him!

Debbie was stunned. Gussie, of all people! And she would be grateful for a chance to repay. A smile of terrible confusion filled her soul. What an odd little twist. Grateful! She stumbled on home, scarcely seeing where she walked. How easily she wept these days! She must be rundown.

At the flat she found David and Noah, having had their fine breakfast of coffee and olives, working with the concertina. Noah was playing, with David instructing, a simple bright tune, the first David had learned from Angelo, perhaps a dozen notes in all, repeated endlessly. They were both cheerful and busy and Debbie had the guilty feeling that she was about to dampen this atmosphere.

"Don't stop for me," she said.

"Mrs. Epstein came over, Mommy, and left that cake. She sneaked over while her husband was out, how's that? Pretty good for old fatso."

"Wasn't that nice of her," Debbie said, straining for her last ounce of good cheer, "just wonderful."

"We didn't eat any," David said, "we decided to wait for you."

"What happened at the hospital?" Noah asked, uneasily watching her face.

"Perhaps I should have gone to Tel Aviv after all," she said. "It's so hard to know what's right."

"I might find Tamar in Tel Aviv," David said hopefully.

"But what about the hospital?" Noah persisted.

She wished he would stop. "Oh, nothing much. Elsa thought I should take some time off. She thought it would be better all around."

There was a small silence, until David said, "You ought to hear Noah play, Mommy; play some more, Noah. Listen!" Noah struck a little tune. "I taught him," David crowed.

"Noah, you've been wonderful, but I must do something, I must make up my mind, really. This is ridiculous. We have a little money. I *could* go to Tel Aviv or Haifa. I just heard from an old friend of mine—she's in Haifa—never even dreamed she was still alive."

"Who, Mommy?" David said.

"No one you know, David honey. She was a friend when I was a girl."

"Really?" David was politely impressed. That must have been the olden times.

"She invited us up. Of course, I've never seen much of Haifa, but I remember the Carmel. It's beautiful. I wouldn't mind living there a bit and I understand they have several marvelous hospitals there, and fine schools too . . . and we've either got to do something here or get out—" She was pacing back and forth and stepped to the window at the sound of the water lorry and Moshe Ben Saul's chant and the customary clamor in the street. In the hall they could hear Rose Epstein running down, her washtub and pail clanking.

"I'd better go down," Noah said. "Get the bucket, David."

"How can we go on like this?" Debbie said half to herself. "A one-legged boy getting our water rations and food, minding us like a one-man bodyguard. It's not right."

"He doesn't mind," David said. "He likes us. At least he likes me."

Debbie had to laugh. And suddenly she felt herself coming alive again. She could think. She had to do some hard thinking.

When Noah returned dexterously balancing a full bucket on his shoulder she said, "Would you stay with David for just a little longer?" She had made up her mind to visit George Stern.

Thirty-four

She waited until the water truck had gone and the streets were again deserted before she slipped up King George Avenue to the Pantilles Pension. The Pantilles was a handsome, unscathed two-story structure above which flew the flag of the United States of America. Here American and British newspaper men were reported to be living in such luxury that all the cats of Jerusalem came to eat the garbage. It must be a strange world inside, she thought. Creatures who come to watch, who debate the fine points among themselves while all about them debate is over and killing has taken its place. Were they touched? she wondered. No, they must be like the denizens of Mount Olympus —going forth among mortal men each day and returning to their godly retreat to live on ham and eggs, drink whisky, and laugh cruelly over the woe of the second-class creatures about them. She loathed them, these demigods. She quickened her steps as she neared the gate and rushed quickly by, telling herself that she had never intended to visit George Stern in the first place and if she had, it must have been a wild thought. Why would he care about her or David? Why should he do anything to help them? She cast about again among her friends; Noah was a nice boy but without the connections to do anything. There was Karl, of course—Karl had the connections but he believed against her. Elsa—how could she consider Elsa? And all her friends at the hospital —doctors, nurses—they would either be afraid like Elsa or she had no right to impose on them. Dick Alpert would want to help, but she would do him injury to ask, and of what help could he really be? Ben Kronstein? No, he was mouse-sized, even if he had the bigness of soul to forgive Vic for having taken his job . . . one by one she dismissed them as she walked, and as they toppled from her list of hopefuls something very close to panic seized her. There was only

Aronowitz, Vic's attorney, a name in Vic's letter, or George Stern. And Aronowitz had done his best to save Vic and failed.

She thought of Stern again as she made her second tour around the Pantilles. Something about the way he had listened to her, a subtle knack he had of picturing and feeling what she was saying, encouraged her to the boldness of coming here. He could not be hurt by helping her. It was a chance. And she recalled from her mythology, sometimes heartless gods like George Stern did help poor mortals—if only for the sport of it, and to prove their strength to the other gods. She would take her courage in her hands and go in. After all what could he do more than refuse her? She knew in her heart, though, she was risking more than that. She was risking hope. She would be dignified. She would not grovel or beg him to help. She would ask him. Leave him plenty of room to escape if he wanted. He was probably busy. She would ask as though it meant little to her. It would not seem even important or as if anything depended on him. She would let him know there were many others anxious to help her.

The third time round she started toward the entrance. The door opened and she saw three men coming out. He was among them, laughing at something one of his friends had said. Quickly she dodged behind a parked jeep and watched the three men get into a Fiat parked before the pension and drive off toward the Center. She felt relieved, as if she had escaped by a narrow margin. Now she marched bravely into the Pantilles Pension. She waited in the dark lounge and called tentatively, "Anybody here?"

After an interminable wait an Arab, cautious and withdrawn, came from the kitchen and stared at her.

"May I see George Stern, the American?"

"Just went out," the Arab said. "Everybody out."

She looked about the barren lobby—a small oak table with a few back-number English and American magazines, and several oak chairs. "I guess I'll wait," she said nervously.

The Arab looked at her dolefully and, inclining his head, backed into the kitchen.

She read the magazines from cover to cover. She wished for a drink, but didn't dare ask the Arab. She wished for a cigarette but found none. Twice she nearly ran out in panicky haste. Home, home, to close the door and bar the way and pack up and get out. To forget. It was almost two hours before George Stern came back with the other two men. The others looked older than he, possibly because his thin sandy hair concealed the gray. Such weird self-assurance! How could any mortal in this world be so sure and easy? And he looked so unsubstantial. A strong wind— She knew she was trapped when he saw her. Now she could never escape. She wanted to get out, pretend not to have seen him, but he was standing beside her.

"Hello," George Stern said pleasantly. He recognized her, but there was a bare instant of puzzlement while he ran down her identity.

"You know this girl, George?" one of the Americans said and he grinned pleasantly at Debbie. "I'm Harry Talbot," he said.

"This is Mrs.—Marmorek, isn't that the way you say it?" George said.

"Marmorek," Talbot said and his own memory did a quick rundown. "Oh, oh yes, I remember."

"Would you mind coming upstairs?" George said and she nodded. Her knees felt weak and she wanted to run. What had she got herself into?

George led her into his room and shut the door. His window led out to a balcony much like her own; this one overlooked Arab lines less than a hundred yards away. The room's sparse furnishings included a table upon which was an open typewriter.

"Sit down," George said. "Make yourself comfortable."

She could hear another typewriter clicking in the adjacent room. "You have a fine view." She walked to the balcony, looked out over the Old City.

"Well," he smiled easily, "till a couple of nights ago we really never got much chance to admire the view. Those are enemy—well, Arab—emplacements right there. You can see them. I slept under the bed out in the hall like everyone else, although one night we did all go up to the roof to watch the mortars from there."

"It must have been colorful. Actually breathtaking, I suppose." Why couldn't she conceal the bitterness in her voice? Had she no sense? Everything made her angry these days. "Did you send your paper anything about my husband?" she asked. She must keep cool—give him a way out.

"Not really anything special, only the official version—Horowitz's version anyway—and even that hasn't got past censorship. What worry warts these censors are! Here's a city defending itself against incredible odds, a terrific story—not about your husband . . . I mean the whole story of Jerusalem—and they're afraid to let a word out. All the people back home get is what comes from the Arab side. The correspondents here are as sore as hell." He was just giving her time to settle down.

"You said the other night, Mr. Stern, that if I needed help I should —well, tell you."

His manner changed. "Why, yes, sure. Is there something you think I can do?"

"I don't know. I don't even know why I came, or what I'm doing here. I honestly don't. It's quite stupid of me. I can't think what I could have had in mind. There's nothing you can do for me, is there—really? There's nothing anyone can actually *do*. I mean nothing that would help. Oh, I'm sorry if I sound foolish, but it's my own fault." She shook her head and for a few embarrassing moments said nothing. She had to try to think, to be careful, to conserve. She had so little left. "I suppose the first help I need—is for someone to tell me what help to ask for." Her voice quivered and she heard herself giggle in a nervous spasm and she twisted wretchedly in her chair. "Mr. Stern, I just need help of any kind I can get." She found herself getting ready to cry. It was awful. She must sound calm and collected. If she could only think. "It isn't anything I suppose that's really important. Nothing compared to the important things that are happening these days in Jerusalem. It's just, well really nothing, only that David can't go back to school any more. It sounds silly, I suppose. Oh, I told you that, I'm sorry. And now they've put me off at the hospital. I suppose you really can't blame them in a way, Mr. Stern, but what am I going to do?" She bit her lip trying to control herself. "What am I to do?"

"Well," George Stern said, "you'd better tell me from the beginning about this hospital business and try to take it easy. Do you drink whisky?"

"Oh yes, yes, Mr. Stern. Thank you, I do, and I could use one, I honestly could."

He poured her some bourbon in a water glass and she took a long drink. It did steady her. Reminded her of Horowitz, the drink did.

She talked then, not what she had meant to say at all, not with dignity, but in disorder. Whatever came into her head. Lord, she thought, I'm disgracing myself. I'm being terrible. But George sat and listened so nicely. He let her talk and she felt she had to talk just as she had the first time she met him. Everything came pouring out in a gush of ideas and feelings and impressions. She told him about Elsa at the hospital, and Karl's going off to Tel Aviv with Lil, and Karl's advice to go to live in Tel Aviv. She told him about Noah, and Dick Alpert's note, and the Epsteins across the way, and the terrible funeral, and Gussie's invitation. And if she did cry as she spoke it was not because she meant to, or even knew that she did, because she had vowed not to. But the words poured out and George Stern sat and listened, not hurrying her or asking any questions, but always willing to hear more. Toward the end she was conscious again of a typewriter going next door. She felt as though she had been making a deposition and the man in the next room was taking it down, perhaps soon she would be there on a fresh sheet of paper in George Stern's typewriter. A little paragraph of disaster. Her misery stripped naked for the titillation of readers in America, in—where was it?—yes, Boston. She was an insect squirming on a pinpoint while an entomologist studied her from every side; she dared not look at George. At last she had no more to say. She felt drained and not much better because she had behaved so badly.

"I'm sorry, Mr. Stern," she said, "to be such a crybaby. And of course you don't even know if I'm telling you the truth. I know that.

You don't know me at all. It isn't very nice of me to throw my troubles at you. But what am I to do, Mr. Stern?"

"Well," George said, when she had come to the end of her torrent of words, "one thing you can do right away that's very simple. You can stop calling me Mr. Stern. I feel too old and respectable that way, as if you were saying Sir. We're not formal here. My name is George."

"Please," she said, "please don't tease me. If you don't want to help me, I don't blame you. After all, why should you? But don't tease. I used to be quite a tease myself, always felt I could banish anything serious with a trivial joke, but it doesn't work. Oh, I'm changed, Mr. Stern. I'm not like me any more."

"Okay," he said unsmiling now, "no teasing. Now, what's your name?"

She told him.

"Deborah? Really? That's my sister's name, now isn't that odd?" For some silly reason they were both pleased. "Now what are we going to be able to do about you? Mmmmmm . . . I suppose your biggest problem, right away, is your job, isn't it? There ought to be something we can do about that. Don't the nurses have a union? Aren't you members of Histadruth?"

"Yes," she said, "I pay dues."

"Well then," he said, "they ought to be able to take care of it in a couple of days. We can see your delegate or shop steward and I'm sure we can get you reinstated."

She wasn't enthusiastic. "I don't know if I'd want that, Mr. Stern," she said. "How can I force my way back?" He could understand that at least.

"Sure, I know how you feel," he said blandly. "But don't you need your job? I don't mean just the money, but to keep occupied too."

"Oh," she said, "I don't belittle the money either. It's very important to me, but somehow, I just don't know. That isn't what I need, *just* to keep my job if I know how everyone feels about me . . . how can I explain it to you? I need my friends. David needs his friends. We want our old friends back. We need . . . I don't know, help . . . sympathy . . . someone to mourn with us . . ."

"That's a rough order," George Stern said. "That'll take time."

"You have to understand," she said, "we traveled a long way getting to this city where we're at home, where people would take us in for friends and we'd take them in and we wouldn't have to hide in cellars and pretend to be somebody else. Where we'd never have to worry over the dark secret things they might be thinking of us. When we got here I felt like pretty nice people for the first time since I was a small girl. And don't think it was easy to get here. We were all scared to death. But we took the chance, we came and it was worth it. Oh yes. We were so happy to have made it. Happier than you realize because you're an American and for Americans it can't be quite the same."

He took a drag on his cigarette, reaching for a thought, sorting alternatives.

"Yup," he said, "Americans are like Chinamen. Can't tell one from the other. I suppose you could move to Tel Aviv. I could help you get there, if that's what you want. It's near, and it's a lot safer. I'm sure you wouldn't have trouble making new friends there."

"I don't know," she said. "Just like that, go to Tel Aviv, change our name, get lost in the crowd. It wouldn't be easy. I just don't know. You see, it's not only David and I. There's Vic to think of. Oh, I know what you think, but it's not possible for me to believe he's gone, it's just not possible. I know he's somewhere, somewhere near, somewhere watching. I've always felt that about my Mama and Papa. I've done so many things all my life because I thought they'd like it and I've tried to hide things from them they wouldn't like. Sometimes they're more alive to me than when I was a girl and we all lived in the same house. And so with Vic now. Perhaps I need to feel that way. We all do, you know. We're a little odd that way. We have so many more dead than living. Do you understand what I mean?"

"I guess so," he said uncertainly. "It's like a religious feeling, you might say."

"No, probably just illusion," she said. "It has nothing to do with God or Heaven or Hell. But it's more real to me than religion. A superstition, I guess. Superstition can be awfully real, sometimes it makes me feel creepy. You see, I feel as though Vic were right here with me. Just now I would swear it. I suppose you think I'm a case."

"No," he said after a moment. "No, I was just trying to decide whose problem we're trying to work on. Yours and David's, or your husband's. Try to look at it practically. If you go to Tel Aviv, somehow you'll start again. After all, there'll be so many newcomers now you'll get lost in the shuffle. That would take care of you and your son. I'm sure they'd be glad to get a graduate nurse anywhere. And your boy can always make new friends. But that isn't what you want, is it? I detect resistance."

"I just couldn't do it to Vic. He fought, he worked so hard for Jerusalem. It's difficult to explain. He's been so devoted, really dedicated these last months. He worked much harder than I ever did. He helped build the new road. Did you know that? He was one of the engineers. His job was important and dangerous. Oh, I saw him afraid many times. He could never fool me. Of course, we're all afraid sometimes, but he was as brave as anyone I know and always good and wonderful to me and David. If we went to Tel Aviv now, changed our name, got lost in the crowd, after a while I suppose maybe we'd be fine, but we'd be proving a great big lie about Vic, wouldn't we? We'd be admitting everything they say. David would go on believing it. I think he believes it now. And he'd always be worried that someone would find out who his father was. Maybe his best friend or his girl or somebody. The way I used to worry in Vienna that someone would discover I was a Jewess. Do you worry about that in America? That would be just awful for him."

"Well," he said, "I doubt if it would turn out so melodramatically, but if it isn't what you want, I wish you'd tell me what you do want."

"Oh, I wish I could myself, I'm so mixed up," she said. "What I really want I suppose is to go back to last week, to go back when I knew Vic was coming home from the Road, and I was waiting for everything nice, for the truce, for peace and a normal everyday life with my own little family. I guess what I want is to undo what's been done. That's silly, it's impossible, I know. I'm not being helpful, am I?"

"Neither am I," he said, "but maybe we're getting somewhere. We can't undo much, but is there *anything* we can undo?"

She gulped her whisky almost absent-mindedly while he rose and paced behind her slowly. "The least I have to undo is what David thinks about his father. That's why I could never hide in Tel Aviv. Or lie about who we are."

He walked to the window, glanced out briefly and blew three careful smoke rings.

"I owe that much to Vic anyway."

"You *owe* him?" he said and he sounded surprised for the first time.

"Yes," she said and felt herself blush for she knew he had almost probed a delicate spot in her own mind and what irked her was that she scarcely knew what she meant herself. She told herself it was nonsense. She had no idea what she could be thinking.

"Please don't be angry because I ask you anything so personal," he said, "but I think it's important. I assume you did love your husband, didn't you?"

"Oh yes," she said, "yes I did, I did, yes."

"What makes you so sure he didn't do this thing?"

"Because I knew him. I knew him better than anyone. There was one time when my brother was afraid he might be doing something foolish. Something just like they say he did. Well, we talked about it. He swore to me he'd never think of such a thing, to help *them.* Even though we had English friends, oh, he was conscious of the danger and we talked it out. He was just too intelligent to do such a thing. You see I'm not very bright, but you should have known him. He knew so many things—not just his own field, electricity, communications, but—he got along with all kinds of people. Rich and poor, Jews, Christians, Arabs. Vic was a very unusual man. He never, never could have done anything like this."

"Well," he said slowly, "I don't know just how much we can undo, but we can try. If you're sure that's what you want."

She tried to concentrate. She tried to feel. "I think it is," she said slowly. "I want them to know that Vic wasn't just an innocent man, not just that, but that he was a tremendous guy, too. A great man. I want David to know it. Him especially. I want it burned into his mind. And I want that little Horowitz to know it. I want him to know that he killed a man who was better in every way than he can ever be himself. I want—O Lord, what good would any of it do?"

George Stern covered his face with his hands and inclined his head as if he were trying to concentrate. When at last he looked up he spoke slowly. "The way things are right now we'd have to prove him innocent beyond any small shadow of a doubt, far beyond what the courts call reasonable doubt. It's going to be a damned difficult job just to get anyone to listen. It'll be hard going. Weeks or months, maybe years, and it'll be expensive."

She said nothing; she watched him pace as if he were winding himself up. "Hell, when you get right down to it though, why *shouldn't* you try? Why *shouldn't* your son get to go back to his own school? Nobody says you or he did anything, do they? Why should you have to run off to Tel Aviv! This whole thing's fantastic when you get down to it. Isn't this the sort of thing the Nazis did—what was it they called it? —*Sippenhaft*, wasn't it?"

"Yes," she said, surprised that he should know. "*Sippenhaft* is what they called it."

"The guilt of the whole clan," he said. "Papa gets on the black list so the SS boys take it out on the wife and kiddies. Well, where I come from that witchcraft went out with the bow and arrow. You know," he turned on her suddenly and shook his forefinger at her, "even if you're a hundred per cent wrong about your husband—not that I say you are, but even if you were, there's no good reason why you—" He ground out his butt. "We'll have to find some way to make people understand that much anyway. Deborah, if I can manage it, I think I might be the fellow to do it. Wait right here for me. I'll be back. Just stay put."

He started downstairs suddenly, and from the window she saw him jump into his Fiat and drive off. She sat on the bed hearing the typing from next door, peering aimlessly about the small room. On the bureau she saw three photographs; on the desk beside the typewriter, two piles of books; and in the open closet a variety of clothing and equipment. What, she thought idly, might these bits of evidence tell her about the man into whose hands she seemed, with no discrimination, to be putting her case, this stranger from halfway round the world, who might believe her.

She smoked several cigarettes out of the package he had left, and sat at his desk examining his books. Surely there was no privacy about a man's books. Several concerned people or were written by authors she recognized: a large *Life of Gandhi*, a small volume by Benedetto

Croce, another called *Persons and Places* by George Santayana, an English translation of short stories by Kafka, and the *King James Bible,* of which certain passages in the New Testament were underscored as though George had been identifying them in his own Palestine travels. The books which meant nothing to her were *The Late George Apley,* plays for the theater by a Maxwell Anderson, *Selected Opinions of Justice Holmes, Inside USA,* an assortment of pocket-sized murder mysteries with lurid covers depicting bosomy victims of foul play, several children's comic books dealing with a character called L'il Abner and a paper-covered green pamphlet entitled *Decennial Report—Harvard College, Class of 1937.* Attached to that pamphlet was a scrawled note: "This just came. Thought you might like to check up on your classmates. Will write soon. Father and I send love. Be careful out there. Mother."

She opened the *Decennial Report,* which consisted of biographies of class members. Turning to the "S's" she found:

STERN, GEORGE LYMAN–Journalism
408 West Coolidge Road
Brookline, Mass.
Business Address–*Boston Evening News*
37 Boylston Street
Boston, Mass.

Married 1939 to Barbara Lesser (Wellesley). 1946 divorced. Daughter Carol Ann born 1940.

"For three years after graduation I lived two blocks from the Yard studying the law of the Commonwealth, and had barely been presented with my LL.B. when I discovered this was not my dish of tea. Instead I got a job as a reporter for the *Boston Evening News,* over the heads of a dozen graduates of the Columbia School of Journalism. *They* have no doubt all become big wheel lawyers. By coincidence my editor (who hired me) turned out to be the fellow who was married to my sister. Just when I was becoming of some value to the paper, I received so flattering an invitation from the President of the United States that I couldn't turn it down. Within a short time I found myself in khaki, first in Florida, later in Louisiana and ultimately in Africa and the Middle East, where I had occasion to visit and live in places with exotic names like Cairo, Monrovia, Abadan, Karachi, Tel Aviv and Jerusalem.

"In the Air Transport Command among many duties I even got to practice law on half a dozen occasions, when I served as Defense Counsel or TJA in Courts-martial.

"Back in Boston I found my old desk at the *Boston News* (my brother-in-law was 4F and held on not only to his own job, clever fellow, but mine too) and have completed a series of fascinating little assignments–including a few features–the most recent of which was a one-man exposé brilliantly entitled, 'The Truth About Judge Crater's Fate.' By the way what the hell *did* happen to Crater?

"My brother-in-law, having observed the growing professionalism of my weekly expense accounts, soon realized that I was born to be a foreign correspondent. Thus my latest assignment: The Middle East. (These lines are written from Beirut.) From here I will cover Palestine also, to which I look forward, partly because I spent many happy days there on leave during my ATC days, and partly because I believe in this year 1947, that little country seems on the edge of a dangerous but exciting new adventure in history.

"At present I have only one fixation–my daughter, Carol Ann, whom I calmly and judiciously consider to be the ideal and most beautiful six-year-old in America."

Something about the passage annoyed her, although she could not put her finger on it. Perhaps it made him too real and at the same time frivolous. He might be an enthusiast who could rush up blind alleys and make matters worse for her and David. She turned her attention to his clothes draped over the chairs and in the closet—old American uniforms without insignia, the kind she had seen on American pilots on leave during her first days in Jerusalem—and two business suits. On the shelf of the closet she saw a tennis racket.

The photographs on the bureau were of a handsome woman in her fifties with an inscription, "To my first-born, with all my love, Mother"; of a plumpish pleasant white-haired man also in his fifties; and of a blonde, skinny but glowing little girl who looked just like George Stern. This would be Carol Ann. Debbie had been alone for two hours, had finished all the exploration she dared, and had begun to worry about leaving David with Noah so long when she heard George's footsteps on the stairs.

"Say, I'm sorry I was so long," he said throwing himself into a chair. "I've just spent an hour with your pal Horowitz. He's a real hard man to make out. I just get all steamed up when I can't get through to a guy. Polite, but inscrutable, like an Indian. Kills me. And is he a nervous guy! Keeps twisting his hair into horns; brother, there's a real case of war nerves. Reminds me of a colonel I knew in Monrovia. Always having trouble with the bush boys. Shoot first and have inquiries later. This guy told me three times how he'd spent hours in the synagogue before confirming the sentence. Very religious fellow. Too damn religious."

Debbie said bitterly, "I hate that man enough to kill him, and someday I may."

"Well, you can feel sorry for the guy too, to tell the truth. Anyway he told me where to reach Aronowitz. I had to drag it out of him. I've called and we have a date for tomorrow at four. He sounds okay, Aronowitz does. He's out in Katamon."

"Vic wrote some nice things about Mr. Aronowitz," Debbie said lamely. Everything suddenly seemed to be going too fast.

"Maybe he'll give you an idea of what to do next," George Stern said.

"Thank you. I really have to go. I've left David alone so long."

"Sure," he said, and they walked downstairs to the lobby together. "You mind if I walk along?"

"If you want to," she said.

"You have enough food over at your place?" he said.

"Well, we have a little."

"Would you like some sardines? Hey, Ibrahim!" He walked toward the kitchen. "Ibrahim!" Ibrahim came running. "Got some sardines?"

"Yes. Sure. You know." Ibrahim grinned broadly.

"Six cans," George said and Ibrahim disappeared. "He must have nine million cans of that stuff. The boys won't eat it any more. They'd starve first."

"I feel like a squirrel in Stadt Park," she said, "with my food for the winter buried in my secret pockets."

"There's an awful lot of squirrel in people," George said, "when bombs start falling."

For a while they walked in silence. "I looked at some of your books," she said. "I hope you don't mind."

"Why should I?"

"Who's Judge Crater?" she said.

"Oh, *that book*," he laughed, and it was the first time she had heard him laugh at anything. "He was a judge back home who disappeared about thirty years ago. No one ever found him. It was a great mystery."

"I think you like mysteries, don't you?" she said. "I noticed all those mystery murder books."

"Yes, as a matter of fact I do," he said, "very much."

"You like to solve them too?"

"That's the best part of them," he said, "finding the solution."

"And is that why you are so interested in—Vic?" she asked.

He walked in silence. "Partly," he said at last, "only partly." They had come to her house. "So long," he said. "I'll pick you up at three-forty. Peace." He said that one word in Hebrew.

Thirty-five

Next afternoon he came for her. She'd made up her mind exactly what she must say to Aronowitz. As they rode out beyond the railroad station through the destruction and wrath of last week's war in the Greek and German colonies, George talked. "I've been checking on this Aronowitz. He's a big wheel in civilian life. Represents labor in Jerusalem and a few of the individual unions too. Probably does mighty well for himself. He's bound to be a big man in government, if there ever is a government. Everyone says he's brilliant but volatile. Changes from day to day. Until he's sold. Our problem is to get his mind working in a straight line." He parked before an old unpretentious Arab house in Katamon.

At the entrance the guard examined George's credentials without a word; he looked at Debbie's labor card. "Wait here," he said in Hebrew and disappeared. After a few moments a noncom asked them to follow him, and led them upstairs into a large dark room containing a single small window and furnished with only two desks at one of which sat Boris Aronowitz.

He was a small, thin, almost ascetic man in his late forties. His khaki looked too large on him.

Debbie saw sharp gray eyes first, too large for the narrow head in which they were set, eyes framed by high cheekbones and fortified with a sharp straight nose. His mop of hair was iron gray, receding at the temples, but combed pompadour as if he were trying to make himself taller. When he spoke it was sharply incisive, but she detected a slight speech defect, not quite a lisp, but an aspirant suggestion of one. Altogether he looked volcanic to her and she was frightened of him.

"I'm sorry to have to meet you under these circumstances, lady—very sorry indeed." He spoke Hebrew to her, then turned to George and in guttural English said, "Mr. Stern. What can I do for you?" He was correct, but not cordial. All she could think was here is the man who saw Vic to the last moment. Here is the man who took my place. What can he tell me, do I dare ask him the thing I really want to know?

"We'd like to get some information," George said offhandedly. Aronowitz swung around, abruptly on guard, and leaned his chair back against the wall, balancing it on two legs. "We want to know more about the case against Mrs. Marmorek's husband."

Aronowitz looked away. "What is it you'd like to know?"

"Well—the details, and after that your opinion."

Aronowitz said coldly, "I'm afraid I can't give you details. Nothing is cleared with Tel Aviv and no statements are permitted except the barest outlines."

"Well now, look, we're talking to the man's wife. That's not very much help, is it?"

"What kind of help are you looking for?" Aronowitz asked sharply.

"She's convinced her husband wasn't guilty. She was hoping that maybe you—"

Aronowitz interrupted quickly. "Since you've asked my opinion, Mr. Stern, I may as well tell you, I have the opposite view, I regret."

"Look," George said, "I have no ax to grind. I never even met the man. I'm trying to nail this thing to the mast. His wife swears he's innocent. She's so positive . . ."

"So he did, too," Aronowitz said. "Did you expect something else?"

"Well," George said easily, "I think she's entitled to some consideration, even from a government at war. Back home she'd damn well get a hearing or there'd be the devil to pay. I've asked around about her—and before this happened most people thought she was quite a gal. Everyone I talk to says the same thing." She wondered who had talked to George. It was embarrassing to be discussed as if she weren't there.

"So I've heard." Aronowitz was unimpressed. He swung forward and placed his fingertips carefully on the edge of his desk. "Listen, the man is gone. When the case started I thought maybe he's innocent myself. The story he told me made sense, but the longer I knew him the more I became convinced he'd sold out. Don't take me wrong—that doesn't mean I didn't work till the last minute to save him. But the better I knew him the more I worried about our case."

"But can't you tell me what he was supposed to have done?" Debbie said.

"It's all in today's paper. The charge was that he turned over to the British lists with addresses of buildings our side was using for ammunition depots, military headquarters, machine shops, our crucial places, wherever Pearlman asked him to put in telephones. Then the English turned your husband's lists over to the Arabs and they used them these last few weeks for target areas, and we suffered terrible losses. No question about it. Almost cost us the city. All that's corrected now, but, my God, look at the cost and such a waste of manpower. Our men have better things to do than tearing down and relocating machine shops, or moving ammunition. It's wasteful. Not to mention our dead."

"But I'm sure Vic couldn't have. He never did anything like that," Debbie said. "That would be so stupid. I just don't know how to tell you so you'll believe me, but it's just not possible . . ."

"Even if I believed you," Aronowitz said impassively, "what could I do now? What could anyone do?"

"Well, aside from that," George said, "what makes you so sure?"

Aronowitz shrugged. "I am not at liberty, I just told you."

"Did you consider the evidence airtight, as a lawyer, I mean?"

"What evidence? Who had evidence? This is Jerusalem, young fellow, not New York. It's a military trial, not civilian. We have no communications with anyone here. We're cut off and the mortar shells are pouring in every day and we have pressure from north and east and south. Well, we had testimony. Not the fullest testimony, but enough to prove a pretty good case. Sure, a little hearsay evidence was admitted. Marmorek changed his story, not once, twice. He blew hot and cold, admitted everything, denied everything."

"Look," George said, "I'm a pretty skeptical guy. You've read the letter Marmorek wrote to his wife, haven't you? Did that sound like a guilty man?"

"Well, they showed me the note before they released it to her," Aronowitz said, knitting his brows and squinting. "The only way I explain it is he wrote for his family, for you, lady, and your son. For afterwards. It was the only thing he could leave you."

"Seemed to think quite a bit of you," George said.

"Well, God in Heaven, I was after all his counsel." Aronowitz softened just perceptibly. "The man took quite a beating. I was the only one to give him any encouragement. The others barely talked to him. Besides shooting him, they were very rude. I did my job the best I could, but when it's all over I have a right to my opinion."

Debbie was trembling, almost as though she were fighting for Vic's life, as though he were alive and she were trying desperately to save him. "Are you *so* sure?" she cried. "Are you like that awful Horowitz?"

"Please," Aronowitz said and leaned forward abruptly. "Don't put me in a class with Horowitz."

"Well," Debbie said, her voice scarcely audible, "my boy's been pushed out of school and I've been turned out of my hospital. Lost my job . . . Our neighbors . . . I have to do something . . ."

"What can I do?" Aronowitz was grim and hard. "I did what I could *when* I could. I'm sorry for you and your son, but I fail to see what can be done now. It would be pointless."

"Not even if we brought you new evidence?" George said.

"But why?" Aronowitz was exasperated. "What new evidence?" He looked at George sharply. "The man is gone. Try to understand."

"What evidence do you think would be helpful?"

For a fleeting second Aronowitz looked as though the thing he most feared was about to happen. " 'Lock him up,' I said. Some people know everything, it's like talking to a wall. Authority does it, oh, I've seen it. Odessa in twenty-two. I saw the Bolsheviks. Goes to the head, it's a chance to play God. I'm not crazy about hearsay evidence in the first place. All right, afterwards we can get *all* the evidence. Then if it's against him, we shoot him. If not, we release him. Suppose we make a mistake, a hundred to one shot, but suppose." He whistled. "I told them the man's done fine work on the Road. Wait. You can never be sure. I spoke to Horowitz myself. I begged him to submit it to higher authority. This should go all the way to the top, don't take it on yourself, I said. Frankly, I doubt he had the authority, and even if he had he shouldn't have exercised it. Why stick his neck out? I tried everything. But now? For what?"

Debbie had difficulty in following him. He rambled and threw his arms about as he spoke, she saw him in a haze, but George was nodding as if he followed every word.

"What evidence do you need?" George said, and Debbie could

see he was beginning to be excited and she felt the excitement too. She was sure in her heart that Vic could see them, somehow knew.

"What's the good?" Aronowitz said. "Unless she and the boy are trying to make a claim against the government for damages. I'm not interested in that kind of case. And if I were I wouldn't recommend it."

"Let's just say it's a matter of justice," George said. "We'll leave the precise mechanics to you. Think of it as pure justice. Distilled. Money could be the method, or maybe some other way. But if the man is innocent don't you think he ought to be cleared? Living or not. What evidence do we need to get?"

Aronowitz looked at Debbie and his gray eyes were bright and alert. His aquiline nose made him as forbidding as an eagle and his nostrils bristled. "If the Arabs break this truce we're only going to push them back further. They're on the run, Jerusalem will live. And so will I. That's quite a thought and I haven't got used to it. I even think of the future a little now. I'll be back in private practice, maybe soon. To sue the government for Marmorek or his family, will this be good? Lady, I represent the National Federation of Labor and labor will be government. I may go to the first parliament. If I stir this up, can it help my government? My government is important, lady. It will be our first in two thousand years. You know what that means? Will it help the army? Will it be good for the Aronowitz family—for Mrs. Aronowitz and the three girls? They gladly share all my burdens, lady, but can I ask them to share your burdens also? You see, in all fairness, I try to be blunt."

"And what about me and David?"

"It will be better even for you and him. Will you please take my advice? Drop it. People will forget. Those who are the bitterest today will realize soon. You and the boy, what have you got to do with your husband's sins?—and they'll be falling over each other to apologize and help. That's human nature. This I must say: In the whole proceeding not one word against you, lady. Not a suggestion. It will be known. If not soon, then later. You're young, attractive, and that helps. Already you see you have interested one American reporter. You have a good reputation, and how long can folks be angry at an eight-year-old boy? You see? But start a rumpus, make a tumult, attack the army, sue the government, and there'll be hell. Everyone will take sides. These things have happened before. It's nothing that hasn't been tried. Passions will be roused. Horowitz will be attacked and he'll fight back. Don't underestimate Horowitz because he's clever enough to know that if your husband is vindicated he's done a tragic thing and Horowitz doesn't want to have done a tragic thing. He'll fight anyone who says he has. He is, as the saying goes, an honest man, a difficult man to fight. You see this is no Dreyfus case and you—" he turned to George and spoke almost banteringly, "you're no Zola."

"But my poor David. Does he have to go on being the son of a traitor? Not only having others believe it, but believing it himself? What will become of him?"

"Lady, you're trying to make me do something I can never do, will you understand that?" He rose from his desk and paced slowly to the far corner of the room. "So . . . I know. 'The world rests upon the breath of the children in the schoolhouses.' " He returned to his desk and sat again. "Ah, but believe me, it would be a terrible mistake, I promise you that."

"I just can't believe it," Debbie whispered half to herself. "My husband wrote me such wonderful things about you. I expected—I just expected—someone so different—so—" She could not finish.

Aronowitz glared, but he said quietly, "Lady, you're sure he's guiltless. Isn't that enough? You're sure." His voice sharpened. "Or is it possible, lady, you aren't absolutely sure? Are you asking me to do something quite pointless and quite dangerous, to satisfy your curiosity?"

Debbie flushed angrily. She could feel her own resentment rise and drain her. "No," she whispered, "no, no, no. But there's a big lie about Vic and I have to kill it."

"I did everything I could," Aronowitz exploded, "while he breathed. Far beyond my simple duty, I promise that. But now? It's an idle postmortem. It might damage the Intelligence Section and the stability of the army itself, and it's a brand new army. It's the only one we have. We have to treat it like a baby."

"I have to get out of here," Debbie said. "I'm sorry, I'm sorry . . ." He persisted in speaking of Vic as if he were dead, as if he did not matter.

"And if you lose," Aronowitz said ignoring her words, "if he *was* guilty and it's proved with all the t's crossed and i's dotted, then what?"

She was shaken, but said nothing.

"Look, Aronowitz, what evidence would we need?" George said and he spoke slowly and smiled persuasively.

She was amazed at George's casual self-control. Even in her fury she could admire it and it calmed her a little.

"You'd never be able to get it," Aronowitz said, rising and escorting them to the door. "It's impossible, don't you see? You'd have to go to England to get all the records. And in England, who would care? Who'd help? The British took every sheet of paper with them. You think they'd give an Israeli access to the archives of the Communications Ministry? Ha! The records of the Telephone Department? You think you could find those lists? Marmorek said he destroyed the originals, but who could believe it? You'd have to find the lists, the physical lists, that's first and absolutely essential. And it's also impossible."

He started back to his desk. "And can you imagine trying to get testimony—depositions—from Walker, what's his name, Reginald and Enid Walker, his wife? You think they'd testify about their relationship with Marmorek, their true relationship? Never. They'd have to agree to submit to cross-examination by the government. Don't you see how impossible such a thing is?"

"How about the names of the principal witnesses?" George said. "Maybe we can get their stories and do a little checking on them. We could probe for soft spots."

"Sorry," said Aronowitz abruptly. "This is a security matter. There's not a chance."

"You're real shifty today, Aronowitz," George said. "And not very helpful."

Debbie looked from one man to the other. George was staring at Aronowitz, but the lawyer had paused in his pacing, was looking uneasily out the little window, then sat at his desk.

Abruptly he said, "I'm sorry I can't give you any encouragement. I've talked too much already, and I certainly don't plan to be court-martialed myself."

At last Debbie found her voice to ask what she had on her mind to ask. "Did you see my husband, Mr. Aronowitz, right up to the time—"

"Yes." Aronowitz softened. "I was there from beginning to end." He closed his eyes to put aside a moment of unwilling recollection and she felt she was in the presence of a vision too terrible to bear.

"How was he?" She scarcely recognized her own hoarse voice.

"Brave," Aronowitz said. "Very quiet and very brave."

"Was he terribly frightened?" Debbie said.

"Lady, he didn't act it, but I'm sure he was. He didn't tell me and I never asked him."

"I would have asked him," Debbie whispered. "O Lord, I would have comforted him. I would have loved him."

"I'm sure you would, lady." He turned suddenly on George. "You're an American, young fellow, and that's why I talk to you at all. My son-in-law served with your Colonel Marcus. Terrible tragedy, Marcus, terrible. He was an extraordinary man."

"Don't worry about my discretion," George said.

"I don't. Probably it's only an instinct, but I follow my instincts," Aronowitz said.

"So long," George Stern said, "and thanks."

Aronowitz nodded gruffly, and without rising again, put his hand out to Debbie. "I'm sorry, lady."

In the Fiat driving back to the Pantilles neither said a word for a few moments.

"I had great hope in Aronowitz," Debbie said listlessly. "I suppose I can't really blame him. He's got other things on his mind and he's got to think of himself."

"He's okay," George said. "There must be a chink in all that fancy armor. He makes himself out a real hard man, but somewhere in all that stone there's a soft spot. We'll have to find it. I'm not sure he knows his own mind completely."

"But he said so clearly—"

"I hardly ever listen to what people say," George said, "I like to watch the way they behave."

"You think so?" Debbie said hopefully. "But he *was* an infuriating man." This American made her feel better, lifted her hopes until she thought suddenly, why am I so cheered? And she fell instantly silent and began to wonder what she would do with all Vic's things—his tennis racket, his clothes, oh what gruesome little problems! If she could only pull a shade over her mind. George drove back to the Pantilles, but made no move to get out of the car.

"What are you going to do now?" he asked.

"I don't know."

"What'll you do about money and food rations? What about keeping busy, and how about David?"

"I don't know."

"I've been kicking around an idea," he said cautiously. "We had a girl here at the Pantilles, an Armenian kid who took care of the place. She served the meals, cleaned up, did the laundry when we had water, made the beds, all that stuff. She left last week, got married, and we've been struggling along with only Ibrahim. He's a Christian, pretty good boy. But he just cooks, if you can call it cooking and that's about it. I suppose you notice the place was crawling filthy." She hadn't. "The boys have to make their own beds now, get their own breakfasts, and they're spoiled. They're used to being waited on. Would you want a job like that? Twenty pounds a month plus tips. I'm sure they'd be tickled to have hospital corners and I guess a nurse knows what it means to keep a place clean."

"What about David?"

"No reason why you couldn't bring him along. There's room for you both, Maria's old room. And if the truce does break, the old Pantilles is as good a place as any. We have thicker walls than most and canned goods."

"But my house, all my furniture . . . All our things . . . What'll I do with everything?"

"Leave them—or move them."

"Oh, I suppose I'm being foolish," Debbie said. "Vic always said I never got over being a child. Here I should be thanking you for the chance. I'll be glad to keep house for you all. But are you sure it will be all right with the others?"

"I'll talk to them. I'm sure they'll be pleased pink. The two New Yorkers are the majordomos—house committee we call them. Service comes hard these days and it rarely comes wrapped in such a nice package." He drove her home and told her to wait there. He'd come for her in the evening.

She felt brighter as she climbed the steps to the apartment. She had somewhere to go, someone to look after her, and a job to do.

George Stern came shortly before five to fetch them and help with their bags. She could not resist kissing Noah as he stood forlornly beside the Fiat just before they took off. David followed behind the car, on his precious bicycle and in less time than she believed possible, without fuss or feathers, she had installed herself in the large dirty kitchen of the Pantilles alongside Ibrahim, and was serving supper to sixteen hungry American and British correspondents. The prospect of living as a kitchen fixture had no special appeal for her, after her years over a Roman stove. Mama had never been able to set foot in a kitchen either. And Ibrahim's cooking did nothing to improve Debbie's attitude. He could do things to canned food so horrible that it seemed scarcely possible. But she held her nose, closed her eyes and said nothing. The Americans and Englishmen were immune to it. Eating away from home was an occupational hazard, and they used Scotch whisky to destroy the taste of the food. It was a far cry from the hospital—catering to these sixteen healthy, hungry foreigners of assorted ages who had come, she thought, like ghouls to watch impersonally and without regret the destruction and death of her city.

George gave David a small horseshoe magnet at the first dinner and showed him how to attract the silverware with it and make a pin jump. David giggled with delight and was his instant and lifelong friend.

In spite of the kitchen and Ibrahim's concept of hygiene, Debbie began almost at once to feel at home in the Pantilles. The sixteen men she served were bright and not unsympathetic and many of them treated her, right from the beginning, with kindness that never became oversolicitous. They took her into their jokes and confidence, partly because they could see she belonged among them, partly because they thought she was pretty cute. And belonging was a sensation she hadn't known since the days when Papa used to tell everyone she was the prettiest girl in Vienna. The atmosphere was a little like Lindenhouse's, when all the actors and journalists and directors had gathered in happier days, except that what was real and hard fact to Debbie was phantom and fantastic to them, and the other way round. Their reality could only be dreamed of in her imaginings. Nevertheless, talking to these foreigners was engaging. They helped her forge for herself one link to the world of everyday. They reminisced to her about the theater, New York, the nightclubs of Paris. Several remembered Vienna with her. Two of them were writing books, one about his experiences in Palestine before and during the war; the other, a fascinating dark and curious man who had come from Egypt and Lebanon, was doing an exposé of the Arab political positions—Maynard Appleton his name was, and he promised faithfully to send her a copy. He was only at the Pantilles a week and was gone before the second siege began.

George was unfailingly attentive and considerate. Although he had his work to do, she knew without his telling her that he had been thinking about the mission he had undertaken for her. She knew he would talk to her when he was ready.

Meanwhile she wrote to Gussie, begging her to come visit in Jerusalem and expressing inadequately her great pleasure in Gussie's letter. She didn't mention Vic, but she sent along an old photo of David.

The nights were hard, morbid with imagery as she lay in bed, sometimes terrifying her, for she had to live with Vic the hours before his execution a thousand times.

At other times she would feel him beside her, oh so sweetly and tenderly. She slept fitfully and sometimes had erotic dreams about him, the kind of dream she had never had since the few vague childish ones that upset her in her teens. This was something a widow could never speak of, this hunger and need to be loved. To lie quietly waiting and at last to give and be given, to find the secrets of another being and to tell your own. Oh, that was so lovely to wait for, no matter how long one had to wait. Who could speak of it, and to whom could she confess it if she chose to speak? She could only mourn.

Many nights, long after they were both in bed, she was startled out of her own troubled sleep by David's sobbing or moaning, and on the first two of these occasions she called to him, softly at first, then louder, but he continued to sigh and weep, then stopped just as suddenly as he had begun, his even sleep-breathing returning, never awakening. In the mornings he had no recollection of it, and no memory of unpleasant dreams. But the recurrence of the phenomenon three or four times a week made her nights worse.

Jerusalem and all Palestine waited for the thirty days of truce to run out, and wondered if the fighting would start again. It began to look as though the UN would be helpless to stop it. Only two days before the last day of truce George returned from the Information Ministry with a cable which he showed her in triumph. It read:

OKAY GO ENGLAND IF SHE PAYS EXPENSES
BUT WAIT TILL SURE SHOW OVER
ELLIOT

"Who is Elliot?" she said.

"My sister's husband," he said. "He's also my boss, my friend, and a pretty decent guy, once you get to know him. He fascinates women especially, even though he's slightly fairyish, but he knows his business."

"What does he mean?" she asked studying the wire.

"Well," he said, "I couldn't get a wire through to him, you know the damn censors are blocking everything, but I managed to get an airmail letter out with Appleton and I told Elliot the whole story. I must have written him ten pages. I told him I wanted to go to England. I had a hunch he'd let me."

"He's also a great mystery fan?" She could not help the sarcasm and when she saw his hurt look she said quickly, "I'm sorry, really, I shouldn't snap. Why do I snap at the ones who are helping me? Would you really go to England just for this?"

He took the cable from her and folded it carefully.

"What does it mean, 'if she pays expenses'? If who pays?"

"You," he said.

"I? That must be quite a lot of money. How much is air fare to England?"

"About two hundred pounds," he said, "round trip."

She was silent. "I have that much," she said slowly. "I've nearly four hundred pounds. I may as well use it. Papa always used to tease Mama, 'Always saving for a rainy day, but you can't recognize the rain.' Poor Mama was still advertising for a chauffeur after Hitler came to Vienna."

"I don't want you to think I'm an altruist," he said lightly. "You see once I get to England, I plan to hop on home for a few days. It's really a big opportunity for me. It'll give me a chance to see Carol. I miss that kid."

She shook her head in disbelief. "You're really going then?"

"Only if you want," he said. "I happen to think Aronowitz is on the right track. How else can we accomplish anything?"

"But it seems so elaborate, so—do you think you can accomplish anything?"

"If you think it's too expensive, we could try something else. I could write to our London bureau. Bill Murdock there is one of our top men—I'm sure he could get hold of the Walkers."

"No, no," she said, "it's not that. I'd like you to go. I wouldn't want anyone else to do it. I'm sure Redge and Enid would help if it were you. It's just that, O Lord, see how easy it is for you. That American passport takes you anywhere, doesn't it? Why, England is just another world to me. Although David could have gone, you know. Enid offered to take him when she left. Did I tell you that?"

"No, you never did. We have to have a long talk about this Walker guy and his wife and your husband sometime before I go."

"Of course I'll have to get the money out of the bank," she said half to herself. "When will you be going?"

"I don't know yet," he said. "I can't go until I'm sure this lull will last. The way the Arabs are carrying on with Bernadotte it isn't going to last much longer. We've only got two days to go and I'd be surprised not to see it break out again."

"O Lord, no, please not. Maybe at the last minute, they'll compromise. It's hard on our nerves, those mortars. Poor David will grow up with some terrible complexes, won't he? But not any more than my own."

"Probably not any more than mine," he said. "Of course, you know even if I go, there's always a chance you're throwing your money away. I'd guess a damn good chance, too."

"No, I'm sure Enid will help," she said. "I'll write her myself. She's really very nice and Redge was always fond of Vic."

"Well," he said, "I'll start making arrangements." He seemed to take it as a matter of course that he should be going to England. "Oh, and one other thing, Horowitz has sent for me. I wonder what he wants."

Thirty-six

On the last day of cease-fire, Karl and Lil got back to town and weary as they were came at once to visit Debbie at the Pantilles. She'd scarcely realized how much she had longed for a familiar face. In the moment she saw Karl her love welled up and she forgave him everything on the instant. She could not even tell him how she felt. She knew the tenderness, the warmth, that each had given the other a thousand times since childhood. She wouldn't dwell on Karl's recent lapse of faith; mustn't think of it again.

As they embraced she scarcely knew what she was saying. "Oh, but I'm glad to see you both. How's Clara? Did she have her baby? A girl? What's happening in Tel Aviv? Tell me everything from the minute you left."

Lil was no less cordial than Karl. They were both bubbling with news of Clara's new daughter, of Tel Aviv bustling with victory, of the roads crowded with Arab refugees herding toward Bethlehem.

Not long after they arrived, George came in, and she was glad Karl and Lil had this opportunity to meet him. All went smoothly until Debbie told them George was going to England, and why.

Karl was shocked and Lilith clucked grimly.

"Mr. Stern," Karl said, "may I say something? I certainly appreciate your helping my sister. But I wish you wouldn't do that. What's happened to my sister has got to be forgotten—just as soon as possible, don't you think? Stirring it up, how's that going to help her? People will just never forget it if we don't let them."

"For Debbie's own good," Lil said. "Oh, absolutely. And even more for David."

"Well," George spoke carefully, "it's what your sister's asked me to do. And she has a point, I think."

"She's in no condition to know what she wants," Karl said. "She'll be sorry. And so will I. You know, everything that happens reflects on us."

"I guess that's so," George said. "I suppose you're all under a cloud. But you see, I was brought up to believe everyone's entitled to a fair shake. Now, you take your sister. What's she done? What's she even accused of?"

"Oh, Mr. Stern, please. People can't help believing she knew what her husband was doing."

"Right," George said. "So you see, in order to put your sister and David back on the track, we can't fight their battle, the one that ought to be fought. We have to go around the block, we have to fight the battle of Victor Marmorek. Your sister's hostage for her husband, and the only way we can set *her* right is to prove *he* wasn't guilty."

"And you plan to prove it, true or not?"

George brightened and spoke with cheerful belligerence. "Yep. You've got right to the bare bones of it."

"Oh, no!" Debbie said. "We have to be sure, I mean we really—"

Both men and Lil were staring at her, and she knew she had given her secret away.

"I'm sure Vic didn't—" Her voice quavered, try as she did to make it firm.

Karl turned suddenly to Debbie and there was urging in his plea. "You shouldn't be living here at all, Deb. This is no place for you, in the same house with Britishers. Can't you imagine what they're saying in town? First Vic, and now you move here with foreigners. Why we even heard about this in Tel Aviv."

Debbie reddened with resentment.

"Lil and I have talked it over," Karl continued. "Come live with us, Deb. It's where you and David belong, and we want you."

"Please," Lil said warmly. "Stay as long as you like. If you're not satisfied with us you can move out any time."

"This isn't spur of the moment," Karl said. "We've talked it over."

Debbie was touched in spite of herself, even more by Lil than by Karl.

"We don't care what Vic did," Lil said, trying to be kind.

Debbie knew, in spite of their generosity, she could never accept their invitation.

"May I come for a visit, Lil?" She could almost feel Karl wince. He looked more tired than ever. "I promise to come if the Arabs hold their fire."

They said their good-byes, sadly, she thought, and Karl turned to George hopelessly. "I wish you'd drop this trip, Mr. Stern. Try to imagine how you'd feel if Debbie were your sister, or David were your son."

George shook hands with Karl and Lil cordially, but did not reply. After they had left, he said to Debbie, "Horowitz finally cornered me this morning. He got wind of Elliot's wire and gave me a thorough going over. He wanted to know what I hoped to accomplish going to England. I instinctively clam up when I'm being pumped. But he went on at a great rate. He said it was a fool's errand, utter waste of time, he's full of these original phrases, you know, and he rambled all over the place—talked about the security risk the government might be running to readmit me after I'd been to England. Mumbled about correspondents' accreditation being a privilege and not a natural right. He was careful to be friendly all the time, a real pal, you know, smiling and smiling to beat hell. I love the way he takes that nice fatherly attitude. 'Mrs. Marmorek, the poor dear girl, I'm sure she wants to try to forget it, to be left alone, to get back to normal. Believe me, old chap, I've met the poor girl and I know quite well how she feels.' He did everything but put his arm on my shoulder and call me son."

Debbie was so enraged she could say nothing.

"Somehow," George said, "Horowitz's being that worried I take as a real sign of encouragement."

On the morning after Karl's visit the sickening familiar crash of mortars began unexpectedly at ten. The Arabs were ahead of time. What about that, Mr. Bernadotte? She could hear Vic laughing. "Don't count on Mr. Bernadotte." The mortar fire was not heavy, almost as though Abdullah's Legionnaires were giving fair warning. Either that or she was used to it.

The days and nights that followed lacked some of the terror and hysteria of the first siege; Debbie's oppression over having to sleep under the bed in the hall with David was scarcely worth mentioning. Perhaps her own circumstance made her indifferent, although she took every possible precaution to remain thoroughly alive. A more likely explanation was that she, along with her fifteen remaining employers, sensed the quick coming of peace and final Israeli victory, for the news was encouraging.

One of the New Yorkers had a powerful radio on which Radio Tel Aviv and Voice of Jerusalem told of Israeli victories everywhere. The Arabs were on the run and refugees were clogging the roads to Bethlehem and to the east. Despite occasional setbacks, the Army of Israel soon had control of the Jezreel valley and the Galilee, including Nazareth. Jerusalem forces took Ein Kerem. Haifa and Jaffa were secure. Acre was safely in Israeli hands; supplies were coming into Jerusalem by the Burma Road, the Palmach was pressing everywhere in the Negev along the Egyptian border, and in the Jenin triangle in the north. Only a few years ago these names were foreign sounds to Debbie, they might have been towns on the moon, or if they were on this earth, they were to be found in the *Arabian Nights*. Today they were as familiar as Snow Mountain, Stadt Park, and the Ring.

Thus the siege ended as suddenly as it had begun, to the surprise of practically nobody. The only question had been whether the Jews would agree to cease-fire before they had captured all Palestine. But the second cease-fire came on July 17, eight days after the new fighting began.

During the first weeks after the siege George and the other newsmen never stopped going. They attended conferences, investigated incidents, reported shootings and demonstrations, went on conducted convoys and briefings, argued with the censors and visited Bernadotte's headquarters.

But as the cease-fire seemed more final, their pace slowed. They awoke later and came back for dinner earlier. Six of them flew to Rhodes to cover the armistice negotiations.

She could see George had something on his mind when he came down to breakfast early on the second Monday after the cease-fire. He sat alone at the long table, peeling a fresh orange she had fetched him and popping the sections into his mouth as he talked.

"Well, I'm packed," he said. "We'll have to have our talk later today, shall we? I'm driving down to Lydda early tomorrow with Talbot. I'll be in London by Wednesday."

"But I haven't given you the money yet."

"Well, I've laid it out myself," he said.

"Oh, but you mustn't. I couldn't let you do that. You'll have to let me give it to you."

"Okay, if you'd rather."

"After all, I'm trying to keep as much of my self-respect as I can."

"Sure," he said. "That's okay with me. Of course it might be safer if you gave me the money when I got back. After all when I get to England I plan to go home to take a look at my daughter. David's made me homesick, you know. And once she gets her hooks into me, I may never come back."

She studied his face, which was stern and serious, and for an instant her heart sank. At last he could hold it no longer and he grinned at her broadly.

"Thanks," he said, "for that look on your face."

She breathed deeply with relief. "You mustn't scare me like that!"

"Can I talk to you this afternoon?"

She smiled wanly. "I'm here all day. Just look for the mop, I'll be right behind it."

After breakfast Debbie went to Barclay's Bank to draw out her money. She was looking forward impatiently to seeing George that afternoon. But George failed to return at two; before he could get back, Prince Bernadotte was murdered by Jewish terrorists just a few blocks away. That sent the newsmen into a frenzy of activity. There were statements and police action, arrests, charges and counter-charges, predictions of violent moves by Britain, the UN, the Arabs, repercussions over half the world; and there was the removal of the casket from the city. George must have filed a dozen stories in two days. There was suspense, and then—nothing.

During the midst of this busy week she managed to find an opportunity to give him the money one evening. Without counting it, he put it in his pocket and never referred to it again. Two hundred pounds. In no way did he indicate that he knew it was half her fortune.

It was almost another week before he was able to take off. Talbot was to drive him down to Lydda in the Fiat. The evening before he left he asked her to come to his room after the dinner dishes and they talked, while he took notes. He wanted to know how Vic got his job, and about Vic's history with the Telephone Office. He asked about the Halliwells and Redge and Enid. He wanted to know if there had been any correspondence with the Walkers since they'd returned to England, and she fetched him the few letters she had received from Enid before postal service stopped.

"He did give David that bicycle, didn't he?" George asked. "And I've heard there was a refrigerator and a washing machine for Hanukka or Christmas or something. Of course, that's only what I've heard." George could be irritatingly insistent.

"Then you quarreled with Vic about these presents?"

"No. We did discuss them though."

"Perhaps quarrel is too strong a word. Was there some difference of opinion?"

"Mmm. You might say . . . something like that." She knew what he was driving at, and she went on the defensive again. "But you don't think anyone like Vic would have done such things—for a refrigerator or a bicycle, do you? Vic was earning over eighty pounds a month, George. I have no idea what salary a reporter gets, but I'd guess Vic was making almost as much as you do."

"I'll complain to my editor," George smiled.

"You see. And I was making thirty-five. So we could afford any of those things ourselves, if we'd decided to get them."

"I see. And did you buy *them* Christmas presents?"

"The Walkers? Why yes, of course. Perhaps not such expensive things. Gloves, scarves, ties. We did get Lloyd a lovely brocaded Yemenite costume that was quite unusual and expensive."

"You think Redge had any special interest in you?"

"What do you mean?"

"You know what I mean. Special interest. You're an attractive girl."

"Oh, that. Mmm . . . I never thought of it, to tell you the truth."

"Never?"

"Well, I liked Redge, but he left me feeling so blah, I just didn't think of him that way. Oh, I mean not really. The way he divides his hair right down the middle. When you meet him you'll see. It reveals a state of mind. As if he uses geometric instruments to get it just right. Now come to think of it, occasionally he'd hold my hand and once or twice I got the feeling that he was trying to look deeply into my eyes. But I always felt I was looking into something opaque, like the glass eyes of a stuffed owl and I had all I could do to keep a straight face."

"And how about your husband—uh—Vic, and Enid?"

"Mmm . . ." she thought carefully. "Oh, there was nothing like that, I'm sure. I guess Vic rather liked Enid, always seemed to, and never made any bones about it. She's quite striking. You'll see for yourself—tall, blond, has a lovely figure, and a nice person. I really was worried about Vic at first. She's much more magnificent than I am and always mistress of every situation too. How I envied her! She took quite a fancy to Vic, too, I believe. Everyone did, of course, at least women. But Enid was rather special to him, I suppose. Glamorous, and his boss's wife. He couldn't help being flattered. Nothing more than that, I'm sure, in spite of any of Horowitz's filthy innuendoes. I think he may have given her a few tennis lessons with the children, and that's about the size of it."

"How did Redge and his wife get along?"

"Splendidly." She could think of no other word to express the unimaginative relationship she suspected. That was it. "They make a grand couple." She could not quite eliminate the slightly derisive amusement from her voice.

In many ways it was a comforting evening, for she had the feeling that they were making progress, clarifying her memories, sorting impressions. She tried to hold nothing back, although she was surprised at how little she really knew about the details of Vic's job, of specific procedures and policies at the Telephone Office. "I was so busy with my own job," she said apologetically, "and there was David to tend to."

They explored Enid's offer to take David to England, Ben Kronstein's being discharged, Vic's promotion. He asked about Pearlman, but there was little she could tell about him.

When he seemed more or less satisfied, they went downstairs and he put a call through to Evelyn Maney in Tel Aviv. Evelyn represented one of the American press services there, and although she had heard of the Marmorek affair, she told George she had not considered it of special interest. She said a foreign press conference was scheduled four days later with Ben-Gurion, and she promised to try one or two questions for George, who filled her in on the details. She would try also to reach Ami Ben Kepelow, the prosecutor, now in Haifa.

"If I'm not here, Ev," said George, "report to Talbot."

He hung up and she took her courage in her hands. "George, would you mind if I went to Lydda with you in the morning? Please? I've never had a day off, you know. I think I'd like the change. And Noah's agreed to mind David."

"Wonderful!" he said. "Sure. Fine." He looked relieved. "We'll leave at seven. Good night, Debbie."

Alone in the lobby she wrote a brief note by candlelight to the Walkers. She was conscious of using Vic's pen, the same one with which he had written his last note.

Dear Redge and Enid,

I am sending this through George Stern who has been a friend and a great help to me during these most nightmarish days of my life, when I have greatly missed the few dear friends Vic and I had. George will tell you what happened here and how you are involved. Please talk to him and give him what help you can and you will be helping me and David beyond anything you can imagine. Our circumstances are not nearly as chipper as they once were. You can picture how folks look upon us here because of what they believe Vic did, but I'm sure you agree with me that Vic could never have betrayed his own people, and I'm equally sure you, Redge, would never have led him to do so. Please, please do anything you can to help, for the sake of Vic's memory as much as for David and me.

Love to you both and David says remembrances to Lloyd.

DEBBIE

She read and reread the note several times, wondering if she ought not to try to make it friendlier or warmer, and finally put it without change, into an envelope which she addressed from her address book. That George would be delivering this letter to so far a place day after tomorrow seemed less than plausible.

At breakfast before sunrise, when David discovered his mother was going to Lydda he pleaded to go along. He begged, wept, and went to the verge of tantrum.

George was not down yet, but Talbot stopped sipping his coffee and tugged at his chin in annoyance.

"Why don't you let him?" he asked. "He's getting stir-happy. It'll do him good."

She agreed but with misgivings.

"If Mr. Talbot will help me take care of you and you promise to be good."

"I'll be so good," David said, "you'll think I'm dead."

David was on his best behavior with Talbot in the back seat, straight and proud because he knew the American standard above the fender gave him special privileges of immunity. If Lloyd could see him now!

Twice they were stopped by unsmiling sentries for examination of papers—more grimly formal than she had ever remembered Haganah troops before.

At last they were bumping along Vic's road. The Fiat took a trouncing because the Burma Road had a surface with little to recommend it. They saw convoys limping into Jerusalem and passed abandoned vehicles, burnt-out trucks, pushed aside by bulldozers.

David was grievously disappointed to discover that this rugged trail was his father's famous road. "It must get better later on," he reassured himself.

The trip consumed more than five hours, although normal time to Lydda was not much more than one.

At Lydda, George went inside to check on his flight. Debbie had never seen an airfield, and the three huge planes on the taxiways gave her the shudders. Planes like these had dropped the leaflets during the Anschluss. It was the sound of planes that brought terror to Rome. In spite of herself the sound of engines overhead made her stomach sick.

But David hopped out of the car and ran like an escaped jack-in-the-box, pointing, exclaiming, shrieking.

"I'll show him around," Talbot said, "you go ahead and find George." He took off after David.

In her pocket she felt for the letter to the Walkers, her inarticulate plea for help, and she hurried into the bare waiting room.

A pasty-faced military inspector was elbow deep in George's valise, stirring his clothing like a thick soup. George waited there so thin and vulnerable. Helpless almost. Finally the inspector slapped stickers on the bag. This was the moment when she might express her thanks, to tell George how she felt about all he was doing. But what could she say? I feel Thank you, and yet something more. I don't know exactly what, but something much more than only Thank you.

But she couldn't. Not a word.

George removed a book from his bag and led her into the glass-enclosed waiting room sticky hot in the afternoon's desert sun. "Well, we're lucky. We're getting off in a few minutes. Sometimes you wait around places like this for hours. Especially at fields like Lydda."

"Oh, I'd have been glad to wait, George. You see, to me it's worth anything to be here now."

They watched the plane taxi clumsily toward them. "Don't you feel queasy setting foot into such an illogical contraption?"

George sighed. "All right, I'll tell you my darkest secret. I'm terrified. I get the screaming meemies on every takeoff and landing, but I'm a sucker for going somewhere. Anywhere—some place new, some place old. It hardly matters. You know what I mean?"

"Yes, I suppose you love traveling. You're full of curiosity, aren't you? Besides you always go first class." George frowned. "I'm sorry, I didn't mean that. Really. Don't be angry." He relented and smiled. "As for me," she went on, "my own curiosity was satisfied long ago. I don't know exactly when or how it happened—it might have been the time we crossed the Austrian border at Gmünd and a Nazi lady stripped me and Mama and robbed her of her watch. Or it could have been the good ship *Petah Tiqva,* my only Mediterranean cruise. Terribly difficult getting good accommodations. It seems Mediterranean cruises were all the rage that year. And we had trouble with the tenders when we got off at Haifa too, you know. And the immigration authorities were so strict. Couldn't have been less hospitable. We had to swim part of the way, I recall. Terribly gay, but unfortunately we did lose several passengers—from drowning, I believe. Of course, we didn't know them too well so we hardly missed them. I just don't know precisely where it was, but somewhere along the line I lost my wanderlust."

"You'll get over feeling like that," George said gently. "You're just too curious not to be interested in every place."

"You'll never believe me, of course. But no, I never do expect to get over it," she said. "I'll tell you something else too, and you probably won't believe that either. I'd gladly swap my feet for roots, actual roots, out of me into the ground, on one pleasant comfortable spot that would be my own. Absolutely mine. I'd be glad to be a nice tree. I'd try to get a place next to another pleasant tree, or a whole forest of other trees perhaps. All the same kind, naturally, like the lindens at Snow Mountain, they were so lovely, or cypresses—that would satisfy me. But all the same type, it would never do to mix the types. No,

I'd be too uncomfortable, standing there wondering if the birches were whispering about me. 'Look at that queer cypress. You know, she never sheds! What do you make of her? She's unnatural. Perhaps we should get rid of her.' I couldn't stand to face the anti-cypress propaganda. No, all the trees would have to be exactly my type. We'd each have our own private piece of earth and when we got lonely we could whisper together, but my one spot would be my own. Without having to fight for it, or struggle over it. Oh, I would do my part. I'd give shade, plenty of nice shade. And if I was the kind that had fruit I'd give it gladly. But whenever the rain fell on my spot it would be my rain. And when the breeze blew across it, it would be my breeze. You think I'm exaggerating, but you're wrong. I just don't want to be a tourist. I lack the imagination for it."

George laughed.

"You become most positive when you're most wrong," he said cheerfully. Before she could answer he turned businesslike. "While I'm gone, see if there's anything you can dig up. This fellow Pearlman may know something. Or Colonel Steinmetz. If you don't get anywhere at all, when I get back maybe we'll run over to Tel Aviv."

"I'll try."

The great letters TWA revolved into view as the plane swung round. George took Debbie's hand. "Bye-bye. Here's something to keep you out of mischief. Read it while I'm away. I'll try to get back soon, couple of weeks maybe—as soon as I can make it."

She took the book. "Good-bye." She could think of nothing further and she said something fatuous, "Have a lovely trip," or something. He mumbled something also, held her hand more tightly, until her fingers hurt, then let her go suddenly, turned, and started up the ramp. She walked slowly through the hall to the waiting room, back out to the Fiat. She had to sit down, she felt weak, exhausted, the way she did in the hour after David was born. Hollow. There was so much more she might have tried to tell him. But she was terribly tired.

The book he had given her was a thick black volume called *Inside USA* and she wondered why he had selected it. Thumbing its pages she found an encyclopedic slangy dissertation on places, politicians, and people in America. On the flyleaf, in ink, it said, "To George, from John." Well, reading about America would be much easier than having to go there.

She heard the four great engines roar and the silver plane stood poised, then shuddered, and sped down the runway. She was spent from the terrible excitement of knowing that there was one other person now irrevocably committed to her mission. She had enlisted help. It made everything real.

Thirty-seven

No one at Haganah Headquarters would tell her where Pearlman was stationed, but an ingenious bit of sleuthing by Talbot among several members of the Palestine Philharmonic paid off. Sam Pearlman was supervising shoring and repair operations at the remains of what was once Notre Dame Hospital, the crucial New City strong point which was being reinforced against the day of fresh attacks by Abdullah's Legion, whose sentries paced uneasily a hundred meters away. Talbot wangled a pass for her, and she found Pearlman hauling sandbags on the story overhead. She stood at the foot of the ladder.

"Would you come down, Sam? I want to talk to you a minute."

"How did you get in here?"

"I have a pass, see? Please come down."

"I have nothing to tell you, Mrs. Marmorek."

"Don't you have any feeling at all, Sam? All I want to do is talk."

"I'm busy, Mrs. Marmorek. Can't you see, and these bags are heavy. Fifty kilos each."

"Come down, Sam. You owe me that much. David and I need help. No matter what you think of Vic you know I didn't have anything to do with it, don't you?"

"I don't know anything," Pearlman said gloomily.

"You think David's a spy too? Now, Sam."

"He'll recover. I'm not worried about him. He's a musician. Big talent. He'll be okay."

He placed the sandbag upon a pile of others, surrounding a gun emplacement. "Don't you know there are security restrictions here, Mrs. Marmorek? No one's allowed in Notre Dame. Especially security risks."

She fled in fury.

Perhaps Ben Kronstein could tell her something. Ben's wife, poor Willie, had been buried during the siege in the wreckage of her own kitchen. Maybe Ben, who could understand the meaning of a loss, could be persuaded to help. But he was not at the Telephone Office. He was in Tel Aviv for a week on government business. The girl at the desk, Esther Schamel, whom she knew only slightly, was solicitous, and promised to have Mr. Kronstein call as soon as he returned.

She tried to tackle Army Headquarters in Jerusalem. They would know about the case. She would go straight to Colonel Steinmetz, to the top. At the Agency when she asked for him, a graying panicky officer came down to see her.

"Can I help you?"

"I'd like to see the colonel about the Marmorek matter. I'm Mrs. Marmorek."

The stuffy officer frowned, rubbed his chin reflectively and made an ugly grimace as if he had just swallowed something unpalatable. "I'm sorry, Madam, I'm afraid that won't be possible. The colonel is terribly busy."

"Well, I could come back some other time."

"I'm afraid it would be no use."

"It's terribly important to me, Captain—I'm sorry I didn't get your name."

"Levy. You see we have no information at this headquarters," he said in measured tones. "No information at all."

"Perhaps you don't understand," she said forcing herself to smile a smile of ice. "My husband has been shot. It's a matter of the greatest seriousness to me. It's also a serious matter to our son. I'm sure the colonel can spare five minutes under the circumstances."

Captain Levy backed away. "I'm sorry, I know how you feel, but this headquarters had nothing to do with it. We weren't consulted. We have absolutely no information. It's a matter for Intelligence. Why don't you see Colonel Horowitz?"

"You must know Colonel Horowitz has gone back to Haifa. Let me ask you, Captain, didn't Colonel Steinmetz have to approve my husband's sentence?"

"This headquarters knows nothing about the case. That's all I'm permitted to say. You must realize we have to look on the matter with detachment."

"Well, don't you think that was rather high-handed of Colonel Horowitz? Just speaking with detachment of course. He was the only husband I have, you know. The only father my son has. But if that's too personal we'll push that aside, shall we, and talk theoretically? Shooting is serious business, don't you agree, Captain? At least I take it quite seriously and I take it personally, Captain, I certainly take it very bloody personally."

"Your husband had a full trial, Madam. He had a lawyer. He had three judges. It's war time."

"And what am I supposed to do, Captain? Fade away? Disappear? Not be a bother to anyone? I suppose that would be terribly convenient! I couldn't care less for it."

"If you were to submit written questions, I'm sure the colonel will be glad to answer them for you."

"How nice! That's sweet of the colonel! You're too kind, Captain."

She snatched her pen from her pocket and wrote on a sheet from her notepad:

> Did you confirm the death sentence of Victor Marmorek?
>
> Have you reviewed the case at any time before or after his execution?
>
> If newly uncovered evidence indicates that the verdict or sentence were in error, would your headquarters be prepared to reopen the case?

She signed her name.

As she handed the torn sheet to Captain Levy, she noticed the brown numerals burned into his forearm.

"Which concentration camp were you in, Captain Levy?"

"Bergen-Belsen," he said.

"Pity you missed the best part of the camp," she said sweetly, "the ovens. Speaking theoretically, of course. Nothing personal, you understand."

Captain Levy said nothing, and she left fuming, but ashamed of herself.

The next day a courier left a note for her written in Colonel Steinmetz's own hand.

> Since all the questions you ask bear on the subject of internal security, it is not possible to be directly responsive, much as we would like to be.

The curt note was signed L. STEINMETZ, COMMANDING OFFICER.

On Friday morning Evelyn Maney called Talbot from Tel Aviv. At his press conference the Prime Minister had offered nothing new. She had asked if the Marmorek sentence had been reviewed and confirmed by his office before being carried out. The Prime Minister said it had not. So far as he knew neither had any other office in Tel Aviv confirmed it. It was a Jerusalem matter. Jerusalem, he reminded the roomful of reporters, had been for all practical purposes cut off and on its own. The final decision in such matters as internal security had been the military commander's in Jerusalem, during hostilities.

Had the Prime Minister received any word on the case since the execution? He had not. As soon as he had time he would make an inquiry.

Was he aware that the widow of the executed man was claiming her husband's execution to be a miscarriage of justice? He was not aware of it, but he was not surprised by it. That seemed a natural enough reaction for a widow.

When would he order an investigation of the matter? The Prime Minister had smiled. The Prime Minister is trying to get on with the business of governing and if he does not get on with it there will soon be a new Prime Minister. The Prime Minister excused himself. He had not seemed to resent the questions about the Marmorek affair, nor did he appear at all interested in the subject beyond paying polite attention.

As for Ami Ben Kepelow, he had refused to be interviewed beyond saying that he was satisfied that Victor Marmorek was guilty and had received a full measure of justice.

Thirty-eight

Debbie wondered occasionally whether Gussie had received any of the three letters she had written and consigned to an uncertain mail. But at the moment of Gussie's arrival at the pension, Debbie was on her way out, with David, to visit Beth Hakerem for Lilith's birthday.

Now on seeing Gussie she was too startled to say anything. Gus stood silent, framed in the front door, carrying a clumsy black suitcase. Debbie would have known her anywhere in spite of the tremendous change in Gussie. For one thing her friend was now vastly handsomer. No one would accuse Gussie of being actually attractive, but the adolescent fat was gone and she had acquired the appearance of quiet physical strength that was also something more than physical, which made her almost handsome in spite of her unlovely features, which her prematurely gray hair now succeeded in softening. She looked better than Debbie could have imagined, dressed as she was in a ludicrously unbecoming yellow flowered print, doubtless a castoff of some generous American or South African lady in an old-clothing drive for immigrants. Gussie stood for a moment as if she were uncertain it was her old friend, until Debbie said in a low voice, "It's me all right, Gus."

Gussie put down the suitcase gingerly and embraced her without a word, something she had never done even in their giggliest girlhood days. Gussie had never been an arms-about-the-waist companion.

Debbie, lapsing into German, said, "You look so wonderful! I'd have known you no matter what, of course, but you've grown—I don't know—better and better!"

"You think so?" Gussie smiled warmly, but no longer shyly. "No doubt my outdoor life. Exercise and fresh air. You're the same, aren't you? Not a line on your face. You still look eighteen. And this is David?"

Debbie bent to David. "This is Aunt Gussie, dear. An old friend of Mommy's."

"From Vienna?" he asked gaily.

Gussie and Debbie exchanged glances. "Yes, dear, from Vienna."

Debbie held Gussie at arm's length and examined her. "It's good to see you. It's so good." Then she smiled to herself. "Where did you get that dress?"

Gussie turned about, showing off her new creation. "Isn't it gay? I received it as a gift."

Still the same Gussie. She had no idea how outlandish it looked on her.

Then seeing David's hair slicked, his clothes immaculate, Gussie said, "David is so beautiful, too. So dolled up. Were you expecting company or going visiting?"

"We're going to see Uncle Karl and Aunt Lil." Before Debbie could stop him, David said, "It's Aunt Lil's birthday."

"Karl!" Gussie said. "Of course! You know I wrote him from Prague that time. Right after you left. In fact I wrote him several times, but I guess no mail went through in those days. How is Karl?"

"Fine," Debbie said.

"He's with Egged," David said. "You should see the bus he drives. Huge. He drove us to the cemetery."

"How long can you stay, Gus?"

"Only the weekend," she said. "I have a wonderful job in Haifa, you know. I have eight girls under me in the factory. Sewing cheap dresses. But the conditions there are so bad, really, you have no idea."

"And your friend, the one you wrote about? I think that's so wonderful for you."

"Oh, Emil's sweet. Much older. He's fifty. We came from Prague together. Emil's a lawyer and, of course, he can't do a thing until he learns Hebrew and then he has to go back to school again. At fifty, imagine! There are so many different kinds of law for such a small country. Ottoman laws, Napoleonic laws, English Mandate laws and Biblical laws and all the new ones. Poor Emil's discouraged. But he'll go on with it. That's the kind of man he is, and what else is there for him to do? Meanwhile I earn enough money to get us by and we're both happy to be here. It's home you know, in a way."

"Stay at my place, Gussie, for the weekend. I have a nice flat in Rehavia. I don't suppose I'll be able to keep it much longer. But right now I'm paying rent for it. You can drop your things there now and then come with us to Karl's. I'm sure he'll be pleased."

As they walked to Gaza Road, Debbie saw how graceful Gussie had become; she walked lithely, proudly, with almost a swagger.

Baumerstock, who was sitting in front of his store, rose ostentatiously, turned his back and went indoors as Debbie passed. Others peered at her queerly as if she were a costumed carnival creature.

As Gussie unpacked she seemed to become more affected by the emotional impact of their meeting. "If you only knew what it does to me to see your face. A face I know from the nice days. It's like no other face."

"I know," Debbie said.

"Ten years ago I'd have wept," Gussie said. "But you know it's not possible to cry any more. That's true, your tear ducts stop functioning. Something happens in the glands or maybe it's a vitamin deficiency. It's the funniest feeling. Something terrible or wonderful happens, and there's a great choking in your throat and you're sure you're going to cry and all you can do is choke. Isn't that the limit?"

"It's a blessing," Debbie said. "We've had enough tears for the century." She noticed that Gussie's old habit of blinking had disappeared.

Gussie looked about admiringly while Debbie made her a cup of coffee. "I haven't seen a place with a piano in ten years," she said somewhat wistfully, tapping the keyboard. She fingered the photograph of Vic in his Sokol uniform, Debbie's favorite, which she kept on the piano. "He's so beautiful, isn't he? How I envy you because of him. Don't they know such beauty could never hide a mean heart? Men are so stupid. Women would know things like that better. I'd never let the government get away with it. Never." She sat and stirred the saccharin in her coffee and sipped it carefully. "Good," she murmured. "You know coffee gives me strength. Every time I had to kill anyone in Bratislava I had three cups of coffee, sometimes four. Before, it gave me courage and afterwards it was a comfort." She spoke so matter-of-factly, Debbie thought she had misunderstood.

"Whom did you kill?" she asked lightly. "Anyone I know?"

"Oh, no," Gussie said, and she smiled gently. "Only Germans and one collaborator."

"Really?" Debbie was no longer laughing.

"Of course. How else could a girl like me get by? I was a Partisan. I joined the Reds, of course. We were the only ones who were really effective. The others were so namby-pamby. Rabbits. You could never trust them. They were worse than the Nazis."

Debbie was becoming uncomfortable. "You must've had to be so—uh—strong." It wasn't the word she meant to use.

"Of course," Gussie said. "I'm quite—as you say—strong." She used the word with the same off-center emphasis. "We were able to use only ropes and knives. We had to be quiet."

"Lord!" Debbie tried to laugh lightly. "It would never do to cause a rumpus, would it? Wouldn't be ladylike!"

Gussie smiled. "I promise you I never forgot for a minute that I was a lady. A well-brought-up girl from a fine upper-class family."

"I can just picture Froelich, the old bat," Debbie said. "If she could only hear us!"

"Oh, Froelich, I haven't thought of her," Gussie laughed, "since I stopped curtseying."

"All those piano lessons, French lessons, the waltz classes, my God, when you think of it!" Debbie laughed. "How could any of us forget we were ladies?"

"I never forgot," Gussie said. "Not for a minute. No matter whom I was choking. Your mother's words would ring in my ears: 'Remember, girls, there's nothing more important than your manners.' "

"Manners!" Debbie was thinking unaccountably of Angelo and her own behavior. "My poor Mama! She was never satisfied with me. Too frivolous, and the boys would never have enough respect. Oh God, when I think of it! I'll bet they had respect for you, Gus!"

"In Bratislava," Gus said with heavy sarcasm, "I never slept with a comrade without always saying 'Thank you,' afterward."

"And 'please' beforehand," Debbie reminded.

"Of course," Gussie said, "I was *always* a lady. It made all the difference." By now they were both laughing, laughing harder and harder, at last almost hysterically. They were only a couple of schoolgirls from Vienna, closer than they had ever been at home.

They gossiped on the bus like two teenage girls, while David was all ears, eyes open wide, taking in every word. Debbie sketched the years in Rome and the trip to Haifa and her months working at the hospital. And Gussie told how she had been rescued by Partisans and had left Prague for Bratislava, crouched over one whole night in a sack in a truck carrying great bags of fertilizer—disguised as fifty kilograms of manure. She told how their small band, ten men and two women, had lived from hand to mouth foraging for food, preying on German Army units, committing railroad sabotage and trying to make the Nazis miserable. Through all her talk ran one strong political theme. The Communists had furnished the only effective resistance to the Nazis. "It was the same in Yugoslavia, my dear. Tito's people were fighters. Mikhailovich was worse than a Nazi. When your side is right you can't equivocate, you can't be squeamish. If you're going to worry about a man's innocent wife or his poor old mother or his children you'll never kill him and sometimes it's extremely necessary to kill him. You see, now at least we've made all this known in Czechoslovakia. The people want us at last. They recognize. You know since Masaryk jumped out the window and Benes has gone, real strength is coming to Czechoslovakia. It's the best thing that could have happened there. And here it will be the same. Ben-Gurion and his stupid old Socialists are weak. They vacillate. They will serve their limited purpose and then they must go also. You'll see."

Debbie said nothing. She had always sympathized vaguely with Histadruth and Ben-Gurion's leadership, for Debbie believed in moderation. Everyone she knew had been bred on it. Vic had preached it.

They had both hated Etzel and the Sternists. They hated the terror of hanging English sergeants, explosions at the King David and the massacre at Deir Yassein. She had the impression that Gussie was watching her for her reactions, but she wanted nothing less than to be drawn into political discussions.

"I haven't been following developments in Prague, except in a general way," she said vaguely.

"You see? You think Palestine is an isolated island too. Where do you think your army has been getting guns? All those bombing planes that fly over Cairo? From Czechoslovakia, from *us*, my dear." She spoke now as if to a child. "And if dear sweet Mr. Benes and Mr. Masaryk would still be there, do you know what you'd have got? Neutrality. Like the Spaniards got. But then you were never interested in politics, were you? Vic was your world."

Debbie watched the barren countryside change abruptly to evergreen forests. It soothed her. "Politics isn't my specialty, but there's been more to my world than Vic alone, I promise you."

Gussie was delighted with Beth Hakerem. The neat rows of houses and apartments set among the spruces pleased her sense of order.

Karl was genuinely glad to see Gussie, and Lilith was most cordial. In many ways Debbie was grateful for her old friend's presence, she relieved so many of the small tensions of the afternoon.

When the conversation sagged, it was Gussie who came to the rescue. She told with great relish the story of her flight from Bratislava to Haifa. Gussie could be quite gay; she seemed to have enjoyed the experience, and even more to tell of it.

"Here we are," she said dramatically. "You see it's one of those freezing February nights in Bulgaria, no February night is quite like a Bulgarian February night, they're pre-frozen. Nine of us, one a ten-year-old boy, about like David, and we're a traveling band of gypsies dressed like for a carnival. With a horse and wagon. Who thought all this up, I don't know. But someone has a bright idea: In Bulgaria and Turkey gypsies are more popular than Jews. That's a comfort for you. All right, I'm willing to be a gypsy. All the way across Bulgaria people take us into their houses everywhere. It's all arranged in advance.

"Where it's not arranged, I have to sing gypsy songs and play the guitar. You should hear me. I do drinking songs in Swedish, an American Indian chant, an old Yiddish lullaby. I tell you, I'm a born gypsy. Quite an organization, this underground, but you have to be on your toes, you need talent. Everyone has his own job and you never know, you can never be sure. At last we come to the Turkish border, it seems as though we've been traveling and hiding for months, and there's this huge Turk soldier, nine feet high, with a mustache, looks like Stalin's, only droopier and bushier. He's standing like the Eiffel Tower. No expression, only big. He screams at us, Stop. He has these three other men with him, midgets, about seven feet tall. The Turks are small, you know, but they must hire their border guards from the circus, and the big one talks only Turkish. Gobble, gobble, gobble, we don't understand a word. Finally he screams in German, Jude? We shake our heads. No, no, no. Such an insult! Is he implying we gypsies are Jews! Some nerve. We try Czech, German, one man knows French. No speak. Especially the big one. When he shrugs, it's quite a movement, frightening. We're afraid we'll all be arrested and sent back and we'd come pretty far. Finally he screams in Yiddish as if he's going to *kill* us, at the top of his voice, as if he's so mad he is going to have us shot on the spot, carrying on like a Nazi—for the benefit of the midgets, of course. 'Welcome, friends! Welcome to the road to Israel. When I wave, move fast, please. Run as if you're scared to death of me and straight up the road three kilometers you'll see a building with a green light in the window. There you'll find friends. May God protect you all. My men think I'm talking gypsy talk. They think I'm a genius. Now hurry!' He curses in Turkish and all this time he's been yelling so ferociously his mustache is hopping all over his face and the ground is shaking, but we feel good. Of course, he looks like he's going to eat us alive, then growls like a dog and chases us across the Turkish border and starts to go after us. His friends are laughing like crazy at the sport he's having with us poor gypsies. They have no idea he's a Jew, or maybe they are, themselves, who knows? Who knows how long we can get away with it? A short while and then they'll have to find another point of entry. So it goes. That's the biggest Jew I ever saw. He is equal to five little ones."

"Must have been awful," Lilith said.

"It was a riot," Gussie said. "I loved it. After all, the outdoor life hardens a girl. But I feel sorry for this man's wife. Probably some tiny creature, and if you ask me, she's not long for this world. This is something I'd like to watch."

"Gus was a Partisan," Debbie said interrupting abruptly, "during the war, in Bratislava."

"You, a Partisan? Not really!" Karl said, impressed.

"Yes." Gussie was matter-of-fact. "How else would I have stayed healthy? We had no good fairies to guard us, you know. The Nazis called me the Witch of Bratislava. The work was not very difficult after a while. In fact I got to like it. There were various compensations. Those were exciting days. Why do you look so shocked? People have strange appetites in times of danger. Aren't your girls all in the army? Killers. They've done the same."

"But you, Gussie, I can't believe it of you." Karl stared.

"You probably wouldn't believe other things about me, if I were to tell you, but I won't shock you."

"What would your father have thought?"

"I was thinking of him most of the time," Gus spoke with grim satisfaction. "I think he'd have been satisfied with me."

"It's a long way from old Vienna, isn't it?" Karl said lamely.

Later in the afternoon Karl took them out to Deir Yassein to show them where some of the fighting and the great massacre of Arabs had taken place; it was like a guided tour to an old battleground of another age; the old picturesque town was filled with brand new immigrants in transit and a few soldiers quartered in ancient buildings. The massacre and fighting of a few months ago seemed already to be as unreal as history. The dead were buried and the living had fled. The old Mukhtar was forgotten, and people met and talked there, the new ones who had replaced the old, as if nothing had changed, as if they had lived there forever. So tenacious we are, Debbie thought. How frantically we try to hold to our normalcy. Above principle, above heroism, above history. Even above justice. What we really want above all is to be as normal as everyone else. To live as though nothing of importance had ever happened to us or to our world, and if by some mischance something has happened, all our effort is to appear not to notice it and if we're so unfortunate that we can't help noticing, at least we try not to inconvenience others by mentioning it.

Karl took them to the village's main office, where the small staff that ran the Deir Yassein camp carried on its work, and there they met the camp director, who lectured like a kindly schoolmaster to the group, explaining who these newcomers from Cyprus were and how they were being cared for, after their long internment by the British; he showed David through the improvised kindergarten where Hanukka candelabras were made by the children from discarded Coca-Cola bottletops and glue. When they got back to Karl's house they found Ben Kronstein, whom Lil had asked to drop over.

Lilith was in a continuous maneuver all afternoon to put them together and Debbie realized with an unhappy start that Lil was matchmaking. Debbie and Ben Kronstein. Lord, what a combination! Poor Ben, wheezing and simpering, a precise, dainty man with his pince-nez punctuating his comic face, his humorless mind.

Still she could not entirely blame Karl and Lil. After all, she'd done the same thing herself—she and Vic had had Jacinta Van Bern and Dick Alpert up half a dozen times, hoping something might come of it. But Dick Alpert was quite a different story. He was appealing, even his taciturnity had a charm; that was a match worth trying to make. But Ben! Yet Karl and Lil would consider Ben highly eligible. Sound, university man, loyal, steady.

He must have seemed ideal to them. She looked slyly at the gargoyle face. Poor Ben, she had everything she could do to keep from laughing aloud, it was so ludicrous. What did they think she was?

As soon as poor Vic could no longer defend himself, as soon as his back was turned, they were ready to betray him, and they were tempting her to forsake him too, in the most obvious way, to turn her back on their love. A temptation which she had not even recognized, which revolted her, was being vaguely defined. A young, pretty widow alone, sweet old Ben, and the eternal loneliness of humankind. That was what Karl and Lil were saying to each other behind her back. That was what they were really hoping. All they wished was for little sister Debbie to be safe, she supposed they really wanted that much for her, and for Vic to be forgotten, buried in the memoryless past with the last of the six million corpses of Europe. That was what must seem to them quite sensible and safe. But they're barking up the wrong tree, she thought. All my senses for that kind of love and feeling died when Vic died. Oh, that nice warmth of feeling, that softness of feeling. Only in my dreaming forevermore.

Ben was at her side now, speaking to her in an undertone. "Miss Schamel gave me a message that you'd been to the office to see me, Deborah. Was it anything special?"

She wondered vaguely if she could talk to him about helping her now. No one knew more about telephone operations than he, at least until he left the department. Could he really have been a witness against Vic? She studied the neat, odd face, but it was a puzzle. Surely this was not the moment to ask him. Then she knew Ben would never help. She would only humiliate herself if she asked him for anything.

"No, Ben, nothing special. I just stopped in to say hello. Habit, I suppose."

Lilith set out a small spread, tea and an austerity cake adorned with a single candle, gaily crying "Happy Birthday, Lilith!" to herself. They all kissed her and ate hungrily and gossiped cheerfully. After moments of aimless chatter Lilith said, "When are you coming back to the hospital, Debbie? We need you like mad there, we're so short-handed. All these newcomers to Jerusalem and I swear half of them are pregnant, the Orientals anyhow—our Catholics, I call them. To them contraception is about as simple as relativity. And we have our Jewish Moslems, too. Some of the men come in with two wives, from Yemen, Morocco, all the Arab states. Wives who aren't more than children themselves—fourteen, fifteen, mind you. And some of these sheiks bring their concubines, I swear, not married at all. They're absolutely a different breed. Absolutely. I often wonder what makes them anything like us. What makes *us* responsible for them? They could be Indian or Malayan or Chinese, they're so different. And yet here they are. Like it or not."

Ben Kronstein broke in with measured precision: "You're not suggesting we keep them out, I hope? Of course it means sacrifice for all of us. Now some people think the only kind of sacrifice is economic, but we'll have to make greater sacrifices than just having less to eat.

We'll make greater social and cultural sacrifices. The culture will come *down.* These Orientals need two generations to catch us Europeans. But we'll have to do it. These people are gentle people at heart. Take these Yemenites. They are delightful. I have two at the Telephone Office."

After each sentence she noticed his sidelong glance—he no doubt thought he was looking at her slyly—as if he were making certain that she of all those present was following his somewhat pompous dissertation.

"Of course," Lilith said, "you're absolutely right, Ben. I'm only talking clinically, you know, not socially, you're absolutely right, of course. I was only trying to get Debbie back to the hospital to help. There are so many sick ones, too, Deb."

"One in three," Ben said dutifully, "needs medical treatment. One in five should be in a hospital. I've become interested in this immigrant problem."

Debbie spoke deliberately, "I don't think I could work with Elsa again. Maybe I could get myself assigned to Maternity if I ever come back. I think I'd like that. But then I'm not being honest or fair, either, am I? It's more than just Elsa. I just don't want to be embarrassing everyone. I'm going ahead, you know, I *am,* about Vic's case." She could sense Ben stiffening. His eyes grew watery, expressionless, and he stared ahead. "I'm afraid there'll be people who aren't going to like it. Not just Elsa, but some of the old fuddy-duddies on the Board. It will embarrass them. Even the government won't like it. I just heard this morning Ben-Gurion said he's heard nothing official about the case. Vic's gone, I saw him buried with my own eyes, but it's nothing official, you see. Well, they're going to hear something official before long. Mighty official too. Then maybe I'll be able to go back to the hospital. After they admit what they've done."

"How do you propose to make them admit it?" Gussie asked.

"I have a friend—this American. Karl's met him. He's gone to England to get new evidence."

"And you expect them to listen? You expect anyone to pay any attention?" Gussie spoke softly, but with the assurance that accompanies authority, and the longer she spoke the more vehement she grew. "You're so much on the wrong track, Debbie, I'm sorry to see you beat your brains and your heart out. You and this American friend. New evidence and all that. Suppose you find new evidence, even suppose it's conclusive. Oh, yes, of course, so they'll be embarrassed, the big shots, but that will lead you nowhere. These wishy-washy weaklings, a government of namby-pambies—and worse. Hypocrites. They'll never do anything decent for you of their own accord. You have to push, fight, make trouble for them. Inquiring discreetly in government offices, pleading privately, begging for justice in whispers and whimpers is nonsense. Absolutely nonsense. For years I lived among you futile people—polite, decent people, who protested, who investigated, and waited each year for the elections. I was the same. What a waste! Remember what your father told me? His lawyer would soon bring my Papa out? His Mr. Jarcho was a big lawyer! I half believed him then. I suppose I needed such a hope to go on with. But in my heart I don't think I ever believed him. Well, what happened to my Papa and yours, and your mother? To Mr. Jarcho too, for that matter? Long ago I stopped having my old nightmare, where I screamed in my sleep for justice before those terrible menacing brutes and had that awful moment when I realized that the men who made justice were the same beasts. But after years of those dreams I woke up one day to the truth. I found that the men who make justice are no bigger beasts than those who make injustice. I learned when I awoke that the only answer is to be among those who *make* justice—who promulgate what is good and what is not. Trials, hearings, investigations, what are they? Nothing but mechanics. A tool of the society. Everything is known and decided by those who make the justice beforehand, it's predetermined by the ruling class. Do you think there's any difference between Mr. Benes and Mr. Ben-Gurion? Never! They're both craven cowards to their core. What else could you expect? They're put there by cowardly societies. To move them, you don't cry Justice, you cry Revenge! You become hysterical. Down with the government! Death to their storm trooper beasts! and so on. Then you will see how quickly the yellow cowards come round. Agitate, agitate, agitate! It's not necessary to agitate for justice, but only for what you want. The world has long since passed justice by, and Israel, even if you don't know it, is part of the world. Let me ask you, is Israel itself justice for the million Arabs who were chased out of their homes and who are starving in tents? For them, some justice! Nobody dares mention them. Not here. You see, my justice may be your injustice. You want to do this thing right? Agitate. Write open letters. Arrange mass meetings, factory meetings, sympathy meetings. Appear publicly with David, dress in black. Pose for newspaper stories. Weep publicly. Tear your hair. Reporters will hunt you out. Tell them your story. Make a villain. This—this Horowitz is convenient. Lift your voice. You'll see, friends will raise funds to carry on your struggle. Friends you never knew you had. They will rise up. There'll be shouting and pickets, radio announcements, street fights. On the walls, small boys will smear 'Justice for the Marmoreks.' If the government can be discredited, brought down, perhaps with luck, you'll have strong allies. This will begin to mean something to those tea drinkers. When they feel the boat rock, when they feel the storm blow, that will be genuine embarrassment. Then something will be done. That I promise you."

They were all looking at Gussie, Karl more open mouthed than the rest.

"Of course, being a Communist," Debbie said lamely, "that's what you believe. We don't believe it."

"I've killed six men," Gussie said sharply and her eyes were fierce. "I don't even know who they were. Probably no better or worse than millions who are living cheerfully today. You think I killed them for some small abstract justice? No, only for a greater world. I know how things can be changed. You're politically illiterate, you admit it yourself. If you can't see, I'm sorry. It's an old-fashioned thing to say, but still true. One person moves nothing, many can move the world."

"I don't think I could do it, Gus," Debbie said, but she spoke reluctantly, for she could feel the impulse to follow Gussie's advice. To bang on doors, to cry out, to insist until she was heard, through the length and breadth of the land. My Vic was innocent! I'll pull down the house if you don't listen! It seemed as if it might be successful. But could she? It was a temptation.

Ben Kronstein could not contain himself. "I've heard things in this room," he quivered almost in falsetto, "I've heard things said which I never thought to hear in Israel. Bring down Ben-Gurion! And from what lips? While you were murdering people indiscriminately in Bratislava, you admit it yourself, I never heard any woman say such terrible things! You haven't the right to mention the name of Weizmann, Jabotinsky, Shertok, Ruppin, Kaplan, Ben-Gurion, strong-headed men, they fought, even with each other, if necessary, but those men and smaller ones like myself were out here pioneering in this place, so you would some day have a home to come to! We fought for it. And you came! But we don't need such people as you! Go back to Bratislava, witch!"

He rose abruptly and taking Debbie's hand said briefly, "Don't listen to her, Deborah. Don't listen. She speaks with the voice of the devils of our century!"

He patted her hand hastily, as if his pat would restore everything, and without another look at Gussie, stalked out.

After a few moments Karl moved then to the upright and played a school ditty which David sang in his treble voice; in a little while all of the oppression of Gussie's advice and Ben's resentment had evaporated and they were at a family birthday party that could have been anywhere.

Thirty-nine

Ordinarily Debbie never saw the extreme left wing Tel Aviv newspaper, and now it was next to impossible to get any kind of Tel Aviv paper in Jerusalem. Nevertheless within twenty-four hours of its publication she had two copies of the issue of *Worker's Day* which editorialized about Victor. Noah was the first to come and show it to her:

MURDER AND TYRANNY

As is well known, one Victor Marmorek, a resident of Jerusalem, was condemned by court-martial and shot in that city on a charge of furnishing information to the enemy. The details of his military trial have yet to be released to the press and public. For some time the public has assumed he received a full and fair trial, secret though it might have been, and that his guilt was proved beyond reasonable doubt.

Word has now been received by *Worker's Day* from a source considered by it to be reliable, that the trial was neither full nor fair; that there remain grave questions as to the guilt or innocence of this man (who incidentally performed important and at times heroic work for Haganah). But above and beyond this comes evidence that no responsible agency reviewed the testimony or the sentence of the court, which was composed of three field officers. Only Colonel Julian Horowitz, Chief Intelligence Officer in Jerusalem, reviewed the findings and confirmed the sentence. Everything was done, including the execution of the sentence, from start to finish, in six days.

What is worst of all is that the governing clique now sits on the case, doubtless protecting the officers who perpetrated the "trial" and stonily refuses to recognize the legitimate claims of the widow and son of the executed man, even for a rehearing of the case in the full light of day, which is possible now that active hostilities are at an end. Thus an innocent woman and child are ignored in a tyranny of pygmies, the timid tremblers who, alas for Israel, hold all the machinery of government in their hands. As is well known, these vacillating and spineless imitators of their European models, Leon Blum and Edward Benes, posing as friends of the worker, are leading us haltingly down the same false paths those inglorious "leaders" led their people—to infamy, weakness and ultimately to self-destruction. Our only hope is to stop them in time. We must alert the people.

It is not denied that Marmorek was no Communist, nor even a progressive thinker. He was, perhaps, nothing more than a typical bourgeois employee of the same kind as our present leaders. Nevertheless he was a human being and entitled to a proper trial, with constitutional protection. He should not have been deprived of life as cruelly and pointlessly as if he had been a horse-fly. His wife and child are entitled to an open explanation and, if appropriate, an apology and adequate compensation from a government of dwarfs which now wants only to forget them and deny its own responsibility. All workers, all progressives, and all people of good will should make this clear to the Ben-Gurion clique which "governs" us, if we can call this governing. If they will not act, steps should be forced by the will of the people.

While she read, she heard Noah shouting from the lobby for David to come out of his room, away from the exploits of Superman for a minute. Noah sounded so excited that she turned to see what he wanted. Standing just behind Noah, half-hidden, was Meyer Van Bern. Her heart leaped up. David's friend. Yes, the children would come to their senses first. That should have been obvious.

"Hi!" David said, unconcerned and outwardly unaffected.

"Hi!" Meyer mumbled, equally indifferent, then turning to Debbie, "My mother said to give you this." He handed her a newspaper-wrapped package which she opened hurriedly. It was a small cake with real icing, pink and delicate. The word "Peace" was written in icing. In the package was also a scrawled card: "We came together on the ship. I've always thought we were good friends. I don't know about you, but I can't afford to lose so good a friend. Can't we get together soon?"

"Hey," Meyer said looking about in awe, "is this house yours? Hey, this is some place! Is that the dining room?"

David doubled up with laughter, putting it on a little thick. "It's a pension, jerk. You never even *heard* of the Pantilles Pension? Millions of men live here. Reporters, Americans."

"Yeah?"

"Want to see something I got from one of 'em?"

David produced the magic horseshoe and lifted a spoon with it. "Magnet it's called."

Meyer's eyes popped. After he had got over the awe of the magnet, he said, "Hey, you have *some* yard. I have a ball here."

David looked at his mother who had not yet permitted him out of the pension alone.

"All right," she said cheerfully, "just in the yard."

Lanky Meyer with his cadaverous face, and arms dangling, sauntered out behind David saying, "René Blum is trying to tell me, if I come over here he'll cut me all up. How d'you like that? Some character! You know, he's got his father's knife. He's nuts."

"He's a *real* jerk," David said with deep passion. "If he cuts you up, I'll magnetize him!" Both boys roared.

Noah and Debbie watched at the window, saw them chatter and throw the ball. Noah said, "He's been needing someone his own age. I was beginning to be a problem to him."

"You'll never be a problem to anyone, Noah."

"I think," he said, "things will be better for you both all the time now. Now that folks are beginning to feel normal and this—" he shoved his thumb at the paper, the editorial from *Worker's Day*.

"I'm not sure I like that editorial."

"It's only a straw in the wind," Noah said. "Things will be better now, I promise. Excuse me, I'm going to watch the kids."

Debbie received her second copy of the editorial at about nine, quite unexpectedly, from George Stern. For a moment she could scarcely believe it was he standing in the lobby, his gaunt face drawn and pale from fatigue, the newspaper rolled impatiently in his fist. When he took her hand she realized she had turned cold in that instant, her palms were moist. She'd had no idea how desperately she had depended on his return, how hard she'd been waiting.

She heard herself say something inane. "You look tired, George. You must be hungry. Can I get you some supper?" But she was studying his face, every shade of his expression for a hint of what he knew.

George was evasive, trying hard to be gay. "I'll try the good old sardines," he said lamely. "Haven't had a good old sardine in three weeks."

She ran off to get his meal, her heart sinking. He was not bubbling over with good news. Instead he looked exhausted and disappointed. O Lord, she hoped she was wrong.

He ate without relish, and asked about everyone at the pension. Stirring his coffee, he took a deep breath.

"Well, I saw Redge," he said.

He lit a cigarette and pushed it between her lips, then lit one for himself. It was an unexpectedly intimate gesture.

"Debbie, have you thought at all whether you still want to go ahead with this business?" His smile was twisted as though he were in physical distress.

"No," she said. "I haven't been thinking about it, I've been going ahead."

He waited, undecided. "Well," he said finally, as if he were about to plunge into an icy sea of unpleasantness, and waited again.

She waited too. It was interminable.

"Redge tried to be nice," George said slowly. "Unfortunately, I'm afraid he's taken to hitting the bottle, and when he's under the influence, he clams right up. Gets real secretive. But when he sobered up he couldn't have tried harder. He gave me everything he could. I got the photostats of the lists, which I'm sure he took out of their files at personal risk. Got 'em right here."

She examined them hungrily. These were the lists then, she recognized the letters of Vic's portable typewriter. She recalled the nights he'd worked on them at home.

"These are all of them?"

"That's what Redge gave me. He had only the photostats. The originals had disappeared. He didn't know where."

The lists were names, addresses, phone numbers—all the phones installed between last October and this February. Vic's signature was on each sheet. What was the meaning of them? Could these lists be betrayal and espionage?

"You see, Redge was taking all kinds of hell from the ministry, because a couple of doctors in Talbieh complained they'd been unable to get phones. So, under pressure, Redge asked Vic to give him a list of all the phones he'd installed since October, how long each applicant had waited, why, and so forth. He asked for the list to show the ministry that no unauthorized phones had been put in, that they'd been following the priority system established by the ministry, and the doctors would have to wait their turn."

George nibbled his last sardine. She waited.

"After he'd got these lists from Vic, Redge wrote his own report to the ministry, saying he'd made a careful check of all installations and the doctors would just have to wait their turn. He never transmitted the lists themselves, just kept them as documentation in case his own report was questioned. But he wouldn't let them out of his office. In fact he filed them away in his personal file, to keep them under cover. Only trouble was, he had this assistant, Halliwell. I tried to see him too, but he wouldn't have any part of me. Anyhow, good old John got the lists from Redge's file, had photostats made and turned them over to British security people to run down the addresses. And apparently those boys did a real thorough job of it. They went out on personal inspection trips and tagged every Haganah installation. About one in five in that file of names turned out to be Haganah. Well, it seems Halliwell had this Arab buddy, Moustapha el Houri, and as his last act of good will before he left for England, he turned the lists over to Moustapha, nicely marked up with CID checkmarks beside each Haganah phone. A perfect list of targets."

"But then Vic had nothing to do with it! It was John Halliwell. You see?"

"Well, it would be nice if it were that simple," George said. "The only trouble is this: *Redge* knew when he saw those lists that they were bad news for Haganah, going around. He was sure they had Haganah numbers, that's why he tucked them in his private file drawer. *Halliwell* knew right away the value of those lists to the Arabs. How come your husband didn't? After all, he wasn't stupid."

"But he had no choice. Redge asked him for the information. It was his job to give it to him. We weren't at war. He was doing his job."

"Maybe so. But even Redge thinks he could have safely left the Haganah phones off. As a matter of fact, Redge never did check the completeness of the lists."

"*Redge* thinks!" she snorted. "How could Vic have known that? If he'd left those numbers out, it might have created more suspicion. Then Vic would really have had trouble. And how was *he* supposed to know which phones were Haganah?"

George wrinkled his forehead and walked across the room to unpack his valise. "Oh, gosh, Deb, I'm afraid he knew. If only he'd told Pearlman there *was* such a list and that it was out of his hands! If Pearlman had known, that would have made all the difference. I have a hunch, it's just a hunch, and I could be way off, but I think that's where your husband's defense got hung up. Why the devil didn't he warn Pearlman?"

Debbie felt the blow, and she had no answer. Why, Vic, why? She would have to think about that.

"Did you see Enid?"

"Yeah. Funny thing. She and Redge are living separately. She's up in Chelmsford. Redge is in town."

"That's strange. Did you find out why?"

George looked troubled. He behaved as though he had only half his mind on what they were saying.

"No. Couldn't figure it out. But it looks like they're not getting on. She's got Lloyd with her."

"And was she able to help at all?"

"No. She was unhappy about the whole thing, but I couldn't get much out of her. Quite a gal, as you say. Seems to have it all over Redge. But she just didn't know a thing. She felt terrible about you, though."

He was only talking to waste time.

"What do we do next, George?"

Again he waited an incredibly long time before answering. His eyes were closed, as though he hated to respond. "You want my honest opinion?"

She was barely able to whisper. "Of course."

"Couldn't we do—nothing? I've had time to think now, Debbie. I'd say your brother Karl's probably right. What we've got isn't conclusive, you see. And the fight's not even necessary. The people you know will come around sooner or later. Once they get over the first shock. Once they stop thinking of you as a freak. As soon as they can face you without embarrassment. I've talked to people at the airport and the taxi driver coming over. They're beginning to see your side of it. It's swinging your way. All you have to do is wait—like Karl says."

What he was saying was true. She thought of Meyer and Jacinta

Van Bern—she had made up her mind to see Jacinta soon—of Elsa's food tins, and Lilith's birthday party.

"See, even the Communists have come into the act. They're ready to make a saint of you."

There was the barest trace of irritation in the way he shoved the Communist editorial at her.

"But that's not my doing. I've a friend—"

"So I see. He must be a real intriguing fellow."

"It's a she. Gussie Goldenberg. I knew her in school in Vienna." George's trace of belligerence receded.

"They're not interested in you, these people, you can be damn well sure of that."

"I haven't seen this girl for years, George. We just poured out everything to each other. We were very close in Vienna, you see. She went with the resistance movement in Slovakia during the war. She says she killed six Germans. That's what she tells me at least."

"Mmmm. She must be a real gentle creature. I'll bet ten pounds she never killed more than four—five at the outside. These Commies can't resist bragging. She sounds like the Pauker type. You know, with a friend like her to help you, you really don't need a fellow like me at all."

"Oh, George, don't tease. I can't stand teasing."

"Well then, I'm not teasing. The editorial is just typical of what you'll be letting yourself in for. I'd hate to see you hurt any more, Deb. I couldn't forgive myself. Maybe you've wasted your two hundred pounds, I don't know. I'm the kind of fellow who finds it hard to admit he's been wrong, but I just feel it in my bones this time. Give it up."

"For my own good, I suppose?" she said wryly.

"It's going to be hard and expensive, and it'll take the stuffings out of you, and even so I wouldn't say no, if I thought you had a chance, even an outside chance. But I don't."

"George, what changed your mind?"

"I just told you," he said doggedly. "Common sense, reason. That guy Aronowitz talked sense. So did Karl. I'm trying to help you see it. I did a lot of thinking while I was away. I even tried to do some feeling. While I was waiting for Redge to get those lists, I took a few days and flew home to see my daughter. That kid's got me in the palm of her hand. She's growing into a real lady. And she's got marvelous judgment in men. She thinks I'm about the finest there is. I've got it all over her stepfather, she says, and I happen to agree with her. Well I go all haywire when I see her. And on the way back that set me to thinking too . . . I tried to imagine she was David—Karl was the one who put that in my mind. How would I feel? And I saw you beating your heart out over this thing. And not doing the boy a bit of good. You have so many positive things to offer. You're a rich girl that way, a lot richer than any I've met. There's so much you can do that'll give you satisfaction and mean a lot more to David. I hate to see you throwing away your energy, all your passion, on a mirage. Passion is a precious thing. It shouldn't be wasted."

"I counted on you so." Her hope was ebbing, her strength was sapped, but she held together somehow. "I was sure you'd persevere."

He took her hands in an instinctive gesture. "Let's sleep on it, Debbie. I'm real dog-tired."

"Oh, George, don't be so kind!" She yanked herself away from him and fled to her room. She had to escape from this sinister temptation. To abandon Vic, to abandon herself and David. To give up only because it would be hard. Only because success was not sure. She had to get away from both the temptation and the tempter.

When she approached her room behind the kitchen she heard David sobbing in his sleep as he so often did, but this time her coming awakened him and he began to cry uncontrollably. It was all in the dark and was weird and shuddery for her. She tried to comfort him, but he wailed and talked incoherently, almost wildly. "He made me kill her; I didn't want to, but Daddy made me do it, Mommy. But I didn't want to, I didn't want to. Please don't make me do it . . . Daddy . . . Please, Mommy, Mommy . . ."

All she could do was huddle his shivering skinny frame to her and say softly, with a calmness she did not feel, "It's only a dream, David, sweet, only a silly old dream."

But he took no comfort from her. He went on crying out, "No, it's really true, Mommy, it really happened, it really happened . . . Tamar is dead . . . She's dead . . ."

And then while the vitality of his delirium was ebbing, he nodded slowly into sleep again as she hummed his old baby song, over and over, monotonously, droning him to sleep. "Someday we'll all come to a place that's nice and warm . . . a place where everyone will be David's friends . . ." and soon he was asleep again.

Setting him back on his bed, Debbie felt herself shaking. This was one of her longest nights, but unlike other long nights, not filled with terror or soft memories of Vic. Tonight she'd have to sharpen her mind, take counsel with herself. George had forsaken her, that much was clear—Vic, Papa, George, all her defenders had forsaken her. Now she would be her own defender. Her mind twisted from thought to thought, but not aimlessly. She had to think hard.

What could be behind the sudden change in George? Had he found that Vic was guilty after all? She was sure she'd have known that at once. She'd have to think carefully. What did she know? What did the lists mean? Names, addresses, innocuous phone numbers. The names danced before her eyes, and the guilty addresses shone into the darkness of her mind. She saw the rubble and dust of Ben Kronstein's building. And Elsa's place. Tamar's house—she recalled now they were running a machine shop in that basement—gun repairs, she'd heard. David's own golden-braided Tamar. But was Vic to blame? He never imagined any harm could come of these lists. Oh, it would be comforting to be *sure*.

But her only certainty was that each step she took now could be a wrong one, however brave and uncompromising and right it might seem. Perhaps that was Vic's error—nothing more than a terrible miscalculation. Survival and success were not a matter to be decided by bravery and being on the side of the angels. There were times when a little cowardice in a dark corner of the inner mind, with no witness, might be the right answer. It need not be cowardice, it could be caution. After all, how could one be sure of anything? In the romances she had read, in some of the cinemas from Hollywood, duty or love pushed aside everything, even death was not too high a price for heroines to pay. A reader could weep and feel cleansed over someone true blue and a little unbelievable. But to decide for herself, here, today, in Jerusalem, she knew the most heroic step might prove to be the most foolhardy and terrible and cowardly she could take. It might do terrible harm to David. There was no direction sign, no clearly marked road, no advice except that her closest friends and her brother and almost everyone said Go back. Could they all be wrong? Here in the midst of the darkest part of the night she could secretly ask herself this question, which she had avoided asking herself a thousand times. What if Vic had done it and it were to be proved again? . . . Something inside her shuddered.

Considering the risk, was it worth having to go out to face hostile people, to knock on unfriendly doors, talk to indifferent men, try to force them to do what they did not relish doing, having to be insulted, humiliated by a succession of officers, bureaucrats and politicians, as she had already been insulted? Could she tolerate the endless pinpricks and heartaches to be endured? An awful terror seized her that she would abandon her course after doing herself injury and without coming to the end of the road. "I'd hate to see you hurt any more, Deb." George would not be the only one to hate it!

Her only help had come, after all, from Gussie and her rather odd friends of *Worker's Day*. Start a row, perhaps they were right. Agitate, agitate. But as she twisted in bed she knew she had to turn away from Gussie and her friends. George had put his finger on it. The Reds were using her and distorting her purpose.

The note from Jacinta Van Bern and Meyer's visit clamored unreasonably for her attention. David had seemed normal and happy again with his old friend, and yet tonight he had had one of his most terrible nightmares. What else could she do but go on struggling? Still David was so young, he'd remember little, if anything, of this whole part of his life. He might not even remember Vic clearly . . . And she knew sooner or later she and David would have to learn to get along somehow without Vic. Missing him, remembering him, but without him. In her deepest honesty she knew it was not going to be necessary to justify Vic to make her own life bearable. Why then did this persistent voice within her keep driving her on and on along this fruitless path? Why did she insist on trying, trying to find justice for a man who was beyond justice or injustice, right or wrong, heroism or cowardice? Why did she feel she had to free herself this way from Vic?

Now, whatever had made her think that? She had no wish to be free of Vic. He had been the loveliest part of her. By far the loveliest. Then what in the world was driving her?

She couldn't waste any more money, she had only a little over a hundred pounds left. What she needed was a good lawyer—someone who was paid to tell her what to do. Papa had always had great faith in good lawyers. She would not depend on amateurs and volunteers any longer.

She recalled her brief interview with Aronowitz with a shudder. Perhaps someone more sympathetic. She couldn't stand many more interviews like that one.

Aronowitz. She recalled George's words. "Somewhere in all that stone there must be a soft spot. We'll have to find it." But where? She could see Aronowitz's piercing, knowing gray eyes, and the memory of his sensitive mouth set in that gaunt, almost ancient small face, made her think that one last appeal to him might work. He had children of his own, and a wife. Yes, he had mentioned them. Suddenly, she knew whom she must see. It was the *wife* of Boris Aronowitz. Through another woman she could say what had to be said. Another woman would be less fearsome.

Forty

Mrs. Aronowitz was thin and somewhat shorter than her husband. The impression Debbie got was dark and hot. The woman's eyes were burning black, matching her unkempt cropped hair, but the sallow yellowish skin and her deceptively soft-featured face was beginning to sag and crinkle with fatigue. She moved almost like a cat as she led Debbie back through the large dark library into the kitchen, where she was setting breakfast out for two. She'd given no response when Debbie told her who she was, except to nod recognition and mumble, "Come on inside."

She motioned for Debbie to sit at the table and she herself squatted on a high kitchen stool, her legs spread and drawn up, like a child.

"Coffee?"

"No, thanks," Debbie said.

Mrs. Aronowitz's expression was almost grouchy. "I'm not fit to talk to before coffee. Hate everyone." She gulped her drink and spoke rapidly as if she could not get finished in time. "You're the woman whose husband—? Sure, I remember. What d'you want with me?"

The words were abrupt, but Debbie felt no underlying animosity, and she was sensitive to animosity these days.

Before she could answer, her hostess cupped both hands over her mouth and shouted, "Judy! Get up, for God's sake. Breakfast's ready."

And from the bedroom inside a girl's voice, "Ready in a minute, Ma."

"I don't know about other people's kids," Mrs. Aronowitz said, "but mine never want to get out of bed. Judy thinks she's a countess or something. She's supposed to be in school in ten minutes, and I'll bet she hasn't got her pajamas off. Here, why don't you take this coffee? It's getting cold and she'll never have time to drink it."

Debbie wondered how she would ever be able to say what she wanted to this woman. "No, thanks. I—uh—I saw your husband several weeks ago," she started tentatively.

"You did? Well, that's more'n I do these days. Oh, he sometimes passes through the house. Theoretically he lives here. Lately it's just to change his clothes. I'm discouraged about that man. He's *so* busy. Days, nights. Between the *unions,* and the *army* and private *clients* and now *politics*. That's what's doing it now—politics. It's like being a widow."

"I doubt it," Debbie snapped.

For the first time a glance of sudden perception flicked across the woman's face.

"I'm sorry," Mrs. Aronowitz said. "I should have more sense."

Judy came tearing into the kitchen. She was about fifteen, dark and nervous as her mother. She stuffed a piece of bread into her mouth and gulped the coffee. "I'm late, Ma," she said breathlessly as though announcing a disaster of the first magnitude.

Mrs. Aronowitz laughed good-naturedly and as suddenly as her face lit up it darkened again. Judy, still on her feet, took notice of Debbie sitting at the breakfast table. "Hi," she said cheerfully. "'Bye, Ma." She kissed her mother, still chewing the last of her bread, and ran out buttoning her cuffs. "Be back for lunch," she screamed over her shoulder and they heard the door slam.

"You'd have to see it to believe it, wouldn't you?" Mrs. Aronowitz said. "She's a little mad. They're all a little mad. She's actually sane compared to the other two. She's going to the school for design now. Before that she wanted to be a nun. Next year she wants to go to Paris or maybe New York—the daughter of a labor lawyer and she wants to make dresses for rich women! Sometimes I think they've all decided to drive me out of my mind." She cleared the few cups and dishes and put them into the sink.

"May I help?" Debbie said.

"You can dry if you like." She flipped Debbie a dish towel and poured a little water from a basin into the sink. "Now maybe we can talk if that's what you want. Isn't that silence lovely? I never can quite believe it when the three of them are out of the house. You should be here when they're all home! O God. But *you* must know all about that sort of thing. You've a son of your own, haven't you?"

Debbie dried a cup carefully and completely. "David's pretty quiet these days. Not as much trouble as he ought to be."

"Well, no wonder."

"Yes, it's no wonder. Look, I started to say I went to see Mr. Aronowitz right after my husband died. I wanted your husband to help me."

"Help you—in what way?"

"My husband had nothing to do with that business. I wanted Mr. Aronowitz to help me prove it—nice and legally. I wanted him to help me make it known."

Mrs. Aronowitz was placing the cups and saucers into the cabinet. For a few moments there was only the clink of china on china.

"I don't want to be unkind," she said at last. "It's the last thing I want to be. But everyone in the world comes to my husband for help. You have no idea. The poor man is exhausted. I'm not exaggerating. He's been getting three, four hours of sleep a night. I *never* see him. The girls have almost forgotten they have a father. There are other lawyers in Jerusalem. Good ones. Whatever your problem is—I know half a dozen who'd be glad to get a decent case. There's Mike Rosen and Dave Reubens. Oh, I know so many."

"But I need your husband. He's the only one who can really do the job."

"Why? Why poor Boris? He's not a magician. He's a good lawyer, yes, only—"

"But he knows the whole case. After all he *was* my husband's defense lawyer."

"He was *what?*" Mrs. Aronowitz seemed to rock back. Her eyes went wide and Debbie saw a pair of huge black pupils glaring at her in amazement. "He never told me that." She sat down. "What d'you think of that *guy?*" She was talking to herself now. "I could see he was depressed these last few weeks. It wasn't like him. Nothing could snap him out of it. I had no idea. So *that* was it."

Mrs. Aronowitz appeared to be shocked beyond paying attention. She walked into Judy's room with Debbie trailing after her. There were three beds to be made up and she started on the first. Debbie went to work on another. "He always discusses everything with me. We've never had secrets, even military secrets. I'm surprised. I just don't seem to be able to keep up any more."

"Well, I went to see him last month," Debbie said. "But he said there wasn't a thing he could do. He kept telling us it was pointless—now that Vic's gone."

Mrs. Aronowitz swatted the pillow into a full fluff. "He has so much on his mind and a thing like that must nearly have killed him. I know Boris. He takes his cases very seriously. And a thing like that."

"Then why won't he help?" Debbie asked. Her voice was strained and low.

"I don't know. Maybe it's political," Mrs. Aronowitz said abruptly. "Anyhow I can't say I'm entirely sorry. It takes too much out of him. He's not a strong man. He's had his share of trouble—he had an operation for ulcers two years ago, and now his blood pressure's high."

They had finished with the beds and they wandered to the living room, which Mrs. Aronowitz set about straightening, emptying ash trays, dusting, and fluffing cushions.

"By the way, what makes you so sure your husband wasn't guilty?"

"I'm sure," Debbie said quickly. "I'd know, don't you think? Any wife would."

"I'm not so sure any more," Mrs. Aronowitz said reflectively. "I didn't know until you just told me what my husband's been doing. Men can become awfully secretive these days. A girl can't be sure of anything, *I* don't think."

"I'm sure," Debbie repeated dully and flatly. "And we've more evidence now. This American who's been helping me has just come back from England with new evidence. I think we could prove a case now, if your husband would help. But I'm afraid to approach him again."

"I don't know why he *scares* most people," Mrs. Aronowitz said. "He's really harmless. Only of course he's a man. That we can't change, not that I'd want to, God forbid."

The two women worked in the living room for several moments without talking. Debbie emptied three ash trays into the trash basket. "You see, I can't have my son believing his father is a traitor," she said at last.

Mrs. Aronowitz looked up sharply. "That's true."

They walked into the second bedroom where one bed had been

slept in, the other untouched. "You see," Mrs. Aronowitz said. "He hasn't been home in two nights. He's coming tonight, God willing."

"Would you talk to him?" Debbie said. "Would you do that much?"

Mrs. Aronowitz turned away. "It's obvious," she said, "you have to do something. At least if you know he definitely won't take the case, you can go to someone else. You're entitled to a definite answer."

"Your husband is worried about the army. The morale, his own position, all that."

"Well, he's a careful man. He's been fooling around in politics too long not to be. His mind is all cluttered up with complications. That's probably what makes him a good lawyer. It might make him a good politician. But he's tired too. It's a great burden for him, a case like yours. And there are so many younger men. Why don't you go to his office tomorrow and talk to him again?"

"Will you speak to him?" Debbie persisted.

Mrs. Aronowitz raised her eyes expressively. "Who am I? Only his wife. I doubt he'll pay any attention to me. But it's your problem, Mrs. Marmorek. Try his office tomorrow and if he won't take it, get some other lawyer. I'm sure you can find a good one."

There was not much more she could say to this sensible woman who appeared to have understood everything quickly and completely. Debbie could not tell whether she was being brushed off again or whether she had made any headway. Mrs. Aronowitz would not be pushed. Debbie knew she would have to leave it at that.

Meanwhile she'd visit Jacinta Van Bern today and perhaps Dick Alpert and try to pick up the elusive threads of normalcy.

Forty-one

It was two days before she worked up the courage to face going back to Aronowitz's office. She was girding herself mentally for the ordeal while she cleared the breakfast dishes, when two strange men arrived at the Pantilles to see her. One had black scraggly whiskers and the other was clean shaven with almost a babyish face; both were of medium height, had the same watery blue eyes, and in an intangible way resembled each other remarkably. They both wore dark checked open-necked shirts and navy blue trousers. The bearded man insisted that they wanted to talk "privately," and lowered his eyes mysteriously. With some reluctance she took them to her still untidy bedroom, where her visitors made themselves completely at home, the bearded one throwing himself full length on the bed, as though he were exhausted.

"I'm Kolish," the smooth-shaven one said, "and my sleepy friend here's Stepnoski. We're acquainted with your old friend Gussie Goldenberg. She suggested we come to see you."

"Yes? What do you want?"

"All we're trying to do is help you," the man with the beard mumbled as if in his sleep. "We're your friends."

"Have you seen this?" The smooth-shaven man took out a copy of the *Worker's Day* from his inside breast pocket and tapped the editorial. Debbie nodded. "Who do you think wrote it?"

She turned from the man before her to the supine one and had the feeling that she was being trapped or taunted.

"Him," said the beardless one, pointing to his friend, who now had closed his eyes and appeared to be asleep.

"I thought it was quite good," the prone man said sleepily. "My blood boils at injustice." She was barely able to hear him and the thought crossed her mind that he might be ill.

"This must have been a pretty bad shock for you," the other man said quickly. "Do you mind if I smoke?"

"What is it you gentlemen want?" Debbie asked. She was doing her best to remain even tempered in spite of their bad manners, for a voice of caution warned her not to be hasty. These men might be useful.

"We only want to help," Stepnoski said from the bed. "Mr. Kolish here is a lawyer from Tel Aviv. He would like to work on your case. There may be a substantial recovery coming to you from the government."

"You're going to *need* a lawyer," Kolish said.

"Our newspaper will be behind you a hundred per cent," Stepnoski said lazily, rolling on his side. "We've received contributions from readers all over the country. More will come. 'The Marmorek Fund,' we call it. It'll be a great thing for you, bringing out this injustice, and it'll do the country good."

"But why?" Debbie said. "I don't even know you. Why should you want to do so much for me?"

"Like we said," Stepnoski said. "I hate injustice and he hates injustice like I do."

"The progressive people of the country will support you," Kolish said. "The reactionaries betrayed your husband—it wasn't only Horowitz—it's that whole band of Fascists—and they'll try to destroy you. It's up to us to destroy them first."

"But I don't want to destroy anyone," Debbie said quickly. "I only want—"

Stepnoski rolled onto his face, and his words were muffled against the bedclothes. "Perhaps it was a poor choice of words. We want to make these reactionaries sit up and take notice. We want them to confess what they've done. To admit what beasts they've been."

Suddenly he sat bolt upright in bed and faced her directly, speaking in a harsh bitter voice. "We want them to admit they killed an innocent man in cold blood and to make amends to you and your son, however inadequate!"

Debbie turned from one to the other. They were both staring at her. She could not quite believe their melodramatic shifts from whisper to shout, from somnambulism to agitation. "Of course, I'd be glad to get help wherever I could," she said uncertainly.

"You don't have to do a thing," snapped Kolish. "Just leave everything to us. We've uncovered information that absolutely proves your husband's innocence and demonstrates the conspiracy and guilt of the reactionary clique in power now. We understand that in many ways your husband was a—progressive, wasn't he?"

These men confused her. She had thought of Vic as many things. But a progressive? Her stunned look must have provoked Stepnoski to continue.

"He had great sympathy for the underprivileged masses, particularly the Arab masses, isn't that so?"

"Well—uh, yes. He always felt sorry for them. He felt they needed medical care, education, better food, and things like that. Not that he was ever able to *do* anything about it . . ."

"Of course. And we understand he was anti-nationalist—in the highest sense, of course. That he thought boundaries and narrow racialism were abominations. He believed that men who work—of all races and religions and nations—should work together, isn't that true?"

"Yes, I think he believed that."

"Actually—" Stepnoski was lying on his back again and speaking lazily, "actually he was already half-communist and he didn't know it."

"He was not a Communist." Suddenly she wished Vic could be here for this ludicrous moment. She could see him throw back his beautiful head, roaring with laughter. "You gentlemen *are* Communists, I take it?"

"He is," Kolish said, jerking his thumb at Stepnoski. "I'm only a man who thinks they're on the right track."

"Put yourself in our hands," Stepnoski intoned. "This man is good, really a great lawyer. He can make speeches to curdle your blood. He can stir up a crowd, get a demonstration going—you have to see him in action. He lifts them out of their seats. And *Worker's Day* will give you front page coverage. Everyone in the country will know about this raw deal before we're through. The people will be screaming for the heads of these cold-blooded murderers. We'll have the fools quaking in their boots. And make no mistake, we can do it."

They had managed to rouse an element of fear in her. But if she refused them, who else would help her? What chance was there that Aronowitz would change his mind? Perhaps she should put these men off, think about it, see Aronowitz first. Why hadn't she gone to his office yesterday? Then she would know where she stood. Vic would have sent these men packing—or would he?

"It won't cost you a penny," Kolish said. "People will support you with money—all we need."

"What people? Communists, you mean?"

"All kinds of people. Do you mind if I take my shoes off? I don't want to dirty your linen."

"You don't have to decide right away," Kolish said. "Think about it. We'll come back to see you in a couple of days, whenever you say."

It was as if he were reading her thought. Suddenly her mind stood aghast at this weird conversation. That Vic should find champions in two men he would have loathed, who had no interest in her or David or anything except how to make trouble for Ben-Gurion! It was too wild for belief.

"I'm afraid not," she said at last and braced herself for the onslaught she felt was coming, not only from them, but from her own conscience at having neglected a marvelous chance. Still she was powerless to make a different response. "You don't care a hoot about David or me or what happens to us. Just so you can twist some minds and get votes with your demonstrations and headlines. Thank you very much, I don't think David and I are having any. And get up off that bed, Mr. Stepnoski. I was brought up in a house where good manners count for something."

Stepnoski stood up sullenly. He turned on her with a bullying passion. "You're a fool! Haven't you any decent feeling for your husband's memory?" He peered up from under glowering brows, and switched suddenly to weary accents. "Perhaps people like you aren't worth saving anyway." He scratched his beard obnoxiously, as though he were looking for an insect in it, and headed for the door.

Kolish lowered his head. "Don't be hasty, Mrs. Marmorek. If you should change your mind, you can get me in Tel Aviv. Here, I'll write you the number: Four nine four three." He scribbled it in a pocket pad he had, ripped out the sheet and handed it to her.

"I won't change my mind," she said, crumpling the paper.

"Well, we're not going to beg to help you," Stepnoski drawled.

As soon as they were out of the house she had a sense of relief and letdown. She would have to see Aronowitz right away.

She was still changing into her street clothes when George came down after sleeping late, wanting breakfast. As he ate, she told him she had decided to go to Aronowitz again—this morning. Although she'd made up her mind not to take George into her confidence any further, some other compulsion was at work to try to win him back to her cause, perhaps nothing more than loneliness.

George jabbed irritably at his fried egg before answering. "You know, you're doing it against my advice," he said.

"I'm going anyway, George."

He waited before he spoke and pushed his plate away without a bite. "I'd better go along then," he said glumly. "I'll be back after lunch. Will you wait for me?"

"If you want," she said with relief.

During lunch, by an amazing coincidence, Boris Aronowitz stepped into the lobby of the Pantilles Pension, carrying his copy of the *Worker's Day* editorial. He was out of uniform now and looking more skeleton-like than ever.

"Why, Mr. Aronowitz! We were just going out to see you," Debbie said, leading him to her room. George followed.

"Look at this!" he said, angrily flourishing the paper. "If you expect me to represent you, this sort of thing is out of the question. If this reflects your sentiments, consider me off the case."

She was too excited to hear him. Suddenly it seemed as if everything would be better. Aronowitz was here and for this moment there was exhilaration, almost cheerfulness.

"It's creepy, really, isn't it, your coming? Telepathy, sort of. We were on our way to your office. I can't believe it's you. It's an omen, isn't it, George?"

"Well, I've been thinking," Aronowitz said carefully. "Turning everything over. This editorial irritated me. It worries me too. Can't get into the clutches of these people."

"I know," she said. "Two of them were here this morning. They have a fund. And a lawyer."

"Kolish?" he said. "What did you tell them?"

"I want only one lawyer," she said.

"Good. And when you retain Aronowitz I want you to know you get also the services of two fine boys in my office. Genuine diggers. Twins, they are, the Rosenthal boys, and they've done a lot of work on it already. Now can we get started? I understand Yank here just got back from England?"

"Yes," she said. "He brought the lists and he talked to Redge. He's done the things you thought were impossible."

"Good. But before you tell me a thing, can we have one thing clear? No campaign can have two commanders-in-chief." He looked sharply up at George.

George put his arm about Aronowitz's shoulder. "I'm a private in the rear rank, Chief."

Aronowitz turned briskly to Debbie. "We'll prepare a statement for you, to dispose of this," he tapped his copy of the *Worker's Day*. "We can use it at the proper moment. For you, Yank, I have a little chore also. Can we sit and talk here?"

Debbie looked at the small thin man, a cigarette hanging loosely from his fingers, and she felt the fantastic energy locked in that frail frame. Her exhilaration was dimming to a glow of a tremendous but grim satisfaction.

"Mr. Aronowitz, I don't know how I'll ever be able to pay you." She hesitated, because now he looked at her fiercely.

"You should have thought of that, lady, when you first came to see me," he barked, then continued with a still expressionless face, "my fee will be my own personal satisfaction. Of course, there will be expenses, disbursements. We'll try to keep them to a minimum. I hope not more than a hundred pounds."

"Now there's another coincidence!" Debbie said. "I have loads over a hundred pounds." Her last balance at Barclay's was, in fact, one hundred and thirty-four pounds. It was not much, but it was enough. She felt armed to the teeth.

Forty-two

When Aronowitz notified them early in October to come to Tel Aviv they had no precise idea of why he wanted them. They knew only that they were to be in the gallery of the Council of Ministers on Sunday—and were not to expect too much. They gathered that some new development in the case had taken place; and that something might happen on the floor of the Legislature. Aronowitz promised to see Debbie and George for dinner Sunday night, although he was busy with his new governmental duties.

On Saturday Debbie and David made the hot trip in the Fiat with Noah Mendoza and George. Karl gave Debbie twenty pounds for her expenses and promised to take Sunday off with Lilith for the trip; they'd leave before dawn by bus, and they would all meet at the Temporary Council Building at eleven. George took the car because he planned to visit one of the new immigrant camps near Tel Aviv for a series he was doing.

As the Fiat descended into the desert from the Jerusalem heights an appallingly hot sun blistered the car from sky and pavement; the helpless Fiat coughed and struggled with an overheated radiator over the now somewhat improved Burma Road. Sweat streamed into George's eyes; David in the back fanned himself and Noah elaborately to indicate the dire state of their discomfort; and Debbie could feel the trickle of perspiration running down her neck and back. Her clothes were tight and her blouse and skirt clung to her in great wet patches. No one would ever say Jerusalem was not hot in summer, especially in the *hamseen* season, but this was her first experience with the far greater desert heat.

The streets of Ramle and the smaller towns on the road were deserted when they passed through, except for a few dogs hiding sullenly in shady spots. In the countryside, endless sweet-smelling groves of orange, grapefruit and lemon delighted David, who had never seen such vast fields of fruit, and then they were on the steaming outskirts of Jaffa and Tel Aviv.

The sights of stuccoed Tel Aviv were wonders to David, the flatness of the city, so different from Jerusalem; Allenby Street and the other broad avenues, and the bustle of taxis and cars, even though it was the Sabbath, made him livelier despite the heat. Only two and a half hours and what different worlds the two cities were! When they came suddenly upon Yarkon Street to the Hotel Gat Rimon, where they were to sleep, and saw the endlessness of the stirring Mediterranean, undulating forever before them, David sucked in his breath and stared in silence; all that water and beach and pretty blue sky. Debbie felt his wonder too, though she had seen her quota of seas and beaches.

She and David shared a room; Noah and George were down the hall. They all sat together in Debbie's room in silence, watching the sea, until they were rested from their wearying trip.

Later they walked along Yarkon Street, Noah rather agile now with his new leg, and watched hundreds of Sabbath swimmers lying in the fading afternoon sun, and jumping or splashing in the shimmering water. Seeing young couples galloping like colts along the strand or playing in the surf, young parents scolding defiant children or gathering their picnic baskets, and older folks watching the endless waves in contentment, her mission seemed to Debbie remote and unreal and unrelated to the world of every day. If these people knew what had brought her to Tel Aviv what would they think of her? If not mad, at least peculiar.

"Let's go in, Mommy, can we?" David's was the voice of the urgent, stirring world and her own words sounded stiff and unnatural, "We can't, David!"

"Why not?"

"Yes, why not?" George took up the challenge and even Noah said, "I was once a damn good swimmer . . . I wonder how I'd do now. I'd like to see."

"I—we—well, we have no swim suits," she said lamely.

"Everyone down into the car," George ordered. "Come on we're going shopping."

They dropped her at Pavolec's, the only ladies' wear shop open on the Sabbath, and they took David off with them to look for a men's shop.

Pavolec's was a dark store, empty except for the large Yugoslav proprietress, who overflowed her clothes in all directions, and never shut her mouth.

Alone in the dressing room she tried on the suit she liked, the light blue two-piece suit with a shirred top, and when she saw herself in the half mirror, even by the glaring light of a bare incandescent lamp, she felt an unaccustomed excitement, a long-forgotten exhilaration. She was a little girl cutting through the pool at Lindenhouse, diving, sliding, screaming. She was with the family glowing on the beach at Milstätter See. She was back again for a holiday at Santa Margherita in her early teens, watching the water skiers from a pedal boat with Mama. This was the kind of girl she was meant to be—a harebrained fluff of ornament, traipsing from Lindenhouse to the shore, from the Krknos to the lakes. O Lord, how easily she could have taken to being useless and scandalously luxurious the whole of her life!

She stepped out of the dressing room into the gloom of the store, and under the barrage of words from the proprietress, the ooo-ing and ah-ing, and isn't it smart darling, my dear, don't you just love it, she looked at herself in a full length mirror. She *was* rather fetching, she was pleased to see. She could still be quite a gay trick, just when she'd come to believe she couldn't care less. She was admiring herself shamelessly, luxuriating in her rose-colored memories, when she suddenly realized George and Noah were in the store with David, and watching her.

"Say!" George said, "you look real good."

"You oughta see mine!" David shrieked.

Without a word she scurried into the dressing room and scrambled into her street clothes. Vanity, vanity. No question about where David came by his showoffiness. She was furious with herself, out of all proportion, but she paid two pounds ten for the suit, a substantial part of her fortune. She was a wicked wastrel, but a defiant one.

Unfortunately by the time they got back to the beach the sun was down and it was too late to swim, but they promised David and each other they would go tomorrow.

After dinner, while David slept, she and Noah and George sat watching the water and sipped cordials and walked briefly through the streets near the hotel. Seeing the shops and amicable strangers all about, busy, but not unfriendly, Debbie knew she might have come here when Karl had first suggested it four months ago. She was not sure, but, thinking as honestly as she could, she might have been better off. And although it would have been hard to turn her back on Vic, even that much, she had perhaps chosen a harder and longer road than necessary. Then she looked at George who was talking to Noah, and at the same time guiding her gently by the arm. And watching his intense face, his narrow, bony, but somehow confident head, she was not sorry for the course she had chosen. She felt buoyed, renewed, and brave herself, ready to go wherever Boris Aronowitz and George Stern might lead her.

They walked slowly back to the water's edge and the three of them stood quietly, looking at the sea and the ugly old squatters' shanties huddled along the beach, speculating what might happen at the Council tomorrow, what Aronowitz might have up his sleeve, while the warm moon flickered up from the deceptively gentle water, swaying and lulling them all into a sense of well-being and security and peace.

In the morning David wanted to head for the sea even before breakfast, but they found a message from Aronowitz's office asking that they be in the balcony of the Council by eleven and he would meet them later for supper at seven.

Reluctantly, David scuffed his feet as they made their way along the waterfront. He would rather be swimming, but he understood that the visit to the Parliament of Israel was part of what they'd come for and so he made no protest and was even proud to hand his pass to the guard for admission. Inside the building, a converted theater on Allenby and Yarkon, they found Karl and Lilith already seated in the visitors' balcony, with Dick Alpert, Lil's sister Clara and her husband Aaron. They were holding seats for Debbie and David. Gussie Goldenberg was there too on the aisle and seized Debbie's hand emotionally as they went by. Jacinta Van Bern waved. Dick Alpert kissed Debbie on the cheek as she passed him. "We're drowning in *Weltschmerz* at the hospital," he said in a droll voice. "A Viennese diversion might save us. Am I right, Lil?"

"Absolutely," Lil said.

And rows behind her Debbie could hear Elsa's voice, ringing like a clarion, evidently to inform Debbie that even she had come up from Jerusalem. Word did get around, a rumor stirred the pot. A side door snapped open, and Debbie leaned forward to see Boris Aronowitz stride briskly to his desk. He wore a white shirt open at the neck, like the Prime Minister, and his gray hair looked as though it could use a combing.

The presiding officer tapped his gavel steadily and monotonously for order, appearing not to expect it, but after some time he achieved comparative silence on the floor.

"The Chair recognizes the gentleman from Tel Aviv."

A large florid Cabinet Minister was on his feet, nervously folding and refolding his hands as he spoke. So this was the Parliament of the new state! Debbie could scarcely tell whether to laugh or cry. Many wore no coats. Few were handsome, and some scarcely presentable. But this was Parliament. This was Reichstag, Congress, Knesset. Here in this room were the people of Israel. The Minister was saying in monotone:

". . . and will interrupt the consideration of the Communications budget which we were considering at the close of yesterday's session to give the gentleman from Jerusalem the privilege to discuss briefly a matter which he feels and which we feel merits consideration."

The chairman tapped the gavel again until the conversation on the floor was no more than a buzz.

"The Chair recognizes the gentleman from Jerusalem."

Boris Aronowitz was on his feet. Other members continued to mumble and several were thumbing through newspapers or sheets of manuscripts, although some turned with attention to the speaker. The Prime Minister, whom David recognized with excited whispers, sat impassively with several of the Cabinet, one or another of them occasionally nodding in response to a whispered intelligence, several reading documents or notes handed them from time to time.

"Mr. Chairman," Aronowitz started hesitatingly and in a low tone, "may I take a few moments from budgetary matters now under consideration and with the indulgence granted by the Chair and the honorable minister, discuss briefly a subject which I consider to be of urgent interest? What I am about to say has already been conveyed to members of the government and I believe we have achieved a measure of general agreement, at least in the center of this house. The members on the right and on the left have taken different views, but perhaps that's because they are most comfortable when they're in opposition. And perhaps they are thinking of the coming elections.

"During the siege of my city, you recall, one of the greatest difficulties with which we had to deal was espionage. Last June, a man, a Jew, was tried on charges of espionage and treason. As many of you are aware I defended that man before the court-martial which convicted and sentenced him. And the man was shot."

The hubbub in the House stopped almost as if on signal. Debbie was surprised to see the faces turned, full of curiosity, watching as if Aronowitz had become suddenly fascinating. No doubt this was juicier business than the budget, but she had scarcely expected such interest in this room. These are the people of Israel, she thought. They are listening. They are hearing!

"The widow of this man, a gallant lady whom I have come personally to admire, and an American journalist about six weeks ago uncovered evidence gathered in the British Islands, which, I believe, sheds a new light on the matter. My office has also been gathering evidence which was unavailable at the trial. This new evidence, I believe, strongly indicates that Victor Marmorek may very well have been and indeed probably was innocent, as Mrs. Marmorek contended from the beginning. I, who confess I was never completely persuaded of this view even while I defended him to the best of my ability, now fully concur after reviewing the evidence with my own eyes. But Mr. Marmorek cannot be brought back to life. This is a tragic matter, not lightly to be shunted aside. Then what are we to do? If the government has snuffed out the life of an innocent man, orphaned his son and widowed his wife, the government must at the very least be prepared to make such amends as are in its power. I hope I don't sound pretentious, but I hope we are not too busy for one human being here. We will strain our bodies and test our souls during the years ahead, in order to take in hundreds of thousands of the most remote Jews from Shanghai or Buenos Aires or Karachi, who may wish to come home, our millions whom we must receive and comfort, house and educate, feed and clothe, and so we must, but what are we bringing those millions home to? Injustice? Indifference to the fate of any man among us? Are we interested only in faceless masses, or does one human being count with us also? A mistake, no matter how grievous, is human; with deep faith in God, even a terrible and tragic mistake like the taking of an innocent life is perhaps forgivable in time. But to persist in the injustice, to defend it, that obstinacy is never to be forgiven. I hear always the murmur too busy, too busy, I have heard it in my own head, with my own ears, and it may even have been my own voice I was hearing. I have been as guilty as any man. Guiltier, for I had the job of defending him. I should have dropped everything! I should have done better, I should not have failed! A life! We must think of it, each of us, as his own life.

"I understand the government is prepared to support the motion which I have handed to the clerk, directing the Prime Minister to appoint three members of this House to cooperate with the Minister of Justice in conducting an immediate inquiry into the Marmorek affair and to report its findings within the shortest possible time to this Council. I know the government supports this motion with misgivings, for there are valid arguments against reopening a sore spot. Nevertheless it is the government's view that they have no choice. I beseech the members of every party and persuasion to support it also."

Many in the gallery applauded. Debbie could see Karl and even Lilith clap their hands in a measured beat. But she only sat quietly and felt the tightening in her throat and stopped David from clapping his hands publicly.

On the floor of the chamber a few members of the Knesset also applauded their approval, while from the right and left shrill cries were raised:

"Mr. Chairman, Mr. Chairman! Will the gentleman yield?"

The stocky chairman rapped for order for several minutes, waiting impassively for the commotion to subside.

"Gentlemen, gentlemen, please."

Aronowitz called, "I will yield to the gentleman from Haifa."

There were sounds of protest—a long groan from the floor and several brief snorts from the extreme left of the chamber, which along with the right, seemed to contain the focal points of disorder and bad manners.

The gentleman from Haifa, whoever he was, rose in his place at the right, a pudgy man with a pock-marked face and frizzy black hair that could have been kinky wire, standing so straight into the air and away from his head that it looked electrified. What a repulsive creature, she thought. She hated him already. He waited while the chairman restored order and then spoke in a clipped Germanic Hebrew, his whole body so charged that he appeared ready to light up. He was a study in suspicion and incandescent fury.

"The gentleman from Jerusalem surely realizes we are not children!

"Oh, I can sympathize with his natural instinct. Isn't it a normal desire for an attorney who has lost his case once to seek to reopen it and have another crack at it? Even at the cost of rubbing salt into some open wounds!"

Aronowitz reddened. She could see even from where she sat that he was on the verge of losing his temper. His hands were tight and white, but he stood silent while the man from Haifa looked about ominously and went on, almost without pause.

"But, as I told him privately, he is here as a legislator and as a member of the party which, for the moment anyhow, dominates the government. He is not here to conduct his private law practice or to represent individual clients. If these citizens have claims against the government, let them go to the Department of Justice. Or let the gentleman go on their behalf. He will, no doubt, find his way round to the right desk.

"On the other hand, perhaps I do my good friend an injustice, and he has more devious purposes to serve. Those of us who have any knowledge of the armed forces know that there is a strong clique plotting tirelessly to do every possible injury to certain of our officers who share my party's revisionist political views, but who have nevertheless devoted themselves loyally for years to Haganah and to our amazing young army. They have faithfully followed orders with which they disagreed, knowing that we ought rightfully to drive the enemy out of all Trans-Jordan, which is still unredeemed Israel! These officers are known to most of us and respected for their professional ability by all who know them, except those who are so interested in iron political control that simply because these officers differ politically they wish to blacken their names.

"I have the honor to know the two officers in question as my constituents and devoted advocates of our political cause and I will resist the launching of any seemingly harmless inquiry, since the purpose of such an inquiry is solely to blight their careers and to discredit my party. The inquiry has only one purpose, to destroy them and to remove them from the army. But they are among out finest, most selfless, devoted citizens and the people of Jerusalem, even more than the rest of us, owe them a debt of the greatest magnitude. We cannot afford to lose them. The government cannot railroad this thing through. And I refuse to permit the good names of Captain Ami Ben Kepelow and Colonel Julian Horowitz to be brought into question . . ."

There were cheers from the right and polite applause from the rest of the House for the two men he had named.

". . . Certainly not for the sake of a man now no longer living who has been proved a traitor to his country!

"Ladies and gentlemen of the Council, the army is the shield of our state . . . We are threatened by enemies on every border who have sworn themselves to a second round and only our devoted army stands between them and us. To divide our army, to attack its segments, and over a convicted traitor, is suicidal. We must guard it, and every member in it as we would protect a delicate flower. We must nourish it as a mother nourishes her newborn infant. We must maintain its integrity and above all its *esprit de corps*, which is its very life."

The cheers from a dozen men at the right side of the House were now tumultuous and disorderly—although the rest of the assemblage sat on their hands. The Cabinet members, without exception, took no part in the approbation.

Again the chairman pounded to restore order and Aronowitz was on his feet, speaking again in a barely audible voice:

"I was aware of the sentiments of my friend from Haifa, and they are better said openly than unsaid. I can only assure this body as a member whose word may be entitled to some degree of credence, and as a practicing attorney, not without some modest apprenticeship in the truth, I can only assure you all that no army feud is being fought here and none will be. Nor is any political ax being ground. I am not at this moment concerned with Colonel Horowitz's or Captain Ben Kepelow's widely published views on taking Trans-Jordan. I have also the greatest respect for the purely professional ability of the officers mentioned. I have worked with them as an officer myself and I do not seek their posts for me or my friends."

There were a few mild titters, but Aronowitz's voice strengthened and he spoke sharply, snapping his words like whips:

"All I seek, and all the government should seek in the matter is the truth. I know it is difficult to work up a great passion over the guilt or innocence of a man already dead. No pressing need to right a wrong is apparent, the deed of execution being irrevocable, right or wrong. Then why stir up dying embers?

"For one thing, abstract justice for its own sake can never be scorned in Israel. But beyond the abstraction there are two human beings, very living people, a lady and a young boy, who need to be restored to life and self-respect. We cannot restore them with pounds sterling nor shelter nor food. But their need is as great as the need of those who came to us from Bergen-Belsen. Greater! Their lives and welfare hang upon this thin thread. Yes, they would be able to live among us, grieving as they do, for a departed husband and father. What family here is without such grief? But how can they live among us as the wife and son of our greatest traitor? And if we will not have them, where will they go on this globe? Where? Who will have them?

"I need no lectures from my friend on the necessity for unity in the army, and I know, too, we cannot expect every man in the army to hold identical political views, any more than we expect it in this chamber. It would be too catastrophic a condition to contemplate—except that perhaps on rare occasions, it might afford some relief for the Prime Minister."

A few members laughed, the Prime Minister more heartily than any.

"While the army's unity cannot be built on a political monolith, it must be built on loyalty to a question far greater than whether our new nation should or should not seek to expand its boundaries, or should permit the busses to run on the Sabbath. No, the army's unity is built on its faith in something tremendous, something which hasn't been seen in this world for thousands of years, and perhaps has never been seen before in human history; something that is not only a boundary, not only a homeland, but a homeland with a spirit of seeking which belongs to the ages. Yes, we must have *esprit de corps* in the army, but how can we have it without *esprit de corps* in every corner of our land? We must continue to seek what the ages have sought. Why do we work daily here to bring a better life not only to our Jews, but to our Christian and Moslem citizens as well? Why? Because behind everything we do we know there must be justice for all. And hope for all. How we are trying! No one knows better than we do. We know that every day we try to do it, here in this room! We search and seek. And what do we seek? What have we sought these five thousand years? A home with justice for everyone! And hope! Yes, even for those who do not conform in every particular. Such a man was Marmorek. Of course he did not conform. His best friend was an Englishman. He was not a Jew's Jew. Perhaps he did not think like most of us in this room. And he was shot. Perhaps I am mistaken, but I think we must know, we must be sure. We must inquire. This is no popularity contest between Marmorek and Horowitz. We must know the facts, even if we do not admire them or like to admit them. To give birth to any principle, some man must be the anvil upon which that principle is pounded, heated, distorted, defined, and sharpened, until in the end all must recognize it. The soul of Victor Marmorek is our anvil, and we shall pound out the rhythm of truth upon him until every child will know it. All our people must know, so that from the roofs it can be shouted —and heard, from Dan to Beersheba: 'Hear O Israel, Justice Is Abroad in Thy Land.' "

"Will the gentleman yield?"

It was the electrified member from Haifa again, dancing impatiently.

"I will yield."

"Does the gentleman think this motion, so charged with unnecessary, shrill emotion and hysteria, would have been offered if a certain newspaper had not written an agitating editorial on the subject?"

Aronowitz grimaced.

"Oh, I suppose the newspaper article was not wholly without influence in the matter. It was not decisive, but we will not have our monolithic friends on the left giving us lessons in justice.

"However, now that you have brought up this editorial, I should like to read a message which Mrs. Marmorek wishes to convey to you and to the country."

He adjusted his glasses carefully and read the words she had written with emphasis in every word:

> In good conscience I must denounce the editorial in the *Worker's Day*. I do not seek assistance from the Communists; I despise their methods, and do not believe in the honesty of their motives. They are attempting to use me, my son, and my beloved husband's tragedy, and we will not be used. We will not have our purpose distorted. My husband and I married because we wanted to spend our lives together. Almost from the day we married we had to flee and hide and dissemble to stay alive. Only when we reached the shores of our homeland did we have an opportunity to realize our hopes. My husband could not have betrayed those hopes. We were married ten years. Ten years is too short, but it is also time enough to know someone. I knew my husband. I know he is innocent. I also believe with all my heart that my own government will do the right thing, and I have prayed that as an act of humanity the government will seek justice for me and my son, and also for the good name of Victor Marmorek.

"The note is signed by Mrs. Victor Marmorek."

There were sudden catcalls and hisses from the left, and a babble of shouts and sarcasms that was almost threatening. The din raged wildly for several moments. Shouts, whistles, epithets, stamping, members scurrying in the aisle. But the chairman pounded his gavel again and Aronowitz continued. As he did so, Debbie became aware that Gussie was noisily leaving the gallery. She glared sullenly at Debbie and strode out.

"Throughout history," Aronowitz was saying, "other oppressed peoples have from time to time escaped to new places or have revolted against their oppressors at home to establish regimes of their own. And what does history tell us of these episodes? The English pioneers who went to America soon set about hanging their bravest individualists for witches; the Frenchmen who threw down Marie Antoinette quickly chopped off the heads of a few of their nonconformist friends, and the Soviets who did away with Czar Nicholas took to shooting and starving their fellow peasants and workers in far greater numbers than the Czar had ever hoped to do.

"Are we doomed to follow the same path, or can our country escape this historic trap? Can we not tolerate a nonconformist like Marmorek? Can we not even tolerate a decent memory of him? Can we have *unpopular* justice *and esprit de corps,* or in the name of unity must we commit the same crimes against ourselves and our own souls which have lately been committed against us by the Mandatory Regime and before that were committed by the Force of Darkness which had its heart in Berlin? It is something we must give thought to.

"My motion may appear to be an insignificant one. It calls for investigation. But the issue is written large. Are we afraid, in the name of unity, to seek justice?"

Aronowitz turned to the gallery for a moment, and caught Debbie's eye.

"I beseech the members to support the motion. Then the world will know we not only offer pity and generosity for our millions wherever they may be on this earth, but also that we offer justice for every man, woman and child among us. And far more than the world's knowing it, *we* will know it ourselves. Each of us. I will know it, you will know it, and the man in the street will know it. The lady sitting behind me in the gallery will know it, and a young lad who is now scarcely old enough to read will know it. For him that will be something worth knowing!"

Aronowitz sat down, and the House was silent, almost hushed. There was no applause, no catcall, no sound, except an occasional cough.

At a signal from the chairman, the clerk read the motion so rapidly that Debbie could understand scarcely a word of it. The matter was put to a voice vote, as nearly as she could make out, and the overwhelming sentiment in the House was Yes. From the right came a dozen vigorous, almost animal-like shouts of No when the negative showing was called for, and then silence. The vote also had come too fast for its full meaning to be comprehended. So in the end the matter was settled not in fury but in a rush to get it over and done with and pass by an unpleasant subject.

The gavel came down and after several minutes of shuffling papers throughout the House, the Minister of Communications rose and began to describe to the House the details of the capital budget submitted by the Communications Ministry.

Outside the Knesset building a knot of friends surrounded Debbie. Each had a word of encouragement. Dick Alpert said: "If Vic's a traitor, so'm I. After all, I treated Arabs. Some even got well. Guess I shouldn't've—hm? Who did I think I was, a doctor?" He grinned, shook her hand, and hurried off. The rest slowly left her, and Debbie hurried back to the hotel.

She and David had arranged to meet George on the beach as soon as he had filed his story. By the time he arrived, Debbie was lying peacefully in the sun, waiting for him, and David was running madly up and down the shoreline like a prisoner let loose. George brought sandwiches, sodas, and a terrycloth blanket.

Karl and Lil, she explained, had left for Jerusalem after dropping her at the hotel, and Noah had, after a hesitant moment, decided to go back with them. Debbie felt a pang of guilt about Noah. She hadn't given him much of her time or thought, and he no doubt felt slighted. She had thought for an instant of urging him to stay, but at the last moment had changed her mind.

George was fresh and cool in his new khaki trunks. His thin legs and bony pale body, she reflected, were nothing like Vic's. His legs were covered with the same hair that covered his arms, almost light enough to be invisible, and his back was freckled in the sunlight, like hers.

As for herself, while she had been afraid that she would feel guilty on her first holiday, she was instead comfortable and at home lying free on the sand. She felt for the first time in years like the girl she was, Debbie Pretsch of Lindenhouse.

After lunch they lay on the terrycloth, their fingers not within touching distance of each other, and she told him, as a joke, about Karl's efforts to pair her off with old Ben Kronstein. "Poor Karl's so old-fashioned," she said. "He still believes in matchmaking. And he's in such a hurry." He listened without comment, and after she finished, they lay back, each with private thoughts, while David continued to run up and down the beach, accosting other children on the sand or splashing, kicking his feet in the surf and asking, "Do you know Tamar Barnstein from Jerusalem? She's about so big. Eight years old." The failure of his quest seemed not to dampen his spirit and he played happily with some of the children he met, returning to check on Debbie and George from time to time, to report his failure, and to be sure they didn't move, waiting to digest his lunch before they would let him go in.

"You know," George said reflectively, almost sleepily, "beaches are so much the same everywhere, and a beach always has special memories for me . . ." She tried, lazily, to follow the pictures which were flashing through his mind. "The beach I remember most vividly was a huge one, the most spectacular, I think, in the world . . . in New York—Jones Beach, they call it. I remember, they were having a World's Fair near there the year a bunch of us drove up from Boston. Boys and girls, mostly just out of college. We never did get to the fair. We'd swim and lie around in the sand till quite late. And we'd wander back to the snack bar, I remember, and eat about a thousand hot dogs, till we were actually sick and after supper we'd go swimming again by the moon. Quite romantic, except that most of us weren't very romantic. I met my wife on that trip.

"And then there were summers we'd go out to the Cape—up to a town called Dennis where we'd swim on a wonderfully empty beach. Great rolling breakers. You just don't get that kind in the Mediterranean."

She lay back and let the sand run through her fingers like velvet and tried to picture what he meant, what his wife had been like, but it was scarcely possible. *Inside USA* had told her about the Irish voters in Boston, and the anti-Jewish hoodlums, but had neglected all the beaches.

"I learned to swim in our pool at Lindenhouse. Vic taught me to do the crawl and I was so proud when I could actually do it. I don't know whether I still can any more. When I was older I never had a chance to visit the beaches. We used to ski a little, Vic and I. Vic loved the mountains and snow. So did I."

She closed her eyes and felt the warmth of the sun bathe her. She was standing again toe to toe with Vic, kissing sweetly. She could feel his soft lips on hers and his hands on her waist, in the room with the great bed in the Krknos. She could feel the memory work her into a sentimental bitterness and it irritated her. She hated the maudlin feeling and blinked vigorously. She smiled to herself and said solemnly, "It's terrible, you know, when one man can mean so much to you even after—after he's gone. Quite terrible. It dominates you, almost against your will. Perhaps, if I'd loved other men or even let some other man love me . . ." She wouldn't think of Angelo now, she couldn't think of him, she'd never admit him. Never. But she was remembering.

She jumped to her feet, and ran down to the water; George was up and after her.

The water exhilarated her as nothing had for a long time; she felt cleansed and refreshed as she ran straight in and dived wildly through the breaking wave, then swam strongly, directly out to sea. There was no Angelo. For this moment there was only herself and the sea. She was charged, cutting through the water cleanly and then she twirled to lie on her back while George swam up and clucked admiringly, "I'm sure I must have seen you in the Olympics."

"The man who taught me," she said proudly, "*was* in the Olympics in 1928. He swam the four-hundred-meter free style in Amsterdam, and besides he was a scrumptious tennis player. Davis Cup team for Czechoslovakia. Swimming was really only a pastime with him."

"For years," George said, rolling to his back also, "I swam like a rock. My game was baseball. I finally learned to swim in a cold little lake in a boys' camp in Maine with a name I know you won't believe. Mooselookmeguntic."

She tried the name and laughed. "There's no such name," she said. She tried it again and they were both laughing.

Later George took David in, a squealing and delighted boy, who ducked and crawled and literally rolled over in the water. George taught him to ride the waves and he played inexhaustibly for an hour.

When Debbie insisted he come out to rest, he said with the vastest indifference she could imagine, "What d'you think, Mom, I met a boy who knows Tamar. He saw her right here on the beach."

"David! Not really? Are you sure?"

"She's not dead after all," he said to George. "She just came to Tel Aviv, like Loet said. That stupid old Dinah, I'll kill her when I see her. She had me worried!"

"Why, David, what wonderful news! Was the little boy sure it was *your* Tamar?"

"Her name's Tamar and she comes from Jerusalem and she has long blond braids. That's her. This boy says she and her mother are going back to Jerusalem in October. Is October soon?"

"Oh, David, I'm so glad. That's this month. She's such a sweet little thing, George. And she and David got on so beautifully together." It was a sign. This was the sign she had been looking for.

"I missed her," David said, and ran off to play with his new beach friends.

Debbie and George lay on the terrycloth together and this time their fingertips touched lightly. She knew George was studying her and she knew if she looked at him he'd turn away and be looking elsewhere, so she kept her eyes closed.

"George."

"Yes."

"I feel mixed up about everything."

"Like what?"

"What we're doing about Vic. This investigation. I wish I was sure I was doing the right thing."

"It's what you wanted, isn't it?"

"I know, but I'm afraid now, I'm a little scared. When I heard Boris this morning and all that talk; that pock-marked man was so angry I thought he'd burst, and all that about the army . . . and politics . . . It seems like so much to stir up. First it was Gussie—I've lost Gussie for good now, and then the army, and now so much politics. All I wanted was for people to know that Vic hadn't done anything."

"Well, it's not so simple. You must've known that."

"I don't think I did. And now it's so real. It's *here.* It's all so complicated and out of control. Have I done wrong, George?"

"You'll have to ask Boris that."

"Oh, no, I couldn't. Boris is so deeply involved now, I wouldn't dare. He'd think me a featherbrain. Perhaps I'd better not think about it. I don't see how I could go back now, could I? It would mean—so many people are in it—oh, it's just impossible. But I wish I was as sure of what I'm doing now as I was last month."

"Have you ever been on a roller coaster?"

"Yes, once. In the Prater in Vienna. Why?"

George leaned on one elbow, put his long hand over her own painfully thin one and held it firmly. "You can't take half a roller coaster ride. You buy your ticket and you take your money's worth. Nothing less than the full ride. They just don't let you get out while the car's in motion. It's too dangerous." Then in a softer voice he said, "I'll come along for the ride if you don't mind, so you'll have someone to hang on to around the rough curves."

"I'm lucky," she said gratefully.

"I have a little problem of my own," George said, as though he were not sure he should tell her.

"You?"

"My boss, that brother-in-law of mine—he's beginning to make noises like he's planning to move me somewhere else. Writes me a note about my expenses. That's a mighty poor sign. And telling me what a gold mine of news there is further east—New Delhi, Karachi. And what a big step up Karachi would be."

"Oh." She was afraid to say a word, it would doubtless be the wrong one.

"The damn trouble is I can't seem to get excited about going. I guess Karachi's bubbling over and I'd probably get a bang out of it once I got there. But I just can't work up any steam to go. Maybe this place has me under a spell. I try to get some of my own excitement into the stuff I send home, but that brother-in-law of mine doesn't get it. Public's tired of Israel. That's my problem."

"What are you going to do?" Her voice sounded small and quavering.

"Don't know," George said. "Don't really know."

When they got back to the hotel room there were notes from several reporters asking when they could see her and promising to call back. The notes troubled her; she wanted to stay out of the papers.

After David's bedtime, Boris Aronowitz came to dinner. It was no easy matter to talk quietly with him in the dining room of the Gat Rimon, for everyone in Tel Aviv knew Boris and wanted just one word with him. He smiled at friends, waved, and gossiped. He gobbled his dried fish eagerly; his nervous energy was conspicuous in the bounce and buoyancy with which he spoke, when he had time, of their prospects.

"We're coming along, coming along," he said rubbing his hands gleefully together, between mouthfuls and the interruptions of men who sidled to their table for those short whispered conspiratorial conversations out of the side of the mouth which are the lifeblood of politics. After dinner he finally suggested that they go to George's room for a little privacy.

"Those twins in my office have done a tremendous job—tremendous," he said, when they were safely locked in. "They've turned themselves into detectives, psychologists, wizards. They've dug out those small distortions that people always employ on the witness stand because—well I guess because they're people. One girl they've been working on for days. This Esther Schamel. She's completely switched her story. The case against your husband looked airtight to Horowitz four months ago, and now it's coming apart at the seams. I tell you absolutely apart."

"I knew it," Debbie cried, catching some of Aronowitz's excitement. She tried to picture Esther Schamel, but could scarcely remember her. Yes, the girl at the information desk in the Telephone Office.

"Ben Kepelow is stewing up there in Haifa. Burning the wires to a cinder," Aronowitz said cheerfully. "Why not? This makes him look like a donkey's behind. But the big hammer won't fall on him. It'll be poor old Julian Horowitz. I think he feels things growing tight already."

"He deserves what he gets," Debbie said belligerently.

"He's being circumspect," Aronowitz continued. "But that buddy of his, Springer, you heard him today. The pock-marked one. Nothing up here. It's all in his backside. He'll say anything if he thinks he can gain something." Aronowitz continued literally to rub his hands together with pleasure. "Of course, nothing's ever in the bag. But the big fellows are sympathetic, from B.G. down. I'm afraid my job may not be quite as tough as I thought."

"How about the army brass?" George asked.

"No trouble," Aronowitz snapped. "All that unity talk is desperation. After all, who's the army? People. Even officers are people. And how many people do you know who are champing at the bit to go marching into Jordan? No matter how gratifying it sounds. Unredeemed Zion. Unredeemed, my tail. We've redeemed enough for our time. Jordan can wait, another two thousand years, for all I care. But when men like Horowitz and Ben Kepelow and Springer make noises that mean fighting again, they win no friends. They get no popularity prizes except from a few hot-blooded American Jews living in Hollywood, those fearless pioneers."

Boris Aronowitz rose to pace off his energy. "What am I making, a campaign speech? Look, we have gaps in our case to close. There's one great question open. A tremendous question. If we have the answer to that, no one can stop us—unless we get the wrong answer, God forbid, in which case, nothing can save us."

"What's that?" George said.

"Why didn't the man ever warn Pearlman he was giving these lists to Walker?" Aronowitz asked. He put the question almost sadly, as if Vic had somehow let him down personally. "If I had the answer to that one, if I only had that!"

He looked sharply at George. "Tell me that one, Yank, and it's wrapped up. Give me the wrong answer and we're finished."

Aronowitz spoke as though he expected George to produce the reply then and there. George rose from the creaky bed, walked to the window and stared out to sea.

"I wish to hell I knew," he said vehemently.

Aronowitz turned, suddenly depressed and as gentle as eiderdown. "Difficult gamble, you know. We'll probably get our tails burned to a crisp." Then as though he had startled himself with the thought, he asked, "Have the newspaper people been here yet?"

Debbie's heart sank. "Yes, but they missed me."

"Good. I'm glad I had a chance to talk to you first. Lady, I know you've had a tiring day. But there's work to do. I'd like to offer some professional advice. May I speak frankly?"

"Of course."

"Well, then." He took a deep breath. "This thing is going to be knocked around in the newspapers as much as in the Council or courts. We all want to be conscious of it. We may win or lose our case there. Newspaper people aren't famous for kindness, you know. Present company excepted, Yank." He nodded ceremoniously. "All they want is to make a great splash. Big headlines. Our job is to keep as many of them with us as we can." Debbie only listened, not saying a word. "They'll be after you," he said carefully. "When they find you, you have to be ready for them."

"Four of them left cards this afternoon."

"Where were you when they came?"

"We were out—on the beach. They left notes that they'd call again."

"Good. But please don't tell them you were on the beach. And please don't go on the beach any more. All they have to do is catch you cavorting around—well never mind. Just be yourself. You have a natural dignity. I think you'll be fine. I guess there's no need your trying to act pathetic or helpless or anything but what you are. How about it, Yank, agreed?"

George drawled slowly, "Well, like you say, I like her just as she is. I'll go along with you on that."

"And don't overplay your son. Where is he?"

"Asleep in my room."

"Oh. Well, we don't want to make it phoney in any way. If people think it's a tear jerker, it'll boomerang. You have a normal boy, okay. If they ask you about the school, you tell them what happened. Nothing more, nothing less. If anything, understate it."

George nodded.

"As far as your husband was concerned, you loved him, you have faith in him, you never wavered, not once. You were close to him and it's inconceivable to you that he could have done any of the things with which he was charged."

"I see," Debbie said. Everything was to be so pat.

"Nothing can be complicated," he said reading her mind. "This is a one-string orchestra. These English people were your friends, the Walkers. You didn't have many English friends, but you had this one couple. Lots of people did. You and your husband both liked the Walkers. You're sure they were pro-Zion. And if any of the reporters become curious about me, stick to the facts. You asked me to help you, which was natural, because I defended him in the first place, and if they start asking about my fees, tell them we've never discussed fees. Tell them it's not a matter of fees. We may as well get that out of the way because they'll snipe if we don't. And don't answer any questions about evidence. Tell them to talk to me about evidence. You understand clearly?"

"Yes. I'm to say nothing about evidence. Nothing specific."

"Right. Just the flat statement. Your husband was innocent. Now one last thing. They may say something or ask a question that will annoy you. Be calm. Be nice. Be relaxed. Pretend not to understand if there are insults. Control your feelings no matter how provoking they are. But keep your wits about you. And whatever you say, try to picture how it will look in print, in headlines."

"I'll try."

"It's essential."

"Will you be there with me?" Debbie asked.

"No. You'll look better alone." He turned abruptly to George. "How about it, Yank, can we give our client a chance to get a little sleep now? Shall we take a short stroll?"

"The Commander-in-Chief must have some dirty job up his sleeve," George said cheerfully. "Will you be okay?"

"Yes," she said. "I'd better go to bed. I'm dead. That cool breeze from the sea ought to be a help, I may even be able to sleep, and we've that long hot trip back in the morning."

But in her room she lay there listening to David's heavy breathing—his adenoids would have to come out soon—and almost hearing Vic's regular breathing in her mind. She could just about touch Vic. She rolled over. What were Aronowitz and George hatching? There were so many details, mechanics, minutiae that had to go into the building of this structure of logical proof of innocence, a structure that had to be as real and complex as a stone and steel building and more rigid because it was built of intangibles—words, fears, memories.

As she dozed she considered her future vaguely. How much longer could she stay at the Pantilles? And if she should leave and go back to Gaza Road, what sort of work could she do? Perhaps she'd take private cases. That paid well . . . better than the hospital. She had to think about money all the time now. But who would take care of David? There were so many women in the same fix . . . with small children—like Jacinta Van Bern. What did she do about Meyer? Perhaps Jacinta . . . A vague thought formed dimly in her sleepy brain. She would think about it later; her great fatigue and David's regular heavy breathing and her own half-formed thoughts combined to put her into a fitful sleep.

She must have been dozing more soundly than she realized, for she heard the phone ring in her sleep many times before she turned sluggishly, switched on the light, and fumbled the instrument to her ear. The girl at the desk hoped she hadn't wakened her, but there were several reporters who were anxious to talk to her, and since it was only ten o'clock . . . Would it be all right for them to come up?

David stirred and asked who it was. She thought sluggishly of Aronowitz's instructions, and mumbled to send the gentlemen up in five minutes. She would have to gather her wits, get her hair combed, put a robe on. Her face, burned and finely freckled from this afternoon's sun, was drawn and sleepy in the mirror, but she doused herself with cold water and warned David to remain in bed, mind his manners when the newsmen came up, to speak only when spoken to and to try to control his perpetual impulse to astound everyone.

Three reporters, one of them a woman, and a photographer came, and after taking great pains to apologize for their late visit they made a few feeble efforts to talk with David, who only stared wide-eyed at them and said nothing. They must have thought him psychotically frightened, but Debbie knew he was only straining to obey her precautions. The photographer finally sat on David's bed and diverted him by showing him his camera and plates, while the others sat on Debbie's bed, holding note-pads, facing Debbie, who stood uneasily, waiting.

"Mrs. Marmorek," the short bald-headed man started briskly, "may we ask you a few questions? I assume you were at the Knesset today."

"Yes, of course."

"Is Boris Aronowitz your lawyer? I mean, have you retained him?"

"Well, I've asked him to help me. Long before he came to the Knesset. Long before I knew anything about him. Right after the trial, in fact. I naturally went to him. My husband had written me about him."

"Then you knew about your husband's trial before he was sentenced," the rather stern square lady said almost accusingly.

"No, you see, the letter from my husband came afterward. When everything was over."

"You mean you had no idea what was happening until after it was all over?"

"That's right."

"I see. And what led you to the conclusion that your husband was innocent?" The younger of the men spoke too politely.

"You can't live with a man for so long and not know something of his nature. Especially if you love him."

"Well, of course, they say that love sometimes is blind. Did you have any specific evidence?"

"No. I understand there was not much evidence either way."

"Well, there was that marked list. The one they found on the Arab prisoner, wasn't there?"

"I'm sorry, but I'm not free to discuss evidence. Mr. Aronowitz forbade me, you'll have to see him about that."

"Oh." The girl again. "Is it true that your friends in Jerusalem ostracized you when this happened?"

Debbie tried to smile and it was an effort. "Not my friends," she said, "only some whom I'd thought were friends. I had been mistaken."

"What was your reaction?"

"I was sorry. But I knew that many people in Israel are not normal. You cannot lose your entire family in a gas chamber and remain calm and normal, especially about treason. We are not detached or academic. I have many friends who are mentally disturbed. You probably do too. So have we all."

"Isn't it a fact that you were more or less completely cut off from the Jewish community?"

"No. There were always people who understood my difficulty, right from the first day."

"Have you heard from the English people involved in the case?"

"Yes. A short note. They know about it."

"Did this American newspaperman, Stern, go to England just to get evidence?"

"Yes, he did."

"Is there any romantic attachment between you and the American? Do you like him?" It was the woman, of course.

She had almost to smile. "No, there's no romance. He's helping me, because he believes in my case. I'm very much attached to the memory of my husband."

"And you are confident your husband will be exonerated, of course?"

"Yes, I am."

"Is that confidence based on evidence or just—uh—shall we call it faith?" It was the cynical young man again.

"Both, I should say, although I think faith is the more important."

"Is it true that you lost your job at Hadassah and that your son was expelled from his school in Jerusalem?"

"I left my job at the request of the hospital. A leave of absence, they called it. I don't think you could say David was expelled. It wasn't that official."

"They threw rocks at me," David said, when at last he got his chance to talk. "René Blum threw one that hit me here. Bleeded like anything. This guy René came to school this certain day and he had one eye missing." He looked at his mother and seeing she would not resist his telling it, then proceeded to fill in the gory details of the day of the stoning. He did a remarkably coherent and matter-of-fact job and the reporters and the photographer listened intently until he was finished.

"How old are you, David?"

"I'll be nine," he said, "in March."

The lady reporter shook her head. "Well, thank you, Mrs. Marmorek."

"This fellow Stern, is he staying here at the hotel with you?" the cynical one asked.

"Yes," she said.

"Come on," the woman said, "I've got to get back to my shop."

"Who's paying all the expenses for this work?" the bald-headed man asked.

"I am, naturally. My brother helps me too."

"Where'd you get the money?" the young man asked.

"I worked for it. Very hard."

She wanted to tell them all to get out, that it was none of their business. "My husband worked hard too. We saved as much as we could in the last four years. We wanted David to go to the university."

"How much did you save in four years?"

"About five hundred pounds."

"Has it occurred to you," asked the young man almost belligerently now, "that an inquiry such as you and Mr. Aronowitz are pushing can bring very unhappy consequences to Capt. Ben Kepelow and Colonel Horowitz? And their families? Have you thought of that?"

"No," Debbie said, "I have not."

"You know these men have wives too. And children. These men

can fall into disgrace and yet your husband cannot be brought back to life. What do you expect of this, a money settlement?"

"I want to clear my husband's name. I want to return to normal life."

"And if you lose your case, then you will only have gotten yourself and your son from a bad position into an impossible one. Isn't that so?"

"But my husband was innocent."

"I see. But if you knew definitely that this inquiry would ruin the careers of Kepelow and Horowitz, and do Lord knows how much harm to their families, would you do anything to put a stop to it?"

"How could I?" Debbie said. "You must try to remember that those men were the cause of my husband's death. They killed him. Do you expect me to be impartial about it?"

"But they considered they were only doing their duty," the young man said, his face flushed.

"I am only doing mine," Debbie said quietly.

"And to whom do you feel you owe your duty?" he asked, now almost sneering.

"To David and myself—and my husband, above all." She thought a moment. "Also I think there will be many strangers who will be glad to know that injustice cannot be the rule in our country."

"You're quite a purist, Mrs. Marmorek," the young man said sharply.

"Perhaps," Debbie said. "Like the rest of us, if I'm psychotic on the subject of justice, I owe it to the deficiencies of my past."

"Come on, boys," the woman said. "Take your pictures, Abe, and let's get out of here."

Abe took flash portraits of Debbie and David. Separately and together. The reporters shook hands and left.

"Good luck," the woman said, and they left.

David fell asleep instantly, but she was awake half the night wondering how this would look in the papers and whether she had said the right thing.

In the morning the desk gave her a collection of morning papers, left by Aronowitz, marked with red crayon and accompanied by a one-line note from Boris. "I wish I were as good a lawyer as you are a client."

It was true; the tone of two of the news articles was favorable. Her remarks were presented with no attempt to twist or bedevil her meanings and what little news editorializing there was, including descriptions of Debbie, as "modest, but proud and firm in her faith in her husband," was all to the good. There were also longer accounts of the Council session, and pictures of Boris.

Only one of the papers, from Haifa, ran a snide article.

> When asked how she was financing the case to clear her husband posthumously, Mrs. Marmorek explained that she and her husband had saved five hundred pounds out of their salaries. According to offi-

cials of the Telephone Department, Marmorek as wire chief earned seven hundred pounds a year, at the Telephone Department, until in 1947 he was promoted over the head of a superior who was considered less "reliable" by the English head of the Department, at which time Marmorek's salary was increased to eighty pounds per month.

Mrs. Marmorek was asked if she considered the possible tragedy which would face the officers who had conducted her husband's proceedings, and their families, if her campaign were to succeed. She was asked if to avoid such a result she could not now stop the proceedings. Her reply was that she would not even if she could.

Alongside this was an interview with Horowitz and Kepelow in Haifa, both of whom affirmed again their absolute certainty of Vic's guilt.

But in the other papers, even the photos of Debbie and David were helpful. David was staring with wide-eyed fright lost in his pajamas in a great bed, and Debbie looked small enough and brave enough to move a strong heart.

Worker's Day editorially took full credit for the entire turn of events. It made no reference to Debbie's disavowal, and completely distorted what had happened at the Council. To *Worker's Day*, this was another victory for communism.

Forty-three

The drive back in the early morning was cooler than the trip down and their pace was more leisurely. They went round about by way of Rammat Gan, so that George could stop off at the immigrants' tent camp there for background material on a story he was doing about the swelling tide of newcomers to the new country. They drove by a small park, past neat apartments of white stucco, and a huge carousel, before they reached the tent camp.

From the road out front, as far back into the fields as they could see were khaki tents, row on row. On some, family names were scrawled in white paint: Benelli, Katz, Atorshi, names from everywhere. She wondered if the Benellis, like the Pretsches of Lindenhouse, had had their name in neat wrought-iron at the entrance to their villa on Lake Maggiore, set luxuriantly in evergreens and lilacs. Benelli, Katz, Atorshi.

George was leading the way across the uneven terrain, his Rolleiflex held loosely in his hand, while Debbie and David trailed after him, hopping across ditches, climbing and sliding. The stench of sewage blew across at them and in front of one tent thay saw a kerchief-topped woman scrubbing her laundry in a tin basin. George focused the Rolleiflex on her, when a man came roaring out of the tent, waving his arms and shouting in English, "That's right! Take pictures of our misery! Entertain your friends! See the monkeys in the zoo!"

George lowered his camera and they stood a moment, until the man, embarrassed by his own outburst, said, "I'll show you! Come, come inside, look for yourself what we put up with!"

They made their way into the tent. The woman, drying her hands on her skirt, smiled apologetically and tried to quiet her husband. Inside there were two rough cribs covered with mosquito netting, each inhabited by a baby. Another woman, much older than the first, rocked the cradles patiently. Words poured out of the man. He and his wife had come from Alexandria. "I had a good job in Egypt. A respectable job. I was a bank teller. One day two men came to see me in my flat. Come to Palestine, they begged. Come to Palestine, and you shan't have to worry any more because you're a Jew. We'll get you an apartment. We'll find you a job. They begged me! Do you think I would have come otherwise? The riots in Egypt were not so bad as all that. Greatly exaggerated, all those things are. Why I came I don't know." He glowered at his wife. "Ha! Three months I've been rotting here. I could be back in Alexandria with a good job."

"Shhh!" his wife said as the other woman watched him scornfully.

George said, "Can't you get work? With so much to be done?"

"Work? Building sewers! Breaking stones for roads, go on a farm! Me on a kibbutz, imagine! They take your children away. Who wants that? I'm a family man. See, I never did such work. What am I, a peasant? Look at my hands, look, smooth, I'm an educated man. Two years at the university. I'm an office man. Let them find me a job in an office. *That* I'd take."

Debbie thought, Karl with his musical hands can drive a bus. But she said nothing. They saw the squalor of the tent. The other woman sat fanning one of the babies. She watched the man with glowering indifference, almost belligerence.

"Who's she?"

The man shrugged. "A numbskull. Hungarian. She was on Cyprus, she and her husband. Speaks nothing but Magyar. They're used to such things. Her husband took a job on the sewer line. A lump he is. No brains." He spat.

"Joseph," his wife cried. "Don't do that!"

"Unsanitary?" he sneered. "Look, see how we're forced to live! How long can we stay alive? Both babies are sick. We don't know what ails them. No doctors. A nurse comes twice a month and leaves a few pills. And what will we do when the floods come?"

Debbie pushed the mosquito netting back and looked at the older child. She was about two, perspiring freely, staring with glazed eyes, wailing and struggling. She had a high fever and her ears were obviously giving her great trouble, for her small fists were doubled into them. An antibiotic injection would cure her in a day or two. The younger child was undernourished, but not acutely ill.

They said good-bye and walked out and into another tent. Apathy was so deep here that no one seemed to mind their coming, or turned to glance at them. There were ten people, most of them lying lazily on their canvas cots; one was reading, another praying. Three men were sitting on camp stools, beside an elderly patriarch, stretched out on his cot. When George and Debbie came in one of the men held his fingers to his lips. One of the others mopped the old man's brow. His eyes were closed and his skin, what they could see of it beneath his gray beard, was dried, gray and flaky, like the scales of a fish. They ducked out quickly again. As they stumbled down the row of tents a goateed man came up behind them and tapped Debbie on the shoulder. "You're Americans?" he asked in Yiddish.

"He's American," Debbie said in German. "Not I."

"I can tell," the man cried triumphantly. "I have a nephew in America, that's why. I've never seen him, but he writes me letters. Listen here, I need help. If my nephew were here he would do it, but since he's not it may as well be you."

He was a confident entrepreneur. Debbie translated; George listened carefully and smiled encouragingly. "You see, right after the war in Poland I had a big job, assistant to the Minister of Trade, in charge of leather goods. This is a big job in Poland. Leather is big business there. The minute I got back from Siberia, the Minister of Trade sends for me. 'Mr. Wolowsky,' he says—that's me—'you had the largest leather works in Krakow before the war'—it's true also—'so you'll be in charge of leather production for all Poland,' and this is a big job. A big job. This is in Poland, where I'm still a Jew, remember. So even though I have a big job, I hear always Jew, and I can't stand it there any more and I bring my two sons here to the Promised Land. Ah, if only my nephew were here. Well, I was a fool, I should have gone to America. He's a big man with charity, my nephew, a man of influence, but I've no influence." He paused to let Debbie translate, then continued. "I've no influence," he repeated and Debbie knew now he was reciting a speech, almost from memory. But it was remarkable how much passion he managed to evoke in himself. He spoke hysterically. "For six weeks I've written twice a week to the Minister of Trade—here—*our* minister, for an appointment, just an appointment, see? Only to see me, to give me half an hour. This is the Promised Land! And I don't get even promises. Everyone is too important, especially the Minister of Trade, may his soul rot in hell. I don't even get courtesy, not an answer, not a word. I've mailed out twelve letters and have received—none. That's fair? That's equitable? That's a Promised Land?"

He snorted suddenly and with great ugliness. "In my own country! Where I'm not even a Jew."

George took his name and the man was transformed to a dear friend and thanked him a hundred times. He smiled a golden-toothed smile through the thick goatee and insisted that George take a carbon copy of his last letter to the Minister of Trade, which he produced from his pocket and presented like a Nobel Prize.

They went to the tent office of the camp director, who gave them statistics and shook his head hopelessly. "No doctors, no sanitary engineers, no social workers, no teachers. Idleness, anger, resentment all day. I feel most of the time as if I were under water, trying to reach the surface to breathe. We need money, but not only money. We need trained personnel, people with brains and training, people with big hearts and small appetites."

As they made their way back to the Fiat through the streets of tents, children called, men and women stood in their tent flaps and waved or smiled or watched sullenly. Inside they could see others sitting in debris, locked in the rubbish which transients insist on lugging with them as bridges to the past—glum, weary, praying, reading; from one tent they heard a phonograph blare as they drove off.

They rode a long distance in silence, even David was lost in reflection. They passed other tent camps on the baked desert road, but they passed, too, communal farms in what had once been parched sand, and now were green oases. They could see in the morning's coolness young men and women working the fields. Tractors coughed under the guidance of bare-chested men, glistening as they spread fertilizer or cut neat parallel furrows. Girls in shorts, harvesting vegetable crops, waved, shouted and giggled as they passed. They rode close by the school of one kibbutz and watched kindergarten children singing, sliding and chasing each other about the courtyard.

It was only after the Fiat had started its slow climb into the hills that Debbie began to sort her jumbled impressions. How could all the thousands of sicknesses of the bodies, minds and attitudes surging in from overseas ever be treated and arrested? Getting everyone to speak the same language alone would take generations. Sixty languages, seventy. Everyone spoke Hebrew with an accent from the past and with each accent there was some hidden wound, some injury which was deep enough to be inerasable for a hundred years.

"Are you going to do anything about the little man with the goatee?" she asked idly.

George was quiet. "Might. If I run into the Minister of Trade."

"He was really very funny. Now I understand Ben-Gurion's problem. He *does* have to put up with half a million cabinet ministers—all like Mr. Wolowsky."

"I've seen funnier," George said.

They returned to silence. He was thinking of ways to help that obscure man. George would do it too. She wondered about the sick babies and she knew how much one extra resident doctor or nurse could mean in that camp. She thought of the Egyptian and all his previous education. He had to have a job in an office.

What could *she* do? George's old warning hammered in her heart. "I hate to see you wasting your passion." Passion could take many forms. She thought of Dick Alpert and his comment at the Knesset. She twisted from the idea, but she knew what she would have to do. She would start by talking to Jacinta Van Bern in the morning. What had to be done was clear now and inevitable.

Once she had made up her mind she felt better, a mood of relief, a sensation she had not had since the siege of Jerusalem. She was relaxed and sure and knew that it was right for her. Much of her sense of struggle and conflict was gone. I've been obstinate and spiteful, she thought. I've been concentrating on myself, like that small Egyptian flyspeck of a man. She had known it subconsciously since her trip to Deir Yassein. She hummed a little melody she had forgotten she knew, a sprightly pizzicato she hadn't heard since the day Papa took her to the Grinzing Garden, when she was fourteen.

Forty-four

When Debbie returned to the pension, she found many letters to answer from all over the country as a result of the newspaper articles. Some abused her, many encouraged her, and a few sent money, which she returned with thanks. One letter was touching: "I am ten years old, and I know how David must feel. I'm sending you this one pound which I have been saving for a certain wrist watch, so you can pay the lawyers to show everyone that David's Dad was a good man and not a traitor."

Abusive letters, usually unsigned, made her furious: "It's selfish people like you, interested only in yourselves, who have prevented us from having a country for two thousand years. Your husband sold us out for money and now you're trying to stir up trouble for reasons of your own. People like you should never have been brought in."

While she had been to Tel Aviv, Debbie was told, Tani had called at the Pantilles looking for her—Tani, who had not shown her face all these months, was back. Now all was to be forgiven. She returned again in a few days, shriveled, brown, frightened, suffering from malnutrition, kissing Debbie's hand and begging her pardon in a hundred inarticulate gestures, shrugs, tears and head-shakings. Her words made no sense, tumbling, mumbling words, but Debbie gathered that she wanted to come back, that she had to come back. She would work so hard, Debbie would be able to lick the floor.

Tani's reappearance set Debbie's plans rolling. In George's absence —he was on a trip to the Negev—Debbie arranged for Tani to take over her job at the pension, promising the six correspondents still living there that Tani's services would be satisfactory. Then she moved her own things back to the flat on Gaza Road.

As soon as they were unpacked Debbie took off for the Tourist Bureau, where Jacinta Van Bern worked, to talk seriously to her. They found a quiet corner, and Debbie explained her plan.

"I'll be home from the hospital all day Fridays and you're home Saturdays. We can juggle our hours so that one of us is always with the boys. And we'll have our evenings together and our nights. I'd just be too lonely, Jacinta, living alone. Don't you think you'll find it more cheerful? Oh, I mean just someone to talk things over with. I need someone like you—steady and a friend."

Jacinta Van Bern's face clouded.

"I promise not to disturb your privacy," Debbie ran on breathlessly. "I absolutely promise you that. We'll work it any way you want."

"I'm flattered you ask me," Jacinta said slowly. "You know it took me such a long time to get my flat and all my furniture together. I'm rather used to them. What shall I do with my furniture?"

"You could sell it," Debbie said, knowing at once that she had said the wrong thing. "Or store it, or I know. I'll get rid of some of mine and you can bring yours. Will that make you more comfortable? You can furnish your own bedroom. And think of the boys! They're crazy about each other. They can bunk together in my room . . . I'll sleep on the living room couch . . ."

"Well," Jacinta said nervously, "I'd have to think about giving up my flat. It's so hard to get a flat these days. And if anything went wrong . . ."

"What can go wrong?" Debbie cried. "Don't we get along? Don't the boys get along?"

"Yes, but—well, I'm very flattered, but let me think about it," Jacinta said. "Let me think it over."

"Of course." She could see Jacinta's face creased with worry. It was one thing to befriend Debbie, to spend an occasional evening together. But to move in with the traitor's wife. And yet, Debbie knew, Jacinta was not a fearful woman.

Reluctantly, Jacinta started to come around, under Debbie's pressure. She even managed to work up some enthusiasm for the idea, although she had misgivings. It would be difficult for two women who had been mistresses in their own homes. On the other hand there would certainly be savings. Jacinta was unimaginative but practical. If she could sublet her apartment on a temporary basis, she might see how things worked out. Two days before George got back from the Negev, Jacinta arranged for her furniture to be transferred to Debbie's flat.

At the same time Debbie arranged to put David back in the Rehavia School. Miss Even made no comment, but led him quietly to his classroom. Most of the children behaved as though his return were nothing unusual. As for David, he was more disturbed over finding himself behind in his schoolwork than with René Blum's open hostility. He had Meyer for one sure friend, and although René Blum now had a firm position as leader of the class and forbade the boys to speak to David, there were several who had never made René's gang, outcasts and poor athletes, who were glad to see David again, although they no longer called him King David. Tuvia soon came round to David's camp; so did Loet; and the day that Tamar returned to school, David brought her home in triumph, like a prize, for Debbie and Jacinta to see.

Once David was settled, Debbie girded herself for her first visit to the hospital. She took a mental oath to maintain a businesslike manner to forestall Elsa from going into a diatribe or lecture. She found Elsa in her records office and said Hello as if they had met last week. "I think I've been on leave long enough, Elsa. Four and a half months. Let's face it, I'm not built for lounging. Fun's fun, don't you think?"

Elsa said, "You should have come back weeks ago."

"You're probably right," Debbie said. "Tell me, what are the chances of getting into Maternity?"

"We're short everywhere," Elsa said wearily, with her heavy, conscious tragicality. "In Maternity as much as anywhere and the babies are coming so fast now it's scandalous. Jewish girls acting like Arabs!"

"It isn't the girls," Debbie needled. "It's that *men* behave like Arabs. The girls are helpless. All men are beasts, Elsa, you know that. Brutes. Fiends. Especially the religious ones. Look at the holiest Moslems—five wives. That's what prayer does for you!"

Elsa reacted to the teasing by becoming more businesslike than ever. "Of course, if you're needed for a week here or there I don't suppose you'll mind. Occasionally we send some of the girls to a camp or one of the new settlements, just to get things started. There are many changes."

"Have I ever refused to do any job, Elsa?"

Elsa bit her lip. "No, you've always been one of my best girls, one of my very best, Deborah." She sighed deeply. "I hold nothing back.

I've missed you. I've missed you." Her mouth was twisted almost as if she were repressing tears and she spoke quickly to get the difficult words out.

"I never meant to be harsh, Deborah. You know my trouble? My heart is dried up like a prune or a raisin. Like dust. You know how it can happen? There's no love, not the right kind of love. Someone to really care. I don't think anyone has cared for me since I'm a little girl. I don't say it to complain, but it shrivels up the heart. Maybe I don't feel what other people feel. I'm suspicious and bitter and cynical. Believe me, I love God, but it's harder for me to love human beings. I try to understand what you've had to bear. I try in my prayers to know, but it's so hard for me, Deborah. I'm vengeful, I'm spiteful, I'm full of arrogance. How I wish I could be humble—so God, at least, would love me. But it's against my nature. I believe in you, Deborah. I want to believe in you. I don't believe in myself at all! I wish I could be silly like you and unselfish like you and tough like you!"

She was wringing her hands and struggling with herself, while Debbie was too surprised to say a word.

"Four months! It's dried me up. Ask the girls, I'm changed since you left. I'm not a pleasant person any more. You helped me, Deborah, while you were here. Just for you to be in the building. I promise to be better. I'll try, I'll try. I pray God to help me try."

Debbie let Elsa unwind in this extraordinary self-betrayal. Then she said, "When do I come to work, Elsa?"

"Any time. Tomorrow, if you wish."

"You're sure it's all right with the Board?"

"Of course."

I'll try to think more kindly of you, Elsa, she thought.

"How's David?"

"Fine."

"I'm not used to children," Elsa said honestly, "but I never gave him enough chance. I'd like to try. Let me see him soon."

"I will," Debbie said.

Elsa's admission that she hadn't liked David touched her more than anything before. She was trying with all her might to be honest.

Some of the other nurses and doctors were friendly and welcoming. Lilith was noisily glad to see her back at work. A few were hostile. She was a curiosity, perhaps worse. Well, she could stand it now.

By the time George Stern returned from his trip to Elath, David was at school, Debbie at the hospital, and the Marmoreks and Van Berns were firmly established in the flat on Gaza Road. The Van Berns were not difficult to get along with. Meyer was placid, and what his mother lacked in brightness and imagination she made up with a gentle and patient soul. Debbie did not forget that Jacinta had come to live in the flat with misgivings, and as an act of faith.

The fall and winter months followed one another quickly, busy for them both. George traveled everywhere, devouring and reporting every aspect of life that had the slightest chance of catching an American reader's fancy. He wrote, wrote, wrote; and what he did not write he saved for telling Debbie.

Debbie, too, worked so hard all winter she had no strength to think of herself, and slept so hard that her dreaming stopped.

From the day she started at the hospital, her work in Maternity gave her enormous satisfaction. Each new baby—and there were scores of them—was a personal triumph for her; she felt in some way she imparted to them the spark of life.

For Debbie, like thousands of others, was swept up in the thing that was moving Israel during those months, a contagious spirit that was hard to escape: the sense of participation in something small enough to embrace, and great enough to move everyone—the bringing home of those in dispersion.

A million had to be brought home: a million not of those who had inherited the earth and could bring wealth to this new land, but a million of the most abject, poverty-ridden, diseased wretches, sick in mind and body. A million to be taken in by half a million! Nothing could stop them now.

The fever of participation in the Return had spread as far as America and South Africa and England, where the Jews of rich, free lands had sent a few sons and daughters to help and poured out unprecedented floods of wealth in their own gesture of participation. The drumbeats of this great In-gathering were being heard round the world. From millions in the United States came voluntary hundreds of millions in treasure. And from the sick world came the first two hundred thousand harassed immigrants, in ships and illegally, heading to the haven of Israel. The fever rose to crisis, and Debbie was taken with it. She felt each day as if she were walking with God, purified and devout.

There were moments when she noticed with a guilty start that Vic was completely out of her mind. Her best evenings were with George, and she spent more of them with him than she liked to admit to herself. He sometimes made a fifth in the flat for supper, or took her out to eat, and once in a while went with her to Karl and Lilith's with whom he managed indifferently.

During this time, no decision had come from the three-man investigating committee on Vic's case. The hearings, which were secret, were held in November and December and then recessed until April so that the Israeli delegation in London might take additional depositions from the Walkers and try to see John Halliwell. This, at least, was given as the reason for the delay. The newspapers carried little about the Marmorek case, except for small items when the hearings were recessed. Debbie, when she had time to think of it, wished the proceedings would stop dragging, and paid the modest bills whenever Aronowitz submitted them to her.

Then spring came suddenly as if it had walked in by a door. One day the hills were no longer bleak and brown, a new green surged upward everywhere. She could feel herself stir with the fresh almond blossoms; she felt the warmth of the new sun, reaching beyond her flesh into her veins and into the catch of her pulse beat. She felt new herself, as she walked home from the hospital on an April evening and found the courtyards flowering in Rehavia, the King George Park, and saw the fading morning glories on Gaza Road. How different from the last spring when she had been creeping from door to door, listening for mortars and worrying about Vic out on the Burma Road. Now she would not see him. There was a rude suddenness to her realization right now, almost a year later. For how many months had she known it clearly in her head, but not fully felt it, encompassed it? Now the final realization engulfed her. It was not green grief, but a full grown unhysterical burden. She knew that all the yearnings and hopes of last year were gone into blackness and that all her hallucinations that Vic was still maintaining his watch over her, or that Mama and Papa were still with her were illusions of which she was now unexpectedly and cruelly deprived by the new life of a new spring. Vic was no longer at her shoulder. Life renewing itself, she knew, was not death reborn, but was new in the truest sense, from God Himself. It was renewal, but it was also creation. And her new sorrow over Vic's eternal absence mingled in her mind with hope for the newest of things, and she had scarcely any sense of disloyalty.

George too must have felt the spring that day for he was in the flat after dinner with two tickets to the Philharmonic which was in town. They were doing Smetana's *Moldau* and Sibelius's *Fourth*. And George, whose living musical heroes ranged from Koussevitzky to Menuhin, had decided to go. He kissed David good night like a bear, hugged Meyer, pecked at Jacinta's cheek and swept Debbie out of the flat like a duchess.

"Heavens to Methuselah," she laughed, "you're in a wild fit, kissing everyone in sight from the boys to Jacinta. Lucky Elsa wasn't there."

George laughed. "I hope you don't feel slighted. The omission was absolutely intentional, I can assure you."

"Well, I felt ignored for the moment," Debbie said.

"If I ever started on you, I just couldn't stop," George said. "It's that simple." She could hear in his voice that he had stopped smiling.

She said nothing and they walked into the soft evening of Gaza Road. She felt deeply sorry that he could rouse nothing in her. She would have to waken under her own power. Perhaps now that spring had come again.

"Are you angry?" he said uneasily. "I probably should have kept my mouth shut."

"No," she said slowly. "I'm only sad."

"It would make things pretty complicated anyway," George said. "For both of us." His arm was around her shoulder and she was comforted at the touch of his friendly fingers; her arm went about his waist as they walked quickly, almost marching down Mamillah Road. At least she could make the gestures.

"You've been patient," she said. "But I think something in me is missing, as if part of me had died. If I were Catholic, I'd be a candidate for a nunnery."

"Let's not think about it now, not just yet," he said. "It's my fault for saying anything."

"No," Debbie said. "It's my fault for being less than human. I'm just not all there."

Forty-five

George had bought seats down front, in the laps of the violinists, and although the acoustics at the "Y" were not ideal, she was captured by the first light trickle of music.

Smetana's *Moldau* stirred her more tonight than ever before, not only as music, but as the well remembered river, flowing always more strongly and melodically, racing martially through the auditorium here in the "Y"; she closed her eyes and was for the moments of the music with Mama and Vic and Papa, sitting high up, at a table on the Barrandov Terrace in Prague watching Papa sip his beer, looking idly down on the river far below, bedecked with gay white holiday boats; and she knew in the sad swell of music the waste of Vic and his father and so many Czech people who had loved their native Vltava as few people ever come to love a river. The terrace, the river, the city, gifted with all the beauty of God's creation and man's intelligence, had been blighted by the greatest evils to be conceived by the minds of men. No doubt the beauty was more poignant for the cruelty that had been its handmaiden. How few good people, she thought, had fought for the cause of beauty! Without her knowing it, the music carried her on its tide, filling her mind with lost opportunities and people gone. If the people of Prague had resisted! Well, in Jerusalem she had had a second chance. Her random thoughts made the *Moldau* an experience of beauty and terror. Perhaps she was nostalgic only for her lost childhood, when all struggles were won by the angels, and villains were invariably put to rout. When the music came to its climax and stopped, she was too limp even to clap her hands, while all around she heard the bedlam of applause and vocal enthusiasm.

As the cheering continued unabated and the orchestra, on a signal from the conductor, rose for its bow, she saw Sam Pearlman behind the violinists holding his viola loosely and looking directly at her. That he was staring at her was not pure imagination because he nudged the player alongside and pointed at her and whispered to him under the roar of applause. She watched while both men then spoke to other members of the orchestra, twice pointing down at her; and one or two struck up what appeared to be an animated argument.

As the applause subsided, the conductor bowed again and retired to the wings while the audience headed for intermission smokes.

In the lobby anteroom she heard her name from far across the hall. A small knot of people she did not know were staring openly at her. She tried to ignore them as George lit her cigarette; then behind them an usher approached, and in a hushed whisper asked, "Are you Mrs. Marmorek?"

"Yes?"

"I have a message for you." He handed her a sealed envelope, and George gave him a tip before he scurried off. Her fingers were not quite steady as she opened the note, and she was conscious that the delivery of the message had focused attention upon her. Her heart sank as she read:

Dear Madam:

Several members of the orchestra who served in the Armed Forces and who have recognized you in the audience have refused to play the second half of the program unless you consent to leave the hall. While the management in no way associates itself with this sentiment, may I take the liberty of asking you as a special favor, in the interest of harmony and in the cause of music, not to return for the balance of the program? I am anxious to avoid any unpleasant incident, as I am sure you are also. I regret having to make such an unusual request, and I hope you will understand and forgive me.

A. KOHN, MANAGER

When she looked up from the paper in her hand, she felt hundreds of eyes upon her. She was trembling, more in rage than in sorrow. "George, are people staring? Or do I just imagine?"

"Where?" George said. "Who do you mean?"

"Everywhere, look! Just everyone!"

She could hear the whispers from the far side of the room, as if each person in the vaulted anteroom had his own microphone, wired to her eardrums. "There she is! That one with the dark hair and freckles; the good-looking one."

"The traitor's wife? What's his name again?"

"You know. Marmorek, something like that. Worked for the Telephone Office."

"Say, she's pretty cute."

"The looks come in handy for the sort of thing *she* does. How naïve can you get?"

"Started all this tumult in Tel Aviv! Imagine—she's looking for sympathy! You'd think she'd be ashamed to show her face!"

"I heard she had an English lover."

"I can believe it."

She crumpled the note into a small wad in her palm. "Let's clear out of here, George."

"Why? Don't you feel well?"

"No."

"What's in that note? Here, this way, there's a way out here."

She put her head down and followed him to the nearest exit and they left the building. They were on the winding path that passes the tennis courts and the Stadium behind the "Y," up to King George Avenue, and he took her up that way. George read the note.

"It doesn't matter," he said. "It doesn't mean a Goddamn thing. Really."

They were in the dark with only the smallest crescent moon for light and he couldn't see her contorted face. "Oh, George." Her wall of resistance crumbled and she felt shivering cold and afraid. "It's almost a year, a whole year."

George put his arm around her and led her up the stony path in silence.

They were close to King George Park, and she said, "Let's sit here a while. I'm so tired. I'm so tired of running."

They walked behind the old security wall, and in the almost moonless night, they were hidden from the street lights; they could barely see each other in silhouette. They were, it seemed to her, two disembodied voices talking across vast times and two far civilizations.

"I just can't run away any more, George. I couldn't care less for it. Fun's fun, don't you think?"

He lit a cigarette and she could see a glow and his soft lips set hard, and the tip of his nose.

"I know the feeling. I've been rejected myself, you know," he said slowly, "by experts."

"You, George? Who could possibly reject you?"

"My wife for one," he said. "I found the whole process most objectionable. It always is, I'm afraid. Especially if you've put a lot of yourself into not being rejected. After you've opened up, you know, and made yourself real vulnerable, then wham! It's just old-fashioned, unrequited love—nothing more."

"But *I* don't feel rejected," she said, "I'm just so *mad*."

"Well, maybe you don't realize it, but I think you've fallen in love with an idea," he said. "You've become a little mystical, I think, a little crazy. Maybe you're trying to prove something, I don't know. It's this pioneer thing, but I recognize the symptoms. You're in love, all right. It's got hold of you. I've seen you at the hospital. And naturally a kick in the shins hurts worse when it comes from your lover."

"I won't let them hurt me. I've made up my mind to it. I'll ignore it. Let them do their worst."

"My theory is there are only two cures for unrequited love," George said. "Time or a new love."

"I've plenty of time," Debbie said grimly. "All the time it can ever take. I'm learning to be patient and some day I'll make them eat the insults."

George drew on his cigarette. "What would you think of trying a new love?" he asked cautiously.

She reached awkwardly to touch his shoulder with tenderness in the dark and struck his elbow instead. He took her hand.

"I know, I know, you think you're not ready," he said. "But think about it—will you?"

"I will," she promised.

"And have pity, because I just don't take kindly to this unrequited love," George said as lightly as he could. "And since you don't either, I'm sure we'd make the most compatible couple in Boston. We'll get along real fine."

"Boston," she reflected aloud. It sounded far away and safe and comfortable. "We'd live in Boston, would we, George?"

"Hell, if you'd come with me I'd give up batting around and be glad to settle for Boston. What do I want with Hong Kong or Karachi? And if I do get ants in my pants I'll make tourist trips. But I've got what I was looking for. I could go home now and be content. With you and my daughter and David. I can get a spot in the editorial room. I'm a pretty well-seasoned newspaperman, you know. And I miss that Carol Ann. You'll see what I mean. She and David'll get along fine. We spend weekends together, she and I. Then I have three months each fall with her. I'm sure she'll like you."

"Did you love her mother very much?" Debbie asked.

"Barbara?" George said. "I don't know what you'd call it. It only happens when you're twenty. Like crazy colts we were. It's something wild taking hold of you. Like hunger or fear. Has nothing to do with anything adult, I don't think. Or anything especially human. It's the animal kingdom asserting itself, I suppose. Somehow we lived on it for a few years. Then we began to crop out as people. Just never was in the cards. She's married to a lawyer now in Brookline, quite a big wheel—and fifteen years older than Barbara. They seem happy. They have two kids of their own and he gives her everything I never could. Stability, position, coziness, very satisfactory for her."

"But you were hurt. And now?"

"I've had plenty of time. Three years."

"But no new love?"

"Not until now."

"What you say is tempting, George. It would be nice to go to Boston and never to hear my name again. I'd be Mrs. Stern, wouldn't I? Mrs. George Stern. And David could take your name too. And the word Marmorek would be gone. Vic could be forgotten in peace."

"You'd like Boston," George said. "It has everything. Concerts, theaters, fine hospitals, although you wouldn't have to work there. You could be a lady. Wonderful schools, beautiful homes. Great endless beaches, nice people . . . You'll like my parents—and you'll get away from all this tumult you've started."

"It's very tempting, George . . . and such a nice man goes with the offer."

"And I'm in love with you," George said. "I'm not trying to be an old kind-hearted benefactor. I'm not a sentimental kid. Neither are you. I think we'd get along, like the man says, till death parts us. I'm sure as a man can be. At least this man."

She was silent and he put his hand under her arm for support.

"I wish I could fall into your arms, George, and it could be like the movies. I do wish I could." She turned to look at him and their faces were an inch or two apart. She kissed him lightly and he let her pull away.

"Shall we go home?" he asked.

"Oh, I'm afraid Jacinta will want to know why we're home early and I couldn't be interested less in her questions. Let's go over to the Vienna for a cup of tea. All right? You see it isn't every day I get proposed to. I have to settle down."

"One word'll do it," George said. "It's really quite easy."

What was she to say? George's was not an invitation to be ignored or cast aside or returned unopened. What was she to do? She would have to think! She had to say something!

They were passing a newsstand, and what she saw in headlines at that moment pushed all thought out of her head. For a moment it was more than she could grasp. The words glistened, blurred, and refocused:

"COLONEL JULIAN HOROWITZ ACCUSED OF MANSLAUGHTER," the *Day* said, and the *Post* read, "KNESSET COMMITTEE BELIEVES HOROWITZ ERRED IN MARMOREK CASE." There were photos of Vic, Horowitz and Debbie on the front pages, and the articles were almost identical in treatment. The *Day* said:

The Knesset committee reviewing the Marmorek case, after having examined all the evidence at its disposal, including inquiries abroad, has today reported to the Knesset, through its chairman, D. Spirov, that in its opinion the death penalty was imposed on Marmorek in error, on two counts—first, because Julian Horowitz, Chief Intelligence Officer in Jerusalem, had insufficient authority to approve the death sentence and should have submitted the sentence for review to higher authorities in Jerusalem and Tel Aviv before sentence was carried out, and second, because the evidence against Marmorek was not sufficiently conclusive to justify the extreme penalty, in any case, and it is not beyond possibility that a completely innocent man was executed. Colonel Horowitz, who resigned from the Army last month in order "not to embarrass the Defense Department," was not available for comment in Haifa; and Mrs. Marmorek could not be reached either at her home in Jerusalem or at the Hadassah Hospital, where she works. Mrs. Marmorek has been seeking to clear her husband's name for over a year and it was her activity which led to the Knesset's investigation. Her attorney, Mr. Boris Aronowitz, Mapai member of the Knesset from Jerusalem, refused to make any statement except that he was gratified at the committee's findings. The Knesset reports and evidence have been turned over to the Ministers of Justice and Defense for action by their respective departments, and a reliable source indicated that formal criminal charges will be made by the government against Colonel Horowitz.

"Well," George said, "this is big."

"Yes," she said. "It's big."

"It's what you've been waiting for. How does it strike you?"

"I don't know," she said. "I don't feel anything, I suppose. Only the chills." She looked at the paper again and the shivers ran up and down her frame. Her throat would let no word out. Vic. Vic. The truth is coming. Hold on for it. She was staring at the paper and it blurred again, her picture and Vic's and Horowitz's. The words jumbled and she felt herself sway from side to side. She had waited so long.

"Debbie!" She heard George's voice from far away. So far! "Are you all right?"

She heard whirring voices, and their intensity grew. Louder, always louder. Good Lord, her head! "Debbie! Are you all right?" George's voice was closer now. His arm was about her shoulder.

She took the papers home to Jacinta, and exulted with her. She woke David to show them to him. Aronowitz had been calling from Tel Aviv all evening. She was to see Eli Rosenthal at his office first thing in the morning. Things would move fast now. Karl called, Lilith spoke. She was so happy. Absolutely happy for Debbie. Elsa called. Then Dick Alpert. Nurses and other doctors at the hospital . . . They had to take the phone off the hook.

Alone in her bedroom she was not much calmer. So much had happened in one night! Yet over and over, in spite of the headlines, her thoughts wandered back to the possibility of going off with George. Everyone dreamed of going to America. And this would be with such a nice husband. It was too good to be true. She knew she was beginning to need him, as she had needed Papa and Vic. He was her new rod. And always his phrase, round and round in her head. "You've so much passion for the living. Mustn't waste it . . . Mustn't waste it . . ." And George would be so easy to spend her passion on. She thought of his soft mouth set so hard. And his warm almost naked eyes. Her life in America could be full too. She could become lost there in the crowd. Boston would be more like Vienna. No one would know her, no one would care. She could listen to Koussevitzky, or go to the theater or to the cinema or chat with the neighbors, or walk in the great park there. She could shop in the great stores and try on everything, or sit in the fabulous beauty parlors. She would wear fantastic gowns and have furs for her bare shoulders, and be the kind of lady Mama and Papa had brought her up to be. She would never have to set foot in a hospital again. Not another day's drudgery. And David could go to Harvard University like George—anonymously, one of thousands, and she might have another baby and George's Carol Ann, and they would all be Americans, together, first class. She could take the children from the lakes to the sea to the mountains. She could be very happy. And George was a man she could love.

Run, Debbie, run! She could hear Vic urging her to it. The great American continent, broad and safe. Be sensible—what do you find here—in spite of everything you've done—except this stupid prejudice against you, drab people gone to seed; diseased and distorted newcomers; a barren countryside, with too many people herded and starving in our big new-style ghetto; Arabs on every frontier waiting for their day of blood and revenge? Fly stratoliner to a new world with your new love! Safety, safety, on the wings of TWA. And the warm and tender love of George Stern. It was a tremendous, almost overwhelming temptation. But something gnawed at her willingness. Something spoke against it, not clearly, nor exactly, nor articulately, but only foggily and in a weak voice. If only George would stay here, just a little longer, she had to have more time to think.

But just before Horowitz went to trial George told her his brother-in-law had finally lost patience and ordered him either to come home or to take the Hong Kong post. "If you stay in Jerusalem any longer, George, you just won't be working for the *Boston News*. I'm sorry, but I can't do anything more with His Nibs. After all, it's his paper." In a flurry of cables and with the aid of two long letters he got permission to stay for the trial, but then his time was up. Jerusalem was a dead post. Debbie knew she would have to make up her mind.

Forty-six

Boris Aronowitz went out of his way to get himself appointed special prosecutor for the Horowitz trial; while Horowitz chose as his lawyer Ami Ben Kepelow, who had been prosecuting attorney at Vic's trial. Thus the major participants in this trial were men who had been key figures in the Marmorek trial, and all could be expected to hold highly personal and subjective views.

The three judges of the District Court were Winkleman, Appenzeller and Lakosi—all men of spotless legal and judicial reputation, although Lakosi, the youngest, shortest and sprightliest of the three and a bachelor, had a racy reputation for courting several married women in town. Old man Appenzeller, lanky, bony, shy and pushing eighty, was known in legal circles for sleeping in court. He was easily bored and cursed frequently under his breath at legal ineptness. The word was he heard more asleep than most judges did awake. Winkleman was a legal workhorse, stocky, with slick, oily hair parted carefully on the side. He possessed the unyielding logic of a geometric proposition.

The courtroom at Bezalel and King George was a dingy room in an unadorned building; the pomp, wigs, robes, and rites of legal proceedings under the Mandatory Regime were ostentatiously absent. Aronowitz appeared in a short-sleeved white shirt.

George sat in the section reserved for the press, taking notes like the rest. Debbie was seated in one of the forty chairs reserved for the public. A court attendant saved chairs for her and Karl each day, in the second row, directly behind Horowitz's wife and seventeen-year-old daughter, for whom, with absolute impartiality, he also saved places.

Outside the courtroom, pickets carried a variety of signs. A large one read: JUSTICE FOR THE MARMOREKS; NO LYNCH LAW FOR ISRAEL. Others, cruder, and held aloft by aggressive shouting young men and women, said: DEFENDERS OF HOROWITZ, SAVIOUR OF JERUSALEM. Old Mrs. Heller carried a sign: MARMOREK KILLED JEWS, HOROWITZ DEFENDED THEM.

Before the trial there was a demonstration, when several pickets attempted to attack Aronowitz as he entered the building. The rioters were scattered by police with tear gas.

Newsmen came to interview Debbie at Gaza Road, stopped her at the hospital, accosted her in court, asking questions—most of them silly and often so personal that she had to think hard of Aronowitz's warning to restrain her temper. Her name and picture were in the papers daily. But inside the courtroom decorum ruled, at least for the moment.

At Aronowitz's table were the Rosenthal twins and the regular government prosecutor, an old man who never said a word. Ben Kepelow was assisted by a woman attorney, whose short hair and bushy brows gave her a more masculine appearance than his.

Julian Horowitz, the defendant, sat at Ben Kepelow's side, and appeared calm and confident. He smiled ruefully at his wife and daughter now and then, and waved to friends who came to court during the trial. On those rare occasions when his eye caught Debbie's, his expression became opaque.

David, busy at school, had only the vaguest idea of what the trial was about. "Have a good time at the trial, Mommy," he said ritually each morning as he tore downstairs with Meyer. Jacinta asked no questions.

On the first morning each attorney addressed the court with opening remarks. The *hamseen* was in full swing, and everyone was hot and irritable.

Aronowitz, as State Prosecutor, spoke first. His tone was even and his voice clear, factual and flat.

"On the twenty-eighth of May, 1948, Colonel Julian Horowitz arrived in Jerusalem from Haifa to assume command of the Intelligence Sector of the new Army of Israel. Upon his order, on the fifth of June, a little more than a week later, Lieutenant Victor Marmorek, then working as an engineer on the new road in the vicinity of Latrun, was arrested and brought to Jerusalem, charged with having committed treason and espionage on behalf of the enemy. Colonel Horowitz convened a court-martial, and in secrecy Victor Marmorek was tried on June seventh and eighth before three officer-judges. He was represented by counsel appointed by Colonel Horowitz, which counsel was given two days to prepare a defense and summon witnesses. He was found guilty on June eighth and was sentenced to be shot. Julian Horowitz, as Chief of the Sector, reviewed the trial transcript, findings and sentence of the court. Marmorek, through his attorney, presented arguments urging that execution of sentence be delayed, argument to the contrary was also presented by Captain Ben Kepelow, the trial judge-advocate. On June eleventh Colonel Horowitz ordered that the sentence be carried out without delay. Victor Marmorek was executed by a firing squad of six men on June twelfth, 1948. It is the contention of the State that the ordering of this execution by Horowitz constituted an act of manslaughter on two counts—first, that Colonel Horowitz, lacking full authority for his action, failed to submit the findings and sentence to higher military authorities in Jerusalem or

Tel Aviv for review prior to execution of sentence; and, second, that he refused to postpone execution until such time as certain evidence and witnesses could be secured to confirm or deny assertions made at the trial, and in this manner condemned Victor Marmorek to death on insufficient and incomplete evidence. It is the contention of the State that Victor Marmorek was, in fact, not guilty of treason or of espionage, but had devoted himself with unusual loyalty to the construction of the road, which was the salvation of Jerusalem, and prior to that had performed invaluable service for Haganah as chief engineer of the Telephone Office. It is the government's contention that while human error is to be expected in time of war, if the error has the grievous degree of usurpation and negligence encountered in this instance and the terrible consequence of death to an innocent individual, that error is criminal at the minimum and murder at the maximum. The State, therefore, obtained an indictment for manslaughter on these two counts, as most fairly taking into consideration all the factors involved."

Aronowitz bowed almost imperceptibly to the three judges and retired to his seat. He moved with great confidence after having spoken without once breaking his monotone. Old Judge Appenzeller was already beginning to nod his head and his eyelids drooped. He was going to be a hard man to keep awake. Judge Winkleman drank an incredible amount of water.

Ben Kepelow rose and now Debbie saw him clearly for the first time. He was strikingly handsome, she thought, rather sallow, Arabic, with bright white teeth and an engaging smile. Apparently charm was his long suit and he played it to the hilt for the benefit of the court. Speaking affably and conversationally to the judges above him, he was respectful, courteous and above all informal, almost chatty.

"If it please the Court, may I recall the circumstances which existed during the Battle of Jerusalem? Property damage, you recall, was appalling, loss of life so great that we are still without a complete count. But only the military leaders were aware of the degree of Jerusalem's real desperation. The enemy seemed to know every building, every post of military importance; they attacked them with mortars and damaged or destroyed them wholesale. The situation was so urgent, and counter-intelligence so desperately required, that Colonel Horowitz was transferred here from Haifa.

"As luck would have it, the day after he arrived an Arab Legionnaire was captured and had on his person lists of most of our important and sensitive positions. The lists consisted of addresses, telephone numbers and names. Many of these addresses were those of ordinary citizens, but the ones of interest to us were those belonging to Haganah, because the Haganah posts, all listed under fictitious names, were identified on these lists by a clear checkmark. The lists found on the prisoner were photostats of a report prepared and signed by Victor Marmorek and sent to Reginald Walker, the Director of the Jerusalem Telephone Department, at Walker's request, and was ostensibly a compilation of all new installations made since October, 1947.

"Marmorek was arrested and tried. He had a fair trial. The transcript of his trial will be part of the record of this trial. We believe it to be the only relevant evidence.

"If, as we now understand, new evidence is going to be introduced here bearing on Marmorek's innocence or guilt—and incidentally we haven't been given an opportunity to examine that evidence—it seems to be a pretty closely guarded secret—we believe it to be irrelevant; because it was upon the evidence presented at the trial and not upon *new* evidence that the judgment, sentence and execution were based.

"As to Colonel Horowitz's authority to approve the sentence, the Court is doubtless aware that the lines of authority were fairly muddled in those days in Jerusalem. That understates it a bit. It was far from clear or precise what authority existed for each individual officer, and personal initiative was not only the order of the day, but necessary. And it's a good and lucky thing that officers like Colonel Horowitz used their initiative; otherwise three Arab judges might now be sitting on this bench and all the participants at this trial would probably long since have been as dead as Victor Marmorek. That small fly in all this theoretical ointment about abstract justice is something I beg the Court to keep in mind. How this thing happened, the context in which it happened, these are important elements, aren't they? We were fighting for the lives of a hundred thousand people, we were fighting to save our city, the city which historically has meant more to civilized mankind than perhaps any other. We grant that a charge of overzealousness might be sustained here against the defendant. If too much zeal, too much conscientiousness, too much devotion to duty is a crime then perhaps Colonel Horowitz was guilty. If the love of Israel was a crime, then perhaps Colonel Horowitz was guilty. Instead of having to defend himself before this tribunal, the defendant should have high awards for service far beyond the call of ordinary duty. But that is not the business of this Court, and we don't want to stray. We are confident we shall be able to prove his innocence of any wrongdoing whatever in the Marmorek affair to the full satisfaction of the Court."

There was sudden and spontaneous applause and someone whistled enthusiastically.

Judge Appenzeller, who had been asleep, opened his eyes, grimaced as though to make certain his false teeth would not fall out and mumbled, "Thank you, young man. Anybody makes another sound, out you go, all of you. This is a courtroom, not a theater."

The stenographic record of the Marmorek trial and all its exhibits were introduced in evidence by Aronowitz, and the judges adjourned the trial for three days to permit themselves to read the transcript.

When court reconvened on Sunday Ben Kepelow made a motion at once to dismiss the indictment on the basis of the Marmorek trial transcript, but it was evident that he had no hope in this maneuver.

The motion was denied and the Government was asked to present its case.

Aronowitz placed himself on the stand as the prosecution's first witness and Eli Rosenthal questioned him.

QUESTION: After Marmorek had been sentenced by the court-martial will you tell us precisely what you, as counsel for Marmorek, did?

ANSWER: I went immediately to confer with Colonel Horowitz at his office.

QUESTION: Officially, or unofficially?

ANSWER: Officially, as defense attorney.

Q: Can you tell the Court what was the substance of your conversation on that occasion?

A: Yes, of course. I told Colonel Horowitz that I had been given insufficient time to prepare my case, as I'd told him repeatedly before, and that there were still several questions and matters which disturbed me, that I would like to see cleared up and which might have pertinence on appeal.

Q: What did he say?

A: At that time?

Q: Yes.

A: Well, he said he wanted to read the transcript and he would talk to me after he had read it.

Q: I see. You didn't discuss the substance of the case then until he had read the transcript?

A: That's right.

Q: And did you see him again after he had completed his study of the transcript?

A: Yes, the next day.

Q: And what transpired then?

A: Well I told him that I had studied the transcript myself all night and that I was only reinforced in my view that there were these questions I thought ought to be cleared up, investigated for an appeal. I wanted time to look into them. I told him that the trial itself should have been held up in the first place, and in a normal time any judge would have granted delay to investigate and study these matters.

Q: What was his reaction?

A: He said he didn't think there would need to be any appeal. He said that in his opinion it was an open-and-shut case. He asked me if I myself didn't think Marmorek was guilty. I told him I had no idea, but I thought these matters should be investigated, and that there should be more time.

Q: Were you able to persuade him?

A: Well, he said he was going to the synagogue, that it had been too long since he had been in one and he felt he had to go.

Q: These matters you felt had to be cleared up, could you tell us what they were?

A: Well, Marmorek claimed that he had submitted these lists of new phone installations to his boss, Reginald Walker, but that he had absolutely not put any checkmarks next to the Haganah numbers. On the contrary, he said, he had maintained the fictional listings of these Haganah numbers so that it would be virtually impossible for anyone to know which were Haganah phones and which were not. Nevertheless, the photostats of the lists found in the possession of the Arab prisoner had the checkmarks. If Marmorek made those marks, there would be no question of his intent, they would be clear proof of a traitorous design. But if he hadn't made them, there was a grave doubt as to his intent. He might have done something foolish, but with no intent to commit espionage. The question of intent seemed to me to be of paramount importance. I thought we ought to be able to pin down precisely just when these marks were made and by whom, in other words to trace that path to its bitter end. That was point one.

Q: And how did you propose to do that?

A: I wanted to question a man named Chaim Yehuda, who was the only photostating expert in Jerusalem I knew of qualified to tell from a photostat just what the checkmarks were made with, crayon or pencil or pen, so the checks could be matched against Marmorek's signature to see if they were made with the same writing instrument, whether possibly the photostat found on the Arab couldn't have been a photostat of a photostat that had been checkmarked. That was a theory of Marmorek's.

Q: What did Colonel Horowitz think of that?

A: He said Marmorek was getting pretty far-fetched and desperate and he couldn't give credence to a theory just because a desperate man under sentence of death suggested it. Besides he didn't think the question of whether the lists had checkmarks or not was relevant. He maintained that once the lists were out of Marmorek's hands, even without checkmarks, the damage was done. The rest was follow-up. Anyone with half a brain, he said, knew that of the new phones installed in that period from October to February a large percentage would be for Haganah. They were, if nothing else, lists to work from and Marmorek would have to be unbelievably stupid to let such lists get out of his hands. He asked me if I didn't agree.

Q: And did you?

A: I told him I could not read the compulsions of another man's mind. I couldn't guess why he'd given the lists to Walker as he had except that he'd been asked for them. His reasons might have ranged all the way from stupidity to false pride, from blindness to fear, but none of these things make espionage or treason; the penalty for stupidity is not the same as for wartime espionage.

Q: Did he give your arguments any weight?

A: Not that I could see. He only said people had been killed every day as a result of those lists. He said if Marmorek had the smallest ration of guts he'd have left all Haganah numbers off the lists. He told me of a whole series of disasters, most of which I knew about —stemming from the lists. I told him it might be advisable to wait until we could talk with Mr. Walker and question him directly, but Colonel Horowitz said he wouldn't believe what Walker said in any case. And he didn't think any Israeli judge would.

Q: Was there any other reason for his not complying with your request?

A: As far as I know, only the trial transcript itself. It was airtight to him, he said. As the transcript shows, Esther Schamel, the commercial girl for the Telephone Department—she was also a member of Haganah—testified that she had seen Marmorek's lists on Walker's desk, the originals, and while she could not recall for certain if the checkmarks were on them, it had seemed to her that they were, although she was not sure. That was the most we were able to get out of her.

Q: But the originals of these lists were not available at the trial?

A: No. All Telephone Office records had been moved to England. Only the photostats found on the Arab prisoner were available. As a matter of fact, Marmorek claimed he had got the originals back and destroyed them. That was another reason I wanted Walker. If he could supply the originals then Marmorek was lying. If the originals had disappeared that would tend to verify Marmorek's testimony.

Q: Then the substance of your plea to Colonel Horowitz was not to do anything about the sentence until there was an opportunity to get more conclusive evidence? Is that correct?

A: Yes.

Q: And his reaction was negative?

A: He said he was satisfied as to the completeness of the evidence, as any reasonable man would be, and he suspected that I was myself. He said that he had been to see Marmorek personally since our last talk and his sixth sense told him here was a man who was guilty and frightened and desperately telling all kinds of far-fetched stories. He said he was a pretty good judge of character, that he'd had a great deal of experience at this kind of thing. He said he had sought guidance in the only place where one could seek it in such matters—across the street.

Q: At the synagogue?

A: That's right.

Q: Was that the entire substance of your interview with Colonel Horowitz?

A: Officially, yes. But as a fellow-officer I urged him privately not to assume full responsibility for an execution. I tried to convince him to submit it to higher authorities in Jerusalem and if possible in Tel Aviv.

Q: What was his response to that?

A: He said he was sent out here to clean up a messy situation. He said he could understand my position, that I was trying to do a conscientious job for my client and I probably had to urge all these points, but his job had to be done also and he was going to do it. He said that this wasn't the English Army with red tape and protocol and passing the buck. He'd had about all he could take of buck-passing with Wavell in Africa. The unique talent we Jews had, he said, was initiative. He wanted to get on with his job and couldn't devote the rest of his life to the Marmorek affair. The man was a spy, he'd been given soft jobs by the British in return for this information, he'd probably gambled on the British staying on forever, he'd miscalculated and now he had to pay the piper and that was all there was to it. He said I'd done my duty, completed a very ugly piece of work quite conscientiously, and in his mind the case was closed.

Q: Was that the end of it?

A: I said I couldn't quite see the harm in waiting, and he said if he followed my advice, to get more testimony, more evidence, have more investigations and then submit the trial record to higher offices in Jerusalem and Tel Aviv with all the headaches those fellows were having already, why the Arabs would take over and we'd both be dead before Marmorek. And Marmorek would probably end up getting a medal from Abdullah and preside at our funerals.

Q: So you urged delay in putting the sentence into effect and Horowitz decided otherwise?

A: That's right.

Q: Do you know whether he consulted higher authority?

A: Well, I didn't know at the time. I assumed he had even though he wouldn't admit it to me. I couldn't see the sense of his sticking his neck out. But a couple of days later I learned that he hadn't consulted anyone.

"That's all," Rosenthal said. "No more questions."

"Why don't you go back to Russia, Aronowitz!" someone shouted. "They know how to treat your kind there. You're a disgrace to Israel!"

Judge Appenzeller mumbled, "Please remove that person from the courtroom. See that he doesn't return."

Then the ancient jurist raised his head from its normal position, chin on chest, and opened his eyes long enough to nod at Ben Kepelow. "Do you wish to question the witness?"

Ben Kepelow stood up and circled slowly, craftily, as if he were facing a dangerous and treacherous enemy.

Q: The defense of Marmorek was an assignment you were given, was it not, Mr. Aronowitz?

A: Yes.

Q: You didn't volunteer for the job out of a spontaneous desire to defend a man you believed to be innocent—or anything like that?

A: No. I was assigned the job of his defense just as you were assigned the prosecutor's job.

Q: And as a conscientious member of the bar you defended him to the best of your ability and used every device open to a lawyer in a case of this kind, such as maneuvers to delay, maneuvers to postpone. Is that right?

A: I did everything I could that I thought would serve the best interest of my client.

Q: But at no time in the course of the trial, not even in your summation to the court, did you urge flatly that your client was innocent. Isn't that what the transcript shows?

A: I don't know. I never studied the transcript from that viewpoint.

Q: Well that's what you'll find, if you're interested. Now let me ask you this. Did you encounter anyone aside from Marmorek who believed him innocent after all the evidence was in? I mean absolutely anyone who had access to all the evidence?

A: Well, there were only the three judges and yourself and Colonel Horowitz and the court stenographer who had access to all the evidence. I never discussed the opinion of the court stenographer with him.

Q: Weren't all these appeals of yours for delay just to salve your conscience that you were doing all you could for your client, when you yourself knew him to be guilty?

Rosenthal was on his feet to object and was sustained.

Q: As defense counsel you were supposed to do everything possible in the interests of your client, don't you agree?
A: Yes.
Q: You knew quite well who Colonel Horowitz's superior officers were. You knew that Colonel Steinmetz was commander of all forces in Jerusalem, and that Colonel Bar was Chief of Intelligence in Tel Aviv, did you not?
A: Of course I did.
Q: Then why didn't you appeal to these officers directly, *yourself*, instead of leaving the matter to Colonel Horowitz?
A: It would have been unheard-of procedure, counselor, and as a former officer you know it quite well.
Q: Was protocol so important? Talk about passing the buck. You keep saying a human life was involved. *Wasn't it rather that you yourself believed your own client to be guilty?*
A: Well, since you press me to it, I have a confession to make, Captain. I did, in fact, write to Colonel Bar and to Colonel Steinmetz both. Confidential notes that I have never previously discussed with anyone.

There was a moment of silence as Ben Kepelow almost physically rocked back on his feet. But he blinked rapidly and seemed to recover with great vigor.

Q: Then these officers were always aware of the intentions of Colonel Horowitz?
A: I don't think so. My letters didn't say what Colonel Horowitz planned to do, because I myself didn't know. I only presented what I considered flaws in the case against Marmorek and urged clemency at the time when they would review the case. I hoped that would force a review, frankly.
Q: Did you send a copy of these letters to Colonel Horowitz?
A: No.
Q: Wasn't that a rather extraordinary omission?
A: Yes. I didn't think he'd like it and I was still in the army, directly under his command.
Q: And what reply did you have from Colonels Bar and Steinmetz?
A: None.
Q: So that they appeared to have confidence in the decisions of Colonel Horowitz. Wouldn't you say that indicated without doubt his authority to carry out the sentence?
A: I'm afraid that might prove to be an unwarranted deduction.
Q: I have no further questions at this time.

Ben Kepelow backed away as if he were afraid to let Aronowitz out of his sight and Aronowitz joined the Rosenthals.

The second witness for the State was Colonel Emil Bar, Chief of Military Intelligence. The colonel was a tall thin youngish man wearing civilian clothes. Aronowitz conducted direct examination.

Q: Can you tell the Court your mission during the war, Colonel?
A: After April, 1947, I was in charge of counter-intelligence in all theaters.
Q: Did that include the apprehending of informers, spies and other agents of the enemy?
A: Yes, that was one of our primary functions.
Q: Did you succeed in apprehending a large number of enemy agents?
A: Well, sir, large is a relative term. We arrested a number of them.
Q: Were all counter-intelligence men assigned to various theaters under your direct command?
A: Yes, they were.
Q: Who assigned Colonel Horowitz to the Jerusalem theater?
A: I did. He'd done a good job in Haifa and we needed a reliable man there. We felt our counter-intelligence in Jerusalem was ineffective until Colonel Horowitz was sent here.
Q: Can you tell the Court your reasons for selecting Colonel Horowitz for this job?
A: I suppose primarily we selected him because of the results he had obtained in Haifa. Previously he'd been a captain in Military Intelligence with the British Force in Africa. He had a thorough knowledge of Arab methods of infiltration and he could speak Arabic. I always felt he had a sixth sense, a certain intuition that is a most important element in this kind of work.
Q: Who gave Colonel Horowitz his orders before he left for Jerusalem?
A: I did. Verbal orders only, there were no written orders.
Q: I see. Can you recall what you told him?
A: Precisely?
Q: As precisely as you can, it's rather important.
A: Well I don't remember with any great precision, but as nearly as I can reconstruct I told him the seriousness of our position in Jerusalem. That the city had no piped water supply and was short of ammunition, manpower, had no electric current, and was surrounded by strong enemy forces in the hills about the city with elements firmly intrenched in the Old City. Background material, really. I told him that according to our information the entire defense of the city was on an improvised basis and that he would have to improvise also. I told him he could take an officer or two with him to help organize his section and that an office for him in

the Agency had been arranged for. I told him, now specifically getting to his personal mission, I told him that while for reasons of Jewish morale we had publicly maintained that the destruction by Arab mortars was wanton, purposeless and nonmilitary, actually there had been a frightening number of direct hits on key posts and sensitive spots—so much so that it threatened the military safety and survival of the city. I told him I believed the enemy had developed an excellent system for obtaining valuable information and that I was leaving it to him to destroy that system.

Q: I see. Did you tell him he could convene courts-martial and approve sentences of capital punishment?

A: No. We did not discuss that. I gave him orders in general terms. I assumed he would develop a penal plan in Jerusalem with the commander there. Courts-martial are generally a function of command.

Q: Did you intend for him to exercise supreme authority in a case involving capital punishment?

A: No.

Ben Kepelow objected angrily after Colonel Bar had given his reply; testimony should be confined to what Colonel Bar had said and not what he may have thought or intended. The objection was sustained.

"No more questions," Aronowitz said with self-satisfaction and returned to his desk.

Ben Kepelow was his old affable self.

Q: Colonel Bar, you received a confidential letter from Captain Aronowitz, then acting as defense counsel for Marmorek, urging you to intervene in the case?

A: I received a letter setting forth arguments in favor of clemency. He didn't urge me to intervene. They were only arguments for clemency.

Q: What did you do about that letter?

A: I filed it. I intended to refer to it when the case was referred to me for review.

Q: But it didn't occur to you to intervene?

A: No, I was pretty busy. And I expected the case would automatically cross my desk for review.

Q: Colonel Bar, when did you first hear of the death sentence of Marmorek?

A: In June, I believe. Sometime, I don't recall the exact date, but I read it in the newspaper. The sentence had already been carried out.

Q: When you received this notice by way of the newspapers did you institute any disciplinary action against Colonel Horowitz?

A: Uh—no, not at that time, sir.

Q: Did you institute any disciplinary action at any time?
A: Yes, sir.
Q: When exactly?
A: In March of this year.
Q: You mean five months after the Knesset Investigating Committee had been authorized? After the newspaper editorials? After the pressure had built up?
A: I don't consider that my action was a result of pressure.
Q: But not prior to March did you do anything on your own initiative?
A: I have just told you disciplinary action was commenced—
Q: I know, nine months after the alleged misdeed had taken place. Nine months after you knew of it. Can you tell the Court why you didn't act earlier, Colonel?

Colonel Bar was rattled. He fidgeted in his chair a moment, then spoke clearly.

A: I had no reason to believe Colonel Horowitz had made an error. I assumed Marmorek was a spy, that the facts against him were absolutely conclusive. Probably that he had actually confessed.
Q: Thank you, Colonel. Those are interesting assumptions. Now, you told Colonel Horowitz that the entire defense of Jerusalem was on an improvised basis, you say?
A: Yes.
Q: And that he would have to improvise himself. Is that correct?
A: I don't know if those are my exact words.
Q: That's what you said in direct testimony. He should improvise himself. Those were your instructions. Thank you, Colonel. That's all. No more questions.

Colonel Steinmetz, the stoutish, rather pompous Military Commander of Jerusalem, next took the stand to testify that according to instructions he had from Tel Aviv he was responsible for all operations in Jerusalem and there had been no exceptions mentioned to him by the Chief of Staff. He considered the convening of a court-martial, if required, would have been one of his duties, rather than Horowitz's. He was certain that Colonel Horowitz was responsible to him for any action in Jerusalem, in fact he had reported to Colonel Steinmetz on his first arrival in the city.

When Ben Kepelow asked the witness about Aronowitz's letter appealing for clemency, and whether he had taken any disciplinary action against Horowitz, after he learned of the Marmorek execution, the Military Commander growled that he probably should have intervened, and probably should have taken disciplinary action, but he did not consider the precise moment when the city was surrounded by hostile Arabs as the propitious one for disciplining high officers in the Israeli Army.

Colonel Steinmetz was the last witness on Sunday.

After court Debbie and George met for a hasty supper at the Café Ben Yehuda. George was unusually quiet and preoccupied, and Debbie covered his hand with her own. "George, what is it?"

"Oh, I don't know. I just keep rather wishing this trial had never come to be. It worries me."

She smiled. "It's like you to be worried about me, of course. But I'm a big girl now, George. I won't be hurt no matter what turns up." Her smile took effort.

George sipped his coffee doubtfully. "Raking over all this, how can you help but be affected by it? I keep worrying over what it'll do to you."

"Nothing can do anything more to me," she said.

"Unless you lose this case," he said.

"I try not to think of that," she said. "We have to win it."

George studied her. "Or you may win," he said, "and be sorry."

"Why, how do you mean?"

"I don't know myself," George said hastily. "But things happen that way sometimes."

"As long as it comes out right for David," she said. "As long as Marmorek stops being a dirty word. And David can start with a clean mind about his father."

"Well," George said, "trials are funny things. You can be sure you're right, and sometimes—" He shrugged expressively. "Judges are weird people. I sure hope we do good."

"George," she said almost angrily, "you're not the faint-hearted type, are you?"

His face twisted into a wry grin. "Maybe I've just seen too many trials," he said.

As if by agreement, they never spoke of George's proposal now or during any of the days of the trial, but it was never completely out of her head and she knew it was uppermost in his mind. Perhaps he was hoping, in spite of himself, that they would lose, so she would flee with him to Boston. But they must not lose. Now and again she tried to imagine Boston and Carol Ann and George's parents . . . She might think of a visit . . .

The next day Esther Schamel testified. Debbie recognized her as the girl who took applications in the Telephone Department for new phones. Aronowitz had mentioned that the Rosenthals had worked hard on her story. Now he handled her carefully and politely.

Q: Where were you employed at the time of Victor Marmorek's trial, Miss Schamel?
A: I worked at the Telephone Office on Jaffa Road. I still do. I'm the commercial girl there.
Q: I see. And were you also the commercial girl during the entire period when Victor Marmorek was chief engineer and Reginald Walker was general manager?
A: Yes.
Q: Will you tell the Court what other activity you were engaged in during the time that Mr. Walker was in charge?
A: I also worked for Haganah.
Q: Can you tell the Court precisely what you did?
A: Well at first Mr. Kronstein and then later Mr. Marmorek would give me the names of people who would be coming in during the next day or two to ask for phone service and I understood from them that these were Haganah phones. For instance they would give me a name like the Brandeis School or Dr. Zises and I would know when people came giving these names, making applications in these names, I was to process their applications without formalities. Of course the application had to be approved by Mr. Marmorek and Mr. Walker. Those which weren't Haganah, we always made little difficulties for them. We would insist every detail be correct and sometimes we could delay those applications for two or three weeks longer than usual because there were only so many phones and we naturally tried to favor Haganah.
Q: Mr. Walker was not aware of this?
A: I hope not. I don't think so. He left almost everything to Mr. Marmorek.
Q: And what were your relations with Mr. Marmorek aside from Haganah business?
A: Well, I saw him all day in the office.
Q: Did you ever go out socially together?
A: Oh, no, sir.
Q: Would you say you admired Mr. Marmorek?
A: You might say so, I think.
Q: Could you say what in particular you found to admire in him?
A: Well, I thought he was a brilliant man. He was quite good looking, you remember, and very cultured. He played tennis with Mr. Walker and Mr. Halliwell. I'd never known another man like him. Not a Jewish man at least. He was like someone from another planet to me. Almost like an Englishman, and I knew he was taking chances to get these phones in. I knew if the British caught him he could have been shot.
Q: Weren't you taking the same chances?

A: Not as serious, no. I could always have covered up, I think. And the British never shot girls.
Q: You say you never knew another man like him. Would it be correct to say you thought Mr. Marmorek was glamorous at one time? That your feelings about him were of a rather personal nature?
A: I suppose, you might say, at one time, anyhow.
Q: And how did he feel toward you?
A: He never thought anything about me, I guess. Other men seemed to like me, but he never had any of the symptoms. At first I thought he was too high and mighty. He was always polite though. And then I knew his wife. She's a charming woman, pretty and so much more than I could ever be. So I just mooned over him like a silly girl. Of course, I was younger then. That was two years ago.
Q: Did anything happen to change your feelings?
A: Yes, sir.
Q: What happened?
A: Well one time when Mr. Walker was away in Tel Aviv I saw Mr. Marmorek at the King David Bar with Mrs. Walker. They were drinking together and having quite a gay time of it. I'd come to deliver some papers to Mr. Walker, to his room, and I saw them from the front desk. I'm sure they didn't see me. But the way they carried on together, you might say he was carrying on *something* with Mrs. Walker, because they kept looking at each other in a funny way, you know.
Q: Did you say anything to anyone about that?
A: I tried to tell myself I was imagining it. But I noticed other things. She was always coming to pick him up for tennis lessons and so on, the days when her husband was out of town. I felt it was no way to treat his wife. She so nice and all.
Q: Was that your state of mind when you were asked to testify at his trial?
A: Well, yes, and I began to have other suspicions about him too. Things I couldn't understand. I saw those lists on Mr. Walker's desk and I wondered about them. But then Mrs. Walker went back to England and right after her husband left, in March I think, Mr. Marmorek went to work full time for Haganah on the road and Mr. Kronstein came back to take over the Telephone Office.
Q: Now, Miss Schamel, you testified at Mr. Marmorek's trial, and this one very important point we have to clear up. You were asked if the lists you saw on Mr. Walker's desk had checkmarks alongside the Haganah phones, and you said the checkmarks were there. Is that correct?
A: I said I *thought* they were. I wasn't sure.
Q: Well, yes, you said that but you finally said you did *think* they

were. You weren't sure, but you *thought* perhaps there were checkmarks. That's what the transcript shows. Now may I ask that question again of you?

A: I don't remember, Mr. Aronowitz, I really don't. You might say my mind is completely blank about it. I've thought and thought about it.

Q: Then why did you say there might have been marks if you didn't recall seeing them?

A: I really don't know, Mr. Aronowitz. I don't know why I said anything one way or the other. I just don't remember. Maybe I did think so then. But I've thought my head off you might say, and I just can't remember any checkmarks. And besides I had no idea they were going to shoot Mr. Marmorek. If I'd any idea like that, if I'd known, I probably would have thought harder. Maybe I'd have remembered *something,* somehow. But I can't remember. Honestly. I swear it. When I read he was shot, when I bought the paper I was sick right on the street right there where I bought the paper. May God strike me dead, Mr. Aronowitz, I didn't know what to think or say to my God. But I couldn't remember any checkmarks. I only saw the lists a few seconds, I just couldn't recall.

Q: But you don't remember seeing checkmarks, is that right?

A: No. No, sir, I don't really remember seeing any.

Q: Now just one more question. After you testified at the trial, did I ask you further questions privately?

A: Yes, you did.

Q: And what did I tell you when we finished?

A: You said you thought there were no checkmarks, but you never told me he would be shot, you never told me that!

Q: Did Captain Ben Kepelow ever interview you again?

A: No. No, never.

Q: Did Colonel Horowitz?

A: No, sir.

Q: Thank you, Miss Schamel. No more questions.

Ben Kepelow looked at her darkly with his sharp black eyes.

Q: Miss Schamel, I won't keep you long. I just want to clear up one point. When you testified and I spoke to you before the trial, Mr. Marmorek's trial, did I indicate in any way what I expected you to say?

A: Oh, no, sir.

Q: I asked you questions and you answered them. Is that right?

A: That's right.

Q: You had no idea what answers I expected?

A: No, sir.

Q: Colonel Horowitz never attempted to influence your testimony?
A: Oh, no, I never even met Colonel Horowitz.
Q: And you did see the list on Walker's desk?
A: Yes, sir.
Q: And the list included Haganah phones?
A: Yes, sir.
Q: And you were uncertain about the checkmarks, and you are still uncertain. Is that correct?
A: That's right, sir, only I'm pretty sure I don't remember seeing any marks, but of course I only saw the lists a few seconds.
Q: That's all, Miss Schamel.

Aronowitz called Chaim Yehuda, the photostater. Ben Kepelow objected, this time with less vehemence, but with greater tenacity, and an argument of fifteen or twenty minutes ensued between Aronowitz and Ben Kepelow, the details of which Debbie could not quite grasp, except that Ben Kepelow insisted that any testimony by Yehuda would be irrelevant and not germane to the issue of Horowitz's guilt or innocence.

"If it please the Court," Ben Kepelow said in his most ingratiating manner, "we aren't retrying Marmorek here, are we? Or are we? Is that the purpose of this trial? I'd like to know. What kind of facts does the State propose to introduce, except to attempt to create another link in the chain of Marmorek's innocence? We hold that the defendant acted properly within the framework of his mission and knowledge, regardless of what new evidence may be introduced at this late date."

Aronowitz shook his head. "The testimony of this witness is tied directly to the first witness's allegations that he asked Colonel Horowitz to contact this witness during the Marmorek trial. We plan to show the witness could have been found and brought for testimony within a reasonable time."

Judge Appenzeller grunted and shook his head quickly at Ben Kepelow. "The indictment charges insufficient diligence in securing evidence, the approval of the sentence on insufficient evidence. Let's hear the witness."

Chaim Yehuda was a shriveled, bespectacled man, not taller than four feet ten, and terrified when he took the stand. He trembled throughout his testimony from the moment the oath was administered, although Aronowitz did his best to calm him.

Q: Can you tell us, Mr. Yehuda, what you were doing during the war?
A: Me? I was in Tel Aviv. I wasn't here at all. I worked in Tel Aviv.
Q: And what were you doing there?
A: Me? Working for Haganah. I already told you in your office.
Q: I understand, but now I want you to tell the Court.

A: Working in Tel Aviv, like I said.
Q: Where were you stationed?
A: In the city. In the Records Office. I did photostating, mimeographing, duplicating. That's my business. But who could do any business then? So I went to Tel Aviv. I'm an office man. Do I look like an infantry captain, or a flyer, maybe?

"Just answer the questions the counsel asks," Judge Winkleman said softly. "Confine yourself to direct answers."

A: Who me? Yes, sir. Yes, sir.
Q: (Aronowitz) During the time you were in Tel Aviv were you ever asked by your Commanding Officer to come to Jerusalem to testify at a court-martial?
A: Me? No, sir.
Q: Were you asked by Intelligence or informally or in any other way?
A: I just said no. No, sir.
Q: Would it have been difficult to locate you if someone had wanted to find you?
A: Me? I was in the same building for the whole time. My family knew where I was. Since 1947. Always right in the same room. Everyone knew where I was.
Q: If you had been called to Jerusalem, would you have been able to come?
A: Well, I could have come in that little plane if my captain would let me. But he was very strict, our captain, especially with old men like me. He was only a boy, spoiled, I guess. Headstrong, but what I was doing wasn't so important. I could have gone for a day, I think. Why not? But you never knew with that boy. Maybe yes, maybe no.
Q: Thank you. No more questions.

Ben Kepelow was up and studying the old man with interest.

Q: Mr. Yehuda, do you think you could look at a photostat of something, say a letter, and you could tell just by looking at it if it were a photostat of the original letter or a photostat of a photostat?
A: Absolutely.
Q: And do you think if something were written on the first photostat in the same handwriting and with the same ink you could distinguish what was in the original letter and what had been added to the first photostat?
A: Me? I think so.
Q: Have you looked at the lists that Marmorek made?
A: Yes.

Q: And you can tell whether those checkmarks were on the original lists or added to a photostat?
A: Me? Of course. The checkmarks were not on the original. Never. That's positively.
Q: How can you be so sure, Mr. Yehuda?
A: How can I be sure red is red and green is green? You just know it. You can't explain it, so I know it, that's all.
Q: You consider yourself an expert, Mr. Yehuda?
A: Me, I'm pretty good. I do first-class work. And business is pretty good too. Come to my shop any time, see for yourself.
Q: Have you ever seen this photostat of a letter before?
A: No. (*After examining the exhibit*) No, I don't think so.
Q: Well part of this letter was original and parts were added to it on the first photostat. Can you tell the court which parts are original?
A: (*After the witness had studied the letter for a few moments longer*) I don't know, I could try.
Q: Will you please do that?
A: It will take a couple of hours, maybe three, four hours. I'm a busy man.
Q: If the Court please, may we call this witness tomorrow morning to complete his cross examination?

The three judges conferred briefly.

"Very well," Judge Appenzeller said. "You can step down, Mr. Yehuda. Be in court tomorrow at nine."

It being only a short time before recess, Benjamin Elihu was called for brief testimony. Debbie recognized him as the bearded soldier who had come to summon her to the Agency. He was still in uniform, his sausage side locks still grotesque. He testified that immediately on Horowitz's arrival in Jerusalem he had been assigned as his aide.

Q: Could you testify as to the personal habits and behavior of Colonel Horowitz as you observed them?
A: His habits?
Q: Well, was he always calm and deliberate?
A: Most of the time, yes. But maybe not when things got complicated.
Q: Can you tell the Court what you mean?
A: Well, during the Marmorek case he was jittery. He used to snap his fingers a lot when he got nervous.
Q: Anything else?
A: He drank a little too, especially during the Marmorek case and after. Relaxed him, made him happier, I think. I used to feel sorry for him.
Q: And that was all?
A: Oh, once in a while he would lose his temper. Like the time I

couldn't find Mrs. Marmorek for him fast enough. He got so mad! I thought he would shoot *me!* But like I say, I felt sorry for him. Such a pfui job he had. I wouldn't wish it on a dog. Such people all day! Crooks, spies, Arabs, liars, women, my God, such women! Sometimes you'd think the Agency was running a regular "house." You know what I mean?

Q: That's all, Mr. Elihu.

Ben Kepelow shrugged. "No questions."

Court was adjourned for the day.

Forty-seven

George and Debbie took supper again at Café Ben Yehuda and read the account of the first day of the trial in the Tel Aviv papers. Most of them took a dispassionate view and none of the tension that pervaded the courtroom was reflected in print. The papers and radio appeared to be making a deliberate effort to play it down, like Deir Yassein, as something to be forgotten quickly, something necessary, but shameful in an undefinable way.

"I think the Schamel girl was helpful," George said. "Effective in a way. She must have had quite a crush on Vic."

"In all those years I scarcely noticed her," Debbie said. "Imagine that. And all that frustration tied up in her. To make her tell, well—almost a deliberate lie. Enough maybe to make the difference for Vic between life and— How could *anyone?*"

"She was only a kid," George said, "confused, scared. They probably showed her the photostats, and she went blank. What was the easiest thing for her to say? Maybe. Maybe yes, maybe no. Your husband certainly must have been a damned attractive guy."

Debbie ate in silence for a few minutes.

"He attracted me," she said vaguely. And she was thinking of Vic as he would look just after tennis, hot and happy and exhausted. "That Schamel girl might not have been very bright, but she certainly had big eyes, didn't she? She saw everything, didn't she?"

"You mean the lists?" George said with deliberate denseness.

"No, I don't. You know what I mean. Suspicious little bitch."

"Well," George was trying to be helpful, but was finding it difficult. "Suppose he did have a—well, a little something with this English girl, what's her name, Enid, probably didn't mean a thing to him. Lots of men . . . She's attractive enough . . ."

"I can't believe that," Debbie flared. "I'd never be able to believe it. Oh, I know he flirted with Enid and she with him. They were fond of each other, but it was harmless fun, they'd never think of anything beyond that."

"But suppose he did," George said lamely. "You might have to get used to that idea. Just try to suppose it."

She was suddenly furious with George. She could see exactly what he was doing. Trying to kill Vic for her, too. Once and for all, he probably felt. Men could be like animals almost. They hadn't changed since the days of the cave. And she spoke, suddenly bitter. "Don't you think we can get along, George, without maligning poor Vic? He—he can't even . . . Oh, it's sickening!" She rose from the table hastily and half ran to the hospital, but George made no effort to follow her. So she spent the night tending her sick children and slowly regretting her own stupidity. George had never said a malicious word about Vic to her, except right after he got back from England, to dissuade her from continuing her lonely crusade. And slowly it dawned on her. So that was it. That was why George wanted to forget the crusade. So suddenly. He was afraid of what she might discover. He'd talked to Enid. He had his own suspicions . . . Now wasn't that like George, he didn't want to see her hurt . . . How stupid could she get?

But there were two very sick babies in the ward and she had no help tonight . . . she'd have to think about George later. And Vic. There was the night of his promotion, when Elsa had pneumonia, and yes, he'd met Enid. And all the nights of working late for Haganah . . .

Before the third day's testimony began, Elihu Rosenthal called Debbie aside in the courtroom and asked her to come to Aronowitz's office directly after court.

At nine-thirty Chaim Yehuda returned to the stand and Ben Kepelow continued his cross examination.

Q: Well, Mr. Yehuda, have you studied the photostat?
A: Yes.
Q: And can you identify the parts of the letter which are original and those which were added to the first photostat?
A: No. It's not possible the way you've done it.
Q: Thank you. That's all.
A: But it's not the same as the list. The list I can tell.
Q: But in the case of the letter, you can't. That's all, thank you.

Judge Appenzeller raised his head slightly and looked at the witness. "Just stay put a minute, Mr. Yehuda. Can you explain why you can tell in the case of the lists and not in the letter?"

"Because, Your Honor," and the little man quivered, "the checkmarks are obvious, but this letter was made specially to mix me up. Very carefully. The same ink, the same handwriting, also this photostat is not very clear. The second one. And the first must have been very, very clear, so it's not easy. But with the list it's different. There's a difference in size, in texture."

Judge Appenzeller dropped his head back on his chest. "It's a matter of degree then?"

"Yes, sir, a question of degree."

"You may go now, Mr. Yehuda."

When Aronowitz called his next witness he did so without fuss, underplaying the moment. "The State calls Mr. Reginald Walker of London, England."

Debbie was startled when she heard Redge's name and when she saw him she was shocked. He had put on thirty pounds, his face was gross and his eyes were bloodshot. He smiled at her as he ambled toward the witness chair, two soldiers before him and two following.

"The State has considered it necessary to guarantee Mr. Walker complete physical protection, not only because of his nationality, but because of certain aspects of this case which might make him a target for anti-British hotheads. The Government has guaranteed his safety."

Judge Winkleman tapped his gavel at the growing demonstration of hisses. "The demonstration must stop, or the court will be cleared."

"It will be necessary for me to question the witness in English, if it please the Court, and my questions and answers will be translated for the record by Mr. Pirosh, the government translator."

The judges conferred. "If the defendant wishes to employ an independent translator it will be permitted."

But Ben Kepelow shook his head. "My client," he said, "is of English extraction. If there are any discrepancies in translation he will call them to my attention."

Q: Mr. Walker, during what period were you stationed in Jerusalem?
A: From 1944 to March, 1948.
Q: And what position did you occupy?
A: I was director of the Telephone Office for Jerusalem and its environs, sir, under the Communications Ministry of the Mandatory Regime.
Q: And can you recall just when Mr. Marmorek was taken on by your department?
A: Yes, sir. It was in December, 1945.
Q: Do you recall the circumstances of his employment?
A: Yes, sir. He was recommended to me by Mr. Benjamin Kronstein, our chief engineer at the time, who suggested we take him on as wire chief. We'd been without a wire chief almost a year, Mr.

Kronstein doubling up, and our service had suffered. I knew perfectly well that Marmorek was an illegal immigrant, that he had no certificate, but since it wasn't my job to detect illegal immigrants and since we desperately needed technicians, I took him on. I might also say that I was impressed with him not only as a technician, but as a man, right from the first day. From the moment I talked with him. He was my kind of chap.

Q: And over the years of his employment, were your relations anything more than that of employee and employer?

A: Yes, indeed. I became quite fond of him and of his wife also and the sentiment, I'm quite certain, was reciprocated. We visited each other's homes, went to concerts and theaters together, and so on. You might say we became close friends.

Q: Witnesses at Marmorek's trial testified that you made gifts to his family. A refrigerator, a bicycle, and a washing machine were mentioned. Can you explain why such elaborate gifts were given by a social friend?

A: Well, sir, Marmorek was managing on a limited salary, an income far below my own. He and his wife had lost everything in Europe. It's always more difficult for people who've had everything and lost it. They'd been accustomed to gracious living, rather, and I considered him my equal in every way. To be frank, I considered him my superior. I felt much the same way about his wife. There were no other people in Jerusalem I felt so close to, including English friends. We were *en rapport*, so to speak. You can say that, and I wanted to show it in some tangible form. I was pro-Jew and Vic Marmorek was my kind of Jewish chap. Here was a fellow I could really like.

Q: So you got him these gifts more or less to satisfy yourself?

A: Well, sir, not entirely. I always had the feeling that it was rather important for him to feel a certain sense of position for himself. Of being more exalted somehow than run-of-the-mill. That was what gave him his greatest sense of security, I rather think. He was pleased that his lad and my son played together and our wives were friendly. So was I, for that matter. You know it got so every Englishman was automatically taken for anti-Jewish. And vice-versa. But that was quite an oversimplification, you know, and that attitude used to irritate me. Matter of fact, I admired the Jewish cause and Victor Marmorek personified all that was best in the Hebrew. He was my kind of fellow, if you can understand that. So my gifts, I suppose, were given primarily because I knew they would give him pleasure. And also because it was my gesture of defiance against this assumption that we were all anti-Hebrew. Of course, I had no idea such gifts would be misunderstood or used against him.

Q: Didn't it occur to you that in view of the political situation—?
A: No, Marmorek and I avoided political discussion. We had a gentlemen's understanding not to talk politics. We played tennis together, we had a certain sense of sportsmanship that we recognized in each other, we went to concerts together, ate together, traveled together, talked shop together, but never politics. We had a kind of belief in each other as human beings that was beyond politics. Let me put it this way. We both thought strife and hatred a terrible waste. We looked upon ourselves as builders, as constructive in a literal sense. We felt if there was more contentment to go round, there would be less bloodshed. That's how we felt, I think. So we were really on the same team.
Q: I see. In 1947 did you dismiss Ben Kronstein from the Department?
A: Yes, we did.
Q: Why?
A: Well, Mr. Kronstein was an irritant. He brought his politics to work. He antagonized the Arabs working in the office, stirred up the Jews, and annoyed Mr. Halliwell from morning to night with Zionist propaganda, which, after a while can become tiring, and to an anti-Zionist like John, rather irritating.
Q: I see. And can you tell the Court why you appointed Mr. Marmorek to his job instead of anyone else?
A: Well, who else was there? He was the only person in the office qualified for it. He was next in line, as a matter of fact.
Q: I see. Now early in February, 1948, you asked Mr. Marmorek for a list of all phones which had been installed since November, 1947. Is that correct?
A: Yes, since October, in fact.
Q: Why did you ask for that list?
A: I'd received a memorandum from the Minister raising the devil about the time lag in the installation of some extra phones for a police station and for a couple of doctors, one Jewish as I recall, and one Arab, who had complained they'd had to wait months for phones. So the Minister asked me to review our priority system and give him a complete report. Simply as part of this process, I asked Vic Marmorek to give me a list of all phones installed, dates of applications and installation, and so forth, and a list of all phones applied for that were never installed, and the reasons for the delays or noninstallations.
Q: Do you have a copy of the memorandum you received from the Minister?
A: Yes, sir. Right here.
Q: Thank you. May I submit this in evidence, if it please the Court? Now, did you have any suspicions that the purpose of this memorandum was to locate Haganah nests?

A: I had no such knowledge, sir, and I don't believe so today. The memorandum did not ask for any lists. It asked for a general report on our procedures. My report to the Ministry included no lists. The only one who had the lists at all was me. It was my idea to ask for them. When I got them I put them in my personal file. I intended that they should stay there.

Q: Why didn't you file them in the ordinary way, in the open file?

A: It occurred to me that Vic Marmorek's tabulation might have phone listings that were illegal. I mean to say, your underground army, so I thought it safest to keep the lists out of anyone's hands.

Q: Why did you go to all that trouble?

A: Well, it was no trouble, and as I say I had the greatest admiration for the pluck of the Jews.

Q: That's quite unusual. Wasn't such an attitude considered by your superiors to be—shall we say—disloyal?

A: No, sir. I don't think so. We were neutral. We had made clear our intention of leaving the country. The UN had voted. We were committed to getting out. In my opinion, during those last days, helping the Arabs would have been quite unneutral. Locking the lists up in my personal file was an act of the strictest neutrality.

Q: Who had access to your private file?

A: No one except myself and my assistant, John Halliwell.

Q: And your wife?

A: Yes, of course, my wife. I used to leave my car keys in that file and sometimes when I was out of town and she wanted to use the car she'd get the keys out of the file, so she did have the key to it, of course.

Q: Then after you put the lists in this file did you ever look for them again?

A: Yes, in England, when this American chap, Stern, came and asked for them.

Q: Did you find them?

A: No. Not the originals at least. I found photostats of the originals. I was never able to learn what happened to the originals, although I did discover who had made the photostats.

Q: Can you give the Court that information?

A: It was my administrative assistant, John Halliwell. I asked him about it and he quite cheerfully admitted that he'd gone to my file, taken the originals and had several sets of photostats made.

Q: Did he tell you his purpose?

A: Yes, indeed. He said he had turned all the photostats but one over to the CID for investigation, but he had no idea what they had discovered. He hadn't bothered to check with them, which quite frankly I believe is a lie. We had quite a row over it. I told him what'd happened to Vic Marmorek, but he took a fairly dim view of the Jewish cause and although I think he liked Marmorek as well as any, and regretted his death, he felt thoroughly justified. John was one of those fellows who just had to get his licks in against the Jews. Of course, we were in England by then, your war was over, and there was nothing to be done.

Ben Kepelow objected to Redge's hearsay testimony about Halliwell after it was translated, and Judge Appenzeller sustained him.

Q: Do you have those photostats, Mr. Walker?
A: No, I took them from the files and gave them to the American newspaperman, Stern. He came with a letter from Mrs. Marmorek and I gave him the photostats.
Q: Are these the ones?
A: Yes sir, they are.
Q: If the Court please, may I submit them in evidence?

Suddenly from outside in the street a shout was heard and a storm of voices.

The four Israeli soldiers alerted themselves and automatically closed in about the witness as a rock crashed through the window.

"Kill the British spy!" a woman screamed from the street.

The spectators in the court stirred uneasily and craned to see what was happening outside. Sharp commands were heard in the street, then shouts of defiance, the muffled shot of tear gas, and finally the scampering of feet.

Aronowitz looked up at the judges, expectantly.

"Proceed, Counselor," Judge Appenzeller said casually.

Q: May I respectfully call to the attention of the Court that there are no checkmarks on these photostats? Now, Mr. Walker, during the month of June, before Marmorek was killed, were you questioned in England by anyone representing the Israeli Army or Government in connection with this affair?
A: No, not until two months ago. Mr. Spirov from the Israeli Parliament came and we had a talk. Of course, the American had come even before that and I talked to him as I've said.
Q: Yes, but I mean *before* Marmorek was shot. Did anyone from Israel see you or attempt to see you?
A: No, sir.
Q: Would you have been willing to talk with a representative of the Israeli Army or Government, say in June, 1948, at the time of the Arab-Israeli War?
A: Certainly, sir.

Q: And so far as you know, no effort of any kind was made to get in touch with you for this purpose?
A: No, sir. Not until Mr. Spirov from the Parliamentary Investigating Committee came to visit me, as I said.
Q: When did you know about Marmorek's death?
A: When I read it in the *London Times*. A very small article, just a sentence or two. In July, I believe.
Q: Thank you. The Government appreciates your coming all this way for this testimony. It's been a generous gesture. I have no more questions at this time.

Ben Kepelow's attitude of cordiality which he had used toward all witnesses changed completely and he addressed the witness arrogantly throughout cross examination, to the clear delight of most of the audience. His eyes flashed and his words were whips. But since his questions were addressed in Hebrew to the interpreter, much of the impact of brash informality was lost.

Q: Are you a rich man, Walker?
A: Well that depends . . .
Q: Don't quibble. Would you say you were worth a million pounds?
A: No. Not a million, not half a million. I should say I could be called comfortable, if money could purchase comforts any more, which it can't, at least in England.
Q: And yet you were able personally to purchase a bicycle for young David Marmorek, a refrigerator, an automatic laundry machine and smaller gifts for the family? Did *your* family have any of these machines?
A: Well, we lived at the King David, we had no use for them.
Q: Nevertheless, you bought the Marmoreks these expensive articles although you didn't have them yourself?
A: Well, my son did have a bicycle.
Q: I take it you were more or less Marmorek's patron, something of that sort, is that it?
A: I wouldn't put it that way, no, sir. I never felt more than his equal.
Q: I see. And do you have the bills of sale for these articles?
A: Bills of sale? No, sir. I threw them out long ago.
Q: Or canceled check vouchers?
A: No, sir.
Q: Or anything at all to indicate that *you* purchased these things with your own personal money?
A: I could call upon the man who sold them to me. Mister—uh—Liebling, I believe. Why, who else do you suppose would have furnished the money, Counselor?

Q: I'm asking the questions, Walker. You answer them. Did the Telephone Office or the Communications Ministry or any other branch of the Mandatory Regime, such as British Military Intelligence, furnish the funds for these so-called gifts to Marmorek?

A: No, sir. Why should they?

Q: I leave that to your imagination, sir. Now can we get off the gifts a moment? When you received these lists from Marmorek, you say you put them in your private file because you knew at once that those lists in the hands of the wrong persons could be very damaging to the Israeli cause. That's why you used your private file. In other words, you, as an Englishman, knew immediately the dangers and implications for the Jewish Army if these lists got out?

A: Of course. The CID could track down these places by their addresses and they might discover ammunition depots, workshops and so on.

Q: Good. So Halliwell knew the dangers to Haganah also. And the value of these lists to the Arabs?

A: Yes, sir.

Q: The only one who seems to have been completely unaware of this danger was Marmorek, who blithely handed you the lists and seems never to have given the matter another thought. Doesn't that seem strange?

Judge Appenzeller peered up from examining his fingers and squinted at Aronowitz for objection, but Aronowitz was doodling quietly.

Judge Winkleman said sharply to the stenographer, "Remarks of Counsel after the last response will be struck from the record. If Counsel wishes to sum up his case now he is free to do so, otherwise he will confine himself to asking questions."

Q: That finishes my examination of this witness. That's all, Walker.

Court adjourned for the day.

When Debbie told Karl she had to see Aronowitz at his office, he was glad to come along. They hurried away before George could reach the street. She felt so helplessly stupid about George. She had only a few days more of him and here she was, avoiding him. Karl walked beside her briskly. Now, he wanted to participate with her. Karl had grown steadily less antagonistic about Vic ever since the day Aronowitz made his speech in the Knesset and one might even think he had brought the whole thing about himself. He sat proudly beside her at all times and Debbie, grateful for his changed attitude, was uncritically pleased to have him there. As they walked down to Aronowitz's place in the Center, Karl joked about Yehuda, the great photostat scholar, and reluctantly admitted that there was much to admire about Reginald Walker. "Perhaps I misjudged the fellow," he said. "It's so rare to see an Englishman with his views. Even so I can't help thinking he looks down his nose at us. Gotten damn fat too, hasn't he?"

"Prejudice will surely get you prejudice," Debbie scolded, "and you're always standing first in line for your portion. I'd like to talk to Redge again, perhaps Boris can tell me where he's staying. I'm surprised he hasn't come to see me, you know. I think he was rather sweet on me."

"Vanity," Karl laughed. "You're all vanity."

"I take after my son," she said.

At Aronowitz's office she was disappointed to find that she wouldn't see Boris himself.

"He's out with another witness," Elihu Rosenthal said mysteriously. "Very important witness."

Rosenthal wanted to go over Debbie's testimony with her. She was to take the stand in the morning and there were a few points to be clarified.

Most of Debbie's testimony would deal with the day she learned of Vic's death, and even going over the events tended to agitate her. She was glad Karl was with her, because he kept her calm. When they were finished Rosenthal thanked her, almost gallantly.

"You'll be all right on the stand tomorrow? I mean it won't be too difficult for you? We'll do our best to make it as easy as we can, and I don't think Ben Kepelow will dare attack your testimony. He might not even question you. But if he does, just answer his questions honestly. You're too honest a person to be rattled."

He was a gentle young man and made her feel as though everyone was concerned with her welfare. "You overestimate me, Eli, but thanks."

"How's it coming, Counselor?" Karl asked, man to man.

"Hard to say," Rosenthal said. "Anything can happen in court. Judges are funny people."

"What does Mr. Aronowitz think?"

"He's hopeful."

"Tell him I'm furious with him," Debbie said cheerfully, "to find he has some other witness more important than me. Heavens to Methuselah, I've always considered myself his favorite client. Whoever can it be, Mr. Rosenthal?"

"Do you think he tells me anything?" Rosenthal shrugged and smiled. "See you tomorrow, Mrs. Marmorek. You go on first. About ten-thirty."

"Sure thing. And Mr. Rosenthal, have you any idea where I can get in touch with Mr. Walker?"

Eli Rosenthal avoided looking at her. "I'm sorry. I don't."

Forty-eight

When Debbie took the stand, her knees shook and her hands fussed. The solemn but curious expressions on the faces of the judges made her feel that this was indeed judgment day.

But whenever she looked at Horowitz sitting placidly or peevishly beside his lawyers, she grew stronger. As her testimony unfolded she became surer of herself and at last she sat there feeling for all the world like a great avenging angel. Here they were—the judges, Horowitz, and Vic, through her. She had brought them here. She had made them listen. In the press section she saw the score of men and women from all over the world. Her countrymen would hear and the world would hear.

Her quavering voice became a trumpet. She was a giantess in that chair. A goddess! If Vic could see her at this instant!

Aronowitz used her testimony to establish further Horowitz's jitteriness and pounded the fact that she was not notified of the trial, sentence, or the review until after Vic had been executed. He struck home his thesis that Debbie, who was the one person with the necessary motivation to move heaven and earth to save her husband, was given no opportunity to seek help. Aronowitz appeared to be satisfied with her responses and Ben Kepelow refrained from questioning her.

When Debbie's testimony was completed, Aronowitz addressed the judges. "We have one last witness, gentlemen. She has come to this court at great personal sacrifice and since she is under considerable strain, may I beg the indulgence of the Court and request that she be treated with courtesy by Counsel for the Defense and others who question her?"

Judge Appenzeller opened one eye and after what seemed to be one long wink, closed it again. Judge Winkleman nodded solemnly. And for the first time in the trial Judge Lakosi looked up with interest. Judge Lakosi was famous for his gallant treatment of ladies in distress.

"Our witness," Aronowitz continued, "is Mrs. Enid Walker of Chelmsford, England. May the record show that she has flown here at the expense of the Government to testify in this case, but her coming has been voluntary."

Enid was called and entered the room timidly. She had changed less than Redge. She looked tired, almost listless, a little thinner, but in spite of her strain and fatigue, she made a stunning figure with her dark-gold braided hair forming her crown. She wore a becoming white linen suit which accentuated her high color.

Q: Mrs. Walker, you are the wife of Reginald Walker?
A: Yes.
Q: And you lived in Jerusalem during the entire period he was stationed here?
A: Not quite. I came here a month after he arrived in 1944 and left four weeks before he returned to England.
Q: How long have you been married?
A: Twelve years.
Q: Now, after you returned to England, were you ever notified that Mr. Marmorek was on trial for treason and espionage?
A: Yes, Mr. Aronowitz. I received a cable from you asking if I could make a deposition touching on several matters. But your cable was eight days in transmission.
Q: Do you have a copy of that cable?
A: Yes, Mr. Aronowitz.
Q: If the Court please, may we submit this cable in evidence? Now, what was your response?
A: I replied that I would be willing to do so. I sent my reply by cable to you in Jerusalem, but I understand you never received it. By then it was too late in any case, wasn't it?
Q: Do you have a copy of your cabled reply?
A: Yes, I do. Right here. And also an affidavit from the Telegraph Office in Chelmsford, which prepared this copy, that the cable was actually filed by me—June sixteenth.
Q: May we submit these in evidence? And when did you learn of the execution of Victor Marmorek?
A: Not for several weeks. In a monthly review I ran across a small article.
Q: Your husband testified that he read an article in the *London Times,* I believe. Is that correct?
Court Stenographer: Yes, a small article in the *Times.*
A: Well my husband and I were living apart. We were preparing for legal separation. He was in London and I was in the country.
Q: So although you were willing to make a deposition, and you replied in that sense, the fact is you never were able to testify, since by the time you received my cable Victor Marmorek had already been executed. Is that correct?
A: That's right, he was gone by then.
Q: A bit louder, please, Mrs. Walker, so the Court can hear you. At any point did you receive a message of any kind from Colonel Horowitz or from Captain Ben Kepelow?

A: No.
Q: I have no more questions at this time, Mrs. Walker, but it may be necessary to ask you a few more questions later, perhaps tomorrow or early next week. Are you prepared to wait over?
A: Yes, I'll be glad to.
Q: Thank you.

Judge Winkleman nodded across at Ben Kepelow. "Do you wish to question the witness?"

Q: Yes, Your Honor. Mrs. Walker, just how well did you and your husband know the Marmoreks?
A: What do you mean?
The witness reddened.
Q: I didn't intend to offend you by the question, Madam, I meant did you socialize with them, have them to dinner, play cards with them, that sort of thing?
A: Yes, of course.
Q: Did you have other Jewish friends?
A: Yes, we did. But the Marmoreks were our closest.
Q: Are you aware of the fact that your husband gave rather elaborate gifts to the Marmoreks?
A: Yes, I am, of course.
Q: Did you approve of his giving them?
A: Well, it was my idea to give them the refrigerator. It's so difficult to keep food fresh in the heat here and Mrs. Marmorek was out a good deal of the time at the hospital.
Q: I see.
A: But I must confess that the automatic laundry machine was my husband's idea and I thought it a bit extravagant of him. Although as long as he was willing to do it, I approved. My only fear was that I didn't want the Marmoreks to feel beholden to us in some way. As if we were lords of the manor and they mere pensioners. I had too much respect for them.
Q: But it *did* occur to you that they might feel in some way beholden to you and your husband? Pensioners, as you say?
A: Yes, I thought they might. I hoped not, but I knew there was that possibility.
Q: And your husband was fully aware of this possibility?
A: I suppose so, but he thought if it were offered in the proper spirit, there should be no question over it.
Q: But it occurred to *you* that the receiving of such large and widely known gifts from an English family might compromise the Marmoreks in the eyes of their fellow countrymen?

A: No, it did not. That is not what I said.
Q: No more questions, Madam. You may step down.

Judge Appenzeller snapped his fingers at Aronowitz. "Your next witness, Counselor."

Aronowitz rose at his desk and said flatly, "We have no further witnesses. We will rest, but may we reserve the right to recall Mrs. Walker if we deem it necessary?"

The judge nodded, looked across at Ben Kepelow and said glumly, "Does the defense wish to commence its presentation now, or would Counsel prefer to wait till morning?"

"Your Honor," the defense lawyer replied amiably, "I should like to make a motion to dismiss. I have listened carefully to the prosecution's case. We believe the evidence here has been totally inconclusive and I submit that the State has failed to make a prima facie case. In the first place . . ."

The judges heard Ben Kepelow out, and reserved decision. Court was adjourned until the next morning.

Debbie scrambled out of her seat and tried to catch Enid outside. As she stepped into the sunlight, she saw Enid being helped by Aronowitz into an American limousine. "Enid!" she called, "wait a minute!" But Aronowitz pulled her friend into the car after him and they sped toward Zion Square and out of sight.

She wondered through the night at the hospital why Enid had come all this distance. The testimony that she gave was neither conclusive nor very helpful, Debbie thought. Puzzling. It scarcely seemed possible that Aronowitz had brought her from England simply to demonstrate again that Horowitz could have sought her out and didn't. It was certainly clear that Horowitz had been in a hurry and had sought no one out. Oh, her mind was becoming sharp as a razor. She was thinking like a lawyer these days. When would she be a woman again? She'd have to find Enid tomorrow or Sunday and they would have a long talk.

The defense motion to dismiss was denied and Ben Kepelow was asked to commence his presentation.

"I have only three witnesses," Ben Kepelow said quietly. "I should like to call Mr. Samuel Pearlman first."

Ben Kepelow conducted all his direct examination with the same geniality and warmth that he had used in his cross examination of all hostile witnesses except Redge.

Q: Mr. Pearlman, according to the transcript you were a volunteer in Haganah. Can you tell the Court during what period you served?

A: Well, when I was thirteen, I guess you might say I began. It was not Haganah then, just cells. I took messages from one cell to another. I carried small arms, grenades, ammunition. I started my way up, you might say. Nineteen thirty-two I started, as a kid.

Q: And what was your mission in 1947?

A: I was supposed to find quarters for various establishments. Arms dumps, first-aid stations, machine and repair shops, observation posts. I was doing this work since 1946.

Q: And what did finding such quarters involve?

A: Well, I had to get a house, an apartment, a cellar, any place, make sure it had room for the purpose and electric service, phone service, good visibility, good arrangements for warning in case of raids, and so forth.

Q: And how did you arrange to get phone service?

A: Well at first it was difficult. We worked with Kronstein. He was a reliable man, but he was frightened and timid. His work was slow. He was a great patriot in conversation, but when it came to action he was—well, slow. Although don't get me wrong. He performed great service. Naturally, all our installations had to be falsified for the records of the Telephone Office, and exactly how he managed the records down there, that I never knew. That was *his* business. I had plenty to keep *me* busy. During this time I found there was a new man—Victor Marmorek—in this department. I found out also from Kronstein that Marmorek was advertising for a teacher for his son for concertina lessons. Nice boy too, David. Talented. Well, so I play the viola in the Palestine Philharmonic, also the saxophone, and tinkle the piano a little. It's not exactly the concertina, but it's all music, so I practice the concertina for a week and apply for the job. I'm hired. Not much competition, luckily! And while I'm teaching David, I'm studying the father. He doesn't talk like a patriot, but you can't always tell from talk. On the day the UN voted, he says It's a cup of hemlock. But the big talkers, like I say, you never know. So I drop him a hint, if he ever wants to do something he should let me know.

Q: And did he?

A: Yes. Just a little after Kronstein is fired and our requirements for space are getting heavier, around September he tells me he's ready. To me, it's a godsend.

Q: What did you give him to do?

A: Well I don't know what he expected, but I explain I need phones, three, four a week. He was disappointed. I think maybe he expected to go out on shooting raids—Commando, a musketeer. I explain to him how important the work is, one phone can save a dozen men, so, while he doesn't like it, he agrees and he's better than Kronstein. That I must say. Although once in a while he worries me. But we got better service than the British Army. Valuable man. At least so I thought.

Q: I see. And how often did you meet Mr. Marmorek?

A: Once a week at the boy's concertina lessons. Wednesdays.

Q: And did you continue to meet weekly as long as Marmorek was at the Telephone Office?

A: Of course.

Q: And he continued to install phones for you?

A: Yes. Right up to the day Walker and Halliwell left, in March.

Q: Now, you say he worried you. Was there anything specific that gave you concern?

A: Well, just after the UN vote, he tells me he's quitting. Quitting the phone company, going to Tel Aviv. This worries me, of course. So I tell him to think it over. But I'm beginning to be not as sure about his reliability.

Q: What happened?

A: Well, after a couple of days he calls me up. Changed his mind. He's going to stay. Believe me, it's a relief. But I'm always thinking about his reliability after that. He makes me nervous. He's going, he's staying, he's staying, he's going. This way and that. He's like that, can't make up his mind.

Q: Did he at any time tell you that he had given his boss lists of new phones including all those that he installed for you since October?

A: No, sir.

Q: Did he ever imply or in any way indicate that your phones had been tabulated and listed and were out of his hands?

A: No, sir. Although when I think back, he behaved worried.

Q: If he had told you, what would you have done?

A: We'd have been able to move all our installations. Transfer them. It would have been a terrific job, but we'd have had no choice. And we'd have saved a lot of men and equipment.

Q: Did it make any difference that the listings were camouflaged by using doctors' names, sanatoria, schools and the like?

A: What's the difference? The CID would send agents to each address, to check up. You couldn't camouflage the address. Actually the CID people did come and we never discovered it. So they knew every installation Marmorek listed.

Q: The only way you could have known about it was for Marmorek to tell you the lists were out?

A: That's right.

Q: Do you have any idea why Marmorek never told you?

A: I can guess.

Aronowitz got to his feet, but before he could open his mouth Ben Kepelow smiled grimly.

Q: Perhaps you'd better not. Can you tell the Court the number of casualties that resulted from mortar fire on these targets?

A: I have only approximate figures which have been tabulated over the last six months. Haganah members dead, 182; injured, 86; stores of materials destroyed or lost, approximately seven hundred tons, much of it irreplaceable machinery. Those figures don't include civilian casualties, men, women and children.

Q: Thank you, Mr. Pearlman. No more questions.

Aronowitz yawned. "I have no questions."

Ben Kepelow's second witness was the Arab prisoner, a small, smooth-shaven youth who entered court wearing his fez jauntily. He looked constantly behind him, as if he expected to be followed.

He was questioned and replied in Arabic and evidenced lively interest and even amazement at the simplest questions.

Q: Ask the witness if this was the document that was discovered on his person at the time of his capture by Haganah troops.

A: It is the same document.

Q: Where did he get it?

A: From his commanding officer.

Q: Were there many such lists in existence?

A: Yes, many. The commanders of most mortar teams had copies. He says this list was known as the Legion's Fifth Column.

Q: What was it used for?

A: Each night the commanding officer would indicate on the lists the places to be attacked that night by each particular gun crew, and with the aid of field glasses and published city maps, that crew would attempt to hit the one or two buildings designated as its target for the night. All rounds for that night were fired at those targets, so that the same buildings might be hit two or three times or oftener in one night and never attacked again.

Q: Does the witness know the origin of these lists?

A: Only what he heard. He is aware, of course, that Marmorek was shot for preparing the lists.

Q: Did the witness testify at Marmorek's trial?

A: Yes.

Q: And he testified that it was common gossip among the Arabs that the lists were the "work of a Jew in the pay of Trans-Jordan." I'm reading from the trial transcript.

A: That's correct.

Q: Does he think these lists were of great value to the Arabs?

A: He says they called the lists Jordan's atom bomb. They were of tremendous value also to their morale. He says if the Legion had had a little more luck they could have taken the city.

Q: Thank you. That's all for this witness.

Aronowitz: "No questions."

The last witness was Julian Horowitz testifying in his own defense. He took the stand with dignity and exuded strength, and, although he was stooped and physically unprepossessing—his large horn-rimmed glasses and loose clothing did not add to his glamour—he created nonetheless an illusion of command. His nonmilitary bearing had a military effect. Spectators sat straighter in their seats and leaned forward attentively. He insisted on testifying in English, which required more translation.

Q: Can you tell me the circumstances of your assignment to the Jerusalem area?

A: The circumstances were desperate. We had only a handful of useful troops. The British, bless them, had seen to it before they left that our position was the worst possible. We'd held on because of the willingness of a handful of men and women to risk everything to hold the city. They used anything they could lay their hands on. Improvising this and that stratagem.

Q: What were your specific instructions?

A: I was advised that military targets were being hit with regularity by mortar fire. That the enemy was all about us and among us. Arab lines were forty meters away; it was impossible to know where spies or saboteurs might be. It's not difficult for a clever Arab who has a working knowledge of Hebrew to pass as a Jew. Colonel Bar told me to clean up the situation. He indicated confidence in my ability based on the counter-intelligence job I'd done in Haifa.

Q: Did Colonel Bar ask you to submit court-martial decisions to him for review?

A: No, sir, never mentioned it. On the contrary. He told me to improvise, to do whatever had to be done.

Q: Did he ask you to submit such decisions to Colonel Steinmetz?

A: Absolutely not.

Q: Did he tell you that you were authorized to convene courts-martial from among your staff at Jerusalem?

A: Not specifically. It was the usual procedure to apprehend suspects, and not to try them.

Q: When you reported to Colonel Steinmetz did he specifically ask to review any court-martial findings?

A: No, sir. He simply said he was damned glad I'd come, that he needed help, that there were spies everywhere.

Q: Did the question of capital punishment come up?

A: It did not. It's implicit in the work. Spying and espionage during hostilities historically, traditionally and militarily always imply capital punishment, don't they, really? It's the only logical punishment, a necessity, in a way.

Q: You say that the usual procedure was to apprehend suspects, but not necessarily to try them. What made you order the trial of Marmorek?

A: It was clear to me and my staff that we were dealing with our prime culprit—that Marmorek was not just a sometime spy, but that he was our master antagonist, the classic traitor. We were dealing with naked wickedness and betrayal. Everyone's blood reached the boiling point during the interrogation.

Q: Was this your own private conclusion only?

A: No, sir. It was yours as well as that of your assistants. I have always believed it was the conclusion also of Marmorek's attorney at the trial, at which he was given every imaginable opportunity to present his case. It was also the opinion of three judges who had no reason to be prejudiced against him.

Q: After the sentence of the court was referred to you for review, will you tell the Court the steps you took?

A: Yes, sir. I read the transcript of the trial carefully, twice. I conferred with Marmorek's attorney twice. I conferred with you, the trial judge-advocate, twice. I interviewed Marmorek personally on three occasions. And I prayed.

Q: Were any one of these factors conclusive in your decision to approve the sentence?

A: I'd say looking back that no single factor was absolutely conclusive. I think my interviews with Marmorek swayed my mind against him as much as anything. I saw a picture of absolute guilt.

Q: Did any factors enter the picture during your interviews with Marmorek that didn't appear in the trial transcript?

A: Well, yes. At the trial he maintained that he had retrieved these lists from Walker's private file and had destroyed them. Completely unable to explain the existence of the photostats found on the Arab prisoner. Simply couldn't understand it. He would not explain how he could have had access to Walker's personal file. But after the trial he told me privately Walker's wife had got the lists for him. Why she should've done so he absolutely refused to say at first. Then later as the time approached for his execution he said he and Mrs. Walker were lovers and she'd done it for him at his urging. Well, now really! This struck me as preposterous. And he could still not explain why he'd never warned Pearlman that he'd given Walker those lists in the first place, or how the photostats came into being if he'd destroyed the originals. He became incoherent. Kept saying he'd intended no harm to Haganah. That his intention should count for something. The lists, he said, had remained in the files six days between the time he'd given them to Walker and the time Mrs. Walker retrieved them. Someone might've made a photostat of them during that period. Well, it soon became apparent to me that he was improvising from minute to minute. Lying and trying to cover himself, and he was getting in deeper all the time. When we asked about his gifts from Walker and his rapid promotion in the Department we drew a complete blank. He fell back on his friendship for the Walkers. Well, I've been friendly with a good many Englishmen. I was an Englishman once myself, in fact, and not one of them has ever bought me a refrigerator or a washing machine and I might say my wife could use them both. The man was twisting, turning and lying more deeply with every breath. He was as guilty a man as I've seen. He'd sold out his people, his city, his country, and if you can believe his remarks about Mrs. Walker, he'd sold out his wife and family as well.

Q: So that in your mind there was no doubt as to his guilt based on the evidence and based on what he told you privately?

A: Absolutely none. The man was guilty, in my opinion, a conscious spy in the pay of the English. His pay came in the form not only of material gifts, but of this prestige we've heard so much about, job advancement and this feeling of equality with members of the Mandatory Regime, which feeling was apparently of the mightiest importance to him. There are chaps like that, y'know.

Q: Was there any question in your mind as to your authority to approve the sentence?

A: None. Colonel Steinmetz was up to his neck. Colonel Bar was in Tel Aviv. I had work to do. We had to get on with it. I didn't want to make a *cause-célèbre* out of a common spy. I'd do the same today under the same circumstances. After all, we lost six million chaps in Europe. And here was a man who'd betrayed them all. Not to mention all the living.

Q: Thank you, Colonel.

Judge Appenzeller nodded to Aronowitz, who rose and stood silent before Julian Horowitz a long time. When he spoke it was quietly, gently, but Julian Horowitz sat erect now, stiffly on guard. He squinted as he replied to Aronowitz's restrained questions.

Q: You heard the testimony which I gave as a witness for the government, relating to the conversations between us after the trial.

A: Yes?

Q: Is there any particular in which you feel clarification is necessary, or are you content to confirm those conversations?

A: I think you gave a substantially correct version of our talks. Quite fair.

Q: Then can you tell the Court as you have never satisfactorily told me, either when I was attorney for Marmorek, or more recently, why you refused to submit the findings of the court and your own recommendations to higher authority?

A: I did just explain that. It wasn't necessary. I told you then and I repeat now, under the circumstances as they then existed, with mortars shattering our key points, good soldiers being lost every day, I couldn't see then and I can't see now why a great to-do should be made over the life of a traitor, who was so clearly guilty that I thought he'd received rather overcareful treatment as it was. Anywhere else in the world he'd have been taken out and summarily shot without trial.

Q: Wasn't that actually what happened?

A: No, sir. There *was* a trial. A stenographic record was kept. You have it. He was defended by counsel. You defended him. He had a full opportunity to explain his actions. Every safeguard.

Q: I see. Now you just said he was so clearly guilty, I think those are the words you just used, "clearly guilty," and yet you refused to wait, you refused to pursue either of two possible courses, one, to wait until the balance of the evidence was available or, two, to submit the matter to higher authority. In view of your feeling that Marmorek was, as you say, clearly guilty, why were you afraid to wait for absolute confirmation? Why were you in such a hurry?

A: I didn't need confirmation. I was already two hundred per cent certain.

Q: But you're only one man. Wouldn't it have been wiser—?

A: I was the man vested with the authority to make the decision, Mr. Aronowitz, and I made it. I was well and faithfully advised. Two of the judges I appointed were attorneys, specially chosen because they were. I was advised by you. What you said was not persuasive to me at our two meetings, but I listened to every word. Every word. A decision had to be made. And it was necessary that there be an example for the population and to deter other would-be spies in the city.

Q: Ah, you needed an example. You had to deter spying. And was it not important that the person selected for this purpose be absolutely guilty?

A: You're putting words in my mouth, Mr. Aronowitz. In this case there was the perfect combination. An example, and an absolutely guilty man.

Q: But making an example was an important element to you, was it not? You never admitted that before. That would explain your haste. Didn't you deny it to me in our conversation?

A: I don't recall one way or the other, old man.

Horowitz began to twist a lock of his hair slowly, thoughtfully, into a short horn.

Judge Winkleman leaned forward to clear his throat.

"May I ask the witness a question?" The room stilled. "The defendant served in Intelligence of the British Army. Was it conceivable to you that any Intelligence Officer, regardless of rank, in His Majesty's Army could have had authority to convene a court-martial, review the verdict and sentence, and in the case of capital punishment, order an execution?"

Horowitz blinked. "When I served with the British Army in Africa, no circumstance of that kind arose in my presence, sir. The British Army had ample personnel. We had a completely staffed legal department. But the situation in Jerusalem was quite different."

Judge Winkleman cleared his throat again. "As I understand military law in most countries, the armed forces usually have a legal department of one kind or another to handle courts-martial. Is that correct?"

"Yes sir, but we had none in Jerusalem."

"In the face of no clear orders, directives or commands from superiors and no clear regulations, wouldn't you as a former officer in the British Army, have been justified in falling back upon customary international military usage and merely turned your prisoner over to the legal department for trial? Even if that meant you had to hold the prisoner and wait until a legal department could be constituted for the army in Jerusalem?"

"I suppose so, Your Honor. Theoretically I might have, but I don't think such action on my part, such fine points would have reflected the realities of the hour. There are millions of dead chaps. Their views had to be taken into consideration also."

"Very well," Judge Winkleman said nodding to Aronowitz, "you may proceed."

Q: What made you refuse to send for Chaim Yehuda? You heard him testify that he was available.

A: Not necessary. All that about checkmarks, a tempest in a teapot. The lists were out. Marmorek had given them out. They bore his signature. Whether he'd put the marks there or not, he'd given out the lists. The enemy had them, the enemy used them.

Q: And you admit that you refused to wait till we could call Walker and Mrs. Walker?

A: Not necessary. Not necessary at all, my dear fellow. They were English accomplices. The judges would never have believed them.

Both hands were at his temples; he twisted his hair with greater urgency.

Q: But death is so final. And a little time might have answered all these questions. Didn't you want them answered?

A: None of these steps was necessary. The man was guilty on the evidence and now that all this so-called new evidence is in, you see he's still guilty. You've had your say, Mr. Aronowitz, and I've listened to it, and I still say the man was guilty. He committed crimes against his own people, atrocious crimes, costing scores of lives. If you ask me his punishment was too damn quick and merciful! I've listened to it all. I'll be glad to hear any more on the subject, but nothing has convinced me or ever will convince me that this man Marmorek was anything but a blackguard directed by the most unworthy of desires and I did only what I thought right and just and necessary.

His hair, where he had twisted it, stood erect, like tiny horns. Debbie had a desire to see him literally strangle. She had never felt so cruel.

Q: Thank you, Colonel Horowitz; you may step down.

Judge Appenzeller looked to Ben Kepelow, who taking Horowitz's elbow and leading him to his seat, said to the judges, "The Defense has no further witnesses."

Aronowitz looked about and then as if he were in some confusion said to the judges, "If it please the Court, may I recall Mrs. Walker? I should like only a short time with her."

Ben Kepelow shrugged and Enid was sent for.

Enid Walker was composed when Aronowitz questioned her again. Her hands remained folded in her lap and she kept her attention steadfastly on Aronowitz. Debbie now found it impossible to catch her eye.

Q: It was stated by Mr. Marmorek at his trial last year that after he gave these lists of phones to your husband he recovered them within a short time and destroyed them. At the trial he refused to say how he had recovered the lists. Miss Schamel testified that only your husband, you and Mr. Halliwell had the key to his private file. Did you obtain these lists for Marmorek?

A: Yes, Mr. Aronowitz, I did.

Q: What prompted you to do so?

A: He asked me to. He told me it was terribly urgent for him.

Q: And you did it as a friend? To help a friend?

A: Yes.

Q: But without telling your husband?

A: Well, Mr. Marmorek told me if I were willing to do it I must do it without telling my husband. If my husband knew, the damage to Mr. Marmorek might be greater, and I understood what he meant. Men sometimes become touchy over their private concepts of duty, which some women, including myself, consider of little importance.

Q: Can you tell the Court what Mr. Marmorek's state of mind was at the time he asked you to retrieve the lists?

A: He was disturbed. More distraught than I'd ever seen him in the years we'd known each other. For a few days before he'd been secretive and obscure and it was plain to me that something quite serious was troubling him. I tried to pry it loose from him and he finally broke down and told me. It was those lists he'd given my husband. No one knew about them except Redge and him, and he felt that it was a mistake for him to have included certain phone listings. I understood him to mean certain illegal Jewish military installations, which he began now to think he could have left off the lists since Redge was making no effort to check them.

Q: Hadn't he told his wife about these lists?

A: No. He told no one. While Mr. Marmorek was very fond of his wife, he considered her almost a child and not really up to sharing these matters. I think he rarely discussed this or most of his other difficult decisions with her. I believe he wanted most to protect her from these realities. There was only Redge and himself who knew about the lists, and then—me.

Q: Did he tell you why he hadn't omitted these Jewish installations from the lists in the first place?

A: Well, he was afraid Redge might have the lists checked and it would have been a comparatively simple matter to see if he'd falsified them in any way. Then the fat really would've been in the fire for the Jewish underground and, of course, for Vic. He'd have been arrested by British authorities.

Q: Had he thought of notifying Jewish authorities of his dilemma?

A: Yes, but he was afraid the Jews would consider him a fool. Especially one chap, named Pearlman, I believe, whom he seemed more concerned over than any of the others. He felt if he could only retrieve the lists before they were put to any use or transmitted to anyone he wouldn't have to tell this Pearlman chap. He felt he'd done a good job for the Jewish Army and after we left, if we did leave, he'd be in line for a position of some importance for his contribution to the Jewish forces.

Q: He felt in some way that if he had to tell Pearlman about giving up the lists, he'd have lost face with Pearlman, is that it?

A: I suppose you might call it that. He was an odd chap in that way. He was most anxious to be in the good graces of his own people, especially the prominent ones, as the time drew nearer for us to leave. He took all sorts of risks. And he was worried that if he told Pearlman about the lists all these installations would have to be moved bodily to avoid detection by the Tommies, and the moving would be done at great cost and hardship, and in the end he would be blamed for the tremendous cost and inconvenience which he might have prevented if he'd been willing to risk his own safety by falsifying the records to my husband.

Q: Did you feel that your going to your husband's private file and getting these things for Mr. Marmorek was in some way disloyal, as an Englishwoman?

A: No. I was doing it for a close friend. To me the personal relationship is the only one. I'm not one for politics or nationalism. He and I were alike that way. Vic, I mean.

Q: And after you had obtained the lists what did you do with them?

A: I gave them to him. To Mr. Marmorek.

Q: And what did he do with them?

A: We burned them.

Q: Where?

A: In my apartment at the King David.

Q: Did you actually see them burn?

A: Yes, I did.

Q: And what was Mr. Marmorek's state of mind afterward?

A: Relieved, hugely relieved. His tension was almost gone. He'd asked me if I'd found any copies or photostats of these lists in my husband's file and I told him there were none. Actually I hadn't been able to go through the entire file, but I hadn't found any, and I thought it unlikely there would be. Miss Schamel surprised me in my husband's office, you see, while I was at the file. I told her I'd come for the car keys. Later I discovered there actually *were* these photostats in existence that I'd missed, but I didn't know it then.

Q: Thank you, Mrs. Walker.

Ben Kepelow glared at Enid sideways from under his dark brows and spoke sharply.

Q: Mrs. Walker, you are a religious woman, are you not?

A: Well I'm Anglican, if that's what you mean.

Q: You believe in the existence of God?

A: I do, of course.

Q: You are trying to tell the truth to this tribunal before your God? And you expect this tribunal to believe you?

A: Well, Mr. Kepelow, I didn't come all this way to tell stories. I came to do what I could to help clear up a tragic mistake.

Q: Isn't it a fact, Mrs. Walker, that you connived with Victor Marmorek to turn vital military information over to British authorities?

A: It is not a fact, Mr. Kepelow. That is a stupid falsehood, which I understand has been repeated, but it is false, no matter how often you may repeat it.

Q: Do you expect this Court to believe that you went secretly to your husband's private file to get something for a man you'd known only as a friend, that you'd do something which you must have known would be considered disloyal by most Englishmen and surely by your husband, simply because you wanted to do some poor fellow a favor?

A: He wasn't just some poor fellow, Mr. Kepelow. He was a very close friend. I'd known him and his wife—

Q: Let's leave his wife out of it, shall we, Mrs. Walker? Isn't it a fact that you and Marmorek cooperated in other ways at many times? You're an attractive woman and an intelligent one, Mrs. Walker. Isn't it true that for some months you and Marmorek were furnishing information to the CID?

A: No, sir.

Q: Isn't it true that for a matter of months you were lovers?

Enid sat for a moment, her expression unchanged. The courtroom was suspended in intense silence.

Then Aronowitz was on his feet with objections.

Judge Lakosi leaned forward with obvious interest, and as the judges conferred in undertones he gesticulated and spoke vigorously.

At last Judge Appenzeller spoke in a low monotone. "The witness will kindly answer the question. The relationship is relevant."

Q: Were you lovers?

A: Yes.

Her voice was barely audible, but Debbie heard it clearly, like a drumbeat.

Q: And did you both not conspire to have him obtain these lists of military information over many months and then transmit them to British authorities? The truth please, Mrs. Walker?

A: No. What I have told you is the entire truth, Mr. Kepelow. I've told you something I've never told anyone else before except my husband. We are separated because of it. Our marriage is on the rocks because of it. But it's the absolute truth. I don't believe Mrs. Marmorek has known until this very instant because neither her husband nor I would ever have done anything to hurt her. She is a completely nice person, deserving much better treatment than she has had at your hands, sir, or at mine. I've told you this truth because I want to persuade you and these honorable judges of the complete truthfulness of everything I've said from this box. We were lovers. But we never conspired to give information. Our relationship had nothing to do with politics. It was a human relationship. Perhaps too human. Now, Victor Marmorek, may God have mercy on him, did one very foolish thing. He gave my husband those lists. He did it, I suppose, partly from fear, partly to stay within the good graces of my husband as long as my husband managed that office. Mr. Marmorek was never certain we British would leave Palestine. Nor, as a matter of fact, was I or anyone else. No one knew precisely what would happen, even after the UNO vote. He was a cautious man, Mr. Marmorek was. But a very nice and charming one.

Q: You mean he played both sides of the fence?

A: I say he was a cautious man. He'd been trained to be cautious. He'd had to be cautious and walk a narrow line in order to stay alive all his adult life. He'd been through all the frightfulness of living under Hitler and Mussolini, his wife's parents were killed in cold blood and his own father was lost, God knows where or how. He was a good man, but he'd learned to be exceedingly careful, Mr. Kepelow.

Q: Thank you, Mrs. Walker, for your spirited defense of Marmorek. Perhaps we can leave these orations to his attorney.

A: Are you finished with me then?

Q: Yes, Madam, you may step down now.

Debbie got up from her seat and ran to the lavatory without a word to Karl or a glance at Enid, and sat dizzily on a toilet in a closed booth, afraid she would black out. She dropped her head between her knees so that the blood would go to her head and then when she was clear-headed she began slowly to rock and sob, like an old woman, as if she had just this moment heard of Vic's death. She saw him now at Enid's bosom, a partner in a series of lustful and far-fetched images. She could hear them pitying her, admiring her, poor Debbie, poor Debbie, that poor child. Debbie is so innocent. Debbie is a goose. While Vic is, of course, a full man and Enid a full woman. She thought that all the little tricks of love and lust which she had taught herself for Angelo, which were necessities like the nightly stories of Scheherazade, variety and ingenuity, the mother of her own stimulation after a while, had not once entered her bed with Vic. She had meant someday to break down and share her secret evils with her husband, but she'd been afraid. Enid, no doubt, had as good an imagination and fewer inhibitions. She and Vic. Yes, Enid was Vic's woman of the world, his mother, his conscience, and slowly as the minutes passed, her sobbing subsided, the images dissolved and she heard Enid's words, "Neither her husband nor I would ever have done anything to hurt her." In half an hour she felt a little more composed and her mind worked harder. Little Debbie had been locked out, locked out, locked out. Out of all the things that had troubled Vic so, because he knew she had too simple a mind and saw things only one clear way. Why shouldn't he have been afraid to tell her? Afraid of her disapproval, for she had locked him out with all her scorn and criticism. She knew it too, and it was a bitter thing to know.

Someone had come into the outside room and was washing and she became aware of where she was. She would have to restore herself to respectability. Karl was no doubt waiting and perhaps George. And then she began to think that Vic was dead. She thought of the burial, of that day he had fallen askew into the ditch. She wanted to get him up, to unbury him, to ask him a hundred questions. To say she was sorry. To say she understood. To tell him about Angelo. To find out what Enid meant to him.

Now was she free? At last liberated from her debt? Free of Angelo, free of guilt, free of everything? She no longer owed herself to Vic. There was nothing to make up. She suddenly wanted more than anything else to see George.

Forty-nine

The person outside turned off the water now, there were rapid footsteps, and she heard George's voice call, "Debbie—are you all right?"

She put herself together, after a fashion, and opened the door. He looked almost as bad as she felt, drawn and frightened over her. She felt a gush of gratitude and warmth for George's concern. Without a word she leaned on his arm, and he led her out into the steaming street, ignoring her red-rimmed eyes.

"Karl had to go meet Lil for supper," he said, and she had a sense of relief. "Where shall we go—Vienna Café?"

"No," she said. "Let's go to your place."

"Why?" he said surprised.

"I want to tell you something," she said. And now she could not wait, the words came pouring out as they walked. "When I was in Rome I knew a man, a rather interesting man named Angelo di Sabatino. He took care of Vic and me. Protected us, got Vic a job. It was dangerous to help Jews in those days, you know. He liked me and he did everything he could to make me his sweetheart right under Vic's nose. It was not very nice, but those were odd days. Anyhow, at last I agreed and we were together. Right in the same room with David while Vic was working nights. He rather threatened to turn us over to the Nazis if I didn't. But I'm sure now he was bluffing. He liked me too much." George walked in silence. "But I wouldn't take any chances. Safety was the big thing. Vic used to say that. And I used to tell myself that I had David to think about."

"I see," George said. He had headed for the café.

"I never told Vic, in all the time we were married I could never bring myself to tell him in words, but I think he knew. Little things he said and did. Not that he ever blamed me. Wasn't that stupid of me never to tell him?"

"I don't know," George said. "What good could it have done?"

"I think it might have done me good. That's why I made up my mind to tell you. I'll feel better. I used to spend an awful lot of time just thinking about it in those days. Me with my piano lessons and French lessons and my perfect manners. Well at least in one field I was a self-taught girl."

She could hear their footsteps as they clomped across the gutter. "The worst part of it was that I enjoyed Angelo. I was so wicked. That's the part I was afraid I'd never tell you."

"Why not?" George said. "Those weren't days for philosophy."

"He was nice and I felt sorry for him too. He had a crippled leg and a huge inferiority complex. I think he really needed me."

They walked a hundred steps and George said, "That was five years ago, wasn't it?"

"Just about. Seems like a hundred."

George put his arm around her waist. "You've had a tough day," he said.

"I've been thinking, George, about going to Boston—and about you. You're so nice. You know I am beginning to become a little more—oh, I don't know—stirred up. At least I think I could be stirred up, George. By you."

He walked more rapidly, but he was heading for the Center. "I don't think you ought to try to decide anything tonight," he said. "It's been a long day."

She pressed on, ignoring his reluctance. "After all, George, it's not as if we were children. We're as grownup as we'll ever be, maybe. And whether I can go with you or not, why should we cheat ourselves? I'm a woman who knows she loves you, George. I know it now. Shouldn't we think of doing something about that?"

As they turned into Jaffa Road at the Square, he said, "Hell, I'd do anything for you, Deb, you know that. But I can't help you get even, can I?"

Debbie said, "But it's not that. I don't want to get even with anyone. I just want you, darling. Really, truly, tonight. Now."

"I'm afraid it's not so simple," George said. "You'd better go to the hospital, like you always do. I'll be with you in spirit."

He was teasing her again, kindly, but still teasing. She was furious with him. It was as if he'd doused her in ice water. But she remained silent. It was a bad day and it would be a bad night.

At the hospital she was called into the hall at about three in the morning. Redge was waiting for her. He shifted his now ample weight from foot to foot and smiled rather frantically when he saw her.

"Debbie, dear. It's good to see you. I just couldn't go back without dropping by, you know. I'd never forgive myself. How are you, my dear? Has this all been a ghastly nightmare for you?"

The words tumbled out, almost meaningless words that covered curiosity and a sadness in Redge she had never seen.

"I try to keep busy. Between the hospital and David, I keep going, Redge. How's it been with you?"

"Oh Lord, the less said the better. We're a regular pair, aren't we? The shy type, we are. Is David well?"

"Yes. Fine. And Lloyd?"

"Quite well, thank you."

Here we are, she thought, two people who have so much to say to each other, the questions she wanted to ask teemed through her mind, but she knew she could never ask them. More than a sea and a continent had separated them.

"It was generous of you to come all this way, Redge. I'd like to thank you."

"Nothing at all," Redge said, and she saw his fingers close and open spasmodically. "I hope I've still got something of the good sport in me."

"Will you be here long?"

"Afraid not. Affairs at home, you know. I may be going to Canada."

"Oh. That should be interesting."

"Well, I hope it shall."

"It was terribly sweet of you to drop in to see me."

"Pleasure was mine," he said. "Are you sure you'll be all right?"

"Oh, yes."

"Quite sure?"

"Yes, thanks."

"Well—good-bye, then. Good luck. Say hello to the lad for me, will you?"

"I surely will."

The summations took most of Friday morning. Aronowitz spoke from notes, in his flattest style. Debbie tried to listen, but his words faded in and out of her consciousness.

"The Government charges manslaughter . . . two counts . . . First . . . the defendant ordered . . . without authority . . . failed to submit . . . to higher officers. Neither colonel delegated to him directly or by implication any such authority. He was restricted to detection . . . questioning of suspects. His spirited assertion that his superiors had more important matters to attend to . . . specious. Convening courts-martial is and always has been a function of command. Without the area commander's signature, the court-martial itself was extralegal . . . But the defendant compounded the evil. The decision to execute . . . was defiant usurpation of authority—naked arrogance . . . tyranny. The State's contention . . . the decision may have resulted from the defendant's personal instability . . . his emotional outrage at what he deemed to be a crime of enormity against this city. He says his blood had reached the boiling point . . . This explains the act, but does not authorize it . . .

"On the second count, the Government has shown that insufficient evidence was on hand for any reasonable man to send Marmorek to his death . . . not enough time was given for the preparation of defense, particularly with regard to Marmorek's intent . . . the quintessential question . . . intent. Was Marmorek's action taken in the hope that the enemy would be advantaged? The evidence indicates . . . not. That he handed Mr. Walker these lists . . . admitted. That he prepared them . . . admitted. That Haganah phone numbers and addresses were included is admitted . . . *but what was his motive?* In a nutshell, was it not to do everything possible to remain in the good graces of Mr. Walker and of the Mandatory Regime, of whose departure he was never fully convinced?

"Well, he began to have apprehensions . . . sought to recover those lists . . . but too late. He failed to inform Haganah. Why? Again, gentlemen, *what was his intent?* He was sure he would be criticized, ridiculed, and above all he wanted to remain in the good graces of Haganah authorities also . . . admitted. Here was a man who wanted everyone of importance to be his friend, to admire him for his courage and fidelity. He too wanted to be of some importance. Is his guilt greater than that of hundreds of thousands of us today who have served alien masters here and in foreign lands, because to do otherwise meant self-destruction? Frenchmen of Vichy, Czechs, Italians, Poles have been guilty at one time or another. Very well . . . being prudent for his own skin, he was imprudent for ours. Was it surprising that Marmorek should have acted as he did . . . a man who had never found a chance to fight for anything . . . perhaps never made his chance? From the day he saw his native country surrendered to Berlin without a shot, through the years when he denied his birthright . . . posed as a Catholic . . . refused to permit the circumcision of his son, to the days when, here in Palestine, he found that cooperation with the British was the safest way of life, Victor Marmorek never fought. All he wanted was to stay out of trouble . . . not so easy. How could he know what to do, whom to work with? He had no crystal ball . . . He hedged. Hedging was a habit . . . How can a man who wants to stay out of trouble choose any loyalty or principle except that of survival for himself and his family?

"But the arresting fact is that the day did come when Victor Marmorek for the first time in his life cast his die. For a man of this kind, it was a decision of heroism. From then on he never faltered.

"After April, 1948, Victor Marmorek worked fiercely . . . left his job, his wife . . . his son, to work on the Road . . . Those who worked with him there told at his trial of his enormous courage . . . his enthusiasm. He saved the lives of two Haganah men at great risk to himself. In many countries he would have received awards, decorations, promotions, but here he was shot because he waited too long. He was shot in temper . . . in fury . . . It was an immoral, unjust, and cruel act. It was also unlawful. It was done to set an example. Colonel Horowitz was a popular officer . . . still is in many quarters, but he must bear responsibility for his act . . . He has thrown a pall over the lives of Marmorek's family, his wife and son, two of Israel's bravest, not only depriving them of husband and father, but also casting upon their name a blackness that will take years of patient living to erase.

"We ask conviction on both counts. However, in view of the circumstances then existing and in view of the exemplary behavior of the defendant in all other respects, and of his record of achievement for Israel, the Government recommends the minimum sentence available to the Court."

There was a hush of silence; Debbie herself was numb. In spite of the heat, she wrapped her scarf more tightly about her shoulders.

The chief judge nodded to Ben Kepelow who stood silent for some minutes. When he spoke, Ben Kepelow addressed the Court quietly also, but he was now grim and strained and he used no notes. Gone was his nonchalant and ingratiating manner.

"I guess we're all agreed that Victor Marmorek gave information to the enemy which nearly lost new Jerusalem forever for us. And he gave the information, if not with the *absolute* intent to advantage the enemy, then certainly with the intent of *risking* advantage to the enemy. An almost fatal advantage, wasn't it? What then is the logical punishment for such a man, even with all this so-called new evidence available? And what, after all, does this new evidence tell us?

"First, that Marmorek knew full well the risk he was running when he handed Walker those lists. Marmorek knew the danger so well that he went to a great deal of trouble to recover the lists. Second, that he was the kind of man who was disloyal, not only to his country and his conscience, but even to his wife.

"What are we to think of such a man? Has this new evidence elevated him?

"After knowing that the lists were in Walker's hands, why didn't he notify Pearlman? That certainly isn't asking too much. Because, as his mistress testified, he was afraid his prestige at Haganah would fall at his failure to maintain the secrecy of these places, and there was just nothing this man longed for so much as prestige. Whether on the English side or our own. Preferably on both.

"He had big-shot-itis.

"Instead of choosing to throw in his lot with his own people he remained carefully on the fence, his feet planted firmly in mid-air, waiting to see which way to jump, and if it is true that he did jump finally, he certainly jumped after everyone else. Here was a man with a calculating mind. Well then let's suppose after that he *was* courageous, after his calculating machine told him to be. Meanwhile the damage he had done was enormous.

"I must disagree respectfully with the State's attorney. When a city is put in hazard by the perfidy of one man, the extreme penalty is *not* too severe. The deaths of scores of persons were caused directly by Marmorek's acts and the destruction of great stores of weapons for defense. What other punishment would have been adequate? What other punishment could have provided sufficient deterrent to like-minded persons? Does the attorney for the Government believe he should have been fined twenty pounds and given a sharp warning not to betray the city again?

"On the evidence and under generally accepted military law, and specifically the unwritten Haganah Code—which was more severe because it was secret, and secrecy was Haganah's greatest necessity—the sentence was lawful, was based on the evidence and was properly approved by Colonel Horowitz."

Debbie's mind flagged and she lost the thread of Ben Kepelow's argument. His words floated meaninglessly over her head. She was dreaming it all, that was it . . . sound and echo all in her head. "More than sufficient evidence," Ben Kepelow droned. *Sufficient evidence . . . sufficient evidence . . . the lists, the lists . . . yes, and Sam and Miss Schamel and . . .* "Areas of jurisdiction," said Ben Kepelow . . . *Of course, jurisdiction . . . jurisdiction . . .* "Lines of authority!" . . . *authority . . . yes . . .* "And improvisation," shouted Ben Kepelow. *Ah, yes, what clever improvisation! . . . Diabolically clever, wasn't it? Ready . . . aim . . . O Lord in Heaven . . .*

Suddenly Ben Kepelow's voice took on an urgency it had lacked. She found herself listening intensely to each word.

"But let us stretch our imaginations, gentlemen, and suppose that Colonel Horowitz was in error. Can anyone say he was guided by evil motives? Can anyone say he was attempting to do any more or less than his duty as he saw it? Suppose then, that in the midst of a war, as a result of an error in judgment, the life of a completely innocent man were taken. Let's just suppose that. It's been estimated that, in wartime, thirty or forty per cent of all deaths result from human errors. An infantryman fails to conceal himself properly or to cover a comrade; a squad commander gives a stupid order; a sentry challenges someone and, misunderstanding the reply, shoots a man like Colonel Marcus; an airplane pilot mistakes a target and strafes his own troops, as happened in the Negev. An overworked doctor makes an error in the operating room. Human errors, errors in judgment, aren't they? Unnecessary, grievous loss of life results. Are all these people later to be called before civilian tribunals on charges of murder or manslaughter? How far-fetched can we get? We are trying to forget war. War is ugly and not the least of its frightfulness is the toll in human lives caused by sheer human error. Let's suppose that that is exactly what Colonel Horowitz made at the worst—an error, a human error, from the highest motives, stimulated by a sharp sense of duty and in a man with a deeply religious sense. It seems to be farcical, as it has from the beginning, to me at least, that he should have to answer in court for doing what he believed was his job. In my opinion, gentlemen, there is no choice. My client must be acquitted.

"Thank you."

The Court adjourned for the Sabbath and reconvened on Sunday morning at eleven. The room was crowded with many standing and again not only the local newspaper people were there, but also all the men and women from the foreign press, who had come back from Tel Aviv and Haifa, to hear the verdict. Horowitz's friends and many of Debbie's were there too.

In a barely audible, dry voice Judge Appenzeller began to read the majority opinion. He and Judge Winkleman found Horowitz guilty on both counts. Judge Lakosi, in dissent, voted to dismiss the first count involving insufficient authority, but concurred in the verdict of guilty on the second count. Following the verdict the sentence was read. Thirty days in prison to run concurrently on both counts; however because of the extenuating circumstances and atmosphere prevailing in Jerusalem at the time of the commission of the crime and as a result of the recommendations of the Government's attorney, the court vacated all but twenty-four hours of the sentence.

To Debbie, one of the most telling passages in the majority opinion were these words of Judge Winkleman:

> We agree wholly with counsel for the defense that in wartime a substantial percentage of loss of life is likely to result from sheer human error or fallibility. It is clear from the evidence that Victor Marmorek had made several grievous errors in judgment. But no traitorous design, no intent by him to advantage the enemy was proved with

even reasonable certainty, according to the trial transcript. Nevertheless, many deaths resulted from his errors. The defendant, in considering the fate of Victor Marmorek, seems never to have pondered this theory of human fallibility so admirably put forward by Counsel now in behalf of the defendant. In passing we note from the transcript also that Captain Ben Kepelow as trial judge-advocate in the court-martial never urged that theory upon Colonel Horowitz, as he has urged it upon us. Thus Colonel Horowitz ignored the concept then which he uses in his own defense now: namely that a human error which has dire consequences is still nothing more than human error. We hold it to be self-evident that to shoot a man for having made errors, even fatal errors, is and ought to be contrary to our moral code, as well as contrary to Israeli military and civil law.

Before the reading of the sentence was completed there was an outraged hoot in the courtroom and a claque of Horowitz supporters began a systematic cat-calling, booing, hissing, and whistling. Shouts of *politics, bribery, lackeys* sent the guards into action and on barked instructions from Judge Lakosi the court was cleared, but not without difficulty; Debbie heard the sickening crush of a club on a particularly vocal demonstrator. Newsmen had already started over to the Telephone Office to call their stories into Tel Aviv and Haifa, while outside the courtroom the shouting and trampling of a small group of organized rightists raged unabated. Inside Judge Appenzeller calmly finished reading the verdict and sentence.

That night the headlines of all Israeli papers from Haifa to Jerusalem shouted, HOROWITZ GUILTY; MRS. MARMOREK'S STRUGGLE TRIUMPHANT; SENTENCE IS THIRTY DAYS; JUDGES SAY LIGHT SENTENCE REFLECTS EXTENUATING CIRCUMSTANCES.

Debbie read the oversimplified leads of each of the articles which gave the impression that Horowitz was totally guilty because Vic was totally innocent.

Dick Alpert stopped her in the hospital corridor, and said, "Always knew Vic was okay. I know only one thing. I liked the guy." Of all the people she knew, Dick Alpert was the only one genuinely on Vic's side, and not simply helping her. She could not help liking that about Dick, even though she herself knew the truth of the matter. What Vic had lived by and everything he had taught her, she felt now in her bones, although she had known it for some time in her head. They had offended together. But she would have another chance.

Most of the newspapers commented in restrained fashion that Israel was stronger for having corrected a terrible injustice. None of them characterized Horowitz as anything more than "an overzealous man in a difficult job," and none of them took any satisfaction in his conviction. At best it seemed a necessary evil.

When she went next day to thank Aronowitz for his help it was not necessary for him to say, as he did, "Please, lady, how can we be pleased? We are two honest people. We did what we could, it was necessary for you and the boy. But did we do right? How can we be sure? You know, Horowitz was not herded here like most of us to this Godforsaken wilderness. He came. He left a free land. He was a pioneer. He helped smuggle thousands out of DP camps into Palestine right after the war, without permits. He was kept in Cyprus by the British for two months. He worked for Haganah from the day he got here. No one was persecuting Horowitz, no, ma'am. There was no Gestapo in England. It is *something* to give up comfort and security and ease of mind. But he did it. Without him would Israel have been possible? Never. Never, lady. And the reward we've given him! Well, you can live in Jerusalem in peace. I hope so. That is something at least."

But Debbie flared up. "That evil little man is a self-righteous pygmy, and I wouldn't dare put a stethoscope to him, because I'm not sure I'd get a heartbeat. You really think there's flesh and blood there, Boris? I hate the man. I'll always hate him. Don't try to take that away, Boris. I wouldn't give you ten like him for one man like Vic!"

Boris Aronowitz hunched his back. He didn't argue with her, and Debbie was grateful.

Fifty

For two days after the verdict she continued to work at the hospital in a state of emotional hangover. Hands were thrust toward her to shake and she shook them. Baumerstock came personally to deliver a dozen fresh eggs and two gallons of Rishon le Zion dry red wine. Bouquets of flowers were handed to her by complete strangers in the hospital corridors or on the street. At the flat she received telephone calls and letters of admiration, although many were still abusive; but nothing much touched her. At first it was as if she were glazed, and everything rolled off, hailstones on a windowpane, clamoring for attention and entry, but unable to penetrate. Only the letter Enid had left upset her:

My dear Debbie,

It seemed so pointless for us to talk, much as I wanted to see you. Mr. Aronowitz was anxious for us not to meet, I think to be sure that I would tell all of what had to be told to clear Vic's name of mischief and I think he was afraid I might hold something back for fear of hurting you. I don't see that there could be much profit for us to talk about these things, but this much I must tell you. Vic always adored you. Even for the brief time I had with him, I always came second. The only reason he had anything to do with me at all, I think, was because he always thought of you as a precious child, to be guarded and loved, but he needed someone idle, someone worthless with whom he could share faults, dishonor and a little wickedness.

Well, I'm afraid there's been no profit in it for either him or me. For my part I can't say I regret having had even his second best, although now I'm paying. I hope Redge will have me back some day. But for you Vic saved his best and everything he did was for you and David. You must know that.

I was rather sorry you kept on with your struggle to clear Vic, because all this had to come out. When Mr. Stern came to England, he sensed where the truth lay, I'm afraid—I've never been a poker-face, you know. He promised me he'd do everything he could to keep you from going on with it, because he knew quite well the hurt you might be in for. But I suppose for you, and for David especially, it was more important to set the record straight about Vic. I keep telling myself it was for David's sake. Well there's a price for everything, isn't there?

Lloyd is fine and sends his love.

ENID

Of course, that was why George had dragged his feet. There was no doubt of it now. She would have to think about George. What was she to do about him? There was no time left.

On the second day Elsa took her aside, her eyes flaring and her face flushed, bursting to tell Debbie something.

"I've good news for you, Deborah. You know they're ready to open the new hospital at Beersheba. You're to go down there in about two weeks. You're to be in charge."

"What? You call that good news? In that black desert? I couldn't care less for it, thank you. Try one of the pioneers who get palpitations over that sort of thing."

"Deborah, it's not going to be a barren wasteland forever. In three years they'll be farming down there. Milk and honey!"

"Oh, you Bible girl! Please!"

"But they're piping water there now. Hundreds of boys and girls are going there to work. They'll be able to settle two hundred thousand, maybe more, down there soon. Our hospital will be much more than a hospital, believe me. It'll be a temple too. That's where they'll come for comfort. Especially with you there."

"Well," Debbie said ragging Elsa impatiently, "if it's going to be a temple why don't *you* take the job?"

"I wanted to, but they won't let me. They want someone—younger. And someone a little nearer to God than I. The trustees know. God knows. And I know it now, too. You see I'm getting more honest with myself every day. The trustees considered everyone on the staff. All they wanted was a good nurse with a tough soul—who was also a holy woman with a sense of humor. Dr. Alpert suggested you."

Debbie thought of the immigrants' camp she had visited and the director's longing, "What we need is people with big hearts and small appetites."

"Once your name came up," Elsa said, "everyone wanted you."

Debbie was almost touched. "But I'm no organizer. I could never."

"We don't organize; we improvise. And now please go home, Deborah. Look at you. Take a few days off. Rest. I can't stand to look at you, you're so exhausted. Go to bed."

"And pray?" Debbie said.

"I'll pray," Elsa said. "You just go to sleep."

It was clear to anyone who looked at her even casually that she was emotionally exhausted. The strain of the trial, of Enid's confession, and of George's still unanswered question were too much for her. She herself felt the need of refuge—total refuge. She was glad to take Elsa's suggestion. She'd pull the sheets over her head and stop thinking, or remembering, or blaming herself or Vic or anyone, even that man Horowitz. She wouldn't think of going to the Negev, or George or anything at all. You've won, Debbie girl, let's concentrate on that. You've really done it. The phone still rang with congratulations and insults from as far away as Haifa and Tiberias. Letters came from strangers all over the world, each letter and call a new assault on her emotions. She took to crying easily and she sometimes found herself giggling for no reason. After the first day Jacinta had the phone disconnected, kept visitors away and tried to isolate her. On the second day when the two boys were off to school and Jacinta to work, she had some time alone with herself, sorting her feelings, trying to think and feel her way out of the maze.

But she had scarcely composed herself, lying quietly in bed, when the mailman came with a special delivery letter from the Minister of Education informing her that the Knesset had established a special fund to be used for David's tuition at the University of Jerusalem or at the Technical Institute at Haifa, whichever he might choose when he was ready to enter college.

The letter was still in her hands, blurring before her incredulous eyes as she sat reading in bed when George came into the flat. Without a word she handed it to him.

"Very nice," he said lamely.

"It's not only the money," she said, a little choked up, for everything was beginning to overwhelm her. "It's that David will be able to do everything we ever dreamed of for him."

"And what about you?" George said. "Will you be able to do everything *you* ever dreamed of?"

"Probably—not," Debbie said. "Can any full-grown person? Take yourself, you have Carol Ann at home. You can't just leave her in Boston and go cavorting about. It's not like you. Any more than I can leave David."

"Nobody's asking you to leave David," George said, almost impatiently. "You surely never thought that."

"Oh, but George, how could I take him to America? This is his country. It's not just like any other country. It's new and he's had to fight for it, almost since he's five. And then we've had to fight for his right to it. Why do you think I fought so hard? It's his biggest and best thing. His friends, his pride, his strength."

"Well, America," George snapped, "is pretty big too. Full of nice people, friends, good kids—all that."

George had been considerate from the day the trial started, had never pressed her to make up her mind. What little time they'd had together had been spent avoiding the subject. And Debbie had not been able to make any progress in her own mind. For the man you love, she thought, you should be willing to chuck everything: to forget your loyalties, and perhaps even the perfect, ideal thing for David. He could settle for less. He was still only a baby . . . He could adapt himself. And this might be her only chance. Why shouldn't she ignore what she'd learned, be glad to make the same mistakes again, and be able to rationalize even desertion? But she had not been able to bring herself to it in her innermost honesty.

Perhaps what she had told George was true, not only for now, but forever—perhaps she would always be less than human. For she was a gladiator now. She had slain dragons. She had made men look up from what they were doing and pause and give her justice. More than justice. She was shining in her new armor. Anything was possible for her now. Elsa recognized it; Dick Alpert saw it; the trustees at the hospital believed it.

Still she heard Vic's voice, *Fool! Childish fool! Who's the romantic now? Try to think of real things. You have a chance. The chance of your lifetime. Fly, Debbie, let's fly on the wings of the twentieth century. America's big, America's rich . . . easy . . . America's safe, and you like this man.*

She was meant for it too, no doubt. The prettiest girl in Vienna. She could sit by the hour having her toenails manicured. The latest hairdo . . . She would deliberate over the proper shade of lipstick to go with her fingernails. She would loll before a television set by the hour. There'd be sailing at Cape Cod and skiing in Vermont. Lake Mooselookmeguntic, or whatever they called it, golf and tennis and baseball for David. She might learn golf herself. And no one to point or stare: "That's the Marmorek woman, see? The pretty one. Oh, *you* know *her* kind."

In America she'd be Deborah Stern, and Marmorek would not be a bad word any longer. It wouldn't be a word at all. And Vic would be pleased anyway because this was what Vic believed. Safety . . . Move on . . . Dignity in a mink coat.

And that passage in *Inside USA* about the hooligans beating up Jewish children in Boston? Vic would laugh. Pooh—pooh! Vic had been ready even to go back to Prague or Vienna. He never understood what that kind of thing did to her. Even though it might never happen again. It *had* happened.

And could she leave Karl? Karl, imperfect, failing in so many ways, but he remembered Lindenhouse with her, and Vienna, and Mama and Papa—she would be giving up all her memories if she gave up Karl. And forever was too long.

There was work to be done. They were sending her down to Beer-sheba. Improvise, Elsa had said.

Still a woman gave up everything for her man. Her mind tried to concentrate on George. He was selfless almost, so devoted, but—she looked at him as she sipped her coffee. He was staring at her in that solemn way he had, curious, not critical, and she felt suddenly sorry for him. And sorry that his sweetness and gentleness could not rouse her to anything more than a desire to be kind. With her free hand she pulled the sheet up to her chin. She wanted to tell him not to mind. She wondered if she could ever love him, force herself to love him, as she knew she had been able to love.

He sat tentatively on the edge of the bed. "A year ago, before I walked into this flat, I'd have sworn nothing like this could happen to me at all. But—" he fanned the smoke from his cigarette away from his eyes. "It's happened. Hell, it's not the clear white heat of twenty-one. I can see the edge of forty creeping up on me. But it's all I have left. Beat a little, but still trying. All I mean is, I think I could spend the rest of my time with you very happily, if you'd care to come with me."

"Could you, George?" She was sparring for time.

"As offers go, it may not be much," he said, and she knew he was trying not to press her. To let her make up her own mind.

His unwillingness to coerce, to insist was so like him. She admired him for it. Vic would have commanded. "George," she said. "I don't think you have any idea how appealing you are."

He smiled self-consciously. "That's why I think I've fallen in love with you. You flatter me. Everything about you flatters me. You make me feel like a real knight in armor. As if every time I do something, I'm a lion or some damn thing."

"You *are* a lion, dear. A scrawny kind of a lion, maybe, because your mane's kind of thin, but you're a true lion with a lion's heart. Only you see you've made a condition."

He stared at her, then turned away.

"You keep saying that," he said impatiently. "I'd thought that was real bait, not a condition. Myself, *plus* America. I thought it was pretty damn generous of me to offer you my country too. Isn't it everyone's ambition to go there? Don't tell me that makes the difference between yes and no?"

Dear George, she thought, what could she tell him? What must she do? Above all, she must not hurt him. She must be kind.

"But you see, George, I *have* a country and a home here and it's all I can handle. I wouldn't care for a new one."

He was silent and spoke slowly. "I suppose that should have been obvious to me."

"And, George, it's awful because I've grown to be so fond of you, too, without even meaning to."

"Well, what do you know," he said, and she could hear he was touched. His voice had an odd, unreal ring to it, high up in his throat. He sat a while and watched her pretend to drink the last dregs of her coffee and at last he broke the silence. "I just don't get it," he said. "My IQ's reasonably high. I don't get all these delicate semantics. I think we'd get along real fine. Day in and day out. Not just on sunny days. Oh, I'm not likely to stand under your balcony with a mandolin or bring roses each morning, you understand. But I'm human, too. I can tell, because I do get gooseflesh when I think of you for too long and I think that's a mighty unhealthy situation. I catch you looking at me with your mouth open like that and I don't know, something goes wrong with me. See, you're doing it now." He put an arm over her shoulder and turned her face up toward him. "You see?"

He kissed her suddenly, rather deliberately, and they rocked backwards and were lying shoulder to shoulder. The kiss stirred her more than she had expected. George seemed so pathetically eager. When he pulled away slightly there was a corner of the pillow between their faces and they saw each other one-eyed over the linen. His voice still sounded strange. "I don't know how you can think so clearly. Like a logic professor. I can't. What difference does it make what part of the world you live in? If the right people aren't there, what good is it?"

"You talk so much," she said. He kissed her gently. "George."

"Yes."

"You're so gentle, much too gentle, I think."

He lost some of his gentleness then. She found herself trying to be more responsive as George grew bolder.

She was going to let George love her. She knew that now. Because he couldn't stay and she could never leave. And because in a way she did love him. He must have sensed it too, for he tried almost like an impatient child to coerce, to consume her. Possession, mastery, the never-ending quest, the animal kingdom seeking what humanity denies, trying to overwhelm all reason. Blindness . . . Unconsciousness. Was it dominion? Oneness? She was too aware through it all, she wanted to cry. And then slowly George was relaxing and she was glad it was over, although it had been so nearly complete for her. Exhaustion, recession . . . Slowly growing feeling of one's self. Separateness . . . Four hands again. Four legs, two bodies. Division . . . Self-possession . . . The sense of loss and twoness. And their problem was poised there between them again, still unanswered.

They kissed, cooler kisses and more longing and sadder ones than before, for they were the kisses of good-bye.

After they had lain still for so long a time that she had lost track, George stirred. "Now," he said hopelessly, "now will you come home with me? You could make an honest man of me."

"Please, darling, oh darling, don't tease at this moment."

"Who's teasing? I'm only trying to get peacefully what I couldn't win by force. You can't go on being so stubborn, Debbie. You're only clinging to some kind of past. Even now you're so stubborn. I'll give you a future, Debbie. I promise. My own as well as yours, for whatever it's worth."

She murmured new words to assuage. "How I'd love to, how I'd truly love to. You're such a special guy. I think you're about the best human being ever invented."

"Don't say another word," George said.

"But—"

"That's the word I was afraid of. I knew I felt another rejection coming." He kissed her lips, her nose and eyes and her fingers lightly.

"I seem to be able to almost bring you to life, don't I? But your mind hasn't really come to life, Deb. I can't seem to stir it up."

She didn't want to argue. Her mind had never been sharper. How easy it would be to say Yes. Yes, yes I'll go, George. Forever, George. But she heard only the voices that said No and they both knew it. Marmorek, her name, was going to be a word, perhaps a symbol now. She would not escape. Aronowitz's work and Horowitz's ordeal and all of her own were not to become cruel jokes without point or meaning. She held George's hand, and whispered, "I'm glad you came today, George. See, I'm more grownup than you think."

"Oh, I've always thought you were grownup," George said. "It's just that I've been a damn fool. I thought I was the guy who could wake you up too."

"Don't grieve, George. It's not you, it's me. Only me. I told you before, I'm not quite all there. Maybe some day when David grows up—he really needs me and he needs me to stay where we are. But maybe after he grows up." She was inventing transparencies. "Maybe someday not too far away."

"I'll keep it in mind," George said, and she knew he was nursing a deep hurt, nothing she could do anything about. She felt unnecessarily cruel and guilty.

"Have I ever thanked you for everything, George? Not ever, I think." It was probably the worst thing she could have said.

"So long, Deb." He kissed her again and she had the feeling when he'd gone out the door and she heard his steps to the street that she would not see him again for a long time.

She pulled the sheet over her head and lay back, exhausted and lonely from her great effort. You see, Vic? I'm still here. I'm going to stay. I may have to go into that damn desert, too. Her lips were forming silent words in something like defiant prayer. I made it, I made it. You see, Vic? I'm going my own way.

She might talk big and brave to Vic or herself, but now she found herself weeping, beyond control, like a child lost, suffering not only from hollow, mysterious loneliness, but also from fear of what was about to befall her. When George left the room, her shield, her security and safety went out with him. All chances for a wonderfully comfortable way of living were gone. She had flubbed the one opportunity which she would never have again. George, she knew secretly, could bring her to life one day soon if she only gave him half a chance, for in these months George had touched her. Now in forsaking him she had forsaken herself. The emptiness in the room and in her soul was hardly to be borne. In desperation she stuffed one corner of the sheet into her mouth and bit hard to stop her own witless crying.

She found it all but impossible to resist the impulse to call George. Next morning she hurried back to the hospital, and on her first day there worked until she was ready to drop. She did the job of three girls.

Toward three o'clock, Dick Alpert came to get her, and with a touch of cloak-and-dagger mystery asked her to come with him. As they hurried through the streets, they met Noah Mendoza, who joined them. Noah was doing beautifully now, as if he had only a minor leg injury which had left him with a slight limp.

They were heading toward Ben Maimon Street when she first heard the drums and bugles. As they moved on, she realized they were taking her to the Rehavia School. Nothing's happened to David . . . Please, God. Neither Noah's face nor Dick's told her anything. She was so afraid of disaster these days. Nothing was sure or safe. But as they approached the school, she saw people standing two and three deep, lining the streets, and the bugles and drums were closer and louder. It was some kind of parade.

Behind them she saw it approaching round the corner from King George. They were children in Scout uniforms—Boy and Girl Scouts.

The buglers came first, playing loudly, and then the drummers rattling imperatively. Behind them a mass of young people in khaki swung into the street, hundreds it seemed, and on either flank, stragglers bringing up the rear; at the head of the winding column a boy and a girl carried great poles supporting between them a huge blownup portrait of Vic, and under his picture were the blazing words: BUILDER OF THE ROAD—HERO OF ISRAEL—VICTOR MARMOREK.

The sight of Vic's face in full color and in such huge proportions was a tremendous shock to her, as if she had got a fiery blast full in the face. At first she was too stunned to grasp it. Then she thought involuntarily, How easily the truth is distorted.

Inside the schoolrooms teachers were interrupting their classes at the sound of the martial music, and children and teachers were filing into the courtyard. David's class—in the midst of an arithmetic examination—followed curiously behind their teacher.

Dick Alpert and Noah led Debbie into the Rehavia School courtyard, and the parade marched right behind her, behind the blast of music. Children and teachers were assembled amid their new plants and young trees, and Debbie saw Miss Even, who nodded and smiled. Jacinta was there with Rose Epstein. Karl and Lil came to stand beside her. Almost everyone she knew was there. The five American reporters still at the pension. But not George. She found herself looking everywhere for George, but she knew he would not be there. Local newsmen had come, too, and two cameramen, who snapped pictures incessantly. Elsa was standing near David; a score of nurses, other doctors from the hospital. She wondered if there was enough staff left not to endanger patients. But she had no time for reflection. Even Ben Kronstein had shown up, and Baumerstock. Alongside Karl, Boris Aronowitz stood, looking a shade uncomfortable, and behind him were the Rosenthal twins.

David was standing in open-mouthed bewilderment as if he could not make head or tail of what was going on. The huge portrait of Vic had stumped him. His father up there! And Debbie could see him slowly spelling out the words to himself. Hero—of—Israel. Then suddenly he smiled in tremendous relief.

Deliberately and with some difficulty several of the Scouts fastened the tremendous banner carrying Vic's portrait to the eastern courtyard wall, which was bathed in sunlight, while the other Scouts stood in stiff military salute.

Outside the courtyard there was a flurry of commotion, and she saw that the Prime Minister, whose Jerusalem residence was down Ben Maimon Street, had entered the courtyard to observe the proceedings.

One of the Girl Scouts, armed with a bouquet, whispered to Miss Even who pointed to David. The girl marched stiffly to him. "In the name of the Scouts of this city and of Israel these flowers are presented in the memory of your father. You should be proud to bear the name Marmorek."

David took them, bewildered and smiling foolishly. The Scout Leader squinted and the bugle corps played a jaunty Haganah marching song and afterward, while all stood erect, "Hatikvah." Miss Even and Elsa were weeping noiselessly. Lilith dabbed at her eyes. The buglers started stiffly out of the courtyard, drums following, and the children stood in silence, listening to the fading of the martial music as it made its way back toward Mamillah Road. David looked at the flowers in some puzzlement, and then seeing his mother for the first time handed them to her. She wanted to laugh and cry. In spite of the ludicrous inappropriateness of all the details, this was a tremendous effort to which so many people had gone for David's sake.

The Prime Minister stepped briskly toward Aronowitz and shook hands, with a warm smile.

"Done satisfactorily, Boris?" He chuckled and vaguely indicated the arrayed assemblage and the banner with Vic's picture. "For a man who deserved less, it's not bad, eh?"

Aronowitz reddened, and said quickly, "May I present Mrs. Marmorek, Mr. Prime Minister?"

The Prime Minister shook her hand solemnly, but heartily. "It's for your son, Madam. All of this, and for you. You understand, I think."

Debbie looked at him sharply. She nodded, unsmiling.

The Prime Minister stepped to David's side, and whispered in his ear. David grinned and shook his head. They clasped hands, the short, stocky white-haired man in a sports shirt, and the small skinny boy, and the Prime Minister waved and left the courtyard briskly.

"Hey, David, what'd he say? What'd he say?" Tuvia yelled.

"He asked me if I'd like to change places with him," David said.

"What's he mean?" Meyer asked.

"Beats me," David said. "I wouldn't want to be *that* old."

"Your son's just been offered the job of Prime Minister," Dick Alpert said.

"I expected that," Debbie said. "But I think he's holding out for King."

"Hey, it's a holiday!" shouted Meyer suddenly. "It's King David's holiday!"

"Oh, no," Miss Even said firmly.

"Hey, David, catch." It was René Blum who had got hold of a basketball and passed it to him. "Come on, let's have a game. It's David's holiday!"

"Children! Children!" Miss Even shouted. She glanced at the other teachers, and they shrugged.

David and René were heading for the basketball court with scores of kids behind them.

"Half-hour recess," the principal declared firmly to the teachers who remained.

Debbie saw Miss Even turn to look at Vic's portrait almost in awe, and she walked up to her and stood silent beside her for a few moments, as if they were at a tomb.

"Take it down after school this evening," Debbie said softly. Debbie looked once again at the huge poster: Vic was so handsome and fearless up there; a giant of a man. "You see, it's not a particularly good likeness of him."

Miss Even looked bewildered. "Very well," she said. "If you wish it."

Debbie forced a polite smile, turned and found Boris Aronowitz and Dick Alpert at her side.

"George called yesterday to tell me good-bye," Aronowitz said. "He's going back to Boston for a few months, and then to Hong Kong."

"I know," she said.

"He's a good man." They walked toward the courtyard exit. "I'm surprised you're still here," Aronowitz said. "But I'm glad you are."

Dick Alpert screwed his face up in surprise as they started back to the hospital.

"Funny thing. It just never crossed my mind you might be leaving," he said. "Where were you thinking of going?"

"Nowhere, really," Debbie said.

A NOTE ABOUT THE AUTHOR

JOSEPH VIERTEL *was born in New York City in 1915. He was graduated from Harvard Magna Cum Laude and took postgraduate work at the Yale Drama School.*

After his marriage in 1939, he and his wife mapped a course: He would join his father in the construction industry and spend ten years there trying to earn enough to retire and write. He spent ten years building homes and apartments from New England to Kansas, housing 150,000 people in fifteen states.

In the same period, he has been a director in a number of concerns: a publishing house, an import-export firm, a theater chain, and some forty-odd real-estate corporations in nine states. During this time, he also managed to write a few short stories which have appeared in Collier's, American Magazine, Story, *and a play,* So Proudly We Hail, *which was produced in 1936.*

Parts of The Last Temptation *were written in Italy and Jerusalem, and the remainder in Stamford, Connecticut, where the author lives with his wife and three children.*